About the Author

As a child Sue Stokes spent hours scribbling in exercise books creating stories. Her ambition to be a journalist was forgotten when a speech given by the matron of a local hospital, at school prize giving inspired her to become a nurse. After gaining her SRN she trained to become a health visitor. On retiring, Sue took up writing classes, her first novel was born from a short story exercise.

Sue is a keen member of her local drama group. She also enjoys reading, and visiting coffee shops selling huge scones.

She lives with her husband and dog in Lancashire.

Dedication

To my husband Ian who has given me so much help with the intricacies of the computer.
My love and gratitude.
Also to my Son, Dan and Grandson Ben who together give me so much laughter and joy.
I love you both.

Susan Stokes

WALKING ON PATHS OF STONES

AUSTIN MACAULEY PUBLISHERS™

LONDON • CAMBRIDGE • NEW YORK • SHARJAH

A CIP catalogue record for this title is available from the British Library.

ISBN 9781398430020 (Paperback)
ISBN 9781398430037 (ePub e-book)

www.austinmacauley.com

First Published (2021)
Austin Macauley Publishers Ltd
25 Canada Square
Canary Wharf
London
E14 5LQ

Chapter 1
Crossdale, North Lancashire 1919

The letter stood propped up on the mantelpiece between Martha's prized pair of china Staffordshire dogs. The envelope was large and brown; the address typewritten, which to Martha could only mean one thing, bad news. She scowled at it.

'One for young Rory, Mrs Watkins.' Smiled George Butterfield, the elderly postman, having stepped up into the cottage to pop his head around the scullery door.

Martha, drying her soapy hands on her apron, had reluctantly reached out and accepted it. Then beginning a cheery whistle, which heightened Martha's panic, for surely it was bad luck to do such a thing in the house, George stepped down out of the cottage door, recovered his bicycle which he had propped up against the stone cottage wall and wheeled it through the small Iron Gate. Mounting his bicycle and still whistling, he rode on down the rough pebbled path.

Martha's hands trembled, as she traced Rory's name with her fingertip. A typewritten letter in the Watkins household was a rare event, and even more so were those addressed to her youngest son. Nervous perspiration trickled down her back, as she clenched the letter in tense anticipation reading Rory's name over and over again.

She walked through the scullery and into her warm, cheerful kitchen. Meaning only to rid herself of the letter's presence, she threw it quickly into the bucket she used for vegetable peelings. She retrieved it seconds later and brushed it clean on her apron, before placing it high on the mantelpiece from where it cruelly taunted her.

Suddenly, the old familiar pain shot through her left shoulder and down her arm. She breathed heavily, trying to rub the spasm away. She moved slowly to her chair, cursing the heat from the banked fire as sweat poured from her brow.

Impatiently, she removed her knitting from the seat, and then lowered herself awkwardly on to the familiar sagging cushion and closed her eyes.

Albert Watkins wiped a large hand over his grimy brow. Black rivulets of sweat that had settled into a lifetime of wrinkles ran down his face until he could taste their sooty saltiness in his mouth. He looked at Jack; his border collie lying outside panting in the shade of a tree. At this moment, he envied the dog; Albert would rather be anywhere than in the stifling smithy attempting to shoe Jacob Pennington's mare.

It was the first day of June. The sweltering heat outside matched the power of the furnace blazing within the dark shed. The sun elevated in a cloudless sky gave renewed hope to a country that had just emerged from the darkness of four years at war.

Albert turned his attention back to Jacob's horse. Somehow, he had to convince the animal that it actually needed to be shod.

Jacob, standing by the horse's head and holding on to the reins, laughed heartily, showing missing teeth as he did so. 'She's got you on the run again, Albert.'

'Just stop laughing and hold her tight, will you?' Albert turned his back, bent over and picked up the mare's foreleg carefully placing it between his knees to remove the shoe. Why was it only farmer Pennington's horse he had problems with!

'You're getting too old for this blacksmithing malarkey,' said Jacob, rubbing a stubby hand over his whiskery chin, as he tightened his hold on the reins.

'It must be a right disappointment that your eldest lad, Thomas, isn't strong enough to take over the business, with his poor heart an'all.'

Albert straightened up, and placing the mare's foot back on the ground, he turned to look at Jacob. 'He could if worst comes to worst. After all, he's been working on the bellows with me all through the war. It's just not the right job for him, he tires easily. I were hoping that the youngest lad, Rory, might learn the trade, but so far, he shows no inclination. Since winning that art prize at school, his head's been full of that painting nonsense. Any road, I don't see much evidence that you can retire either, Jacob; that farm of yours won't run itself. I think it looks likely this is our lot until the good Lord sees fit to take us,' Albert said, shaking his head in despair before bending again to remove another horse shoe.

Jacob fiddled nervously with his horse's reins, as he spoke, 'Aye, well that brings me on to an important matter, Albert. I've been right lonely since my Emily passed on, as you might imagine.'

Albert nodded; temporarily distracted by an obstinate horseshoe.

'The farm is too big for me now that I'm on me own and all.' Jacob licked his lips and ran his fingers through what little hair he had. 'I'm not much of a cook either, so I were wondering if…God in heaven Albert, you're not making this easy for me,' he continued, staring at Albert's unforgiving back. 'Fact is, I were wondering if I might ask your permission to marry your Eliza Jane. She's a fine lass, and I reckon she would make me a good wife and partner on the farm. I'd look after her, you know I would, and she would want for nowt.'

Albert remained silent, as he considered his old friend's words. Fact was Jacob was his own age, they had gone to school together which would make him thirty-five years older than Eliza Jane, and chances are that she would be widowed at an early age. He knew his wife, Martha, would be furious that Jacob should even think of such a thing, though he had to admit he wasn't sold on the idea himself; it didn't really bear thinking about too closely; but then, who was he to decide his eldest daughter's future, best let her answer for herself, after all her chances would likely be limited at her age.

Jacob persevered. 'Well, say summat, have I got your permission to call on her? I take it that she'll be working in Jackson's as usual.'

'Aye, she's working,' Albert muttered, hammering a new shoe loudly in the hope he wouldn't have to say anymore.

'Well then, what do you think, will she have me do you suppose?'

Albert shrugged in a non-committal fashion before letting go of the mare's leg and straightening up. He placed his rough grimy hands on his waist and stretched his back.

'That's your horse done, Jacob.'

'Well ta, Albert, ta very much, lad, for yer warm words of advice; I don't think.'

Albert was aware he had annoyed his old friend with his cursory replies but didn't feel able to pass an opinion either way. He wasn't about to upset his friend and best customer by saying no, and he also knew he couldn't speak for his daughter. He stood to one side as Jacob put his cap on his head and mounted his horse.

'Put what I owe on me bill and I'll settle up with you later. Walk on, Bess.'
He clicked his heels against the horse's flanks. The horse lumbered forward
carrying Jacob out into the street.

Albert watched him go. He fervently hoped that Eliza Jane would not
welcome the advances of a man the same age as her father. Jacob admittedly had
money, but he wasn't known for readily parting with it. At twenty-seven, Eliza
Jane wasn't getting any younger, and also not pretty like her two younger sisters,
Etty and Molly. Sighing heavily, he took up his broom and began sweeping up
the dropped nails and old horse shoes. The struggle with Jacob and his mare had
left him with a thirst and the thought of a brew at home with the missus made
him smile.

Albert had fallen in love with Martha the moment she led a lame horse into
the smithy, thirty-five years ago. He knew she loved him dearly, although she
would never tell him so, of course. Her bark was worse than her bite, he
explained to those unfortunate folks who got on the wrong side of her, of which
there were many. Martha could be as fierce as an army Sergeant Major to the
outside world, but to him, although brusque at times, she could be loving and
kind. Albert would do anything for her and she knew it.

The smithy stood beside Albert's cottage in the small village of Crossdale in
North Lancashire. 'No-man's-land' the locals called it, being situated barely in
Lancashire but not quite in Yorkshire. Stories were handed down through the
generations, of many villagers in Crossdale changing allegiances regularly so
they could claim to be on the winning side in the Wars of the Roses. Grey stone
cottages lined the wide street that ran in tandem with the canal. A humpback
bridge had been built over the water, which led to a small footpath and the village
hall. Jackson's wasn't the only shop in Crossdale. There was a tiny newspaper
and sweet shop combined with a post office that was run by twin sisters, Beatrice
and Jemima Emmet, both in their late fifties. Roy Hughes owned the local
butchers, and next door stood Laycocks antiques, where Martha spent many
happy hours, browsing amongst its many treasures. She particularly liked pottery
dogs, other small decorative pieces of china, linens and old ribbons to decorate
her thick hair, which was her only vanity.

Albert stood in the entrance and whistled for Jack. The dog shot up from
under the tree and was at once by his master's side. Albert removed his leather
apron and hung it on the usual hook. He then checked the fire pit was safe and

hanging his tools back on nails hammered into the thick blackened stonewalls, he left, locking the door behind him.

Standing for a moment breathing in fresh warm air, Albert looked to the right down the street and saw Jacob's horse standing patiently outside Jackson's shop. Huffing to himself, he removed his cap from his head and ran a piece of rag from his pocket over his perspiring brow. Jack began heading for the Bluebell pub across the road, making Albert laugh. 'Not today, boy, let's go, and see the missus.' He turned left, walked the short distance to his cottage, opened the gate and strolled up the path, admiring Martha's neat garden as he did so

Albert's bulk filled the small doorframe, as he entered the cottage. Jack, as always, trotting by his side. Martha had her back to him. She had recovered from her bout of pain and was standing at the sink peeling carrots for dinner. He gazed at her, drawing comfort from the sight of her familiar form. She was heavier and more rounded since they first wed. Her hair had turned from fair to grey, but to him she was still the same girl he had fallen in love with. Spotting an opportunity to have a bit of fun, he crept carefully across the tiled floor, placing his grimy hands over her eyes.

Martha jumped. 'Oh, my goodness me, is that you, Albert?'

Albert laughed as he let her go. 'And who else were you expecting, my girl?'

Martha turned to face him. 'Albert Watkins, you are filthy,' she protested, wiping her eyes on her apron before throwing him a towel. 'Get to that sink and wash yourself; there's plenty of hot water on the range.' Jack crept into his basket in the corner by the range, something was up with the missus, and he was best off out of the way.

'What's up, love? You're right tetchy.'

'You'll be tetchy too, lad, when I tell you.' She moved towards the mantelpiece wiping her hands on her apron as she went. 'Rory's got a letter, George brought it this morning.' She reached up to the mantelpiece and took it down from its position of authority.

Albert suddenly needed the comfort of his armchair; the news of the letter was causing his brain to work overtime and the smell of lavender polish mingled with the aroma of fried onions was making him feel nauseous. Slumping into his chair, he took the letter from Martha's trembling hand and carefully examined the envelope.

'Who could be writing to our Rory, typewritten an' all?'

'I don't know,' said Martha, trying to ignore her returning chest pain.

Albert looked into his wife's blue eyes, and saw his worries mirrored there. 'I can see what you're thinking, love, but you're wrong.'

'Am I?'

'Yes.' Albert got up and walked over to the mantelpiece and returned the envelope to its position between the china dogs. He reached out and grabbed Martha, hugging her tight.

'I'm scared, Bert.'

'Stop your mitherin', woman. When are you going to cease worrying about our Rory? Look, the kettle's boiling; let's have that tea and a slice of Eliza Jane's fruitcake.'

Martha, her pain now receding again, reluctantly smiled at him. 'You're too late for that, Bert. That cake was taken over to Jackson's this morning. I think our daughter has got herself a bit of a fancy for a certain young man.'

'Do you indeed?' Albert laughed. 'In which case, Jacob Pennington will have a run for his money. He was in today with that flighty mare of his. He had marriage with our Lizzie on his mind.'

Martha's anger temporarily over took the importance of the letter. 'How dare he think our Eliza Jane would be interested in marrying him?' She gave an involuntary shudder.

'Don't worry, I gave him short shrift, well, as much as I dare; him being a good customer an all. He was asking me what we'll do when I can no longer work in the smithy; it brought all those worries back to me, I know we've discussed this a million times, but…'

Albert's voice trailed off as Martha interrupted him, her mouth fixed firm. 'Neither of the lads is interested in taking over from you, so don't start that again.'

'But if anything happens to me, where will you live, Martha? We've a bit put by for funerals and such, but having to pay rent on somewhere else to live, well, the money's not going to last long. If Rory took over as Blacksmith, then you'll be able to stay in the cottage.'

'Enough now, Albert, leave it alone. I hope the Lord sees fit to take us together. At least the children will be married and leading their own lives. I'm sure I could park myself with one of them.'

'I wish Thomas was stronger, so I needn't worry about you, love.' As soon as he had spoken, he knew he'd said the wrong thing.

Martha stiffened at the mention of her eldest son. 'There's not a day that goes by without me wishing things were different with Thomas. I don't need you reminding me what a terrible mother I am. How was I to know that Bridie Flannegan's child was ill when I went to help her with the new baby? I was just being a good friend, I had to take Thomas with me, I had no choice.'

The pitch of Martha's voice indicated she was close to tears. Albert looked at his wife. He knew he shouldn't have raised the old subject and felt guilty as he reached out to try to comfort her. 'Martha, don't go punishing yourself where there's no need.' His voice didn't sound as gentle as he would have liked.

Martha pushed Albert away. 'There's every need,' she spluttered. 'How else would you explain Thomas's weak heart? He got diphtheria, and it was my fault.'

'C'mon love, let's have a cuppa, we're both het up and worried by that wretched letter.'

'What letter?' said Rory coming in through the kitchen door. He raised his thick, dark eyebrows quizzically until they almost disappeared into his black hair. A good looking boy, with a high forehead and a wide, well-formed mouth, traces of manhood were starting to slowly manifest themselves in his face in his nineteenth year.

'A letter came for you, lad,' Martha said, nodding towards the envelope in Albert's hand.

Albert drew in a nervous breath of anxious anticipation, as he handed Rory the letter. 'Son, before you open it, there's something we think you should know.' But Rory was already opening the letter.

As he read it, his parents studied his face.

Chapter 2

Eliza Jane was blushing; she knew she was but she couldn't do anything about it. David Jackson had looked her straight in the eye and complimented her. 'Best bit of cake I've tasted in a long time,' he said. They had just finished their morning break in the back kitchen of the living quarters behind the shop and were returning to their duties.

Mr Jackson looked pointedly at his watch, as they returned but continued serving the first in line in the queue of customers. Eliza Jane grabbed her apron from underneath the counter and as she tied her apron strings, she glanced at David then looked away before he caught her looking. She had loved him from afar for many years, and had written him long letters throughout the war to keep his spirits up while away fighting. She had worried in silence about his safety. She had knitted him balaclavas, scarves and socks and sent them out to him without her family's knowledge. Only Miss Beatrice at the post office shared the secret of the regular parcels that were sent to France. Now David had come home, it seemed the letters and all that knitting actually counted for nothing, it was like she no longer existed. It had been worrying her that the Jacksons would no longer need her services at the shop after David's return but luckily for her, Mrs Jackson was immediately called away to Manchester to look after her sister, so her job for the moment was safe.

Eliza Jane took up her position behind the counter. David stood to the side of her, ready to serve.

'At last, I've been in this queue for fifteen minutes,' said a familiar voice. Eliza Jane groaned inwardly. Mrs Fanshawe was a regular customer and known for her acid tongue. A woman whose short legs looked incapable of bearing the weight of her impressive bosom, she wore an array of different coloured hats, each decorated with something that resembled a bird's nest perched on top. The heady aroma of mothballs always announced her arrival.

Eliza Jane smiled politely. 'Good morning, Mrs Fanshawe, what can I get for you today?'

'How come you're so red in the face, lady? It does nowt for your complexion.' She studied Eliza Jane closely, and was strangely satisfied to see Eliza Jane, blush even more. 'Any road up, it's a good job I've got my shopping list or what I need would have gone clean out of my head I've been standing here so long. She consulted the list in her basket. Let me see. I've got enough coupons for butter, some nice lean ham and some sugar.'

Eliza Jane busied herself with weighing out the groceries while Mrs Fanshawe chattered to no one in particular. David winked at Eliza Jane as she squeezed past him. Was it the wink or the slight touch of David's body that caused her to colour up again?

'Its high time the government stopped all this rationing, the war is over and has been for some time but there's no sign of it coming to an end,' said Mrs Fanshawe turning to address the customer behind her. Before the lady had time to reply, Mrs Fanshawe's attention was diverted to the shop doorway for there stood Jacob Pennington looking unusually diffident.

'Why good morning, Jacob Pennington, come away in, no one's going to bite,' she called heartily

Jacob doffed his cap and returned the greeting. 'Mrs Fanshawe, ladies.' He nodded, as he entered the shop. 'I won't join the queue. I don't want serving,' he said. 'I just want a word with Eliza Jane here if that's all right.' He twirled his cap around nervously, and then rammed it under his arm while he retrieved his handkerchief from his pocket to mop his sweating brow. He moved forward and the queue of customers parted to let him through.

Eliza Jane stopped weighing out sugar for Mrs Fanshawe and froze. Why did Jacob Pennington want to see her? He wouldn't propose to her again; would he? Not in front of David and Mrs Fanshawe. She had turned him down once already, unbeknown to her parents and he had replied that she was as plain as a cow's rump and not likely to get a better offer. Slowly, she lifted her eyes to face him as he approached the counter.

Mrs Fanshawe's eyes grew round with curiosity. She nearly passed out, her hat quivering with excitement, when Jacob got down on one knee. Eliza Jane in embarrassment ordered him to get up immediately and sought Mr Jackson's permission to usher him into the back of the shop. Although Mrs Fanshawe strained to hear every word that passed between them, she realised she couldn't hear a thing. As soon as she had paid David, for he had taken over serving her and without waiting for her change, she hurried from the shop. It was her duty to tell the village what had just happened. Scurrying over to the Misses Emmett's post office and sweet shop, she was itching to be the first one to spread the news. She stumbled into the shop and leaned heavily on the counter taking deep breaths. 'Jacob Pennington has just asked Eliza Jane Watkins to marry him in front of the whole of Jacksons shop.'

'Well, I didn't know they were courting, are you absolutely sure?' said Mrs Wimbourne, who was in the post office passing the time of day. She was used to Mrs Fanshawe telling a tall tale or two.

'Sure, as I'm standing here with some of Jackson's best ham in my basket.'

'Well, come on, tell us what happened, what did she say?' Miss Jemima Emmett said impatiently.

Miss Beatrice Emmet looked up from stamping letters from behind the post office counter.

'Well,' noticing that the three women in her audience were riveted, she paused for dramatic effect. 'Jacob got down on one knee, and then found he couldn't see over the counter, so he struggled up again and said…'

Mrs Fanshawe now deepened her voice: *'I'm not getting any younger, Eliza Jane, and nor are you. If you want bairns, you'll have to get a move on; so how about it?'* She lightened her voice again. *'How about what says Eliza Jane?'* Nevertheless, she knew what he was getting at all right. *'I mean to marry you Lizzie,* he said, then he took her hand – and this is the best bit – *I admire you Eliza Jane, and I could give you a good life, so will you marry me, lass.'*

'Don't leave it there, what did she say?' said Jemima Emmet. She removed her reading glasses, revealing piercing blue eyes to get a better look at the bearer of such important news.

Beatrice Emmett's heart lurched. She peered through the grille of the tiny post office counter, alarmed at such news. She had been holding a candle for Jacob Pennington since they were at school together. Although he had never seemed to reciprocate her feelings, she had always hoped that after the death of his wife, he might look in her direction. Her mind was whirling with the possibility that once more, she had been overlooked for romance. Nevertheless, she couldn't see how Eliza Jane would have accepted him; since she knew her heart lay with David Jackson. Beatrice recalled all the letters and parcels Eliza Jane had sent him during the war. Unable to think of anything to say and concerned that she might inadvertently betray Eliza Jane's trust, Beatrice remained silent.

Mrs Fanshawe, the excitement of the morning suddenly making her feel tired, sat down on the chair by the counter to continue. 'Well, now, I don't rightly know what she said, because she took him out back to finish the conversation. I'm fairly sure she said yes, but my ears aren't as good as they used to be. But if you ask me, they're as good as married, you can be sure of that.'

Etty Watkins, Eliza Jane's younger sister, overheard the last words of Mrs Fanshawe, as she stood in the doorway of the shop. She smiled wryly to herself, some unlucky person was the subject of malicious gossip as usual. She looked at Mrs Fanshawe from the doorway just making her out in the darkness of the shop after the bright sun of the day.

'Holding court again, Mrs Fanshawe, what a surprise!'

Mrs Fanshawe was incensed, and pulling herself up off the chair to her full height using the counter for support, remarked, 'There is no need to take that tone with me, Etty, I'm just saying that your Eliza Jane is set to wed Jacob Pennington.'

'What!' exclaimed Etty. 'Where did you hear this? You're making it up. I would have been the first to know if it were true.'

'Well, pardon me I'm sure, but I have just witnessed the proposal in Jackson's shop this morning, not more than half an hour ago,' Mrs Fanshawe retorted.

'How dare he think our Eliza Jane would even consider becoming his wife; why she'd end up being his slave more like?'

'He's a very kind man,' muttered Beatrice in his defence, pursing her thin lips and patting a stray grey curl out of the way of her eyes, as she came out from behind the post office counter.

'Well, we all know how you feel about Jacob, Beatrice Emmet, so you can put your face straight.' The bird's nest wobbled precariously on top of the hat, as Mrs Fanshawe barely paused for breath before continuing. 'So just fancy, your Eliza Jane will be mistress of Pennington's farm. She'll be having a baby or two afore long I expect, and that won't help her figure, lump of a girl that she is. I only hope she has better luck than poor Emily Pennington, God rest her soul, all them miscarriages and not a live baby to show for her efforts.' Mrs Fanshawe sniffed loudly.

'A proposal right here in Crossdale; it's so exciting. Why we haven't had an engagement in the village since…' Jemima Emmet's speech faded, as she caught sight of Etty's distressed face. The shop suddenly fell quiet.

'Since I became engaged to William before he went to fight for his country and never returned,' said Etty, her eyes flashed at Jemima, before gazing at the other women. She bit her lip to stop tears forming. 'I'll take me ma's *Women's Home Journal*, Miss Jemima, and I'll be on my way.'

Jemima replaced her spectacles to look for the magazine amongst the pile of journals below the counter.

'Oh, and Mrs Wimbourne, I'm glad I've seen you; your blouse will be ready later this afternoon. I'll bring i round to you.' Etty was a superb seamstress and had a talent for designing clothes based on illustrations from magazines that the village doctor's wife saved for her. She had many customers in Crossdale, which saved the local ladies a train journey into Lancaster for their clothes.

Etty took the magazine and nodding a brief farewell at the four ladies, turned to leave.

Mrs Fanshawe continued with an innocent air that belied the intended sting in the remark as Etty left the shop. 'At least Eliza Jane won't have to worry about a finding a wedding dress to fit, you know with her being on the large side, because you can make one of your clever designs for her.'

Trying to ignore the intended insult to her older sister, Etty left the shop with gritted teeth. As she stepped out on to the top step of three that led up to the shop, she heard Mrs Fanshawe resume her chatter: something was being said about the poor girl, the war and William.

Etty's anger increased, as she marched over to Jackson's shop. Sparring with Mrs Fanshawe had left a bitter taste in her mouth. She patted her hat straight as if it had been knocked sideways by the encounter, in an effort to restore her equilibrium. With her face, set she burst into the grocer's shop. Luckily, the morning rush was over and it was empty. David and Eliza Jane were just cleaning down the counters and were surprised to see Etty barge into the shop banging the door behind her.

'Tell me you didn't our Lizzie. Please, say you didn't—'

David Jackson smiled at the sight of her. 'Etty, you're looking a right bobby dazzler this morning,' he greeted. 'Is that a new dress?'

Temporarily distracted, Etty, smiled at him. 'Thank you, David; I made this to my own design.'

'Well, you look right pretty.'

Etty, suddenly remembering her mission turned to her sister. 'Lizzie, you didn't accept him, did you?' Etty searched her sister's face for an answer and felt her heart sink to her boots. 'Oh, for heaven's sake Lizzie, you did, didn't you?'

'No! I did not agree to marry Jacob Pennington, and even if I had, that would be my business, not yours.' Eliza Jane had been irritated by David complimenting her sister, although it was not surprising, Etty was lovely with her pert good looks, and hair like ripe corn. Eliza Jane was always being unfavourable compared to her sisters. Her own hair was straight and mousy, twisted into a bun on the back of her neck. She and Thomas shared Da's colouring. Etty and Molly had beautiful fair curls like Ma. Only Rory was dark.

Eliza Jane looked steadily at her sister. 'I couldn't say yes when I don't love him.'

'Thank God.' Breathed Etty, leaning over the counter to grip her sister's arms as if to shake her. 'You could do so much better,' she added.

'I don't know how, it's not as if I'm much of a catch.'

'Why of course you are! Any man would be pleased to have you as his wife; you're the best cook this side of Lancaster, isn't she, David? Wouldn't our Eliza make a good catch for someone?'

'Absolutely,' agreed David, dutifully.

'There, even David agrees, now come on, it's quiet in the shop; let's go home for our dinner.'

Gazing admiringly at Etty, David's voice carried a hesitant sense of hope. 'Are you going to the celebratory peace dance in the village hall tonight?'

'I'll think about it,' said Etty, winding a curl around her finger and tilting her head on one side.

'You must come, Etty. Oh, and you too, Eliza Jane, it wouldn't be the same without you.' Eliza Jane felt a sense of elation. 'And will you bring some of them sausage rolls you make?' he added.

Molly Watkins was cycling home. She usually loved the ride up from the station. The long lane meandered for a mile up to the village, and was lined with mayflower bushes in the spring, interspersed with bramble bushes which came into their own in the autumn. The smell of the mayflower although past its best was still pungent.

Today, however, Molly had no time to enjoy her surroundings or the beautiful sunshine. She was pedalling furiously, her usual soft features and curved mouth that always looked as if she was smiling, was set, and she gripped her handle bars angrily. Within a week, she would be out of a job, having been employed as a ticket clerk at the local station for nearly three years. The previous incumbent, Cyril Henderson, had recovered from his injuries sustained while fighting, and was ready to return to his old job. Not that Molly blamed Cyril; it was all Lloyd George's fault: not only had he passed the *Restoration of Pre-War Practices Act*, meaning men were entitled to return to their jobs after active service – but in a further oversight, he had failed to give young women under thirty the vote. *Stupid man,* thought Molly.

Although she didn't want to work on the railways all her life, it was an inconvenience to lose the job and she'd miss the wage. Molly's real ambition however was to become an actress. Now riding her bike, she was imagining herself to be Marjorie Daw, swept off her feet by Douglas Fairbanks, the day dream caused her to wobble, and she had to put her feet to the ground to steady herself. For some years now, she had contemplated how she could make it happen? Molly was always full of optimism. As a child, she had loved hearing her da read David Copperfield in his rich tones. Mr Micawber had been one of her favourite characters. 'Something will turn up' was Micawber's hope, and soon became Molly's byword. She pedalled on.

Thomas Watkins crossed the street to Laycocks antiques shop. He had seen Constance Haswell coming towards him in the distance and wanted to avoid her. It wasn't that he didn't like Constance, with her auburn curls and green eyes, but he had vowed never to get married, and thus couldn't see the point of pursuing a relationship that couldn't ultimately go anywhere. No woman would want to tie herself down to an invalid? The restrictions on Thomas's life were entirely self-imposed; Doctor Green had assured him he could get married and have children, but Thomas knew that the regular pain in his chest on exertion was real, and had decided otherwise. The army had rejected him due to ill health in 1914, which had left him feeling inadequate and did nothing to improve his self-esteem. He suffered recurring nightmares involving the war recruitment posters; Lord Kitchener's eyes seemed to mock him wherever he went.

Henry Laycock was behind the counter in his small workshop which was more of a cubby hole with a window. His appearance was as dry and dusty as some of his shelves. A confirmed bachelor who was content with his life, he was concentrating on the workings of a watch with his eyeglass in place. As the doorbell jangled, he looked up and smiled at Thomas, as he entered the cluttered shop.

'Ah, Thomas.' Henry got up from his chair and placing his eyeglass on the desk came round to the counter. 'I'm glad you've come in, another of your pieces, has been bought, that beautiful eagle you carved.' Henry Laycock sold some of Thomas's carvings as a sideline to his antique trade. 'Full asking price too.'

Thomas was delighted. 'Thanks, Henry, do you know who bought it?'

'Someone from London, they were just passing through, although they used to live up here somewhere. I can get the bill and check if you like. They certainly admired your work; said they might be interested in more pieces.'

Thomas shook his head; he didn't have much faith in his own abilities but felt pleased at the unexpected praise. 'Not to worry, Henry, let's just hope they come back for more. Now, do you want me to mind the shop while you have your lunch?'

'Will you do that, lad? I won't be long. I'll settle up with you when I get back.'

'Take as long as you need,' reassured Thomas. 'I'm quite happy here.'

Henry Laycock went back to his cubby hole, gathered up the timepiece he was working on and then disappeared into the back of the shop.

Thomas looked around him; he loved this old shop with its varied treasures languishing on dusty shelves. He must tell Ma that some more pottery dogs had arrived; perhaps he would buy one for her birthday next month with his earnings. The faint aroma of wax mingled with the slight smell of damp excited him. He would have loved to own a shop like this; just the sheer delight of the feel of polished wood and the comfort of running his hands over thin porcelain was heaven to him. He moved behind the counter and stood importantly behind it puffing out his chest. He shook his head and laughed at his silliness, imagination was a wonderful thing, for he would never own a shop like this except in his dreams.

Chapter 3

Back at the cottage, Ma gazed anxiously at Rory's shaking hands, as he read the letter. Instead of seeing puzzlement in his deep brown eyes, she saw his face break into a huge smile. He whooped and jumped in the air, waving the letter. 'I've won!' he shouted, whirling his bemused mother around by her waist. 'I've won!'

Ma slumped down on her chair; her face was flushed and she felt the beginnings of a familiar pain in her upper chest. 'Wait a minute, son,' she gasped. 'What are you talking about, what have you won?'

Da went to put his hand on Ma's shoulder, steadying her. 'What is it, lad, what have you won?' he pleaded, worried for his wife.

I've won the National Gallery's art competition.'

Rory took a moment to calm down, then continued. 'You remember that watercolour I did of you in the Smithy, Da? Well, I entered a competition in Mr Laycock's newspaper. It was run to celebrate the return of the paintings to the National after their wartime evacuation. I entered ages ago; in fact, I'd forgotten all about it. I had to send the canvas off to London. Miss Beatrice at the Post Office was very intrigued with the huge parcel, but I didn't tell her what it was. First prize is a camera, and the winning portrait is to be hung in the National Gallery in London.' Da could see excitement dancing around Rory's bright eyes and felt some small measure of his son's exhilaration

'I won it, Da,' he said, 'I can't believe it, I won.'

Ma who was just beginning to recover from the pain in her chest glanced at Albert, patting his hand that lay on her shoulder. Tears of relief moistened her eyes. 'Eh, lad, I'm cock-a-hoop for you, I'm right proud. To think our son's painting will be seen by all those hoity-toity folks in London. What do you say to that, Albert?'

Albert was still trying to make sense of it all. 'So, you won a camera, for that picture you painted of me!'

'Yes, Da, and you'll be hung in the National Gallery.'

Albert considered this for a moment. 'Hung in the National Gallery, imagine that, all those folk gazing at me. I'll be right famous.' He turned to his son, rubbing his hands with glee. 'I'm proud as punch, lad; perhaps I got it wrong, maybe you can make a decent living at this art thing, after all.' A long rumbling laugh erupted from the depths of his stomach. He hugged Rory and jigged him around the room. Ma provided the accompaniment, beating time by clapping her hands.

Etty and Eliza Jane confronted the pandemonium, as they came in through the back door.

'Whatever's going on? What's happened, are you all right, Ma?' Eliza Jane took her mother's hand, puzzled by events. 'Ma, what's—' She stopped abruptly, as she saw Etty gathered up in her father's embrace, and danced around the room. Rory grinning widely. She laughed, although she had no idea why. Ma tapped her feet in delight from her chair, as she looked at her eldest daughter. 'Not to worry, love, it's good news. Rory has won a competition. Remember that painting he did of your da? Well, it's going to be hung in the National Gallery in London.'

'London! That's wonderful,' said Eliza Jane smiling at Rory, who was jigging around the room, having taken Etty over from his breathless father.

Ma took Eliza Jane's hand, bringing her close. 'Rory will explain it later, better than me, I still can't quite understand it.' She shook her head. 'Now I want to hear about you. Your da says that old goat Jacob Pennington asked for your hand in marriage this morning. You didn't agree, did you? That's not what I want for my girl.'

'I turned him down, Ma; though it might be the only offer I get.'

'Don't talk rubbish, lass, I know there's someone out there just for you. In fact, I'm sure of it. Now let's get that kettle on, and we might break open the broken biscuits you bought home from the shop. Dinner will have to wait.'

Etty selected her best dress to wear for the dance that night; she held it up against her then pirouetted around the bedroom she shared with her sisters. Molly and Eliza Jane were sitting on their beds looking at her, amused at their sister's antics. The room was filled with three single beds, two were side by side and the third ran along the wall behind the door and to the side of the window. Ma had made matching bedspreads and curtains in yellow gingham in an effort to lighten the room and a rag rug lay on the floor in the middle of bare floorboards. In the corner of the room was a large wardrobe and underneath the small window was a dressing table and mirror.

'Perhaps I should enter a dress design competition,' said Etty, 'I expect I could win something better than a camera.'

Molly and Eliza Jane exchanged glances and sighed.

'Etty, how can you say that,' chided Molly.

'Well, where does Rory get his talent from, that's what I want to know. I can draw a bit, but only clothes, nothing like Rory's paintings.' Etty had stopped pirouetting and was at the dressing table where she picked up a box of rouge. She gave her sisters a disarming smile through the mirror, as she busily applied the red powder to her cheeks.

'Etty,' Eliza Jane observed, 'Ma will never allow you to go out with rouge on your cheeks.'

'I couldn't care less what Ma thinks. I'm old enough to go out how I please. Anyway, I have to cover up some of this yellow tinge to my skin from the powder I handled at the munitions factory. No wonder they called us canaries.' Etty gazed in despair at her face and hands, was it worth three pounds a week to lose her pale skin.

Eliza Jane slid off her bed and placed her feet to the floor. She walked over to Etty sitting in front of the dressing table. She had been concerned about her sister since she had come home from the factory. 'The war has changed you, Etty,' she said. 'I don't know what happened when you worked in the munitions factory, but you're different since you came home.'

'It was hard work but we always had a laugh living together in the hostel. I was almost sorry when the work finished, and I certainly miss the money. I thought my work in Carlisle would somehow keep my William safe; I thought if I could do something to help shorten the war, it might increase his chances of coming home. Well I was wrong, wasn't I? William didn't come home; he's lying out there all alone, somewhere under cold French soil. I should be with him. Losing William changed me, Lizzy, not the factory.'

Eliza Jane lowered her darkened eyes. 'I know, dear,' she said softly, placing a comforting hand on her sister's shoulder.

Molly sighed, breaking the silence. 'It sounds fun though, Etty, living in the hostel away from here, hard work but fun.' Then with her eyes becoming dreamy, she continued, 'I wish something exciting would happen to me.'

'Molly,' scolded Eliza Jane. 'The last time you said that, we went to war. Be careful what you wish for.'

Nevertheless, Molly was too far gone in her fantasy to be brought down to earth. She stood up on her bed flinging her arms out and bowing deeply. She wobbled precariously which made her laugh, as she collapsed back on her bed. 'Suppose a big film director might visit the dance tonight. Suppose he wants to whisk me away to star in his next film. What would I do? How would I tell Ma?' Molly's face clouded over.

'Suppose you cross that bridge when you get to it, dear,' smiled Eliza Jane.

Molly clasped her hands to her chest. 'I have the strangest feeling. I know something will happen, I can feel it, but don't ask me how or when. I just know.'

There was a knock on the bedroom door. 'Are you lasses ready?' Thomas sounded impatient. 'We're going to be late.'

Molly squealed. She had yet to do her hair; she quickly got off her bed and headed for the mirror that Etty had vacated. She grabbed a hairbrush and briskly gathered her long hair into a becoming upswept style.

'Two minutes,' called Etty pinning a flower on her dress. 'Right, I'm ready, I can't improve on perfection.' She turned to Eliza Jane. 'Are you going to the dance dressed like that?'

'What's wrong with this skirt and blouse? I feel comfortable in it.'

'You wear that skirt every day, Lizzie; you'll never get David Jackson to dance with you looking like that.'

'I haven't got anything else to wear. He wouldn't dance with me anyway.'

'Let me put some rouge on you then.'

'No, Etty, please don't. My face is red enough as it is.' Etty refused to take no for an answer and dragged Eliza Jane over to the dressing table and applied some rouge and powder to her sister's face.

Etty stood back to admire her handiwork completely un- aware of Eliza Jane's embarrassment. 'There you look better already.' She replaced the powders on the dressing table and turned to look at her sisters. 'I think we will be the best looking lasses at the dance tonight.' Eliza Jane made a disbelieving face which Etty ignored. 'Right, shall we go?' Etty and Molly left their room and ran down the stairs chattering excitedly Eliza Jane followed behind them dreading Ma's reaction to the rouge.

Ma met them at the bottom of the stairs. 'Etty and Eliza Jane, go right back up those stairs and take that red stuff off your cheeks. I'll not have my daughters going out looking like a couple of haricots.'

'You mean harlots, Ma.' Laughed Rory from his perch on the arm of his mother's chair.

Martha rounded on Rory, the look on her face was one he knew well and made him stand up. 'And you're too young to know such words; I could still put you over my knee my boy?' She turned back to her daughters to repeat her request.

'No, Ma, we won't,' Etty said defiantly. 'All the girls are wearing rouge this year. God knows we've had four years of misery: a bit of rouge might cheer us all up.'

'Etty, you'll do as I say, please and take Eliza Jane with you. I'll not allow you to go to the dance like that.'

Martha looked to Albert for support but none was forthcoming. Enjoying his after dinner pipe and relaxing in his armchair, he personally thought all his daughters looked beautiful.

'That's typical of you, Albert Watkins, where your daughters are concerned, you're as blind as a bat.' Martha fired at him.

Etty tried to make her case again. 'Ma, I'm twenty-five years old, I'm entitled to dress how I please. I would have been married and running my own home by now if William had been spared. Don't you dare, Lizzie,' she added, as she saw Eliza Jane heading for the stairs.

Ma stood with her cheeks inflated, her fists balanced on her hips. Understanding that she was beaten, she said, 'You will be the death of me, Henrietta Watkins.'

Etty paused for a moment wondering whether to retaliate. Deciding against it, she twisted on her heel, grabbed Eliza Jane's hand and made for the door. She turned to look at her siblings. 'Well, are we going?' Without waiting for their answer, she swept out of the room, taking a reluctant Eliza Jane with her.

After kissing their mother, Rory and Molly followed.

'Don't worry, Ma; I'll look out for them. It's not Lizzie's fault,' said Thomas, kissing his mother's cheek.

Ma grasped his arm as he started to leave, 'I know you will son, I know, but I want you to have a good time too. Promise me you'll have at least one dance with that pretty redhead that follows you about. You know who I mean, Charlie Haswell's daughter. Constance, isn't that her name?'

'I can't promise such things, Ma, you know that. Anyway, she may not want to dance with me, and who can blame her? Two dances and I'm puffing like a train; it's hardly appealing to a young woman to sit out several dances.'

Not long after they had left, Ma was in pain again. She knew it was only indigestion; she must have eaten her tea too quickly. She would make up a potion of bicarbonate of soda later and that would help. She smiled as she looked at Albert snoring by the fire. She was sitting in her own chair opposite him. Poor lad, he worked hard; she knew that, and he was a good provider to the family, let him sleep. She resumed her knitting as the pain began to subside.

Eliza Jane felt silly; she hated what Etty had done to her face. Before anyone noticed her, she quickly took the sausage rolls from the basket she was carrying and placed them on to one of the tables bearing the buffet. Turning quickly with her head down, she rushed off to the toilet to remove the powder. Using the large mirror that was hung up, she rubbed most of it from her cheeks with her handkerchief. Satisfied she could do no more, she wandered out towards the dance floor. The usual sombre hall had been decorated by the village committee with flags and bunting all in red white and blue. There were trestle tables down one side of the hall laden with supper and next to it, a makeshift bar that was attracting some of the young men who had returned from the war. With varying degrees of disability, they stood together happy to be alive for that was all that mattered.

The local band with Henry Laycock on the piano and Roy Hughes, the butcher, on the fiddle were playing a waltz. Eliza Jane watched Etty dance in the arms of David Jackson. She tried to feel pleased that her sister was having such a good time, but it wasn't easy with her own longings for David held tightly inside her. Wryly, she observed Jacob Pennington whirling a very animated Beatrice Emmet around the floor. *So much for his broken heart*, she thought.

'Shall we?' Thomas appeared and extended his hand to her, causing her to smile.

Suddenly, the accusing voice of Constance Haswell interrupted them. 'Thomas, I think you've been avoiding dancing with me all evening. You don't mind, Eliza Jane, do you? After all, no one wants to dance with their brother, do they?'

Firmly taking his hand, Constance pulled a reluctant Thomas onto the dance floor. With great determination, she placed his arm around her waist and snuggled in close to him.

Eliza Jane watched them, grateful that her mother wasn't there to witness such immoral intimacy.

'Do you want to dance, Eliza Jane?' She looked up to find David Jackson standing before her.

'You don't have to, David, I'm all right here.'

'No, c'mon, Eliza Jane just one dance, eh.'

Eliza Jane blushed, as she took David's hand and joined him on the dance floor.

'You look nice tonight; your cheeks have a flush to them.'

'So do you, David.' She winced at her stupid remark. How could she write reams of letters to him through the war but not be able to hold a sensible conversation face to face?

'You brought the sausage rolls then.'

'Yes.'

They finished their dance in silence, and David escorted her back to a spare seat. It was then as David was walking away that she saw Etty give him a nod of approval as she danced by. Eliza Jane's heart sank; he had obviously been instructed to dance with her? She was humiliated.

Molly was having fun; she was much in demand as a partner on the dance floor. She giggled and waltzed her way around the room. Rory, not having much experience with girls was propping up the bar and chatting to friends.

Constance whispered in Thomas's ear, as they danced slowly around the floor. 'Let's go outside for a while; it's very hot in here, and besides there's something I have to tell you.' He wanted to refuse but the thought of filling his lungs with cool air was appealing.

Constance looped her arm through his, and they wandered out to the humpback bridge that crossed the canal. The evening air was cool after the heat of the day and Thomas drew in deep breaths as he began to relax. He gazed up at the sky: the stars glinted like shiny buttons on a new waistcoat. He pointed out Orion's belt and other constellations. Constance listened politely, in awe of his knowledge, but she was also wondering how she was going to tell him her news. She shivered from the cool night air as she perched herself on the low wall of the bridge. Thomas folded his arms and stood beside her.

'I love this village, Thomas; I never want to leave it.'

'Aye, it's a grand place.'

'Do you ever see yourself moving away?'

Thomas considered this question for a while as he lit a cigarette. The yellow glow of the match illuminated her face. 'I would never want to leave,' he said.

'Do you see yourself settling here then, you know marriage and babies?'

'No, lass, I can't see it. I'm not fit, I was turned down by the army. You know that, my war was spent working with Da in the smithy, and I wasn't much use to him.'

Constance paused, trying to gain the courage she needed before continuing.

'Thomas, I think we should get wed.' She held up her hand to silence his objections. 'I know you don't love me as much as I love you, but it would please my folks and yours too, I think.'

Thomas swallowed hard, why had he agreed to come outside with the lass, he should have known. He thought quickly before answering. 'You know, Connie, we've got all the time in the world to think about marriage. Why we've barely been courting and we've only just come through a ferocious war. There's no rush; let's not talk about it now.'

'But that's just the point, lad, we don't have all the time in the world, my family is moving south in two weeks, dad has been given a promotion. If we got married, I could stay here, with you.'

Thomas chose his words carefully. 'Connie, you know I care about you, and I wouldn't hurt you for the world but I can't marry you, lass. I couldn't be a proper husband to you, I couldn't provide for you as I would want. Where would we live? I don't have a job; all I have is the money I make on my carvings.'

'There's a small cottage for rent over the back of the village. We could live there.'

'What Granny Parkers' old place, we always thought that was haunted as bairns, it needs a lot doing to it, it's been empty for a while.'

'It would be ours to do as we please with. Just think about it, just for us. I've been to look at it, and it's not that bad.'

Thomas looked into her eager, green eyes and could almost imagine himself living with her. The idea was appealing, but also very wrong. Finally, he replied, 'I'm sorry, lass, I'm sorry if you got your hopes up. I cannot marry you.'

'But I could look after you. Please, Thomas, I love you. I've a bit of money of my own put by and I earn a regular wage from my job as a secretary in Lancaster. We could be so happy.' She laid a hand on Thomas's rough jacket.

In the silence that followed, Thomas was aware of the music and laughter coming from the village hall which seemed to add poignancy to the situation in which he found himself. *It would be the easiest thing in the world to say yes,* he thought, as he considered his answer but he couldn't allow the lass to support him, he could never hold his head up again. 'I can't let you support me, Constance, it wouldn't be right.'

'I don't mind, Thomas, really I don't. I want to.'

Thomas reached for her hands and turned her towards him. 'Listen, lass,' he said softly, 'you are the kindest, sweetest girl and if I was to marry anyone then it would be you, please believe that, but I'm never going to marry, I'm so sorry, lass.' Was he refusing her because of the physical condition of his heart or was it that he didn't really love her in the first place? He couldn't answer his own question. He watched helplessly, as a tear rolled down her cheek. Hurriedly, he continued speaking devastated that he had caused her to cry. 'Constance,' he placed a hand under her chin. 'My guess is that one day, someone will love you as you deserve to be loved. Go with your family, lass, find that someone and enjoy the adventure.'

He kissed her gently on her wet cheek, then handed her his handkerchief. 'Come on, dry your eyes now, and let's pretend we've never had this conversation.'

With a sob, Constance turned and dashed for the door. As she re-entered the brightly lit hall, she blinked, wiped her eyes and blew her nose hard on the handkerchief Thomas had given her. Finally, when her eyes adjusted to the light, she noticed Jacob Pennington was on the band rostrum with his hands in the air and about to speak.

'Listen up; let's have some quiet. I've an announcement to make,' called Jacob. When the crowd fell silent, he continued. 'There's a lady here tonight that has just made me the happiest man alive by consenting to become my wife. Ladies and gentlemen, please allow me to introduce my—'

Suddenly, a door banged at the far end of the hall and a voice shouted, 'It's Thomas Watkins, he's hurt, quick someone fetch t'doctor.'

Chapter 4

Albert opened his eyes allowing the morning light to filter in. He sighed then yawned. He had slept well, must have been the pint he had at the bluebell last thing before turning in. It had the makings of another warm day. Stretching out his cramped limbs, he swung his legs to the floor and waited for a moment to gather himself before standing to his full height. Martha was still sleeping and looked peaceful, bless her, let her rest after all the excitement and worry of yesterday. It had been such a relief that it was not the letter they had both lived in fear of arriving for the last nineteen years.

Creeping out of the bedroom, he listened at his daughters' door. All was quiet; they must have had a late night after the dance. There wasn't a sound from the lads' room either. Grinning to himself he went downstairs to the kitchen – oh to be young again, he sighed.

Albert sang quietly, as he prepared the tea. This was his favourite time of day: the empty silence of the early morning. As the kettle boiled on the hob, he gazed out of the scullery window and watched the swans gliding by on the canal. A sudden noise broke his contemplation, startling him. He spun around to find Thomas standing before him. 'God in Heaven, lad, you made me jump.' On closer inspection, he saw that his son had a swollen left eye; his face bruised and battered also. 'Whatever's happened to you? Look at your face, your ma's going to be right upset.'

'I'm all right, Da, Doctor Green has looked me over. It's just a few cuts and bruises, and some sore ribs.'

'What happened?' A terrifying image of oozing blood intermingled with white feathers flashed through Albert's mind. He pushed it from his brain, unwilling to believe his worst fears. After all, the war was over. The poor lad had previously had white feathers thrust at him by angry strangers, mostly women, who had not known he had tried to enlist. Albert exhaled loudly. 'Who did this to you, son?'

'I don't know, Da. I was set on from behind. I don't want to make a fuss; just leave it, Da, please.'

Thomas sat down gingerly on his mother's chair by the dwindling fire in the grate. 'If you're brewing though, I'd murder a cuppa.'

'Never mind the cuppa – by the looks of it, you've been nearly murdered. Wait here, I'll take your ma her tea, and then get dressed. It has to be reported to Constable Haswell, let him deal with it, he does bugger all else for the village.'

'No, Da. I don't want a fuss, besides, Constance told me last night that her father's been promoted to Sergeant, and they are all moving south. It will be a while before they replace him. Just take Ma her tea and forget about the whole thing.'

With the tea in his hand, Albert left the room. Thomas winced as he stood up, his whole body ached. He knew who had done this to him, but he would never tell.

In the room above his head, he heard a crash of crockery, the sound of heavy footsteps, then his da's voice, shouted down the stairs: 'Thomas! Thomas, for God's sake get the doctor. It's Ma. Get the doctor, now.'

Asking no questions and quite forgetting his injuries, Thomas headed out of the cottage, hobbling as fast as he could. He made towards the village boundary stone, passing terraced houses with low stonewalls and neat gardens. The doctor's house stood in its own grounds just outside the village. Finally arriving, gasping, and coughing, he thumped on the doctor's front door. He folded his arms around his sore ribs, and bent forward unable to catch his breath. Why was no one opening the door? He banged again, striking the panel with his fist. He heard a car approaching in the distance, which eventually drew on to the gravel drive and stopped beside him… 'Thank God,' Thomas muttered to himself, as he recognised the doctor behind the wheel.

Rory woke to the sound of sobbing from somewhere in the house. Pushing up onto his elbows, he looked across the small room to Thomas's empty bed. His stomach lurched, as he remembered the beating his brother had received the night before. 'Bastards!' he said, his teeth clenched. The crying continued but he was unsure where it was coming from. Throwing back his eiderdown, he put his feet to the floor; snatching up his shirt and trousers from where he had dropped them the previous night, he dressed hurriedly before striding to the door, opening it cautiously, and listening intently.

The sound was coming from his parent's bedroom. He moved closer along the landing to stand outside their door. He could make out a low rumbling voice, which he didn't recognise, followed by Thomas's voice which was clearer. The door opened, and he came face to face with Doctor Green.

'I'm sorry, lad,' he said, placing a hand on Rory's shoulder as he passed him. Rory stood transfixed by the sight that met his eyes. He could see his father was seated at the bedside with his head bowed while holding Ma's hand. He turned to look up at his son, shaking his head, his face wet with tears.

Rory stumbled backwards and turned on his heel. He ran blindly down the stairs, barging past Thomas on the way. He tugged at the front door and ran out into the street. Not knowing which way to go, he looked left then right. Seeing the back of Doctor Green's car driving down the road, he ran in the opposite direction, quite forgetting he had no boots on his feet.

Eliza Jane found him some hours later, crouching behind the cricket pavilion; she sat down beside him. She placed his boots by his feet and put a comforting hand on the curve of his back. They sat together in silence for some time. After a while, Rory spoke in a low voice. 'She's dead, isn't she? Ma's dead.' Eliza Jane nodded.

'How did it happen?'

'Her heart,' whispered Eliza Jane.

'I ran away, Lizzie.'

'Yes, Rory, it's okay, you were in shock.' This said quietly. 'You loved Ma so much, and she loved you.'

I will never forgive myself,' said Rory fiercely. 'Da needed me and I let him down. I let you all down.'

'No, Rory, you've let none of us down. We're all so proud of you. Think how joyful Ma felt yesterday, and that was down to you.'

'I'll make it up to Da, I'll work with him in the smithy, it's what he wants more than anything. I'll give up my painting, I'll do it for him. I'm going to become the best blacksmith there is.'

'Listen to me, lad: the greatest thing you can do for them both is to be happy and painting makes you happy. Why you saw how proud they were of you yesterday, don't throw it all away.' She smiled and nudged his shoulder. 'Come on, put your boots on, let's go home.'

'I can't see Ma.'

'You don't have to do anything you don't feel comfortable with, lad.'

'Sometimes I think I'm going mad, you know. I've always had a strange feeling that there's something missing in my life. It's weird, like not having a right arm or something. Why do you suppose that is?'

'You've just lost someone very precious,' answered Eliza Jane

Rory didn't like to tell his sister he had felt like this long before Ma's death.

News of Martha's death soon spread around the village. Thomas was given the task of greeting the locals when they came to the cottage to pay their respects. Ma was laid out in the front parlour in the finest coffin Albert could buy. Thomas repeated the same words to every caller. *Yes, it was a shock. No, Da was not up to receiving visitors but you are most welcome to come and say goodbye at the funeral.*

On the morning of the funeral, Albert, restless and miserable, wandered into the front garden to pick some roses. Jack joined him with a downcast tail, staying as near to his master as possible. Martha had been very proud of her roses and they were now in full bloom, the early morning dew bringing out their intoxicating scent. Albert selected six healthy flowers, one for each of them to place in with his wife. They would match the rose-sprigged cotton dress: a particular favourite of Albert's, in which Martha was laid to rest in.

Molly watched him through the bedroom window, as he shuffled back along the path to the house. Dressed in his only black suit, with a crisp white shirt and collar, washed starched and ironed by Eliza Jane ready for the funeral, there was no sign of the handsome upright man that was her father; instead he had become weary, old and bent. So much so she doubted whether even Mr Micawber could be optimistic about their future.

Pausing for a moment outside the parlour Albert inhaled deeply. He wanted to pretend that Martha was just out at the shops or visiting a friend, but he knew the reality of what was to greet him as he entered the room. 'I've bought something for you, my love,' he said, gently placing a rose under Martha's hands. He whispered a little prayer then bent to kiss her forehead.

A timid knock on the open door broke the moment. Albert saw Rory standing nervously in the doorway.

'Son, come and say goodbye to your ma?'

'I can't, Da, I can't do it. Please don't ask me. I've only come to tell you that the Co-op is here for Ma; it's time to go.'

With a final glance at his wife, Albert stumbled slightly as he walked towards the door to greet the funeral directors. Rory moved forward quickly to grab his father's arm. Albert looked at him for a moment then patted his shoulder, 'I'm all right son, I'll manage,' he said, as he straightened up and walked steadily out of the door. Rory could hear the undertaker's voices, then Da's, agreeing they could collect Ma.

Rory stood for a moment looking at the coffin from the doorway. Two steps and he would be right beside her, but he had never seen a dead body before. He was scared, what if the *person* lying in the coffin didn't look like Ma. He knew he couldn't bear it, so he turned and walked away, hating himself for it.

'The Co-op did a lovely job,' observed Mrs Fanshawe in the post office a couple of days later.

Mrs Wimbourne agreed. 'Only what Martha deserved. Fancy, she were only fifty-eight.'

'That's no age,' agreed Jemima Emmet. 'They said it was quick, her heart you know.'

'She died in her sleep I believe,' said Mrs Fanshawe, warming to her subject. 'Albert found her dead when he bought up her morning tea. Must have been a shock; I see that Etty was hysterical as her mother's coffin was lowered into the ground, it would have been fuelled by guilt, of course, she and Martha never did get on.'

'Albert's taken it hard,' put in Jemima Emmet, 'they say he's not opened the smithy since. Did you see him at the graveside? He could barely stand upright between them lads of his. Mind, talking of which, those poor bairns left behind without a ma;' it doesn't bear thinking about.' She shuddered dramatically, and then catching sight of Beatrice Emmet's eager face, she added, 'Now then Beatrice Emmet, think on, don't you go getting any ideas above yourself – after all, I can't deny it, Albert is still a handsome man.' Beatrice was about to reply but Mrs Fanshawe widened her eyes and nodded towards the shop door: a familiar warning that someone was coming, and that they should rapidly change the subject of conversation.

'Any road out I'll just have a quarter of mint humbugs, Miss Jemima if you please,' she said hastily. 'Oh, it's you Jacob. We were just talking about Albert, have you seen him?'

Jacob held up his hand as if to stop the flow. 'Now hold your horses, Sheila Fanshawe. First, I need to say hello to my fiancée.'

Beatrice looked anxiously at Jemima noticing her mouth fall open in surprise, as the bag and scoop for the humbugs were held in mid-air. 'What's all this about sister, what does he mean by calling you his fiancée?'

'I'm to be Mrs Jacob Pennington.' Beatrice's cheeks became redder still as she searched her fiancée's face for support.

'Married!' shrieked Jemima. 'What a dried-up old spinster like you to be wed, have you gone soft in the head?'

'When did all this happen then?' asked Mrs Fanshawe, eagerly. 'Why it were only a week ago that you were asking Eliza Jane Watkins to be your bride, Jacob. What are you playing at, lad?' demanded Mrs Fanshawe.

'I realised it was Beatrice that I've,' he hesitated, choosing his words carefully before continuing, 'been fond of all these years. We're to be married as soon as the banns are read.'

Everyone watched as Mrs Fanshawe turned and dashed through the door and down the steps, hot news did not apparently wait for humbugs.

Chapter 5

Albert sat by the fire; although it was a hot day in July, he was in need of the warmth it provided. He gazed at Martha's empty chair which had become a shrine since her passing. Her knitting lay unattended, and the cushion remained flat from when she had last sat down. On the circular needles was the grey wool of an unfinished sock. There was a bitter comfort in seeing it there. Jack was stretched out beside him, rarely leaving Albert's side these days. The dog lay with his shiny black head resting on his white-socked front paws.

Vaguely aware that his arms were irritating him, Albert scratched his skin vigorously until it began to bleed. Doctor Green had diagnosed eczema, and had prescribed cream that now lay unused in a drawer in the scullery.

It was a month since Martha had died, and he rarely left the house. Deep in his heart, he knew he couldn't go on without her.

Eliza Jane called from the scullery, 'Da, I've made soup, and there's bread fresh from the oven?' Albert barely had the energy to shake his head in refusal.

'Knock, knock, anyone at home?' Jacob Pennington put his head around the back door. The aroma of fresh bread hot from the oven compounded his feeling of regret that Eliza Jane had rejected his offer of marriage. He looked over at Albert and the sight of him looking grizzled and bent shocked him.

'I let meself in, Albert,' he said loudly, in case Albert had lost his hearing as well as his wife. 'I've come to see how you are. What's to do, lad, eh?' Jacob sat down heavily in Martha's chair crushing the knitting in the process. Eliza Jane who had come into the parlour on hearing Jacob's voice noticed the look of anguish on her da's face. 'I'll make tea,' she said, disappearing into the scullery.

The men sat in silence until the tea was made and a cup placed in front of them.

Jacob gulped at his hot tea, urging Albert to do the same. They sat in the dimly lit room; the curtains drawn on Albert's instructions shutting out the bright sunshine. He cleared his throat, desperately trying to find some suitable words to comfort his friend. He couldn't remember what had been said to him when Emily had died, and thus had no words of comfort for the shadow of a man sitting opposite him.

'Work is piling up at the smithy, Albert.' Jacob bit his lip – that wasn't the way to begin. He tried again, 'We miss you around the village, lad. When I lost my lass and bairns, I thought my world had come to an end. I do understand – if that's any comfort to you.'

Jacob was concerned. Albert continued to stare blankly at the floor, refusing to even acknowledge his old friend. It was so hot by the fire. Jacob took out his hanky and mopped his brow. 'I can tell you now, Albert,' he said, blowing air up from his bottom lip to cool himself. 'I wished I were dead on many occasions. Oh, folks were kind all right, but I'm not popular, so it didn't take long for them to stop visiting. You know I think of my poor Emily every day. I still miss her, but God's honest truth it doesn't hurt as much as it did. I mean, tek' me now, I've finally persuaded a perfect woman to become the second Mrs Pennington, and I'll be well looked after. Yes, I know I wanted to marry your Eliza Jane a short while ago, but I realised I were too old for her. There's no fool like an old fool, so they say, lad, eh? Nevertheless, you're the lucky one. Oh, you may not think so now, but I can tell yer that you are.'

'Lucky!' exploded Albert.

'Oh, so you can say summat then. Yes, lucky, you have five wonderful bairns to look after you, I had no one. Think on, lad.'

Albert suddenly leant forward grabbing Jacob's wrist. 'Help me, Jacob. You must help me. The family are creeping around, not wanting to upset me, and no one mentions Martha for fear of upsetting me. Do you know what the worse thing is, I just can't forgive her for leaving me? I'm so bloody angry that I don't know what to do with mysel.' Albert trembled violently, as tears coursed down his cheeks. Then as suddenly as he had grabbed Jacob's wrist, he let it go, thrusting his face into his hands.

The others, eager to escape the misery of the house had gone for a walk. There was a road out of Crossdale that led past Doctor Green's house and down to a small pond. They had bought bread for the ducks and had settled themselves on the grassy bank aimlessly throwing crusts into the water. Molly laughed as she watched the ducks squabbling for food.

'Molly,' said Etty coolly. 'You shouldn't laugh; it's not right with Ma only just laid to rest.'

'I didn't mean to be disrespectful, but Ma wouldn't want us to be sad and I miss her so much. You know the other day when Joe Haswell asked me to go for a walk with him…'

Thomas stared sharply at Molly. 'Did you say *Joe Haswell* asked you to go for a walk with him?'

'Yes, and I went, but I didn't enjoy it. I liked him in school but he's changed. He told me something interesting though. He said that his sister Constance asked you to marry her, and that you refused. I don't call that very chivalrous Thomas Watkins.' She thought for a moment. 'What have you got against Joe anyhow?'

'I've nowt against him,' mumbled Thomas, rubbing his neck with his hand.

Etty knew that Thomas did this when he was feeling uncomfortable about something; she thought for a moment then looked steadily at him.

'It was him that beat you up on the night of the dance, wasn't it?' she said.

Thomas looked at the horizon, ignoring Etty's words.

'I'm right, aren't I?' Etty persisted. 'Why did he do it, was it to avenge his sister's honour? It makes me so angry that scum like Joe Haswell are far too wily to get themselves killed in the war and yet there's my poor William, who would never have hurt anyone if he could help it, lying in an unmarked grave somewhere in France. There's no justice in this world.' Etty paused trying to contain her anger then continued, 'Why didn't you say at the time?'

'Because Connie told me they were moving south; it wasn't worth making a fuss. Besides maybe, I deserved it, I broke her heart which means I'm no better than Joe really.

Everyone stared at the water, there was nothing more to say.

Chapter 6

Three days later, Albert went back to work, though it was short lived. He was soon laying back in his bed with the curtains drawn and Jack by his side. Rory knocked on the door and entered the room. As he approached the inert figure on the bed, Jack growled low in his throat, warning Rory to leave the master alone. Rory reached out and fondled the dog's head. 'It's all right, boy,' he said quietly, then he addressed his father. 'Da, you've only been into work for two days, c'mon give it another go. Why don't I come in with you, I can learn the trade, that's what you want, isn't it?'

'I'll go in tomorrow maybe, but now just leave me alone.'

'We lost her too, Da, just you remember that.' Rory instantly regretted his words, as he looked at Albert lying shrivelled and vulnerable in his bed. 'I'm sorry, Da,' he said, 'it's been hard on all of us. Will you at least let me take Jack for a walk; he's not left your side. Come on, Jack, let's go.'

Rory clapped his hands to rouse the dog. 'Come on, boy, let's go.' But Jack refused to move. Rory gave up and shutting the bedroom door quietly behind him he went downstairs. Eliza Jane stopped dusting and looked at him expectantly but he just shook his head in reply.

He sat down wearily at the table in the sitting room; he opened his sketch pad and began to draw. He had promised himself he wouldn't paint again but drawing was different. With a few strokes of his charcoal, he started to draw a picture of a young man. Rory had no idea who he was but he seemed to resemble himself.

Albert rolled over in bed, turning his face to the wall. His eyes felt heavy, his chest tight and his limbs ached. He couldn't face life without Martha, and he couldn't face the children, nor could he stomach the sympathetic gazes of the villagers. Jacob had told him to take small steps; those words echoed in his thoughts. He couldn't even manage one step at the moment. He had barely eaten since Martha's death, and his clothes were hanging off him. He was useless, he thought. Even his children were despairing of him. If only he could see Martha: talk to her, touch her, smell her familiar scent, take comfort from her warmth.

He could hear the voices of the family downstairs – Molly was giggling, Etty was complaining, Eliza Jane soothing. A dark thought invaded Albert's mind and he suddenly sat up, then putting his feet to the floor, he stood up and lurched over to Martha's dressing table. Jack jumped down from the bed to follow him. Albert opened the top drawer and not finding what he wanted, he opened another. He finally found Martha's writing case in the third drawer down. Laying the writing case on the table next to Martha's hairbrush, he extracted two sheets of paper and two envelopes, and then searched for a pencil. He thought long and hard about the letters he was about to write, before assembling his ideas as coherently as he could on the paper. Once finished, he read them through and placed them in separate envelopes and addressed them. Leaving the letters on the dressing table, he pulled on his old trousers and shirt, laced up his boots, collected the envelopes and went downstairs, Jack at his heels.

Eliza Jane rose from her chair, putting her book to one side when she saw Albert.

'Where are you going, Da?' she said, noticing the envelopes in her father's hand. 'I was just about to make some tea.'

'Just over to the post office. I've replied to a couple of the letters I got a few days back. Now you stay, boy,' he added, patting Jack, 'I won't be long.'

Rory and Eliza Jane shared an approving look, perhaps a month after Ma's death, Da was finally on the mend.

Albert delivered one letter to the post box, and the other he took to the Smithy where he sat in silence for a while, before returning home.

Chapter 7

'You'll be the death of me.' Ma's words looped around in Etty's head until she thought she might go mad. Was Ma dead because of her? Was it her responsibility that her da was now grieving alone in his room? Sitting at the dressing table, she inspected her face in the mirror for signs of culpability. Guilt was not an emotion Etty was familiar with. She never wasted time on self-recrimination. What's said is said and what's done is done, and there was no time for regrets. She had to concede she looked wretched though and there was more than a vestige of guilt hiding behind her eyes for the way she had treated Ma. Nevertheless, she would not take ownership of that guilt or punish herself in any way. People died, it was part of life, and life had to go on.

She rose from the dressing table and went to her wardrobe. She found the straw hat she was looking for and put it on. She tied a cream chiffon scarf around her neck and smoothed her blouse into the wide belt around her slim waist. Always dress as if you are going to meet the King, her mother had told her, well, she wouldn't let Ma down now.

Ma was famous for saying many things, mostly warnings about the evil desires of young men; particularly when she had been courting William. Etty shivered when she recalled her mother's advice on how a well brought up young woman should behave before marriage. *Too late for that, Ma,* she thought, remembering how William's hot urgent kisses had made her feel. She missed William so much it physically hurt. With a final glance in the mirror, she left the room and went downstairs and after calling to Eliza Jane, who was in the scullery that she was going out she pulled the door shut firmly behind her. Etty had no idea where she was heading just knowing she wanted to be on her own.

'Quite a few letters for you today, Jacob,' George Butterfield observed handing them over, while standing just inside the farmhouse kitchen door.

'Aye, they'll be replies for the wedding,' said Jacob, as he shuffled through the envelopes. 'I'm asking Albert to be my best man but I don't hold out much hope he'll accept.'

'How is he? I don't see him when I call at the cottage and I don't like to keep botherin' the daughter.'

'He's not good, George, not good at all.'

George nodded. 'It's a sad do Jacob, that's for sure.' He turned to leave before remembering something else he wanted to say. 'By the way, just to warn you, Farmer Hunter has been having trouble with foxes on his land.'

'Ta for the warning, George, I'll keep a look out.'

George touched his cap, climbed back on his bicycle and rode away.

Jacob turned back into the kitchen, surveying with distaste the scene before him. Sooner he was wed, the better, he thought, looking ruefully at the dirty dishes from last night's rabbit pie supper, which was combined with this morning's congealed egg. He pushed the dishes to one side, and sat at the table to read his letters. There were six acceptances to the wedding, and one refusal with regret. He would ride down to the village later and show Beatrice. Picking up the next envelope, he attempted to decipher the bold writing before sliding a buttery knife under the fold of the envelope flap. He withdrew one sheet of paper and looked at the signature: it was from Albert.

A sudden commotion outside distracted him: the chickens were squawking and the sheep were obviously agitated. He dropped the letter and got up from the table to reach for his gun from the rack on the wall above his dresser. Fearing that Farmer Hunter's visiting fox might be worrying his own livestock, he folded the barrel of his shotgun over the crook of his arm before heading out of the door.

Etty sauntered along the road trying to enjoy the warmth on her face from the sun; the birds were singing tunefully, but this did little to soothe her black thoughts. William was uppermost in her mind. She regularly pictured him lying in a field far away from Crossdale, damaged and bloodied. She remembered clinging to William's mother when the terrible news came through of his death. A lump swelled in her throat and stayed firmly in place. She walked on, swallowing hard; she still wasn't sure where she was heading and didn't really care.

Suddenly, she heard her name. Looking around, she saw David Jackson slithering to a halt on the shop bicycle.

'What are you doing all the way out here, Etty? You're a long way from home.'

'I'm just out walking. I needed some thinking time.'

'You've walked a mile or two. I could give you a lift home on the cross bar.'

Etty thought for a moment then agreed: She knew David liked her and a little bit of admiration was just what she needed right now, after all it wouldn't be so unpleasant sitting close to David while he pedalled home and it might be fun.

'Well, close your eyes then, David while I climb on, and no peeping,' she said flirtatiously. David immediately obliged as Etty gathered her skirt through her legs, and bunched the folds in front of her. Still holding on to her skirt, she carefully balanced herself neatly sideways on the cross bar. She wobbled precariously, as David pedalled so he suggested she put an arm around his neck. Taking hold of him meant inhaling his masculine scent and the heady mixture of musk and hair oil excited her. She longed to lay her head on his shoulder and forget her troubles, but once again thought of William.

Progress was slow on the rusty old bicycle and David found it hard to concentrate on pedalling with Etty's arm around his neck He was conscious of her neat waist, and the wonderful smell of clean fresh soap coming from her hair.

A car passing by backfired causing David to jump, wobble and veer off the road. Both David and his passenger landed in a heap on the grass verge.

David lay stunned for a moment then propped himself up on his elbows and looked over to where Etty was sitting up and starting to dust herself down. Her precious hat lay forlornly next to her.

'Look at my skirt, it's ruined.'

'I'm sorry, Etty. Are you all right? Any bruises?'

'If I have bruises, I wouldn't be telling you, David Jackson, that's for sure.'

David smiled to himself, as he got to his feet. This was Etty at her feisty best and he loved her for it. 'Look, why don't we rest awhile. We're both a bit winded and we should get off the road side.' Etty looked up at him as he put a hand out to help her up; she was aware that they were on the verge of the point of no return and although she knew it was wrong, she needed to feel a man's arms around her again. Taking his hand, she stood upright and held his eyes for a second longer, then a single girl should have.

Jacob strode back into his kitchen and hung his gun on the rack on the wall. Whatever or whoever had been worrying his hens and sheep had gone and the livestock not touched. Feeling parched from his exertions and deciding to have a cup of tea before returning to his letters, he moved his kettle back over the hot plate of the range. Jacob stood and looked around his kitchen while waiting for the kettle to boil. Beatrice had said she wanted a coat of paint applied to the walls before the wedding that was the trouble with women; they always wanted you to change something. When the kettle boiled, Jacob made his tea, poured it out and carried his cup back to the table. As he sat, he picked up the letter from Albert again, and began to read:

Dear Jacob

You have always been a good friend to Martha and I and I thank you for it.

I am finding it impossible to live without my darling girl and I cannot seem to find the strength to move forward. I loved her so very much.

By the time you read this, I will have dealt with the situation I find myself in, which will be the best for all concerned.

Please come to the smithy when you get this letter. The door will be locked I have therefore enclosed a key in the envelope. It is imperative you come alone, Jacob, I don't want the bairns involved.

As God is my witness, I cannot go on without Martha… I have failed everyone I love and there is only one course of action left for me

May the Lord forgive me?

Your old Friend

Albert.

'Oh my God, the bloody stupid bugger. What the hell has he done?' Jacob anxiously tore open the remains of the envelope, causing the key to drop out on to the table with a small clatter. He picked it up, grabbed his cap from its hook on the wall and ramming it hastily on his head, made for the back door. Flinging it open, he allowed it to slam behind him as he ran as best he could to the stables. He cursed his fumbling fingers, as he quickly saddled his mare and fastened the strap on the horse's bridle. He glanced at his pocket watch, hoping to God he wouldn't be too late.

'Have you seen Da?' asked Thomas, coming in through the kitchen door. 'He's not at work, the smithy door is locked.'

'He said he was going for a walk,' said Eliza Jane. She was just taking scones out of the oven; Da loved them and with fresh butter and Ma's homemade bramble jelly liberally spread over them it might encourage him to eat. 'It will do him good to get out in this beautiful weather. Etty has gone too – they're probably together.'

'That's good, I'm pleased. Perhaps Da is beginning to adjust. I'm just off to Laycock's to help him tidy up. I'll see you at dinner.'

Finally relaxing in the glow of the sun, Etty idly plucked at a buttercup growing in the grass next to her. She slowly leant over to where David was half lying taking his weight on his elbow and held the flower under his chin. The yellow reflected on his skin. 'Ah, I see you like butter,' she teased. David held her gaze, as he took her hand with the flower in it placing it next to his heart. She sat up, allowing her hand to stay safely in David's grasp. 'David,' she said, 'will you do something for me?'

'Anything, Etty, you know that.'

''Tell me about William, I need to know. I know I've asked you before and you wouldn't tell me but you were there, did he suffer?'

David placed Etty's hand back on to her lap before turning away. He closed his eyes, the image too painful to bear. He remembered agonising screams, William's amongst them.

He remembered how at zero hour when the whistle blew, his friend had clambered over the top with the others. He had been in the reserve trench waiting for his turn to scramble out. He heard later that William had pulled an injured man to safety and had returned to help another of his battalion. He wouldn't have heard the blast – they say you don't hear the one that hits you but when it came, he wouldn't have stood a chance. Someone had told him later that William's legs were blasted away. He couldn't even begin to tell Etty what had happened. He turned back to face her and tried to be light hearted as he spoke.

'Your letters always cheered William up. He looked forward to receiving them and would disappear to the tents to write back to you almost immediately. He used to read me bits of them, news about home, and your work in Carlisle. Lizzie's letters and parcels kept me going too, she was always knitting me something warm to wear.'

'Our Lizzie sent you letters and parcels?' Etty echoed incredulously.

'Yes, and I loved getting her letters; it helped with homesickness, and kept up the morale.' David took Etty's hand again. 'Listen, Etty, whatever you've read about the war, the reality was one hundred times worse. You really don't need to know.'

'Don't treat me like a fool, David. I want to understand what William went through. You were in the same battalion as each other; he was your best friend, so you're the only person who can tell me if he suffered before he died? I have a right to know.'

David thought for a moment, his mouth twisted, as he bit down on his lip to prevent tears forming in his dull eyes. How could he describe to this lovely girl, some of the terrible things he had witnessed? The rats and lice, scraps of bloodied uniform scattered around the muddy trenches – limbs torn from bodies. There was screaming, confusion and the stench of death was everywhere. He still had nightmares, and couldn't stomach hearing a whistle because that meant it was time for them to go over the top. He knew by the look on Etty's face that she wouldn't give up, so he made the decision to tell her a sanitised version of events.

'It wasn't all bad. If you were waiting in the reserve trench, you could share a cigarette; write letters, that sort of thing. If you were on guard duty, they gave you rum to keep out the cold. At night, you might wake up to find a rat sharing your blanket. You had to sleep sitting up, couldn't wash for days and felt demoralised and filthy but we smiled through it to keep morale high. Worst of all' – David tried to form a smile – 'was the endless supply of bully beef and biscuits they gave us to eat. I still can't look at corned beef when serving it to customers.' Taking hold of Etty's other hand, David looked at her earnestly. 'William was a damned hero. I heard that he saved a man's life without any thought for his own safety. He didn't suffer, Etty, I promise you, he didn't suffer.' David's voice died away to a whisper, his heart beating faster and his breathing more obvious, as he lied to save Etty heartache. 'Sometimes, Etty' – David faltered, for now he was telling the truth – 'sometimes I feel guilty that I'm still here, and that I didn't die like so many others. The guilt associated with living is far worse than the pain of dying.'

Tears ran down Etty's cheeks and David pulled her to him to comfort her. He kissed her forehead, her cheeks and then her lips. She froze for a moment – William's face flashed before her, but then it was gone, and she threw herself into David's arms and returned his kisses. Slowly and tentatively, he began to undo the buttons on her blouse, exploring her body with his hands and mouth. Etty knew she should say no but somehow, she couldn't. She wanted this, it had been so long since she had been made love to and she yearned for William's touch.

'God in heaven, Albert! What have you done, lad?' Jacob shrieked, as he hurried further into the smithy his eyes adjusting to the darkness. Albert, a rope tight around his neck, was swinging from the rafters of the building. Quickly, Jacob picked up the fallen ladder beneath him and placed it up against the beam. He wobbled as he climbed the ladder holding Albert's legs in one arm to take the weight of his body as best he could. He took his knife out of his pocket and cut the rope around the beam. Rolling the weight of the body on to his broad shoulder, he slowly descended the ladder, breathless from the weight of his friend, he laid Albert gently onto the ground and placed his ear as close to Albert's chest as he could. He listened for a breath or a heartbeat, anything that would tell him he was still alive, but he already knew it was too late.

With wild eyes, he gazed around the smithy, trying to adjust to the horrific events of the day. He and Albert had been friends for many years, and this was not how he envisaged it ending. He moved from kneeling to sitting on the dusty floor beside Albert while he decided how best to help. His dazed brain wouldn't function properly; he kept looking at the body, not quite believing the evidence that lay beside him. If only he had supported him more, listened to him, Albert had begged him for help and he had done nothing except tell his old friend it would get better. He could have stopped this happening, if only… Suddenly, the fog of grief lifted and the course of action became clearer. Jacob knew exactly how to help his friend and it was the least he could do. For the sake of the family, the nature of Albert's death must be kept quiet. This was surely why he had wanted Jacob to find him. The bairns should not live with the disgrace of their father's suicide. 'I'll be back as quick as I can, Albert, lad,' he said to the inert body, as he scrambled heavily to his feet. Making for the door, he opened it a fraction and popped his head glancing quickly from left to right. When he was sure no one was coming, he slipped through the door locking it behind him. Jacob mounted his horse and rode as casually as he could to fetch Dr Green, hoping that the doctor would also hold Albert's secret.Etty buttoned up her blouse and smoothed down her skirt. David was sitting beside her on the grass. He lit two cigarettes and gave one to her. He drew heavily on it, his muddled thoughts assailing him. He had wanted to make love to Etty for years, but now he felt he had taken advantage of her by using her vulnerability over the death of William. David had loved Etty since school. He and William had fought over her many times in the playground, but he had to admit defeat when she and his best friend became engaged. War was declared before they were married, and William's tragic death separated them.

They were both silent, almost distant. David was the first to speak. 'I'm sorry Etty.' He ran his fingers through his hair. 'I'm so sorry.'

'I'm not sorry.' There was a further silence. 'I've shocked you, haven't I? Today I needed to be made love to David but don't worry I won't hold you to anything in fact I just want to go home.' Etty stubbed out her cigarette, scrambled to her feet and tucked her blouse back into her skirt. She replaced her hat and began to walk away, leaving David sitting on the ground. He noticed she had left her scarf on the grass. He picked it up and called after her, but she didn't respond. Shrugging, he squashed the scarf into his pocket, righted his bicycle and pushed it after her.

Chapter 8

They were a silent and miserable group that morning in July. They sat around the table in the kitchen in stunned silence, aware of the two empty chairs at either end of the table. Thomas fondled Jack's ears, finding comfort in their silkiness. He had been carried home from his master's grave, only to escape, and sit once more, patiently for many hours in the cemetery.

Molly, trying to be optimistic, broke the silence. 'Well, what shall we do?' she said, gazing around the table at her siblings. 'What's going to happen now?'

No one answered her.

'I can't bear this; it's all my fault they're dead,' said Rory dramatically. He covered his face with his hands and rubbed his eyes. 'I'll never lift a paintbrush again. I should have been in the smithy supporting Da, learning the trade. I've let everyone down.' His whole body shuddered, as he placed his forearms on the table and buried his face in his arms. Eliza Jane moved her chair nearer to him and put a comforting hand on his shoulder.

'Enough of the dramatics, Rory, grow up for heaven's sake,' shouted Etty. Why did Rory always have to be such a baby, Ma had obviously spoilt him.

'That's enough, Etty,' Thomas remarked fiercely, 'we are all to blame, one way or another. Now let's stop this, it's not helping. We've to decide what we're to do. The new blacksmith has been appointed, so we can't stay much longer.'

'I hate the thought that someone is taking Da's place. He's been blacksmith here for almost forty years.' Etty spoke for them all.

'What's that illness,' asked Molly, creasing her forehead, 'whatever Doctor Green said Da died from?'

'Bright's disease,' said Thomas, something to do with the kidneys – but the strange thing is, Da never seemed ill.'

'Why didn't he tell us,' asked Eliza Jane, 'we could have helped him more if we'd known?'

Etty nodded in agreement. 'We took Da's strength and health for granted.'

'I never saw him taking any pills,' Thomas remarked

'What are you saying,' Etty challenged, 'that he wasn't ill?'

'Look, I'm as puzzled as the rest of you. All I'm saying is apart from grieving for Ma, he seemed fit, he couldn't have done his job otherwise.'

'Should one of us should talk to Doctor Green,' Rory suggested, 'find out more?'

'If anyone talks to Doctor Green, it will be me,' said Thomas decisively. 'But for now, we have to decide what to do.'

'Something will turn up,' said Molly positively.

'For God's sake, Molly, just shut up! I'm sick of hearing you say that, it's so glib and means nothing.' Etty rose to her feet. 'I've had enough of this, I'm going out.'

'Etty, sit down,' warned Thomas.

'No, Thomas, what's the point? You think you are in charge of us all, now, but I have news for you – I'm old enough to make up my mind about what I do next. Decide for the others by all means, but leave me out of it.'

Standing and scraping back her chair, Etty stormed out of the room, slamming the door behind her.

Eliza Jane placed a hand on Thomas's arm to stop him following her. 'Leave her, Thomas, she's just hurting: we all show it in different ways.'

'We are *all* hurting, Eliza Jane,' said Thomas, rubbing his neck, 'it doesn't alter the fact we still have to decide what to do, we have to find work and somewhere to live and I'm fairly sure we won't find either in Crossdale, we shall have to move away.'

Everyone fell silent.

Etty sat on the low bridge over the canal and brooded on her future. David Jackson had been outside the shop when she had passed by a small distance away on the other side of the road. Sweeping the front step, he had raised a hand to wave but she pretended not to see him: it was better that way. David was one of the reasons why she didn't want to stay in Crossdale. She knew she could never love him as he wanted her to and seeing him every day could be a problem. The other reason was that she had nothing to keep her here: just a dead-end needlework business making clothes for local matrons. There was a whole world out there that could surely make use of her design skills.

She stood up, pacing back and forth, stopping only to kick the bridge in frustration. She searched in her pocket and found her cigarettes; the others had no idea she smoked but she needed the calmness that a cigarette gave her. Etty was furious with her parents, how dare they leave her but even angrier with herself, for the feelings of guilt their deaths were invoking in her.

The following day, Thomas sat nervously in Doctor Green's waiting room. His head was full of nagging questions; things he couldn't fathom.

'I've come to settle Da's bill,' said Thomas, when he was finally called into the office. 'Pay you what we owe you.'

'Sit down, Thomas, now there's no charge, lad, why if I think about all your da has done for me over the years, I must owe him.'

Thomas was relieved. 'Thank you, doctor, and we wanted to say how much we appreciate what you did for him, and Ma.'

'Your father was a man to be proud of. He worshipped your mother, and would have done anything for her. Just think about young Rory's arrival, your da accepted it all without...' Sitting behind his large desk, Dr Green stopped talking abruptly and began to shuffle uneasily on his chair while screwing and unscrewing his fountain pen, finally he started to leaf through some papers. Suddenly, he rose from his chair turning his back on Thomas appearing to concentrate on searching the table behind him.

'Without what?' enquired Thomas politely.

Doctor Green turned to face Thomas. Realising he had been unwittingly indiscrete, he mumbled, 'I'm talking about the comfort he gave Martha after Rory's birth. She had a bad case of depression, and Albert helped her through.' Now, lad, if there's nothing else I can help you with, I must get on. I've many more patients to see.'

Confused by the doctor's demeanour, Thomas left the surgery. He considered what had just transpired as he walked home: Doctor Green's apparent unease, and the sharply terminated conversation. What did it mean? What were the circumstances of Rory's birth and what had Da accepted so easily, or were his thoughts running away with him?

Eliza Jane looked up from patting a mound of butter into shape. She was working with her back to the counter in Jackson's. David, on the other side of the shop, was busily weighing out sugar and placing it into blue bags. The shop was fairly quiet that afternoon and normally, they would have had some banter between them but not today. She was puzzled, there was something different about him, he appeared distracted, and it seemed he could barely look her in the face. Perhaps he felt uncomfortable with her since her father had died, not knowing what to say or do to comfort her. Several people had crossed the road to avoid her recently. They would wave and blurt a quick greeting from the distance, then veer off in the opposite direction. Eliza Jane's nostrils twitched; she could smell mothballs. Turning around, there was no surprise in seeing Mrs Fanshawe standing there.

'Eliza Jane, how are you dear?' she said. 'So sad for you all and both parents too,' she added as if Eliza Jane's parents had died on purpose. 'So, what are you all going to do? It's such a shame that your father didn't own the business, I suppose old Spiers will appoint a new blacksmith, so you'll have to leave your sweet cottage. Such a pity, Martha kept it like a new pin.' She sucked on her teeth before continuing, 'Now dear, if there's anything Mr Fanshawe and I can do, you must let us know: you only have to name it. Obviously, we can't offer you a home, we've only a small cottage as you know, but I couldn't call myself a Christian if I ignored your troubles. Well, that's all I came to say, so I'll bid you good day.'

Turning to leave, Mrs Fanshawe addressed David who was still busily packing sugar. 'Good afternoon to you, David, tell me was that Etty Watkins I saw you with the other day, or were my old eyes deceiving me?' Noting his embarrassment, Mrs Fanshawe continued with relish. 'Yes, I thought it was her – and as I said to Mr Fanshawe – it couldn't have been very comfortable for her riding on your crossbar. It's a good job she had her arm around your neck, otherwise she might have fallen off. But there she was without a care in the world on the same day that poor Albert died. Well,' she said, pleased with her morning's work, 'I can't stand here all day; I've things to do, good day to you both.'

Eliza Jane turned back to patting the butter; tears sprang to her eyes caused by the lump growing in her throat. Etty hadn't mentioned seeing David that day or the bicycle ride. She impatiently drew a hand across her face, wiping the wetness from her burning cheeks. She glanced at David, as he continued weighing out and bagging the sugar. Although he was refusing to look at her, Eliza Jane could see that the tips of his ears, shone like a beacon in the dim light of the shop.

Thomas didn't want to go through his parent's belongings, but it seemed there was no alternative; it had to be done if they were to move. The room felt cold, devoid of any comfort, although it had been warm and cosy when his parents were alive. He opened drawers and cupboards and pulled out clothes which he folded into a box. He had refused offers of help, because he had an overwhelming need to do it alone but he wasn't sure why.

He remembered Ma having a box crammed with personal treasures. If they had been good as children, they were allowed a peek inside as a reward; it must still be here somewhere, and it might contain some answers to his suspicions that his parents had been hiding something.

He finally found it on top of the wardrobe, placed well back from view. It was a large mahogany box with a lid of burr walnut. He opened it carefully. Inside were some pressed flowers, his mother's wedding ring, ribbons, baby bootees, a scrap of material from her wedding dress, several of Rory's drawings and his recent prize winning letter. There was also a bundle of old letters, and a locket. He opened one letter and scanned the contents. They were love letters from Albert to Martha. Hastily, he replaced them not wishing to intrude on their privacy.

Seated on the bed, he turned the remaining contents of the box out onto the counterpane. A key glinted at him amongst the bits and pieces. Picking it up, he turned it over in his hands. A sudden memory of Da using a similar key to open a box containing papers in the smithy flashed across his mind. He remembered Da shutting and locking the box quickly before he could look into it. Thomas heard the front door bang downstairs, and quickly slipped the key into his pocket before quietly leaving the bedroom. On the landing, he could hear the muffled voices of Etty and Eliza Jane rising through the stairs door that was ajar. They were arguing as usual.

There was nothing to tell Lizzie Anyway, that was the day I came home to hear the news about Da – everything went from my mind. David offered me a lift on his bicycle because I was a long way from home – I accepted, nothing more.'

You needn't have had your arm around his neck; if Mrs Fanshawe saw you, no doubt others did too.'

'Since when did you take any notice of what that old bat says; she's poison on legs. I had to hold on to him or I would have ended up in a ditch.'

'No, you didn't have to hold on to him, you could have held on to the handle bars instead.'

'Why would I do that? Who wouldn't want to hold on to David Jackson? I know you would if given half a chance.' Etty knew she was being mean but seriously why such a fuss over a bicycle ride!

Eliza Jane coloured up. 'That's not true, Etty.'

'You can't deny it, Lizzie. David told me about the letters you sent him through the war. I know you're in love with him; it's as plain as the nose on your face. But here's a word of advice, don't waste your time on him because you don't stand a chance.'

Eliza Jane tried to suppress a sob, as she fumbled in her apron pocket for her handkerchief. She turned on her heel, ran to the door of the stairs passing through and banging it behind her. Holding her handkerchief to her nose, she barged past Thomas at the top of the landing and made for the sanctuary of her room.

Chapter 9

It was just after midnight when Thomas, with the key in his pocket, let himself out of the cottage. Shutting the door quietly behind him, he crept the small distance to the smithy. The door creaked loudly as he opened it, causing him to jump. He slipped inside and shut it behind him as quietly as he could. Reaching up to the right, he ran his hand along the shelf to locate Da's torch. The familiar smell of wood smoke assaulted his nostrils. With the torch cutting through the darkness, he began to look for the box.

He searched the drawers, ran his hand along the shelves, and used a stepladder to look along the blackened sooty beams. He highlighted a rope that had been tied around one of the beams in the pool of light created by the torch; it had been roughly cut, the threads hanging lose. The sight made him shudder but he couldn't say why; a horrific thought crossed his mind about the way the rope had been cut, making him wobble, he grabbed the sides of the ladder to steady himself.

He was about to climb down when he caught sight of what seemed to be a bundle of blackened rags wedged in the corner of the beam. Grabbing it, he descended the ladder and carried the box over to the anvil. Placing the box down, he felt in his pocket for the key, dropping it in his excitement. He passed the torchlight over the ground until he located the key and retrieved it. With fumbling fingers, he inserted the key into the box, it fitted and turned. Nestling at the bottom of the box were some papers. In the torchlight, he scanned the first paper; it was a birth certificate. The name of the child was Rory James, born to Elizabeth Tyson on the sixteenth of December 1899 in the Parish of Barton. The father's name and occupation had been left blank. Thomas's thoughts began to race, flicking back and forth in time. He felt exhausted; a sense of fatigue had crept into his legs. The conversation with Doctor Green made sense to him now. The doctor knew that Rory was not ma's child. He hastily put the birth certificate into his pocket and opened up another piece of paper from the pile. He began to read the contents with trembling hands:

Dear Albert and Martha,

I hope you will forgive me for the trouble I bring upon you. Martha, my dear friend, I can only hope that on learning my predicament that you are able to help me. I cannot tell you how desperate I am, and at a loss to know what course to take.

On recently visiting the doctor after feeling unwell, I was stunned to learn that I am carrying a child due to be born in December. You cannot imagine the shock and distress this has caused me. Sadly, the baby's father, whom I still love, is not in a position to offer me marriage. Moreover, he has been prevented by my father from contacting me. I have since heard through friend that he has returned to America with his wife.

As you can imagine, I have brought great shame on my family.

As you and Albert already have four children, I am asking you if you will bring up the baby as your own. I promise I will never try to see the child or contact you.

If you agree to my proposal, please write at once and we can discuss our plans further. Papa will offer you an annual income to help support the child.

I beg of you not to think too badly of me. I have been a fool in love, and that is my only defence.

I remain your devoted friend

Elizabeth

Thomas was never more aware of his heart thumping in his chest until now. He tried to come to terms with the contents of the letter. They had never been told that Rory was adopted, and he was trying to fathom how this news would affect the family. His parents had obviously not wanted Rory to know of the circumstances surrounding his birth and it was not up to him to divulge their secret. He looked further into the box and found an envelope bearing his name. Disturbed by a sudden noise of footsteps, he quickly stuffed the two letters into his pocket beside Rory's birth certificate, flung the lid down on the box and ran to hide it in a drawer.

The door to the smithy creaked open, and a torch light was switched on. Thomas froze in fear, almost unable to breath, until he saw Rory in the flood of light. 'You scared me, Rory,' he said, putting his hand to his chest.

'You're scared,' came the relieved reply. 'I saw a light flash on and off in here through our bedroom window; it woke me up. Your bed was empty, I thought the smithy was being burgled.'

'I heard a noise too,' said Thomas, thinking on his feet to explain why he was in the smithy. 'I've just got here myself; I was using Da's torch to check around everywhere, that's probably what woke you. Everything seems all right. I expect it was a cat. Let's go back home, there's nothing here to worry about.'

Rory yawned, as he got up from the kitchen table to put his cocoa cup in the sink. 'I'm done in,' he said to Thomas. 'I didn't really want to get out of my bed and investigate intruders but as you weren't there, I thought I should protect the girls.' Thomas didn't respond. Rory looked at his brother, worried that he appeared to be lost in thought while rolling the dregs of his cocoa around in his cup. 'It's half past one, and I'm heading up those wooden stairs to Bedfordshire,' he tried again, remembering that this was what Ma used to say when they were children. Again, no reply.

Rory stopped for a moment before opening the latch to the stairs door. He turned and looked closely at his older brother; he looked troubled which belied his assurances that he was just tired. Thomas appeared to be bearing the weight of the family on his shoulders, and at that moment, Rory silently vowed to do more to help.

'Are you all right, Thomas, you seem preoccupied.'

'I really am just tired; it's been quite a night.'

Rory, wondering if Thomas was thinking of Ma and Da, said, 'I miss them both, don't you, it doesn't seem to be getting any easier, everyone said it would.'

Thomas looked up from studying his cocoa. 'It will get easier; I promise you, Rory.'

Turning, Rory opened the door to the stairs, waving his hand behind his head in acknowledgement of his brother's advice.

Thomas watched as Rory lifted the latch on the door to the stairs and disappeared to bed. Quickly, he pulled the papers out of his pocket and with trembling fingers, he opened the envelope addressed to him.

Dearest Thomas,

If you are reading this letter, then you will know that I am no longer with you. You will also have discovered the truth about Rory. Whatever your thoughts, you must remember that he is still your brother. I want you to continue to take care of him and your sisters. Your Ma and I did what we thought was best for everybody at the time, and Rory has grown into a very fine young man of whom we are so proud. He has always been ours in our hearts. He must never know that we are not his real parents, and I charge you with this secret.

Please forgive, your old father for not being with you now as you continue life's path. It is breaking my heart to leave you all but the burden of living without your mother is too much for me to bear, and I have taken the coward's way out and ended things in the only way I know how. I have failed you all and I'm deeply sorry. I know in my heart that you will all be much better off without me to worry about.

I have also written to Jacob Pennington, to ensure that he finds me when it is all over, and not you or one of the others.

Find it in your heart to forgive me, Thomas, for I know that what I am about to do is a sin against God, I hope he will forgive me my trespasses as I hope you can, son.

Be brave; make your way with your sisters and brother into the world with courage and fortitude, and may God go with you. You have the whole of life's journey ahead.

I am so proud of you all.

Your loving father

Albert Watkins

Thomas closed the letter, carefully refolding the lines his father had made. A tear, starting in the corner of his eye, rolled down his cheek; it was soon followed by a deluge. He lay his head on his forearms on the kitchen table and whispered, 'Why, Da, why weren't we enough for you, we loved you so much but you didn't love us enough to stay.' And with that thought, Thomas wept as he'd never wept before.

Chapter 10

Eliza Jane was hurrying to work. It was five minutes past seven, and she was late for her first day at the shop since the death of her Da. Even for the early hour, it was a beautiful morning and the warmth should have made her feel alive, but instead she was tired, weepy and jaded. Today, she had to tell David Jackson they were moving away. She constantly asked herself why she hadn't already told him, and concluded it was probably the fear of his indifference that had prevented her. What if Etty was right and he didn't care whether she stayed or went? That would be too much to bear.

On reaching the shop, Eliza Jane automatically followed her usual morning routine. She reached for her apron from behind the store room door, then having tied the strings behind her back, she took the yard brush down from its hook taking it outside to sweep the front pavement.

David soon followed her out. 'Eliza Jane, are you sure you want to work this morning? Pop and I would understand if you couldn't face the shop, and the Mrs Fanshawe's of this world.'

Eliza Jane gazed at the face she had held in her heart for many years. She looked at him as if for the first time. She noticed his deep brow, partially covered with a sweep of thick fair hair that framed his deep brown eyes. She could pinpoint the very button on his waistcoat she had sewn on, after retrieving it from where it had rolled under the counter. She knew every inch of the neat moustache above the constantly smiling mouth. She loved the easy way he chatted to customers, and dreamt of his long, slim fingers touching hers. Her tummy was in turmoil, tears pricked at her eyes.

'Actually, David, I was going to tell you today that we're moving away.' She was pleased to see the shock register on his face, for she loved him with all her being, and maybe just maybe he felt the same, if only he would reach out, touch her hand, anything to give her hope, but he continued to stand still and say nothing. Biting her lip to hold back the tears, she made a supreme effort to sound confident and happy as she spoke but could barely hold it together. 'The new Blacksmith is coming in a couple of weeks…have to get out…all need jobs…somewhere to live…so much to think about, so I think I need to go home.'

Realising she was babbling, she gave a strangled sob, untied her apron strings and thrust the apron and the broom into David's hands. 'I'm sorry,' she cried. 'I'm obviously not quite recovered yet; it has been a hard-few weeks.' Turning on her heel, Eliza Jane half ran and half walked down the street, crossed the road and passed the smithy before running up her garden path and through the back door.

Eliza Jane banged the door of the cottage behind her, flew past Etty in the scullery and made for her room. The latch on the door to the stairs stuck, as she tried to lift it. She pummelled at it, crying with exasperation until it eventually relented and let her through.

Etty watched her sister's wild entrance with some surprise, but immediately guessed that the tears were down to one man. David Jackson. Loud sobs emanated from the bed room above. What had he said to her? Putting the kettle on the hot plate over the fire, she searched the George the fifth coronation tin for some of the better broken biscuits. When the kettle had boiled, she made the tea. She placed the teapot, some plated biscuits, two of Ma's best cups and saucers, a jug of milk and sugar on the tray and carefully climbed the stairs to the room that she shared with her sisters. Balancing the tray in one hand, she gently knocked on the door.

Eliza Jane sat up on her bed wiping her eyes with her handkerchief as the door opened which Etty pretended not to notice, as she set down the tray on the chest of drawers and began to pour. 'Get this down you,' she said, not unkindly. 'Whatever David Jackson has said, or even failed to say, a hot drink of tea will help.'

'What makes you think this is about David?' Eliza Jane said weakly

'Because he's an insensitive bastard that's why, and I make no apologies for the language, Lizzie, so you can take that look off your face. Like all men, he can't see a good thing when it's right under his nose. You would make him a wonderful wife, but does he realise that, does he hell.'

'He's never said or promised me anything, Etty, and like you said, I know I don't stand a chance, but I love him so much. I wish I didn't, but I do.'

Etty reached out to her sister and took her hand. 'I didn't really mean what I said; I was annoyed at the time and just retaliating to your questions about the bicycle ride.'

Eliza Jane was surprised, Etty didn't usually almost apologise for anything. She smiled a watery smile and gratefully squeezed Etty's hand.

When the tea was drunk, David Jackson had been pulled to pieces and Eliza Jane was smiling once more, they lingered to talk of the future, wondering where they might be in a few months and whether they would still be together.

A short while later after leaving Eliza Jane to rest, Etty went downstairs, put on her coat and hat, left the cottage and marched down the street to Jackson's. David was cleaning the shop window with a tan cloth. He stopped and smiled warmly when he saw her approaching. 'Hello Etty, I haven't seen you for a few days, how are you holding up?'

'Oh, I'm fine, David. I'm tough as old boots, but Eliza Jane, now she's a different matter. She's kind and caring, and because of that, she's very sensitive. Whatever you said or didn't say to her today just wasn't good enough. For heaven's sake, don't you realise how she feels about you, you great lump. She's been in love with you for years.'

David looked aghast. 'What! I had no idea honestly, Etty; I've never given her any encouragement. We've always been just good friends, nothing more. I don't harbour any other feelings.'

'Well, just as well, we're going away then.'

'I don't want you to move away, Etty, or any of you for that matter.'

'We have to, David; we all need jobs now that my father has passed on.'

'Etty, I want you to stay.'

'Why would I want to stay? My parents and my fiancé have died – I've nowhere to live, what's here for me?'

David swallowed hard. 'I'm here, and I love you. No, don't look so shocked, you must know how I feel about you. I want to marry you, Etty.'

'Please don't, David, I can't hear this.' She turned away

'Why not?' His voice grew scratchy and emotional. 'Surely you must feel something for me? Think of that wonderful moment we had together. I know I do. I think of you on that perfect day lying in my arms drowsy from the heat of the sun. You were so beautiful.'

'I admit I've known you were sweet on me, I've known for ages, even before you and William went away to war but I can't give you anything, I don't love you, I'm sorry. The other day was just one of those things. I told you that at the time. I needed someone to make love to me – anybody would have done, that was how I was feeling.'

'Etty, please, you don't mean that, please don't say that to me.' David tried to grab one of her hands but she placed them firmly out of reach. He ran his fingers through his hair in exasperation.

Turning away from his stricken face, she made her way around to the front of the shop, barging straight into Mrs Fanshawe who had been listening intently to their raised voices.

'Well,' said Mrs Fanshawe, her hat feathers quivering with indignation, 'well, really.' She huffed at Etty's disappearing back. It was reported later in the post office that Etty Watkins and David Jackson had been quarrelling outside Jacksons, she had run away, and he had been distraught.

Molly and Rory had been to see Rudolph Valentino, a handsome young Italian actor in the film *All Night* at the Palladium picture house. They were travelling back from Lancaster on the train. The film was a comedy and gradually, they had put their grief aside and laughed with the rest of the audience.

Molly was full of it. 'Isn't Rudolph Valentino handsome?' she sighed, as she smoothed her skirt before sitting down in the train carriage.

Rory grinned. 'I'll take your word for that, Moll.' Molly smiled at her brother, grateful that he had accompanied her that afternoon.

The train pulled into the station at Crossdale. They left the carriage, passing along the platform. There had been a sharp rain shower but now the sun was out and Molly was feeling warm in her three quarter length coat. Climbing the steps that took them over the bridge to the other side, they choked and coughed as the steam from their train enveloped them as it began to gather speed to leave the station.

Molly rubbed her eye; she had a piece of grit lodged there. Hearing her name, she looked over her shoulder to find Cyril Henderson from the ticket office panting after them.

'Cyril, hello, how are you?' she enquired.

'Oh, mustn't grumble, Molly. I just wanted to say how sorry I was to hear about your da. I couldn't come to his funeral because I was working. Both your parents were fine people, and they are a sad loss to the village.'

Molly's face crumpled as she held back the tears. 'Thank you, Cyril. It's been so hard for us all. I still don't think it's hit us properly yet.'

'It all takes time, Molly,' Cyril remarked. 'Now, lass, I hear you're leaving us so I just wanted to let you know that if you need train tickets, you just come and see your Uncle Cyril, I will see you all right.' He gave a knowing wink as Molly stood on tiptoe and kissed his cheek, causing him to blush. 'Thanks, Cyril, you're an angel,' she said.

Thomas was breathing heavily, as he slowly cycled to Pennington's farm. He had some daunting but necessary business to attend to. The day was very warm again and sweat was beginning to run down his face. He wobbled, as he raised a hand to wipe it away. Jack was running beside him, his tongue hanging from his open mouth to keep cool.

'Thomas, lad, good to see you, come on in,' said Jacob on opening the kitchen door to a knock. Thomas rested his bicycle up against the farmhouse wall and entered the cool of the kitchen.

'Now what can I do for you? Eh, Jack,' he added patting the dog, 'you've run a long way, boy, let's get you some water.' Jacob put a dish full of water on the floor, and the dog was soon lapping at it noisily. Thomas watched Jack drinking trying to evade Jacob's questioning eyes, not knowing how to begin the conversation he needed to have.

'Sit thee down at the table, lad, I'll put kettle on, we'll have a nice cuppa,' said Jacob, heartily, masking his worry about the purpose of Thomas's visit. The poor chap looked beaten by life, he thought. Realising it would take more than a cup of tea to rejuvenate the lad, Jacob decided the patent Pennington cure for all ills would be more suitable. He took the kettle off the hob, shuffled to one of the cupboards and extracted two glasses and a bottle of whisky. He set the glasses on the table, pulled the cork out of the bottle and poured two large measures.

'This'll revive you more than tea, son, drink up.' Jacob swigged the contents of his glass down in one, and poured himself another. Thomas, who had only ever drunk ale before, took a sip finding the liquid stung his throat but warmed his lungs as it went down, the sensation finally loosened his tongue.

'I've come about, Jack. We've had notice to quit the cottage, and the new black smith and his family are coming in a few days. We all need jobs, and we can't take much more of the pitying looks we're getting from folk, oh I know they're only being kind but we are all in need of a fresh start.' Thomas, having spoken in a rush, drew a breath. 'We were wondering if you could keep Jack for us, he could be a good working dog, he's fast and a quick on the uptake. We hate to let him go but he was Da's dog really and we can see he really misses him.'

'Well, lad, and you must call me Jacob, Bonnie's getting a bit old now, and I was thinking of retiring her, but perhaps she could teach this young'n a thing or two before she gives up. What do you say, Jack?' Jacob looked down at the dog? 'Do you want to become a proper sheep dog?'

Jack cocked his head to one side, as if he was considering the proposition, then with a swift bark, he headed for the door. 'Looks like he's keen to get started.' Jacob laughed. 'Of course I'll take him, Thomas, lad, he's a bright dog.'

Jacob refilled both empty glasses. 'I knew this would happen one day if owt happened to your da, in fact, we talked about it, but I know that doesn't help you now, lad. Where will you go?'

Thomas gulped, he had still to ask Jacob about Da's death, his heart beat faster, panicking as he composed what he was going to say trying it out in his mind first. He started to squirm in his chair and nervously finished the contents of his glass straight down. 'We're not rightly sure yet. We're thinking of finding a hiring fair.' There was a sudden silence as Thomas almost lost his nerve before continuing. 'I know you found Da, Mr Penn, I mean Jacob.'

Jacob slowly poured out another whisky for them both while considering his answer. He had given his word to Doctor Green that he wouldn't tell a soul of Albert's suicide. He looked at Thomas, noting his drink-flushed cheeks.

'I don't reckon there's much I can tell you, I found him that's all, collapsed on the floor and I called the doctor. 'I'm sorry, truly sorry but I don't know as how I can help you further.'

If Thomas hadn't been quite so giddy with drink, he would have remembered that he had heard those words before from Doctor Green. He drained his glass and rose unsteadily to his feet. He could not bring himself to tell Jacob that he had found his da's suicide letter. He couldn't even bear to think about how Da did it.

'I understand, Mr Pennington,' he said rising unsteadily to his feet. 'I understand a lot more than you realise.'

'Why don't you leave Jack here, lad? I promise I'll take good care of him for you, and for Albert. He were a good friend to me all these years was Albert, and it's the least I can do.'

'I think you have done much more than that for my father, and I'm very grateful to you for it. I think you saved our family from a lot of heartache.'

Jacob extended his right hand to Thomas. 'I'm not sure what you're getting at lad but enough of this maudlin talk, let me wish you all the luck in the world on your journey. Don't forget, you'll always be welcome here with Beatrice and me, any time, and that goes for the rest of the family an' all. Here take this; it might help.' Jacob wrestled with his pocket and produced a florin that he thrust into Thomas's hands.

The three sisters were sitting around the table in the parlour waiting for Thomas to return. Rory was sitting in Da's chair reading a letter and they couldn't tell from the expression on his face whether it was good or bad news? Rory smiled as he looked up from his letter. 'Don't look so worried, it's good news,' he explained. 'It's from the competition people; they want me to come to London on the second of July to collect my prize at the National Gallery.'

The front door opened and closed. 'That must be Thomas now,' said Eliza Jane. They all looked up expectantly, as Thomas lurched into the kitchen and slumped down in Ma's chair opposite Rory.

'My God, Thomas, are you ill?' Eliza Jane went over to him to feel his brow.

'No, I'm fine,' he said, 'but…' He closed his eyes still clutching Jacob's florin.

'He's not ill,' said Etty leaving her chair and looking more closely at Thomas. 'Can't you smell him, he's drunk! Quick, Lizzie, get some camp coffee on the stove, we must sober him up.' Eliza Jane hurriedly left the room.

Rory flung his letter to one side and rose from the table. He walked over to where Thomas was slumped in the chair. 'We needed you, Thomas, we needed you to take care of us, and all you can do is lie drunk in Ma's chair. What do you think she would say to you? Well, you disgust me. Why don't you just grow up?' Rory raged at him.

'Rory, just shut up, lad, this painting success has gone to your head, soon you'll be too grand to talk to us,' exclaimed Etty.

Rory groaned and ran his fingers through his thick black hair, as he returned to Da's chair and flounced down in it.

'I just want everything to be the same as before,' he complained sulkily. 'I want my ma and da. I miss them so much. I want them to see my painting in the Gallery so they can be proud of me. I don't want to be brave anymore, I need to wallow in self-pity but instead I've got to try and be grown up. What does the future hold for us all, tell me that, Etty? You don't know do you, well I can't take any more, I just can't.' Rory raised his head; tears were streaming down his face.

'I want, I want, pull yourself together, Rory, you're nineteen years old for heaven's sake.' Molly shot a warning look at Etty across the table.

'Etty,' she warned.

'No, Molly, this needs to be said, don't you think we feel the same and Thomas too, that's why he's in this state. If you'd had to abandon Jack, you would be lying there drunk too, and what about Eliza Jane, do you think she doesn't care?'

'Doesn't care about what?' asked Eliza Jane coming back into the room with coffee for them all. She placed the tray on the table. Rory lifted his tear stained face, rose to his feet and threw himself into his sister's arms.

'Help me, Lizzie, help me please,' he begged. 'I just don't feel I belong here any more.'

Chapter 11

Thomas felt his stomach tighten with apprehension as he faced old Mr Yeats across a huge expanse of solid mahogany desk, cluttered with files and ledgers. He coughed; the musty smell and collection of fine dust over all surfaces was causing him some discomfort.

The minutes ticked by in the silent office, only broken by the sound of the solicitor, occasionally clicking his tongue as he perused the papers before him. Thomas whose head ached mercilessly from his whisky consumption the afternoon before passed the time by counting the number of books on the dusty shelves but soon abandoned it as there was too many. He remembered the recrimination from Rory, as he lay slumped in a chair. He shuddered, he'd let them all down and Ma would have been furious. He stared through the grubby windows onto Dalton Square and watched an ex-serviceman swinging up the road on crutches. The sight caused him physical pain.

Finally, slowly and deliberately, Mr Yeats opened the ledger and ran his finger down the figures. He looked up and peering over the top of his spectacles said, 'I am pleased to report, Mr Watkins, that your father, being a careful man, had amassed savings of three pounds, seven shillings and sixpence, which is bequeathed to you, the eldest son, in the event of your mother's death. I must of course offer you and the family our sincere condolences on your loss. I believe the death certificate stated that your father died from Bright's disease.'

'I believe so,' mumbled Thomas.

'Do you have any questions, Mr Watkins?'

Thomas swallowed hard, he wondered if the details of Rory's birth were known to the solicitor. Surely, Yeats had dealt with the legal side of his parent's care of Rory.

'I understand Mr Yeats that Albert and Martha were not the natural parents of my brother Rory. Do you have any knowledge of his true family?'

Old Mr Yeats removed his spectacles and looked thoughtfully at Thomas; it was some moments before he spoke. 'I do not. Money was sent to your parents in respect of Rory regularly, but I have no knowledge apart from the name of the firm dealing with the matter, from whence it came. May I enquire if you have future plans?'

'We have decided to try London.'

'I see, well permit me to offer you some advice, just remember the streets are not paved with gold.' Mr Yeats allowed himself a small chuckle which turned into a hearty cough.

At home while eating their evening meal, Thomas regaled the others with tales of the elderly solicitor, mimicking his comment about the streets of London.

'Did he really say that?' said Molly incredulously.

Thomas nodded, and she giggled.

'Ridiculous little man,' Etty snorted. 'What does he think we are – stupid?'

'He was just trying to be amusing,' Thomas said laughing, 'and failing badly.'

'Aren't the streets of London paved with gold then,' said Rory with an innocent air.

'Oh Rory!' they shouted in unison.

Eliza Jane went to say goodbye to the Emmet sisters at the post office. She was fond of the two ladies, and didn't want to leave without seeing them. She glanced through the window of the shop, and groaned at the sight of Mrs Fanshawe and Mrs Wimbourne standing at the counter immersed in a bout of gossip.

Eliza Jane couldn't abide either lady, but particularly Mrs Fanshawe, who was always so unkind to her. No one wished more than Eliza Jane that she was dainty like her sisters, but it wasn't to be. She couldn't help being five foot eight inches tall with big bones and lank brown hair and Mrs Fanshawe did not have to remark upon it every time they met but remark she did. Eliza Jane hesitated for a moment, deciding whether to wait a while and return when the coast was clear, or to brave the viper's nest. Reprimanding herself severely and lifting her chin in defiance, she took a deep breath and started up the steps of the shop. The door was wide open, the women's voices carried outside their heads together not realising Eliza Jane was outside.

'Well, it wasn't his kidneys that carried Albert Watkins to an early grave,' said Mrs Fanshawe, drawing her audience a little closer by lowering her voice. 'I can tell you that much. You remember my sister, the one who lives in a large detached house in one of the better parts of Preston?' The others nodded. 'Well, she happens to live next door to the niece of Doctor Green's cleaner.'

'Who, Agnes Trimble?' asked Jemima Emmet?

'Yes, the very same, now listen, wait till I tell you: Agnes told her niece she had caught sight of some papers on Doctor Green's desk which said that Albert had taken his own life.' She paused before continuing. 'He hung himself.' The ladies were beside themselves. Beatrice shrieked, while Jemima and Mrs Wimbourne fanned themselves with newspapers to recover. There was so much commotion that they didn't hear the strangled sob, or the footsteps running away from the entrance to the shop.

Eliza Jane headed blindly for the bridge over the canal. She sat on the wall and attempted to control her tears. It couldn't be true, not her da. Agnes Trimble must be wrong. Da would never have left them that way; he loved them too much, and they loved him. A horrific image of her father dangling from a rope shot into her head, causing her to scream in terror. She stood up and began to pace back and forward trying to erase the image in her mind. Finally, she sat again, and fresh tears cascaded down her cheeks.

David Jackson, sweeping the pavement outside the shop caught sight of her sitting on the bridge lost in thought. He needed to talk to her, set things straight; he had never meant to hurt her the other day. He rapidly hung up his brush in the back room of the shop and told his Father he was going out for some air. He walked purposefully up behind the shop towards her. Eliza Jane stiffened as she saw him coming pretending not to notice him until he finally stood beside her.

'May I sit with you?' he said and without waiting for an answer, he perched on the bridge next to her. 'I just wanted to apologise for the other day.' Eliza Jane refused to speak or even look at him, in case he saw her tears. 'I wouldn't willingly hurt you – you know that, don't you? I think the world of you, we're such very special friends, and nothing can alter that, even if you move away. You do know that, don't you?' Eliza Jane nodded, she thought for a moment as fresh tears ran down her cheeks, and then she stood up and turned slightly to look at him

'I'm the one who's sorry, David. Etty had no right to discuss my feelings. I know you don't care about me as I do about you so I've succeeded in not only embarrassing you but me too. Now before I say something I shouldn't or you say something you can't possibly mean, I think we should finish this conversation.'

Eliza Jane set off without looking back, but if she had, she would have seen a pained expression on David's handsome face.

Chapter 12

The last few days before leaving for London were spent clearing out the cottage. Henry Laycock found some battered brown suitcases languishing in his storeroom that he gave to Thomas. They packed only clothes and personal items, unable and unwilling to carry anything else. Thomas stacked what little furniture was theirs outside the cottage for sale, and people came from neighbouring villages to poke through the pile. Horses and carts were used to take away items bought for a farthing. Ma and Da's fireside chairs were hoisted on a cart, along with their bed. A grubby looking man took them away, whose wife picked through the pile with disdain. They offered to take the family bicycle as a favour, and that was also thrown on top of the cart with the other goods.

'Clever idea,' Etty remarked, as she watched them drive away. 'Sneering at goods to keep the price down, by the way has anyone seen my pink scarf, I seem to have lost it and I don't want it to go along with the stuff for sale.' No one had.

Mrs Fanshawe and Mrs Wimbourne fought tooth and nail over Martha's china dogs, each claiming they had been promised them, so Eliza Jane was relieved when Henry Laycock offered a good price to take the dogs back, which she readily accepted.

Eventually, anything that did not sell was carried away for a small price to the local incinerator. Rory, adamant that his art material was no longer needed, burned his easel on the kitchen range. The others tried to point out it was Da's wish he continued with his painting but Rory wouldn't listen. He believed that if he had gone to work with Albert, which is what his father wanted, he might still be alive and the business thriving.

Early in the afternoon, the new blacksmith, young and brawny, arrived by horse and cart. They were still cleaning the cottage when the new family arrived. The blacksmith's haughty wife sat beside him: their three children were almost hidden in amongst their possessions on the back of the cart.

It was agony to watch the family invade the house: Bedrooms were chosen by the children. The wife immediately placed an apron around her waist then began to black the range; even though Eliza Jane had done it the week before. The sight of another woman in Ma's scullery was too much for her, so she kept out of the way by taking a walk past Dr Green's house and into the country side. She had many questions ready for the doctor should he be out tending his front garden. By the time she reached Dr Green's house, she was fired up and ready to learn the truth.

The doctor was in his garden, he smiled at her over the wall. 'Hello, Eliza Jane, how are the preparations for London going?'

'Fine thank you, doctor, it's a nice day,' she said, and walked quickly on cursing her lack of courage.

Thomas shook hands with the new incumbent and wished him well. He then ushered his family across the road to spend their last night in Crossdale, in rooms at the Bluebell public house.

The following morning, they walked the mile to the station with heavy suitcases, gripped tightly in each hand. Thomas and Rory also carried a picnic basket between them.

It was a sad group that waited on the platform of Crossdale station that early morning in late July. It had been six weeks since they buried Ma, and two weeks since they laid Da to rest beside her. Everything felt raw. The heavy unseasonable rain did little to lighten their mood. They'd had little sleep the previous night – very aware that the lights on in the cottage across the road were not of their making. Rory felt some small excitement for the journey they were about to make but Molly, missing her usual sense of adventure felt dispirited and low.

Other passengers watched them sympathetically, as they stood huddled together on the platform, their suitcases at their feet. Many walked over to shake hands and wish them well. Cyril Henderson had been as good as his word and had issued them all with railway passes. They were taking the train to Lancaster then changing for the London train. Cyril had also given them the address of his Aunt Agnes who had rooms to let in Islington.

Thomas was weary; he seemed to have aged in such a short time. He looked as if he was bearing the troubles of the world with no means of solving them.

Eliza Jane was doing her best to put on a brave front, but it was difficult to disguise her heavy heart. She had carefully avoided talking to David again since that encounter on the bridge, but now shivering with nerves in the early morning sun that was trying to conquer the rain, she wished she could see him, just once more.

Etty felt strange. She wasn't sure why. Was it delightful anticipation or sheer terror that invaded her heart? Perhaps it was both. Deep down, she felt the family were on the verge of some great change, but couldn't have told you what form it would take.

Hearing her name called, Eliza Jane looked up, and was surprised to see David Jackson pedalling towards her. She stood rooted to the spot as her heart dropped to her stomach before returning to its rightful position. Etty seeing his approach gently nudged her sister towards him. A blushing Eliza Jane shrugged her shoulders. What he could want? He had already settled her wages, giving the cash to Thomas for her. Perhaps she'd left something behind. She watched him, as he dismounted and pushing his bike forward, he walked towards her.

'Eliza Jane, I've come to say goodbye and wish you luck. I couldn't bear the thought of you leaving without seeing you. I'll miss you so much, my dearest and special friend.' Then overcome with the boldness of his speech, he hugged her with his free arm and kissed her flushed cheek. At the same moment, he tried to get Etty to look at him as she stood behind Eliza Jane. He pleaded with her using his eyes to beg her to change her mind and stay with him, but she purposely looked away. David released Eliza Jane, and with disappointment tearing at his heart, he tried to brush Etty's rejection aside. He took a step back. 'Write to me sometime, and let me know how you're all getting on – please, Eliza Jane.'

Performing joyful somersaults inside, she nodded. 'I will, David, I promise to write when we're settled.'

'I'll look forward to receiving your letters,' he said, as he mounted his bicycle and with a smile and a wave to the others, he shouted 'good luck' before heading back to the village.

Eliza Jane watched David's journey with her hand on the cheek he had kissed. Savouring his words, she vowed to store them deep in her heart to be revisited on rainy days.

Etty irritated that David had used Eliza Jane to try to make her jealous, stepped forward saying rather more sharply than she intended. 'You can wipe that smile off your face, Eliza Jane, but I'm right pleased for you.' Her words breaking into Eliza Jane's joy. *The cheek of the man,* she thought privately, *would he never take no for an answer.*

David Jackson pedalled back to the shop; his head full of conflicting emotions; on one hand, he was glad he had made his peace with Eliza Jane. He had meant what he'd said, but on the other, one look at Etty's face told him there was no hope of her ever loving him, which was hard to bear. He parked his bicycle outside of the shop, but instead of going inside to help his father, he went round to the back, through the door to the kitchen and up the stairs to his bedroom. On entering, he immediately went to the drawer of the bedside table, and with great reverence, took out Etty's pink scarf. He thought how beautiful she looked at the station, even in the grey, slanting rain. He sat down on the end of his bed clutching the scarf to his cheek imagining he could smell the whisper of a fresh breeze in a buttercup meadow on a summer's day. Slowly, he exhaled, sighing deeply, for it was the only piece of Etty he had left.

The Crossdale train drew into Lancaster station. 'Right on time,' said Thomas, examining his watch. 'The London train is leaving in twenty minutes, on the other platform.'

The family took up almost the whole of the compartment on the London train, leaving just one seat, next to Thomas, which was taken by a young vicar, who told them that although his parish was in London, he had been at the Priory in Lancaster on church business. He introduced himself as Christopher Howard, Kit for short. Chatting amiably, he told them about his parish in Lewisham and his sister, Grace, who lived with him at the vicarage. His parents had also sadly died he explained, which saw Molly who was sitting opposite, instantly warming to him.

Rory wasn't so sure about him, feeling that the vicar had dismissed his artistic achievement. If it wasn't for his success, the family might well have had to go their separate ways. He sank back and slumped against the window dreaming of the ceremony and beyond, regretting he had promised himself that he wouldn't take up a paint brush again.

Eliza Jane opened the picnic basket she had prepared, and they willingly shared their feast, such as it was, with him. They sat in comfortable silence, munching ham sandwiches, apples and thick slices of Eliza Jane's fruitcake, as the fields rolled by in the hazy sunshine. She then produced a thermos flask full of hot tea.

'What are your plans after attending the prize giving?' asked Kit, as he finished his cake. 'That was delicious, thank you.'

Eliza Jane blushed at the unexpected praise.

'We have to look for work,' answered Thomas.

'And somewhere to live,' added Etty, raising her eyebrows. 'Although we could spend another night at Aunt Agnes's boarding house, if worst comes to worst heaven help us.'

Eliza Jane embarrassed by Etty's use of the word heaven in the company of a vicar gazed studiously out of the window.

'I see,' said Kit. He was concerned; London could be a sinful, evil place, especially for those not used to City life. 'Look, let me give you my address just in case you need it. London is a big lonely place.' He found an old envelope and pen in his pocket, and jotted down his details. He handed the paper to Thomas who carefully placed the address in the top pocket of his jacket.

After chatting pleasantly with the young vicar for some hours, the train eventually rocked into Euston Station. Molly panicked, she didn't want the journey to end; she rather liked this tall and charming young man. Kit stood to retrieve his suitcase from the rack above his head. He then helped Thomas and Rory lift down the girl's cases.

'What have you got in here, Molly, boulders?' he joked, as he pretended to drop it. His hand touched hers momentarily as he gave it to her; both registered the touch and allowed it to linger slightly longer than was strictly necessary.

Molly smiled. 'A lady never discusses the contents of her case, but you're right, it is heavy.'

'Come on, Molly, don't dawdle,' said Etty, peeved that her youngest sister was getting all the attention.

Once they were all assembled on the platform, their suitcases at their feet, Kit bade them farewell. 'I hope we meet again sometime.' He smiled. 'But remember if you need any help or a place to stay you have my address.'

Kit shook everyone's hand, and with a final wave, he disappeared into the smoky crowds of Euston Station. Molly was crestfallen; she had enjoyed his cheerful and reassuring presence. Still, Thomas had his address, which was a comforting thought.

The station was enormous noisy and dirty; unlike anything they had experienced before. Crowds were milling around, passing them in all directions, walking purposefully and at speed. The smoke from the trains lingered in the air, making them choke and cough. Struggling with their heavy bags, they weaved through the people, desperately trying to keep together.

Outside the station, young lads barely old enough to be out alone, waved newspapers and shouted incomprehensible slogans. There were numerous colourful barrows laden with fruit and vegetables, each seller calling out their prices to passers-by. A woman sat on a stool, surrounded by a jungle of flowers, making posies and bouquets.

Etty gazed in awe at the fashions that the women were wearing. Although she had worn her best coat and hat, which were considered fashionable in Crossdale, she still felt shabby in comparison. Eliza Jane kept her eyes to the ground, also feeling estranged in her old boots and threadbare coat.

Thomas led them from the station looking more confident than he felt. Rory immediately feeling at home in the capital placed his cap at a jaunty angle and adopted a swagger; this surely was where he was destined to be.

They knew from Cyril's instructions that they had to take a tram to Upper Street in Islington which departed from outside the station.

Their tram lurched sideways, as it trundled up to the stop. Thomas stood back letting the girls climb the narrow steep stairs to the open top carriage. Then after he had boarded, he hung on for life as the tram set off swaying from side to side making it difficult to climb the stairs with a heavy suitcase.

'Mind 'ow you go ducks,' said the conductress.

Thomas reached the top and flung himself into a seat behind the others breathing heavily. Soon they were enjoying their first exciting view of London. Cars were vying for space on the road with horse-drawn carriages and barrow boys that called out in the air. The pavements were swarming with men in bowler hats, boaters, and flat caps. Attractively dressed ladies, held pretty parasols high against the sun's rays, while a crocodile of schoolboys in knickerbockers were ushered along by their harassed teacher.

The conductress hopped lightly up the stairs with practised ease, to give them their tickets. From his seat, Thomas looked up at her rather liking the dark curls creeping out from under her jauntily angled cap.

'Five to Upper Street please and can you tell us when we get there, we want the stop nearest to Compton Street?' said Thomas.

'Righto, ducks. I'll give yers a shout when we get there.' She vigorously wound the handle on the machine that she wore slung across her chest and Thomas watched as five tickets spewed out.

Molly, wasting no time in her pursuit for work, asked, 'Do you know if there are any jobs going on the trams? I used to work on the railways during the war.'

'Not a chance, dear, it's me last day terday. The men want their jobs back, you see, and us women are not needed anymore. It's a crying shame, if you ask me. We kept this country going for four years and now we're tossed aside like we don't matter.'

'The same happened to me,' agreed Molly. 'I lost my job with the railway just recently.'

'I know ducks – you, me and a few fousand other women. Lloyd George finks me head might explode if I'm given too much responsibility. Ah well, better get back to it. See yers all later.'

'Doesn't she talk in a funny way,' said Rory, after the conductress swung back downstairs.

'She probably thinks we do too,' said Thomas, dryly. He suddenly gave an almighty sneeze, which caused him to pull his handkerchief hurriedly out of his top pocket, along with Kit's address that fell to the ground unnoticed, and was soon swept under the seat.

They fell silent as the journey progressed, hunger and tiredness overtaking them. It had been a long day.

'Upper Street, this is your stop.' The conductress's voice shouted up the stairs.

They scrambled up from their wooden seats, gathering their suitcases, as the tram came slowly to a halt.

'Straight through the gardens and Compton Street is right there.' The conductress pointed in the direction that they were to travel. 'Yer can't miss it.'

'Thanks very much,' replied Thomas.

'Pleasure, my love; anyfing for a handsome lad like you.' Thomas smiled, he was going to like London, he thought.

Aunt Agnes's boarding house stood three stories high, next to similar properties in the tree-lined street. It had been built in red brick with a design of white brick around the front door. It looked like a like a doll's house, with symmetrical windows two to a floor. They gathered outside with all their worldly goods around their feet not quite knowing what to expect. Thomas tentatively pulled the doorbell, and after a short while, a small rotund woman with grey hair and round spectacles greeted them at the front door. She was wearing a white pinafore apron, covering old fashioned clothes. A delicious smell reminded them of Ma's home cooking.

'Mrs Parkinson,' he enquired politely.

'Hello, my lovelies, you must be the Watkins family. Now call me Aunt Agnes, everyone does. Any friends of our Cyril's are right welcome,' she said.

Thomas, pleased to hear a good Lancashire accent again, suddenly felt very homesick.

'Now, you must be tired and hungry, I'll show you to your rooms first then there'll be a hot meal waiting in the dining room. Come this way, my dears. I've put you three girls together, and you two men are on the next floor up.'

Wearily, they climbed the stairs to their rooms. 'There's plenty of hot water in the bathroom, so don't be afraid to use it, and there's wash basins in the bedrooms. Dinner will be in half an hour.'

Agnes smiled at the weary young travellers. Cyril had told her a little of their story, which made her feel very sorry for them and she had resolved to cheer them up.

With hardly time to take in the size and comfort of their rooms, they swilled their faces at the sink in their rooms before trooping downstairs to find the dining room.

Once seated around a large oblong table, Agnes entered carrying a tray of steaming hot pea and ham soup, which she placed down. 'I must say it's good to hear Lancashire accents again,' she said cheerfully. 'Do you know when I first moved here with our Earnest, no one understood a word I was saying so I used to shout at them like they were deaf. Earnest were a Londoner: we met when he came to do the accounts for the mill where I worked in Clitheroe. Our relationship were frowned on, of course, but that didn't worry, my Earnest. I mean to marry you, my girl, he said. Mind you, he lost his job for fraternising, as the mill owner called it, so we got married and upped sticks to London. We lived in this house with his Ma until she died.'

'It must have been difficult for you,' said Eliza Jane, 'leaving your family behind and moving down here.'

'Well, I were in love, and where ever he was I needed to be – that's what you do for each other, isn't it? Of course, Earnest is no longer with us – God rest his soul – but I'm never short of company while I have my guests. Now eat up, there's plenty.' Her gaze fell upon Etty. *Particularly you, lass; you need it most,* she thought.

With hot food inside them, it wasn't long before their eyelids began to droop.

'Get yourselves away to bed, you all look worn out,' remarked Aunt Agnes.

'Let me help you clear the table,' Eliza Jane remarked, feeling guilty that she should be waited on.

'No Love, ta, I can take care o' this, you get off.'

No-one needed a second bidding and one by one, they filed wearily up the stairs. Thomas and Rory had two single beds in their room. The girls had a double and a single. Etty grabbed the single, leaving her sisters to share.

'I love Aunt Agnes, her home is so warm and comfortable,' remarked Etty, pulling her thick eiderdown over her arms, and admiring the gold curtains.

'She's lovely,' said Eliza Jane, who was sitting up in bed reading. She put her book down. 'The story she told us about her Earnest was so romantic, and the smells from the kitchen reminded me of home and Ma.'

'I wonder why she looked at me when she told us to eat up. My clothes already feel tight these days' Etty mused, almost to herself.

'I shouldn't worry Etty, you can cope with a few extra pounds,' said Eliza Jane ruefully.

'Cyril did us proud, didn't he?' Molly remarked, turning from the sink and putting her nightdress over her head. 'I knew something would turn up,' she added, before climbing into bed beside Eliza Jane. 'I wonder what tomorrow will bring.'

Etty yawned, as she slid further down into her bed. 'If we don't turn out the light and go to sleep, we'll never find out, if you've finished reading, Lizzy, I'll say goodnight to you both.'

Chapter 13

The following morning dawned bright and slightly breezy. Aunt Agnes provided a breakfast of toast with boiled eggs from her own hens; Rory picked at his food, he felt slightly sick with nerves. Would his painting really stand up to professional scrutiny, what if people didn't like it and could he converse with all those posh people at the Gallery. Ma had always taught them to speak properly but he still had a Lancashire accent. He wished Ma was with them, she would have known what to say.

Once everyone was fed, washed and groomed, they assembled in the hall with their cases.

Aunt Agnes joined them smiling as usual. 'Well,' she said, 'it's been right nice having you all to stay; like a breath of good Lancashire air blowing through the place.'

'It has been lovely staying here,' said Thomas feeling in his pocket, 'how much do we owe you, Aunt Agnes?'

Agnes raised her hand. Nay, lad, I won't take a penny. You are friends of Cyril's, and that makes you friends of mine. Now, do you want to leave your suitcases here – save lugging them around – you know, come back for them when you've found rooms to let.'

Thomas was touched. 'Thank you but you've done more than enough already,' he said. 'We can't impose on you any longer: we'll take our cases with us.'

'You will all be most welcome to visit anytime, don't forget,' Agnes replied warmly.

Etty, who had really warmed to their landlady, hugged Agnes tightly. 'Thank you for everything,' she said.

Agnes hugged her back. 'Now don't dawdle or you'll miss your tram,' she said briskly, gently pushing Etty away before tears welled in her eyes, she was sorry to see them go.

Waving their goodbyes and shouting their thanks, they walked the short distance down the garden path, through the gate and on to the pavement. Aunt Agnes waved until they were out of sight.

They were early for the ceremony, so they spent some time in Trafalgar square in front of the National Gallery. They gazed up at Nelson's column, in awe of its size. They listened to a guide talking to some tourists, and were stunned to hear it was one hundred and sixty-nine feet high, costing forty-seven thousand pounds to be built.

Pigeons circled round and flew overhead, some of them settling on the heads and shoulders of people. One perched on top of Thomas's cap, and left its calling card. The others laughed, watching as Thomas stood frozen. As soon as the bird flew off, he snatched his cap off his head, screwing it up in a ball and forcing it into his jacket pocket.

'If only I'd got my camera now,' said Rory, relaxing slightly for the first time that morning and enjoying the sight of his brother looking scared with a pigeon on his head.

'Thank goodness you haven't,' said Thomas, not wanting it to be recorded for posterity.

'You might as well put your hat back on,' said Rory, as he snatched Thomas's hat from the pocket, 'you don't want a white mess on your hair, but you have to catch me first.' Rory ran a little distance from Thomas, waving his cap in the air. Thomas darted to grab it but the action made him short of breath so he called to Rory instead. 'You can keep it! I'll just have yours.' He managed to whisk Rory's cap off and rammed it on his own head but it was too small. They both burst out laughing.

Watching them from a distance was a tall, attractive man with collar length black curly hair. Patrick Lawrence was a professional photographer, passing through Trafalgar Square on the way to his club. He smiled, as he watched the two men larking about.

Etty sat on the wall of the fountain trailing her hand in the water which felt delightfully cool even in the heat of the morning. Molly, oblivious to her brothers' horseplay was wandering around the square in awe of her surroundings. She was wondering where the theatres were and hoped she might get to see on or two of them. Eliza Jane joined Etty on the wall. 'Did you hear that guide say that the design of the column was decided by someone winning a competition?' she said.

'Yes,' said Eliza Jane, smiling. 'It just goes to show you what can happen when you enter competitions.'

The square suddenly fell strangely quiet as an open-top bus drove by full of men. They were talking in a strange language. Excited, their speech sounded harsh and guttural. I wonder who they are,' Etty mused, almost to herself.

'German prisoners of war,' said the man sitting on the other side of her, they must be sightseeing before they go home, the bastards. Excuse the language, miss, I didn't mean to offend you.' Etty turned to look at the man who had spoken, noticing the empty sleeve pinned to his jacket where his arm should have been.

'No don't apologise, you deserve to call them names.' She assured him. Continuing to gaze after them, she pondered on what she had seen. 'I've never even seen a German before, strange, they look just like us. You expect them to have two heads or something.' She suddenly felt chilled, these were the people who had killed her William and ruined her life. She felt her hand being squeezed in support from Eliza Jane, but she continued to look straight ahead fearing her tears for William would begin to fall again. The man next to her stood up and touched his cap with his good hand and limped slowly away.

'Time we were going in,' said Thomas approaching the girls, still a little breathless from chasing his brother. 'Where's Molly?'

'I'm here,' said Molly, passing through a group of tourists to reach them. 'Did you see that bus load of men; someone said they were German prisoners.'

'The war is over, Molly, they're just ordinary men waiting to go home to their families.'

'That's easy for you to say, Thomas,' Etty grimaced, 'they didn't kill your fiancé.'

'They were just doing their job, same as our boys. Now come on, let's go and see Rory's picture.'

They crossed the road carefully, the volume of traffic, so different from at home, bothered them slightly, then climbed the steps up to the Gallery entrance.

Patrick Lawrence, using his photographer's eye was, intrigued by the family and followed them into the gallery.

Once inside, they stood silently in awe of the lavish surroundings. Marble pillars stood majestically at the bottom of each staircase. There were four wide staircases off from the main hall. Rory looked up and nudged Thomas. 'Look at that ceiling,' he said. Thomas gazed up at the light pouring through each glass dome, casting huge pools on to the marble floor, making it difficult to see which way to go.

'Where do we have to be, Rory, what does it say in the letter?' he asked squinting in the sunlight.

Rory, having read his letter many times previously and knew its contents off by heart still drew the envelope out of his pocket, opened it up and scanned the details. 'It says the Barry Rooms, but I'm to announce myself at the desk.' His voice sounded loud, as it echoed around the marble hall.

Rory led his family to the main desk. 'May I help you, sir?' The man sitting behind the desk appeared aloof but polite.

Rory having been addressed as sir became temporarily tongue tied. Etty stepped forward. 'My brother is here to collect an award; his name is Rory Watkins.'

The man immediately stood up. 'Mr Watkins, how nice to meet you, if you will follow me, I will take you straight through.'

They all followed the man down a lengthy corridor and through an ornate door. Here the others were told to stay where they were as Rory was led away to be introduced to the Director of the Gallery. The room was large, with more marble pillars and ornate ceilings. Drinks were being served on trays by soft footed waiters. Both Thomas and Etty took a glass of sherry as the tray passed them by.

'Etty, Ma always said ladies do not drink in public,' admonished Eliza Jane.

'Good job she's not here then, isn't it?' Etty replied.

'I can't believe how many people are here,' whispered Molly in an attempt to stop her sisters arguing. The ploy worked, each sister falling silent.

Rory's painting of Da at work in the smithy was unveiled to the applause of a selective audience. Thomas gazed at the hearty, healthy man in the picture before him. Closing his eyes, he tried to shut out the pain of seeing his father looking so alive.

Etty couldn't bring herself to look at the painting for a different reason. The guilt over her parent's death was never far away, and she hadn't been able to rationalise her feelings or talk to anyone about it. Not that she would – since this would have been a sign of weakness in her, and Etty refused to be weak. She turned away and looked around the room, as she sipped her sherry.

Da had been funny that first day Rory had set up his easel. He'd stood stiffly to attention, aware of the responsibilities of being painted. Carrying his hammer in his hand, he kept asking if he was striking the right pose for the painting. '*Just be yourself, Da, let me do the rest,*' Rory had said. *'I want you to just be as natural as you can.*' After some hours of strained posturing, Albert had eventually forgotten that Rory was there, relaxing into his daily routine.

Although Rory would remember his taste of success for the rest of his life, he knew nothing would induce him to take up his paintbrush again. It never occurred to him that his da had died simply because he couldn't live without Martha.

Eliza Jane, gripping Molly's hand, was choking back her tears. With his face flushed in the firelight, Da looked so complete, so content, swinging his hammer. She was sure the poisonous chatter she had heard about his death was a lie. As the picture showed, her da was a wonderfully strong and capable man, whom she loved. She could not imagine him leaving them all so violently, and by his own hand. Molly looked pale and drawn, the painting of Da was too much to bear and she was grateful to have her sister's support.

Before Rory was awarded his prize, there was to be a speech by the director of the gallery. Small, bald and pompous, he cleared his throat theatrically before beginning. He occasionally glanced at the notes in his hand, making his speech hesitant and boring.

'We would like to thank you all for coming. It is so nice to see so many people here today. This competition was organised by the trustees to celebrate the return of our paintings to the Gallery from their evacuation during the war.'

He continued with a lengthy description of how and why the works of art had been packed up and sent away. 'And so you see, we have them back in their rightful place today. But enough of that, we are here today to celebrate the achievement of this young man.' He indicated Rory who was standing slightly behind him and to the right. 'The board of trustees and I felt that this picture accurately portrays an aspect of the rural history of our country. Unfortunately, since the end of the war, this idyll is rare: there are far fewer blacksmiths now, due to the age of automation taking over from the horse, and so few young men returning from the war are taking up the trade. The blacksmith here in this painting is strong and clearly equal to the task ahead of him. He is in charge. The wonderful use of colour and texture recreates the dark interior of the blacksmiths shop, with just the right amount of illumination from the furnace reflected in the man's face. The judges agreed that they could almost smell the fire. It was therefore a unanimous decision to award' – the director struggled to find Rory's name on the sheet of paper he was holding – 'a unanimous decision to award Rory James Watkins first prize. The recipient of the prize shall win a camera, the sum of five pounds, plus the honour of being hung in the National Gallery.'

The director ushered Rory forward and shook his hand as a couple of photographers put their heads under the black cloth of their camera's and held up plates that flashed in front of them. 'To conclude,' he added, 'I very much hope you will all celebrate the safe return of our paintings by visiting our different floors of the gallery. Please enjoy this time today. We would like to thank you for attending, and once again congratulations to young, um, young' – he searched his paper once more – 'young Rory Watkins.'

The director led the applause with a hearty enthusiasm.

Etty glancing around her, noticed a particularly handsome guest standing to the side applauding her brother. He was tall with curly black hair and bright-blue eyes. He appeared well dressed and elegant and she thought him quite beautiful. She caught his eye; he smiled, and moved closer to where she was standing.

'Don't say it,' warned Etty.

'Say what?'

'Oh, the usual – like what's a nice girl like you doing amongst all these dull old paintings.'

'Well, now I might have to,' he teased. 'I'm Patrick Lawrence by the way and what is a nice girl doing here amongst all these dull paintings?'

'They are all dull, except for one and that was painted by my brother. He's just won the prize.'

'Yes, I know. I thought you were related – I noticed you all earlier in the square, your other brother is over there' – he nodded toward Thomas, who was chatting to a member of the board of Trustees – 'and your sisters are right now pretending they understand abstract art!'

'I suppose we stick out like sore thumbs in our clothes and you will have noticed by our appearance that it's our first time in London.'

'You stick out, as you put it, because you're beautiful, and I know my camera will think the same.'

'What am I supposed to do? Be so flattered that I fall into your arms?' Etty said with heavy sarcasm.

'You are a prickly girl; can't you accept a compliment in the manner in which it's given?' He smiled at Etty and said, 'Shall we start again. I'm Patrick

Lawrence a professional photographer at your service, how do you do.' He bowed low.

'Henrietta Watkins,' Etty replied, flattered that an attractive man should be paying court to her.

'I would love to meet your family. Will you introduce me?'

Etty considered this for a moment. She was unwilling to share Patrick with the others, particularly Molly, but for the second time in her life, Etty did as she was told.

Patrick shook hands with Rory and Thomas and kissed the hands of Eliza Jane who blushed, and Molly who giggled. 'That's a fine piece of photographic equipment you have there, may I see it?' Patrick said admiring Rory's prize.

Rory was reluctant to pass over his prize for inspection but on noticing Patrick had his own camera, he did so. Patrick examined the camera carefully, then as he handed it back to Rory, he said, 'Do you know how to use it?'

'I understand the basics I think,' Rory answered truthfully.

'Well, it is an extremely smart piece of equipment, and congratulations to you, your painting is superb. Have you travelled quite a distance? Are you going to see something of London while you are here?'

The group suddenly fell silent. No one quite knew how to answer him, because they didn't know what they were going to do themselves. Rory, without thinking, suddenly blurted out a potted history of their story. Molly interrupted where necessary to add flavour to the tale. 'So, you see, we can't go back to Crossdale. We're hoping to find work and somewhere to live,' she said.

Thomas was embarrassed by his siblings' forthright expressions and said, 'Mr Lawrence doesn't need to know our life story; you both go too far with your dramatics.' He glanced over at Patrick. 'I apologise for my family.'

'No, please, I am keen to hear more,' Patrick replied warmly.

This man is perfect, thought Etty gazing at his animated face. Unconsciously, she patted her hair, and made sure her hat was on straight.

'Rory is an unusual name,' Patrick remarked, 'where does it come from?'

'Ma always said I was named after someone called Rory McAllister, who was a friend of the family that she worked for. Apparently, he was a frequent visitor, and a good friend of the daughter of the house.'

Thomas suddenly recalled Ma's often told tale of how Rory came to be named. It began to make some sense to him.

'I like the name,' said Patrick, his face looking strangely wistful for a moment. 'Now,' he said enthusiastically, 'how about some luncheon? There's a place just a short walk from here, my treat.'

Thomas quickly declined, ignoring Etty's hopeful face. 'Thank you, Mr Lawrence, but we haven't time and as you can see, we have our cases with us. We have to find somewhere to live, so we must get on. I hope you'll excuse us.' He wasn't sure what it was that was bothering him about this man, unless it was the way Etty was looking at him that made him feel uneasy.

'Surely, you must eat,' Patrick insisted, and we can discuss your problems in relative comfort. I may be able to help.'

'I'm going to lunch with Mr Lawrence,' said Etty firmly, 'you can all meet me later if you like.'

'I think the whole family needs to stay together in a strange city, Etty,' said Patrick calmly, 'come on, surely you've nothing to lose Thomas, I promise you I'm quite safe. Today's Thursday, and I only eat people from Lancashire on Fridays.'

Lunch was fun; even Thomas was enjoying the company. Patrick was a great host, amusing and chatty. He had been shown, what had been referred to as his usual table, by a busy little man in a frock coat. The suitcases had been whisked away from the family much to the horror of Thomas, would they ever get them back, he wondered. Extra chairs were bought quietly and efficiently. Three waiters had pulled out the chairs for the girls before they could do it for themselves and crisp white napkins had been gently placed in everyone's lap. Thomas resisted the temptation to tuck his into his collar as usual. The tablecloths were snowy white and the cutlery highly polished. Wall lamps glowed softly contributing to the intimate atmosphere.

Patrick seemed to know a great many people, and when they stopped by their table, he introduced the family, 'as friends of mine from Lancashire.'

Etty was smitten; she had never fallen so quickly for anyone before, even her William. Patrick was the most wonderful, handsome and intelligent man she had ever met. She flirted with him, as only she knew how. Patrick responded in a friendly manner but appeared to treat her no differently to the others much to Etty's disappointment.

When lunch was over, Patrick sat back in his chair and took out a long cigarette holder and a silver cigarette case. He offered a cigarette to Thomas, who accepted, then selecting one himself, he put it into the end of the holder then placed the holder between his lips.

'I'd like one, please,' said Etty vowing to buy a cigarette holder as soon as possible. Patrick raised his eyebrows, passed her a cigarette and held a match to it. Etty seized the opportunity to cup her hand around his.

Eliza Jane went to speak but Thomas shook his head indicating she wasn't to embarrass Etty.

Etty drew heavily on her cigarette then copied the way Patrick draped his arm over the back of his chair as he blew out the smoke.

Molly, who had been watching Etty with a degree of embarrassment for her older sister, looked across the table at Patrick. 'You suggested earlier you might be able to help us, Mr Lawrence.'

'I did, Molly, and over luncheon I have been formulating a plan that may be of interest. I live alone in a part of London called Upper Sydenham, and I own a photographic business that I run from my house. I specialise in portrait photography. My house is large and has five bedrooms.' Thomas realising what Patrick was about to say leaned across the table to intervene, but Patrick held up his hand and continued, 'No, please, hear me out, 'don't take this the wrong way Thomas, but here's what I propose.' He turned to look at Rory who was sitting next to him. 'I would like to take you on as my apprentice at the studio. Rory was thrilled; an apprenticeship to a professional photographer was beyond his wildest dreams. He stood up and offered Patrick his hand. 'Thank you sir, thank you so much, I won't let you down.'

'I'm sure you won't. Now my housekeeper has recently left me to look after her sick sister in Scotland, and I'm becoming very tired of eating at my club. Would that interest one of you?' Uplifted by the sudden turn of events, Eliza Jane, her face hot with embarrassment, seized the moment. 'I'd like to offer my services for the job of housekeeper,' she said, a blotchy red streak running down her neck. 'I'm a good cook, and you'll not go hungry at all.'

'Wonderful, I will look forward to it,' replied Patrick, smiling at Eliza Jane's eagerness. 'The rest of you can take your time to find suitable employment. How does that sound? We could give the plan a trial run, say a month, what do you say?'

'I knew something would turn up,' said Molly beaming, 'and it has!'

Thomas fell sullenly silent; he was suspicious that someone they had only just met should come up with such a speedy solution to their problems. He didn't know what to say.

'My brother appears to have lost his manners,' said Etty, quickly seizing the opportunity to intervene. 'On behalf of us all, I will accept your very generous offer – and thank you, thank you so much, Patrick.' Etty did not want this opportunity to slip through her hands.

'Wonderful, now if you will excuse me for just a moment, then we shall be off.'

As Thomas watched him go, he felt a deep sense of panic rising inside of him. He turned on Etty furiously, 'I'm head of this family now,' he hissed. 'And any decisions made about our future rest with me. We know nothing about this man: how do we even know he's telling us the truth. We should have discussed it first, before you batted your eyelids at him.'

'Don't talk daft, Thomas,' spat Etty, 'this is a God given opportunity, and we can't afford to turn it down. You heard what Patrick said – A trial basis of one month, we've nothing to lose by giving it a try.'

The others agreed, and by the time Patrick returned, Thomas had been out voted.

Chapter 14

Eliza Jane opened her eyes with a start and hurriedly threw back the bed covers. She was convinced she had overslept, and would be late for work at Jackson's before she remembered the train that yesterday had bought them to London. Realising that home no longer existed, except in her memory a terrible sense of home sickness washed over her. An image of David sprang into her mind, and she wondered if he was missing her, as she was missing him. Realising she was indulging in pure fantasy again, she remembered that her new position meant she had several breakfasts to cook, and a new employer to impress. She crept past Molly's bed the occupant of which was still fast asleep and tiptoed to the bathroom. Etty had bagged the single room on her own. The others knew better than to argue with her.

The spacious bathroom housed a huge claw foot bath, a toilet and a large porcelain basin. She washed in cold water as usual, splashing it over her face. She had never used a basin before and wondered why there were two taps; she didn't know that one was used for hot water. After washing, she dressed quickly tying an apron round her waist as she went downstairs. Mr Lawrence had briefly shown her where the kitchen was last night, but she still had to try several doors until she found the right one.

The kitchen was intimidating. She was used to Ma's small scullery at home, and right now she wished she were there. She gazed around the large square room, taking some deep breaths, she tried to unravel the knot that had formed in her stomach. It was a beautiful room dominated by huge painted cupboards and shelves, and a black and white tiled floor. Cheerful curtains hung at the windows and the walls were white, shiny and easy to clean. Instead of a range that needed black leading, there stood a large cooker on four legs, the like of which Eliza Jane had never seen before, and thus had no idea how it worked. Over the other side of the kitchen, stood a white box on legs. Timidly, she opened the door and found milk, butter and cheese, stored within. She put her hand inside, surprised that everything felt so cold to the touch. Why wasn't the butter on a marble slab keeping cool in the pantry like at home, she thought?

'It's called a refrigerator; it's designed to keep your food fresh longer,' Patrick said, noticing her puzzled face as he came into the room. He was wearing a three-piece suit with a white stiff collared shirt and a bow tie.

Eliza Jane's face grew florid, prickly and hot. She felt like a small child who had been caught with her hand in the sweet jar.

'I've never seen one before, or even heard of them,' she said, conscious of her northern accent, and desperately hoping she sounded vaguely intelligent.

Patrick was concerned, he hoped he hadn't made a mistake with taking in five strangers but certainly Eliza Jane didn't seem to know much about the workings of a modern kitchen. 'Can you manage, Eliza Jane, I'm aware everything must be very different.'

'Yes, yes of course, Mr Lawrence, of course I can manage,' she lied.

Patrick, not sure that Eliza Jane could cope decided to call her bluff and replied, 'Good that's fine, I'll leave you to it then.'

Eliza Jane did not reply

'Did you hear me?' Patrick asked, starting to feel sorry for Eliza Jane and concerned that she was near to tears. 'Eliza Jane,' he spoke again, she turned to look at him. 'On this first morning, shall we work out the mysteries of the kitchen together?' From that moment on, Eliza Jane became a devoted employee.

Everyone assembled for breakfast in the kitchen. Patrick refused to have his alone in the dining room, preferring to eat with his "new family". He came into the room waving some newspapers. 'You've made the papers, Rory. *The Times* has a small piece about you, and *The Daily News* has an article and a picture.'

Etty almost snatched the *Daily News* out of his hand. 'Let me see,' she smiled as she looked at the paper. 'Nice picture, Rory.'

'Can I look, Etty?'

'Wait on, I'm reading what it says.'

Patrick aware of Rory's frustration offered him *the Times*. As Rory read the article his smile became broader. 'Listen, it says "Mr Watkins was delighted to have won". Delighted no less, I tell you I was thrilled. Ma would have been so proud of me, wouldn't she?'

'She certainly would, lad,' Eliza Jane answered warmly.

Once breakfast was over, and the kitchen cleaned to Eliza Jane's satisfaction, she spent a little time becoming acquainted with her surroundings. It was such a beautiful house with three reception rooms and a large library and study. There would be so much to write and tell David and the thought of him reading her words gave her a thrill. Back in the kitchen, she found few provisions in the pantry so decided she must go shopping that morning. Patrick had given her some housekeeping money, and Eliza Jane had a mind to be prudent with it – since she wasn't sure when she would be given more, and was too shy to ask. She took a lasting glance of satisfaction around the kitchen, before removing her apron and exchanging it for her outdoor clothes. She put on her hat and coat and set off down Sydenham hill towards the town. The morning was overcast but warm. Eliza Jane smiled and nodded to people as she passed them by, she felt ridiculously happy but couldn't be sure why. She sauntered down the hill swinging her basket making towards Wells Street; this would eventually lead her to High Street and the shops. Patrick's directions had been very clear. Continuing down Wells Street, she noticed a park to her right where she might have a sit down on the return walk. She found the butchers on the corner of Wells Street and High Street and taking the family's ration books out of her basket, she joined the forming queue. Business was brisk, although there wasn't a great deal of meat to be had. The shop smelt of sawdust, and there were one or two whole pigs and sides of beef hanging from hooks in the ceilings. There were two butchers, one older than the other, both were chatty and looked resplendent in their matching aprons, boater hats and bow ties.

When Eliza Jane reached the counter, the younger butcher grinned at her and said, 'Now then, young lady, what can I get yer?'

Tentatively, she asked for mutton chops for her hot pot.

'That's me best neck of mutton mind,' the butcher said. 'Do yer 'ubby proud, that will, I can guarantee it. He'll love you forever if yer put it in a stew for 'is tea.' Eliza Jane flushed and said nothing; she placed the meat in her basket and handed over the money and ration coupons.

The butcher grinned at her. 'Cat got yer tongue, 'as it? Ain't seen you before, where 'ave yer come from then?'

'Lancashire,' whispered Eliza Jane, embarrassed that the queue behind her could hear.

'Blimey, ends of the earth, that is. Anyway, love, you enjoy it, and come back and see us soon.'

Mortified with embarrassment and with a bright red face, Eliza Jane dodged speedily through the waiting queue and out of the shop.

Every shop she went in greeted her in a similar fashion. People were so friendly, and yet hadn't she had always been told that northerners were supposed to be the friendly ones. It seemed southerners took you at face value, unlike those at home who were friendly enough until they found out everything there was to know about you, then only spoke when they saw fit.

She ventured further down the street, enjoying the bustle and throng of the people, the cars and trams. In Crossdale, the only person to have a car was Doctor Green; everyone else used horses, bicycles or just walked. Lost in these musings, Eliza Jane walked straight into a lamppost bumping her shoulder. Rubbing her upper arm, she looked up and noticed that she was in front of the biggest shop she had ever seen.

Cobb's Department Store had several large windows, ranging down the street and around the corner. She idly glanced at each window display, admiring the fashions and the home wares and blushing at the display of corsets. In the last window, near to the entrance, there was a notice that read: Female Staff wanted, apply within. Hurriedly, she re-traced her steps back up the hill to home for Etty needed to know there was a job to be had, and not a moment to lose.

Chapter 15

Etty was less than impressed with Eliza Jane's news of the prospect of a job. 'Why on earth would I want to be a shop girl?' she said. Etty had already mapped out her future and determined to become Mrs Patrick Lawrence; she couldn't believe the style in which Patrick lived. The house on Sydenham hill was magnificent and stood in its own extensive grounds in a wide avenue of other large mansions. There were five bedrooms, a large drawing room with a huge fireplace, a slightly smaller sitting room, a dining room that housed a highly polished table and a study that contained a magnificent desk and shelves crammed with books. Patrick's photographic studio was at the front of the house. She perpetually worried that if Thomas didn't begin to trust Patrick, he would soon ask them to leave. With perhaps only a month to make Patrick fall in love with her, she needed to make every day count.

Her first stage of the plan involved new clothes. This was essential if she was to compete with the society ladies who came to the photographic studio for a portrait sitting. Etty had appointed herself as the studio's unpaid receptionist, and regularly brought her design skills to the fore using feathers, ferns and coloured screens to enhance Patrick's portraits. She was thrilled that Patrick appreciated the flair in which she went about her work. As each client waited to be shown into the studio, she took the time to study their clothes. When they had left, she made a preliminary drawing of their outfit, sketching it on her pad. Then she added her own design embellishments. She begged Thomas (so undignified but needs must) for some of Da's money to buy new material. Thomas had given it to her on the condition she made Eliza Jane and Molly new clothes also. Scowling, she reluctantly agreed, and immediately set off down to the shops to buy material.

Molly meanwhile had been very enthusiastic about Eliza Jane's news of a job. At Patrick's suggestion, she had immediately telephoned the store for an appointment and the following day, she hovered nervously outside the shop, having secured an interview with the general manager. Molly looked at her reflection in the store window, checking her appearance and straightening her hat. Taking a deep breath in, to steady her nerves, she pushed open the large glass door of the store and went in. The shop had an almost over powering scent which pervaded the air, emanating from the perfume counter that seemed to lie towards the back of the store.

The department that held the vacancy was not specified in the advertisement and Molly hoped it wasn't to be corsets or home ware, as she wanted to be part of the ground floor bustle, selling hats, scarves or perfumes. She approached the nearest counter.

'How may I help you, miss?' said the middle-aged woman, looking down her nose at Molly.

'My name's Molly Watkins. I have an appointment with Mr Gambon – could you tell me where I might find him?' Molly's stomach was gurgling in terror. The woman called over her shoulder to an assistant who was working behind her counter. 'Miss Josephine, step forward if you please.'

A pleasant looking girl with beautiful auburn hair swept up into a bun came to the counter. 'Show this lady to Mr Gambon's office – and don't dawdle.'

'Yes, Mrs Roberts, come this way please.' Molly walked quickly to keep up with her guide. 'Is she always that snooty?'

'Always,' agreed the girl, 'we call her the general for obvious reasons, you do not want to get on the wrong side of her.'

Molly thought for a moment, perhaps working here wouldn't be as easy as she at first thought. 'Do you like working here?' she asked the girl.

'I enjoy it most of the time, are you coming to join us?'

'I hope so,' Molly said, 'if Mr Gambon likes me. I'm Molly by the way.'

'What goggle-eyed Gambon; he'll like you all right – you're a woman, aren't you – just watch yourself with him though, you'll find out why soon enough. Come and find me afterwards and let me know how you get on. I'm Josephine, Jo for short, like Jo March in *Little Women*, though I liked *Anne of Green Gables* better because she had red hair.' Jo suddenly stopped and pointed. 'That's his office three doors down on the right. You can't miss it.'

'Well, here goes, wish me luck, Jo.' Molly took the final steps towards the door marked Percival Gambon and raised her hand to knock gently.

'Come in,' came a muffled voice from behind the door, Molly turned the handle and entered a small office. Behind the desk sat a large, greasy looking man with thinning hair and a drooping moustache. He had an obvious squint leaving Molly unsure which eye to look at. She found it hard to suppress her laughter – goggle-eyed Gambon – now she understood.

'Ah, Miss Watkins, I presume. Do sit down.' He motioned in the general direction of a chair. 'I believe you're interested in a job with us at Cobbs.'

'Yes, sir, I am, very interested,' replied Molly perching herself primly on the chair and gathering her skirts around her feet. She didn't want Mr Gambon to see that her boots were in need of repair.

'You realise there are many young ladies queuing up to be given this chance to work at Cobbs?'

Molly had not noticed any queues but agreed anyway by nodding compliantly. 'Thank you for seeing me, sir, and at such short notice.'

'Well' – he stroked the ends of his moustache – 'let's hope it's worth my while.'

'Yes, sir.' Molly was beginning to feel uncomfortable in Mr Gambon's presence.

'Miss Watkins, can you tell me why I should be interested in hiring you, what experience do you have?'

'I worked in the ticket office at our local station during the war, so I'm quite used to serving customers. I believe I could be an asset to Cobbs.'

Mr Gambon nodded. 'Do you have references?'

'Yes, sir.' She reached into her bag that she had been holding tightly on her lap and handed him her references from the station. Although the letter from the Station Master was not long, the minutes ticked by slowly as Mr Gambon read it. Finally, he looked up.

'Your reference is highly satisfactory, Miss Watkins; I can see no reason why you should not become a valued member of staff.'

'Does that mean you are giving me the job?' Molly asked.

'You may start tomorrow on one week's trial. I'll put you in the millinery department under the tutelage of Mrs Roberts. Please report to her at 8am sharp in the morning. You'll work forty-eight hours with Sundays and one other half day off a week. Your wages will be twenty-five shillings weekly and sixpence will be deducted from your wages should you be late for work. Welcome to Cobbs, Miss Watkins.'

'Thank you, sir.' Molly was thrilled but contained her excitement. 'I'll look forward to it.'

Mr Gambon rose from his desk and walked the short distance to open his door, which Molly took as her cue to leave. She smiled and nodded slightly in farewell and as she passed him by, she thought – though she couldn't be sure – that his hand had slightly brushed over her bottom.

Molly carefully walked the corridors back to the millinery department. She saw Jo trying to sell a hat to a very cross looking lady, so she waited, until Jo became free. The lady left without a purchase.

'Difficult customer?' she enquired, as she approached Jo.

Jo groaned. 'They can all be difficult customers, especially when trying to convince them that an expensive hat suits them when it obviously doesn't. Some times, it works; this time it didn't. Well, how did you get on; did you get the job?'

'I did, and it looks like we'll be working together – he's put me on millinery.'

'That's wonderful; I know we're going to get along famously. By the way, did you find out what I meant about watching yourself with him?'

Molly nodded. 'I think so, but I couldn't be sure.'

'You'll learn, none of us ever turn our backs on him.' Jo suddenly caught sight of Mrs Roberts; she had finished serving her customer and was annoyed to see her staff member gossiping when her counter was a mess.

'Looks like the General is giving us the eye; you had best let her know you've got the job. I'm really looking forward to working with you.'

'And me you, see you tomorrow.' Molly walked over to Mrs Roberts to explain she was to start tomorrow. After further instructions from the supervisor, Molly lingered over the hats and scarves. Etty would love this, she thought, as she gazed at the array of brightly coloured scarves. Smiling to herself as she imagined it, she also knew that her sister would sort out goggle-eyed Gambon and his wandering hands in the blink of one good eye.

Chapter 16

Several days later, one afternoon, there was a knock on Etty's door; she lay her cigarette down in the ashtray and shouted '*entre*.' She had picked up the word from the honourable Belinda Carrington, who had draped herself over Patrick, calling him darling, during her photographic sessions. Etty liked the sound the word made but had taken an instant dislike to Belinda.

The door creaked open, and Patrick's head peered around the door. 'Am I disturbing you?' he asked.

'Not one bit,' Etty said, placing her sewing down on the table in front of her.

'I wondered if you'd like to come with me this afternoon. The Duchess of Hampshire has telephoned; her daughter is coming out next season, and Mamma has commissioned a formal portrait of her to be published in the *Tatler*. Unfortunately, the daughter loves horses more than clothes so I was hoping you could accompany me, and help to make her look her best – I've every faith in you. We'll go in my car and be back in time for dinner.'

Etty was ecstatic, a whole afternoon out with Patrick was a dream come true. Not wanting to appear too excited, she took a deep breath and considered her answer for a moment. 'I'd love to help Patrick, but I really have to finish this dress for Molly, perhaps another time.'

'Of course, Etty, I completely understand, it was just a thought I'll leave you to it then, and see you later.'

Etty realised she had been a little hasty; she had hoped that Patrick would try to persuade her. 'On second thoughts,' she said, trying to appear casual, 'a run out might do me good. I've been feeling a little off colour lately.'

'Excellent, be ready in half an hour, I'll meet you by the garage.'

Patrick withdrew and closed the door behind him.

Etty was in a flat spin – what should she wear, how should she act, what should she say? She rose quickly from her chair which caused her to become dizzy. As the room swirled around her, she grabbed the corner of the table to steady herself. Closing her eyes, she waited a few seconds for it to pass. She was right about needing a break; she had been looking a little pale for a couple of days, and hoped she wasn't coming down with a cold. She opened up her wardrobe and selected her latest navy dress in embroidered silk crepe. Instead of wearing a hat, she wound a chiffon scarf around her head, which matched the silk ribbon draped around her slim hips. Pulling on her white gloves, she was confidently pleased with her reflection in the wardrobe mirror.

Sharing an intimate space with Patrick on the drive out was sheer heaven. Patrick was wonderful companion. She tried to sound knowledgeable when he talked of his car: A Morris Cowley Bullnose, with a 1.5 litre engine and 26 brake horse powers. She was genuinely impressed, even though she barely understood a word. They stopped for tea in one of the small villages on the way. She relished pulling up outside the tearooms in an expensive car. Patrick, tall and handsome, dutifully opened her door. Desperately hoping the customers inside the tea rooms were watching, she placed a hand on Patrick's arm, as she climbed gracefully out of the car.

The Copper Kettle tea room was a small cottage with a thatched roof. The interior was dark but cosy and afforded a degree of coolness from the heat of the afternoon sun. They found a table by the window and Patrick ordered afternoon tea. Etty was delighted when the waitress asked him if his wife would like Indian or China tea. Patrick chose to ignore the mistake, and suggested they had china tea.

'We must look married,' Etty told him delightedly, gazing at him with clear blue eyes.

Patrick laughed. 'Yes perhaps we do,' he agreed.

Etty concentrated on confidently pouring the tea. Sipping hers delicately, she looked at her surroundings, admiring the gleaming brassware hanging by the side of the large fireplace. The delicate bone china felt exquisite in her hand. The muted clink of teacups and quiet conversation from the other tables delighted her. The sandwiches and scones were sublime, and although Etty tried hard not to eat – it didn't do for a young lady to eat like a horse – but she was overcome by hunger. The tea shop felt gloriously cool away from the heat of the day. With a start, Etty realised it was the first of August, exactly six weeks since Albert had died. She shared her thoughts with Patrick.

'It must have been a terrible time for you all losing your father so soon after your mother's passing.' Patrick commiserated.

'It was,' agreed Etty. 'If only I could turn the clock back, I would try to be a very different person.'

'How do you mean?'

'Oh, not so rebellious, I think. I caused Ma a lot of worry. Too independent for my own good that's me I'm afraid. I've always been what Ma would call headstrong.'

'I can't believe that,' said Patrick seriously, the corners of his mouth twitching with laughter.

'Oh you,' she replied, waving her serviette at him and laughing.

'Was there anyone special you left behind in Crossdale? You're a beautiful girl.'

'You're a fine one to talk Patrick Lawrence, what about you?' said Etty, thrilled that he had called her beautiful.

'I asked first.' He reminded her with a smile.

Etty sighed. 'I was engaged to a lovely man, his name was William. I loved him more than anything in the world but he lost his life in France in the last year of the war. There has been no one special since.'

A strange sensation passed over her, as she suddenly pictured David Jackson in a field full of buttercups.

'Are you all right, Etty?' Patrick leaned over the table to stir her from her thoughts. 'You were far away for a moment, what were you thinking?'

'I don't know something and nothing really,' Etty said returning his gaze. She skilfully changed the subject. 'What did you do in the war, Patrick?'

'If you mean did I fight, then the answer is no. I was living and working in America. I went in 1911 and I came home in January this year. I was employed by American Vogue magazine. I did most of their fashion photography.'

'All those gorgeous women, and you were never caught,' she teased. 'Why was that?'

'I suppose I'm not really the marrying kind.'

'Where are your parents?'

A fleeting look of sadness passed over his face as he thought for a moment.

'I'm sorry; I didn't mean to pry,' she said quickly.

'No, really, that's fine. I fell out with my parents a long time ago. My father refuses to speak to me, and Mother's not strong enough to stand up to him. He's just a bully, Etty.' He paused for a moment as if trying to shake off the past. 'Now if you have you finished your tea; we'd better be on our way. Etty got to her feet excusing herself, telling Patrick she was going to powder her nose. As she washed her hands in the basin in the cloakroom, she gazed at her reflection in the mirror above it and whispered to herself, 'You are the marrying kind, Patrick Lawrence: you just haven't met the right girl yet.'

Patrick was already in the car when Etty re-appeared; she walked quickly towards it not wanting to keep him waiting. As soon as she was settled in her seat, Patrick cranked his engine and they went on their way.

Epson Hall was an old country seat which had been in the Hampshire family for generations. Patrick drew the car in through the huge iron gates and scrunched the tyres down the long gravel drive which was lined with magnificent topiary. Etty breathed deeply when she got out of the car, her eyes scanning the impressive building before her. They walked up to the front door which was opened by the butler before they had even pulled the bell handle.

'I saw you coming, sir, please do follow me, I will take you to her Ladyship.' The magnificence of the house overwhelmed Etty, as she followed the butler and Patrick through its myriad corridors. The lights, the cornices, the thick carpets and the paintings of previous Hampshire's were a revelation to the girl bought up in a blacksmith's cottage in Lancashire.

The Duchess was sitting on a brocade sofa by the window. She was pleasantly plump with several chins and a highly rouged face, and dressed in a long gown of green velvet that had probably been fashionable when Victoria was on the throne. The Honourable Virginia was seated next to her failing in her attempt to look elegant in her riding skirt and jacket.

'You're quite lovely, dear' – Lady Hampshire took Etty's hand – 'and how very clever of you to wear a scarf around your head instead of a hat. I simply must try it one day; I expect one would be so carefree. Now I would like you to meet my daughter, Virginia.'

Etty held out her gloved hand which Virginia pumped up and down in greeting.

'Ha, so you've come to try and make me look presentable, well good luck old thing, Squiffy Lewis, says it would take a miracle' – she guffawed showing a large set of upper teeth – 'isn't he just priceless.'

Wondering who Squiffy Lewis was and not liking the sound of him, Etty gently suggested they take a look at Virginia's wardrobe.

'Oh, absolutely old thing, come with me.'

Up in Virginia's bedroom, Etty browsed through her wardrobe. She selected a white afternoon tea dress with a cream sash and a lace over skirt, with white stockings and shoes completing the look. She took down Virginia's severe hairstyle and arranged small finger waves to softly frame her face, while the length of her hair was pulled to one side to cascade over her shoulder. Instead of Virginia wearing a pearl necklace around her neck, Etty slipped it around her forehead.

'Oh golly, I actually look quite decent for once; I wish Squiffy could see me now!'

Etty was beginning to realise that Squiffy was rather important to Virginia. 'He will see your photograph though,' she soothed, 'come on let's go and show your mother.'

Later when the photographs were complete, Etty went back upstairs with the Honourable Virginia and Patrick shared a sherry with the Duchess.

'Henrietta is quite delightful, Mr Lawrence. Tell me what fashion house does she work for? I shall remember to visit them, and ask for her services again.'

'Henrietta is not currently employed as a *vendeuse* Duchess but she is an extremely accomplished dressmaker and amateur designer. She has only recently moved to London from Lancashire, and is hoping to gain employment here. I have taken her brother on as my assistant. He's a very talented young man, and will go far under the right guidance from me.'

'You always have been generous to a fault, Patrick, you are such a darling man, but as for Henrietta's talents well that's nonsense, she is wasted as a dressmaker, I shall recommend her to the House of Harding, their previous *deuxieme vendeuse* left them to be married. I shall telephone you when I have secured Henrietta an appointment.'

'That would be much appreciated Duchess. Henrietta will be indebted to you.'

On the drive home, Patrick relayed his conversation with the Duchess to Etty. 'So it looks as if you might have an opportunity, if the Duchess is as good as her word.'

'I'm very grateful to the Duchess, Patrick, but I'm not sure…I mean, I don't even know what a vend… Whatever you said is, what do they do?'

'A *vendeuse* is employed to help clients choose the right wardrobe. They introduce high class ladies to a particular fashion house. You'd work under the premier *vendeuse*; it's a very important job, Etty, and with the Duchess of Hampshire on your side, you'd be an asset to the company.'

'I've seen designs from the House of Harding in Vogue,' she said, wondering how she could tell Patrick she didn't want the job without hurting his feelings… 'They make some beautiful clothes…'

'And?' enquired Patrick.

'And I want to design clothes myself, not encourage folk to buy other peoples work. I want the titled ladies of London to be wearing original designs by Henrietta.'

Patrick smiled as he looked at her momentarily then back at the road. 'Etty, you are a wonderful girl, and I really rather like you.'

Etty was thrilled, he really did seem to care for her, all she need do now was bade her time. No harm in telling him a little of what she was feeling, she thought. 'I like you too, Patrick, very much, very much indeed. She lowered her eyes and placed a hand briefly on his thigh.'

There was only one downside to Molly's newfound success, as she told Eliza Jane while helping her peel carrots at the kitchen table.

'What's that, Moll, I thought you loved your job?'

'I do, but I wish I could see Kit again. You know he was the vicar on the train, I really thought we had a connection but I can't even get in touch to see if he feels the same way.' She had searched everywhere for the address that Kit had given them but without success. She berated Thomas regularly: after all, he was the one to lose the paper. He had mentioned he lived in Lewisham, which Molly had discovered was only a short bus ride away, but how could she wander around all the churches in Lewisham looking for him – Ma would have been horrified at such impropriety.

'I suppose I will just have to try and forget him, there is no other way.'

'It might be for the best, dear,' Eliza Jane said, thinking of David and not really prepared to heed her own advice.

The back door suddenly opened with a crash. Etty rushed through the kitchen with her hand over her mouth. Patrick hurried in after her. 'Etty may need some help, she's just been violently sick.'

Chapter 17

It was now late August and the family had been in London for eight weeks. Molly and Rory were quite settled in their work and enjoying their new roles. Etty finally had an appointment at the House of Harding that day; the Duchess of Hampshire had been as good as her word although Etty had begun to despair of it happening. She had been sick several times since the fateful day in Patrick's car and was beginning to worry about herself. Thomas was not having any luck with finding employment he would go out early every morning to join a job queue of ex-servicemen and coming home dispirited and tired without success. Luckily, Patrick had not mentioned them leaving the house after their trial month, nor had anyone brought up the subject.

Patrick was particularly pleased with Rory's progress. He was a fast learner and used his artist's eye to create exciting and different photographs.

'How is Etty this morning,' asked Patrick, placing his newspaper down and sitting at the breakfast table, in between Rory and Molly. 'Any more sickness lately, she has her appointment at the House of Harding today?'

Eliza Jane placed a plate of scrambled egg before him, and was about to answer his question, when Etty strode into the kitchen. 'I'm absolutely fine, thanks Patrick.' She sat down at the table opposite him but refused anything more than a cup of tea. 'I've my appointment at the House of Harding today, could you possibly drive me there, Patrick?'

'Of course,' he agreed.

'You look so elegant, Etty – is that dress one of your own designs?' asked Molly.

'It is,' said Etty, thrilled to be able to show off her dress, she stood up to perform a pirouette but immediately felt dizzy. She held on to the edge of the table to sit down. 'Trouble is,' she laughed, 'I think you're feeding us a little too well, Lizzie, it feels slightly tight.'

'What feels tight?' said Thomas, joining them in the kitchen and throwing his cap on the table. He looked weary and in need of a cup of tea, as he shuffled to the table and pulled out his usual chair. Eliza Jane made him some tea, silently removing his cap from the table.

'Did you get the job, Thomas?' asked Rory.

'No, it was the usual story,' said Thomas morosely, slumping into the chair at the table. There were forty-five applicants waiting when I got there; all with more experience than me. I didn't want to work in a factory, anyway.'

'Don't give up,' said Patrick, 'don't despair something will happen.'

'God, you sound like Molly, Patrick,' Thomas snarled. Molly started to object loudly to the insult but was soon shouted down. Thomas continued, 'Listen, nothing is going to turn up, do you hear me, nothing. Rory's got work, Molly's enjoying Cobbs, Etty's got prospects and even Eliza Jane has a job, but not me, oh no, useless Thomas, no one wants me.' Spilling his tea as he roughly lifted the cup to his mouth made him swear.

'Calm down and have a cigarette old man,' said Patrick soothingly, handing Thomas his cigarette case.

'Don't call me that' – Thomas waved off the cigarette case – 'I'm not your *old man,* stop patronising me for God's sake. Everyone seems to have forgotten that I'm the head of this family.'

'Pull yourself together, Thomas,' Etty snapped, 'if you stopped feeling sorry for yourself, you might well get a job, but standing in job queues with your defeatist attitude, I'm not surprised no one is willing to take you on.'

'Etty, can't you see how upset Thomas is,' said Eliza Jane, standing at the table. 'He's the rock we all depend on, and he doesn't need to feel the edge of your sharp tongue.'

'Really, Lizzie, is that so?' said Etty, rather more sharply than she had intended. She was feeling dizzy and unfocused. 'I rather think Patrick is the rock we all depend on, don't you?' Wondering how she was going to get from the table to the door, she stood up and walked carefully out of the room. The others watched her go.

'She still doesn't look well,' observed Molly, leaving the table to put on her hat and coat that was hanging on a hook in the kitchen. I have to go or I'll be late, I will see you all tonight.' Molly left by the back door.

'I'll just go and see if Etty is all right,' said Eliza Jane, as she left the room to find her sister.

There was a short silence before Patrick said, 'Don't listen to Etty, Thomas. 'You are the head of your family, and they need you.'

Feeling placated by Patrick's kind words, Thomas calmed down. 'But she's right, Patrick,' he said, softening his tone. 'She is so right. I have so much going on in my mind, I can't even think straight. You don't know the half of what I've been through: I feel like I'm walking on paths of stones. I was continually bullied throughout the war for not being able to fight. Do you know what that's like, Patrick? No, I don't suppose you do. You were born with a silver spoon stuck in your mouth, so you've no idea what it's like to be Thomas Watkins. Well, let me tell you, I'm weak, oh I pretend to be strong but I know things I wish I didn't, there are terrible things tearing and burning my heart. Who would be me, Patrick, eh? Then there's you turning my sisters' heads with your wealth and grandeur. How do you think we can afford to ever pay you back? I was against us coming here in the first place, and now I know I was right to be concerned.'

'What terrible things are you talking about, Thomas?' asked Rory.

'I can't tell you, so don't ask.'

'But I'm your brother; tell me what's bothering you. Perhaps I can help.'

Thomas turned on Rory. 'You're not…' He began but then checked himself. 'You're not old enough to bear the responsibility, so just forget it.'

Thomas looked at Patrick then at Rory. 'I'm going to my room, just leave me in peace.'

He left the room, banging the door behind him. Taking a deep breath, he tried to calm himself. He climbed the stairs, needing the sanctuary of his room. It was large and not over furnished, which allowed him to breathe more easily. He shared with Rory as they had done at home. He sat heavily on his bed then punched his pillow savagely, throwing it across the room. Thoughts of his small room at home in Crossdale invaded his mind; he remembered the smell of newly baked bread drifting up from the scullery, and the lavender polish that Ma used. He breathed deeply trying to calm his heart that was banging in his chest. The technique did little to help, as suddenly he began to feel very anxious again. He was concerned that he had gone too far with his outburst downstairs. After all, Patrick had been so generous to them, and now through stupidity and frustration he had risked their security. He would have to apologise, or his siblings would never forgive him. He was temporarily distracted on hearing Eliza Jane and Etty arguing down the corridor and it upset him, what was happening to this family?

After resolving to make amends, he sighed deeply and made his way downstairs to apologise to Patrick. When he reached the kitchen, he saw the door was slightly ajar. He peeped in through the gap. Patrick was seated next to his brother at the table and was reaching out for Rory's hand while very gently using his other hand to stroke Rory's cheek.

Thomas turned away disgusted. He went back up the stairs and into his room as fast and quietly as he could and gently closed the door on his thoughts.

At dinner later that evening, Etty was excited. She prattled on about her interview at the House of Harding and how she had managed to convince them to employ her as a designer. 'After seeing some of my sketches,' she said, her eyes bright and animated, 'Mr Harding has offered to take me on as a trainee designer. I never thought I'd manage it. I start tomorrow, I have so many ideas, I can't wait. This is a dream come true for me, and it's all down to you, Patrick.' She lightly touched his arm, across the table. 'I want to thank you.'

'They wouldn't have offered you the job,' he said, 'if they didn't believe in you. You did it all on your own.'

'Ma and Da would be very proud of you, Etty,' said Thomas contritely. He was genuinely sorry for his earlier outburst, and was trying to make amends. He was also trying to forget what he had unwittingly seen pass between Patrick and Rory; it was playing on his mind. He thought he might have imagined it, and thus didn't feel he could broach the subject with Rory. He thought he noticed, however, a distance between the two men that normally wasn't there. He had always thought that Patrick was different but had not been able to put his finger on the precise nature of that difference. Perhaps, it was because he was wealthy and artistic, that Thomas found him slightly intimidating. He couldn't be one of those men who…no Thomas was unwilling to even think about homosexuality and cast the idea away. No matter what he thought of Patrick personally, he had to acknowledge they all owed him a great deal.

Chapter 18

'Rory please put that table down and listen to me,' Patrick demanded, 'I was merely trying to help yesterday, show you that you had a friend, I know Thomas had upset you.'

Rory was setting up the studio to make the most of the available light conditions for the photographic sittings that day. The day was bright and sunny outside but casting shadows in the studio. He stopped momentarily and turned to Patrick. 'It was just a bit of a shock that's all. I come from a background where we don't display affection and certainly not between the men of the family, we just don't do it. Perhaps things are different in London, I don't know but not where I come from.'

'I understand, but I could see Thomas had upset you and I thought you needed some support.'

'Let's just forget about it, it really doesn't matter and I do thank you for your support, I don't know why Thomas has turned into such a grouch lately.' Rory shrugged his shoulders as if to ward off the memory of Patrick's hand on his cheek.

Patrick, still keen to make amends, replied, 'You know, I was just thinking the other day of what you have all done for me. I was lonely, rattling round in this house with no one to look after me. Now I've put on half a stone with Eliza Jane's cooking, and you're turning into a very good photographer that could benefit the business, Etty is loads of fun, and Molly is a perfect sweetheart.'

'You forgot to mention Thomas.'

'I make no apology for that. He and I don't seem able to see eye to eye. Nevertheless, in spite of that, I worry about him; he seems to have aged beyond his years. He's much younger than me, but he acts as if he has the weight of the world on his shoulders.'

'It would help if he could find a job,' said Rory, stepping back to view an arrangement of flowers that stood on the table beside the portrait chair.

'Leave that with me, Rory, I have an idea.'

'He won't take charity, Patrick.'

'This isn't charity; if he lands a job, it will be on his own merits, I'll merely point him in the right direction,' Patrick replied mysteriously.

Etty was feeling dizzy again. She was in the middle of a new and exciting design at work, when she had to put her pencil down and close her eyes for a moment. The room was full of desks where three other trainee designers sat beside her. She felt claustrophobic and wished the supervisor would allow an open window. Whatever was the matter with her lately, she was beginning to worry about herself. The feeling eventually passed, and she resumed work, but her supervisor had noticed and came to her desk. 'Henrietta, are you feeling well – you're looking very pale, is everything all right?'

'Perfectly well, thank you, Miss Bell.'

The supervisor looked at the evening dress on Etty's sketch pad. 'This is beautiful work,' she said, pointing at the design. 'I particularly like the long lines of the dress, but I'm not sure the waist is right. A waist at hip level is very bold, and I don't think Mr Harding will approve. I suggest you bring the waist back up to where nature intended it to be.' Violet Cummings, a designer who sat opposite Etty smirked. It was satisfying to see this smug newcomer being reprimanded, it meant that she, Violet, was still Miss Bell's favourite and that is where she intended to stay.

Etty gritted her teeth. 'Yes, Miss Bell.' She continued sketching. *What did old ding-dong know?* she thought, her designs were positively Edwardian. They were on the brink of nineteen-twenty, a new decade, and it was time for change. Now if she could only get Charles Harding to view her design, he might think differently to Miss Bell. Without warning, bile rose again to her throat, and she dashed to the bathroom.

Etty was sent home from work later that morning. Patrick took one look at her wan face and made arrangements for her to consult his Harley Street physician that afternoon.

Eliza Jane was in the butcher's shop in Wells Street again that morning. She was getting to know the cheery man who served her, and rather looked forward to her visits.

'Well, it's only me favourite girl. What does yer 'usband want for 'is dinner tonight then?' He greeted her

Eliza Jane laughed. '6 pork chops please.'

'Blimey, married to a giant are yer, girl. 'ow can any man eat six chops.'

'I'm not married,' she said, feeling the heat seep into her face. 'I'm housekeeper to Patrick Lawrence – the photographer up on Sydenham Hill. My brothers and sisters live there too.'

'Not married, eh, a lovely girl like you! Well, well, well, that's a turn up.' He wiped his hands on a clean cloth, and his arm shot out over the counter. 'James Harrison,' he said, 'but you can call me Jim.'

'Eliza Jane Watkins, but you can call me Eliza Jane,' she replied smartly, ignoring the still grubby hand that was given to her. Jim gazed down at his hand, quickly apologising for its bloodstained state. 'Sorry,' he said sheepishly, 'I agree never touch a butcher's hand you don't know where it's been.'

They stood for a brief moment in silence, grinning at each another.

'Watch yerself; with my brother, he's all charm that one,' warned the other butcher in the shop. He was laughing.

Eliza Jane giggled to herself, as she left the shop to the accompaniment of Jim singing loudly and slightly off key. 'She's a lassie from Lancashire, just a lassie from…' His voice trailed away.

It was a long toil back up the hill, so Eliza Jane decided to have a rest in the park. A band was playing on the bandstand, and the sun was high in the sky. She took a seat and listened to the music, enjoying the late summer warmth. Crossdale seemed a long way away. She thought about David Jackson. She had written to him, telling him all about their luck in meeting Patrick, and David had written a back, a letter full of local news, telling them about Jacob and Beatrice's wedding. For a brief moment, Eliza Jane thought that should have been her, had she accepted Jacob's proposal. Although it was likely her only chance, she was still glad she hadn't said yes. She was pleased to hear that Jack was doing well and had become a very diligent sheep dog. David had also enquired about them all individually. She had shown the letter to Etty, though she had displayed little interest. She did remark, however, that she hoped Beatrice Emmett's wedding dress had been a success on the big day.

Mr Laycock from the antique shop had asked David to pass on a message that he hoped Thomas would send him some more carvings, as they were selling well. A small cheque was enclosed with the letter. It had cheered Thomas up a bit, and he had set out to find some suitable wood to carve a new piece.

Eliza Jane raised her face to the sun's rays for a moment, enjoying the rare sensation of feeling content. Opening her eyes, she smiled at the young children who were enthusiastically throwing bread for the ducks in a nearby pond. She watched as two drakes fought over a small crust. They took to the air squawking at one another: the bread was dropped and another duck swooped in to scoop it up. *Serves them right,* thought Eliza Jane. She held her breath, watching carefully as two small boys sailed their wooden boats. Their nannies were chattering on a bench, and Eliza Jane worried that the boys might fall in, as they crouched over the pond.

Mother's passed by pushing prams, and Eliza Jane wondered would she ever have children? She thought of David again, and then felt hot at such thoughts of impropriety. It would never happen, she knew that, but she could dream, she told herself.

She sighed loudly, then aware of the heat and the pork chops in her basket, she got up to leave, but as she did so, she caught sight of Rory sitting on a seat a little distance away. What was he doing in the park? She raised her hand in greeting, shouting his name but he didn't respond. She watched as an elderly woman approached him, taking his arm and helping him to his feet. Eliza Jane gasped, suddenly realising that it wasn't Rory at all. This man was blind but he resembled Rory in every other way.

'Come a long, Ronald, I've got you,' the woman said, smiling at Eliza Jane as she walked past.

Eliza Jane watched as they walked out of the park gates, and climbed into a chauffeur driven car. She blew out her cheeks in amazement, stunned for a while; she had never seen anyone so like another before. Remembering she had to get the meat home, she got up and leaving the park, she began her toil up Sydenham hill. Puffing slightly from climbing, she arrived home and burst into the kitchen, anxious to tell Rory what she had seen. She made her way to the studio but found that he was busy and could not be interrupted. No one else was at home, so her story would have to wait.

If Etty hadn't felt so sick, she would have enjoyed the ride in Patrick's car to his physician. Patrick had told Etty he would come back for her later, but first he had some business to attend to at Claridges, so much to her annoyance she was left alone.

Feeling uncharacteristically nervous, and in awe of her grand surroundings, the waiting room was plush red velvet furniture with dark green drapes at the extensive windows, she listlessly flicked through some old copies of Vanity Fair.

After sitting for ten minutes, she was finally ushered into Mr Barbour's consulting rooms by a nurse who told her to sit and wait for the doctor. She gazed around the consulting room, taking in similar furnishings as in the waiting room. Mr Barbour's desk was enormous, and standing on it a picture of a smiling woman within a silver frame. Presumably, Mrs Barbour, mused Etty, who personally felt that the lady in question would benefit from wearing one of her own designs, instead of the drab affair she had on.

The photograph was obviously from Patrick's Studio, as it was unmistakeably his style and had his name written just above the edge of the frame. Suddenly, the door opened making her jump.

'Miss Watkins, I am so sorry to keep you waiting. Most unforgiveable of me, I was called away temporarily.'

Mr Barbour was tall, sombre and grey. He wore a monocle in one eye. Everything about him was grey, thought Etty; even the way he uttered her name with the emphasis on the miss, or was that her imagination. He turned to his nurse, as she entered after him, asking for a tray of tea to be brought in.

'No tea for me, thank you, doctor. Tea doesn't agree with me at the moment, perhaps a glass of water.'

Mr Barbour nodded the instruction at his nurse and she left the room.

'Now Miss Watkins, how may I help you, Mr Lawrence informs me you have been sick lately, perhaps you might discuss our symptoms.'

Etty was amused that he had used the term *our* – she doubted Mr Barbour had the same symptoms as she did.

Rory had finished his only sitting that afternoon and, and wandered into the kitchen in search of Eliza Jane. Seeing him arrive, she put the kettle on to make tea for them both.

'Where is everyone?' she asked.

'Thomas is out looking for a job, and Patrick has taken Etty to see his doctor,' Eliza Jane replied.

'Good, she needs to see someone,' agreed Rory.

Eliza Jane warmed the tea pot before adding the tea. She then poured boiling water on to the tea leaves, letting the tea pot stand. She opened up the tin of biscuits in the pantry and offered one to Rory before pouring his tea. 'Listen though, I've got to tell you or I'll burst – you'll never guess who I saw in the park on the way home.'

'You're right, I'll never guess,' Rory said, dipping his biscuit into his tea.

'Rory,' she said, watching him dunking his biscuit. 'Ma hated you doing that.'

'Didn't she just,' he said with a grin, remembering his mother chiding him. 'Bless her heart, she had such standards. Da was always teasing her about it. Anyway, who was it that you saw?'

Eliza Jane dipped her biscuit in her tea too, although she missed Ma and Da desperately, she suddenly felt quite carefree. 'You'll never believe it but I saw your absolute double; his name's Ronald and he's the image of you, in fact I thought it was you, except he was blind, poor man. He was driven away by a chauffeur in a large, posh car.'

'How strange, but don't they say everyone has a double somewhere. Did you speak to him?'

'No. A woman who looked too old to be his mother came to collect him. She led him to the waiting car.'

'Poor chap, fancy looking like me,' observed Rory wryly, reaching for another biscuit.

Thomas opened the kitchen door and came in wearily. He sat himself down beside Rory, flung his cap on to the table as usual and sighed.

'Any luck?' asked Eliza Jane hopefully, as she poured him a cup of tea.

'No, there are no jobs to be had. There are hundreds of ex-servicemen out there, and I think you'll find the prospective employers are all their old regiment top brass or such like, so I don't have a chance in hell. I don't know what I'm going to do. The money for my carvings is meagre, and what little of Da's money we have left is dwindling.'

'The secret is to think like Molly,' said Rory grinning, and now on his third biscuit. Perhaps something will turn up at least I hope it does, meanwhile you do have your carvings, you will just have to make more of them'

'I can't hurry the process, Rory; you know as well as I do that these things take time.'

Rory bit back a sharp retort. Thomas was right irritable these days, he had changed since Da's death, was it only because he couldn't find work, or was something else bothering him.

In the treatment room in Harley Street, Etty was in shock. She stared at the screen curtains surrounding the couch on which she was lying and it crossed her mind what a lovely dress they would make, anything to take her mind off the news she had just been given. The thought had crossed her mind once or twice; particularly as she hadn't had her regular monthlies, but to find out it was true was still a shock.

'Do you understand what I'm saying, Miss Watkins,' said Mr Barbour squinting through his monocle. 'I believe you're at least twelve weeks pregnant, the possible delivery date is April the first, next year.'

'April Fools Day,' muttered Etty wryly, as she rose from the couch behind the screen. The nurse left the room.

'I beg your pardon, Miss Watkins.'

'Just talking to myself, Mr Barbour,' she replied, as he left her to dress.

Etty finished dressing and returned to her chair in front of Mr Barbour's desk. She sat and looked at him, clasping her hands so tightly in her lap that her nails dug into the palm of her hands, but she hardly noticed the pain. 'Are you sure? I mean could there be a mistake. I worked with munitions through the war, and we were always told that having a baby might be more difficult for us.'

'I can hear a heartbeat, and with your other symptoms such as weight gain and morning sickness, there can be no doubt. Congratulations to you and to Mr Lawrence.'

'Oh, he's not the… I mean he's not aware that I'm having a child. He'll be delighted of course, when I tell him the news.' Etty wondered later why she had not disputed that Patrick was the father, but it had seemed so easy to go along with it, after all one day soon when they were married, he would be.

Mr Barbour nodded gravely. 'I am perfectly sure.'

Etty rose from her seat. 'Thank you, Mr Barbour,' she said with as much dignity as she could muster. She offered him her hand as she had seen titled ladies do to Patrick as they left the studio. 'I trust you'll respect my privacy.'

Mr Barbour left his chair and bowed over her hand before walking her to the door. 'Of course, Miss Watkins, that goes without saying. Perhaps, however, I might refer you to a well-respected and certified midwife to help you through your confinement.'

'No,' said Etty vehemently, 'that won't be necessary thank you. I'm sure Mr Lawrence, will see that I have all the help I need.'

'Of course, as you wish, Miss Watkins.' He closed the door behind her.

Patrick was sitting in the waiting room; he stood up as Etty came through. 'Just a bout of gastric flu,' she said light-heartedly, taking hold of his arm and glancing at the nurse with a meaningful look. 'Come along, darling,' she added, and with her head held high, Etty ventured out into Harley Street with the terrifying knowledge that another life was growing inside of her.

Chapter 19

'Watch your back,' hissed Jo. 'Goggle-eyed Gambon is on the prowl – he's coming this way.' Molly hastily tidied up the samples of hat trimmings that she had been showing to a customer. Quickly, she shoved them into a drawer behind her and pressed it closed with her hip before facing Mr Gambon. He stopped by her counter on his way through the shop.

'Ah, Miss Watkins, I believe you've been with us a month now, how are you finding your place of employment: are you happy?'

'Very happy,' said Molly demurely, 'thank you for asking, Mr Gambon.'

'Mrs Roberts speaks very highly of you, so well done.'

'Thank you, Mr Gambon.'

'I have requested that Mrs Roberts spares you from your duties on the shop floor tomorrow to help me in the stock room. I think we have had an over order arrived; it will need sorting. She has agreed to my proposal.'

'Yes sir, of course.' Molly's heart sank, a whole morning in the stock room with goggle eyed Gambon was not going to be easy.

'Until tomorrow, Miss Watkins.' Mr Gambon's good eye passed over Molly's body causing her to shiver involuntarily before he strutted away.

Molly breathed a sigh of relief. Jo immediately dashed over from her opposite counter to sympathise with her friend.

'What are you going to do?'

'You heard him then?'

'Of course, I did; you will have to be very careful, Molly; you know what he's like. The last girl that he took into the stockroom was sacked but no one knows why but we've all got a pretty good idea.'

'Don't worry, Jo, I'm sure I can handle him.'

Mrs Roberts, who had finished serving a customer, gave them one of her looks, and Jo returned to her counter.

The morning proved busy, and Molly and Jo were told to take a late lunch. They ate in the staff restaurant, chatting between mouthfuls of pie.

'Molly, you know you said that this job is just a stop-gap until you are discovered as a movie star?' Without waiting for an answer, Jo continued. 'So I'm thinking you must be very good at acting.'

'It's only my joke really, Jo. I know it could never happen in a thousand years. I do like acting though, and I've performed in pantomimes at home.'

'I think you should join us then?'

'Why, who are us?'

'The Lewisham Players, my brother is Chairman. Every year, we put on a pantomime, and auditions are tomorrow night: we're doing Cinderella this year.

Molly thought for a moment. 'I'm not sure that we'll still be living here by December. We might have to move on: we can't live with Patrick forever.'

'Think about it. If you want you can come home with me tomorrow night for your dinner, then we can go to the auditions. My brother will see you home afterwards.'

'Are you sure your parents won't mind – shouldn't you ask them?'

Jo's face clouded over, she thought for a second before she spoke.' My parents are dead, Molly: they both died in that flu epidemic last year. It's just my brother and me.

'Oh, Jo, I'm so sorry, I didn't know, but I do know what you've been through and I wouldn't wish it on anyone. Listen, I'd better let you know about tomorrow, when I've asked at home. But it sounds like great fun, thank you.'

'Thomas, are you there?' Patrick called up the stairs.

Thomas poked his head over the curved banister. 'Did you want me?'

'Yes, would you do me a favour? Would you go to Claridges to pick up a small package that someone has dropped off there for me? Take a taxicab, just let me know the cost and I'll reimburse you. I'd go myself but I have important clients all day.'

'Certainly Patrick,' said Thomas, thinking that taxis were an extravagance, 'but I'll take the bus.' Thomas went back to his room, put on a clean shirt and combed his hair. He caught the bus a little way down Sydenham hill on the other side of the road. His search for a job meant he was becoming very practised at getting around London on its transport system.

Thomas stood on the other side of the road and gazed at the expanse of Claridges hotel. The building stretched down one road and round the corner to another. It had a majestic entrance before which stood a gentleman in livery and a top hat. As cars were queuing up outside, the gentleman was in perpetual motion of opening doors for the hotel guests. Each guest received a smart salute, as they climbed out of their car, heading inside the imposing building. Their chauffeurs then drove away turning immediately right after the building. Thomas supposed it was to an exclusive parking area. He continued to watch for a while, thinking how busy the gentleman was. After a while, he crossed the road and headed for the entrance.

As soon as the doorman noticed him, he came towards Thomas. 'Can I help you, sir?' he asked politely.

'I have a package to collect for Mr Patrick Lawrence,' Thomas replied, feeling slightly in awe of the man with the gold braid standing before him.

'Certainly, sir; walk straight through the hotel foyer, turn to your right, and ask at the desk.' He saluted Thomas, as he passed through the door, before returning to his position.

Once inside, Thomas immediately removed his cap. Following instructions, he passed through the beautiful lobby with its gold edged pillars, glittering chandeliers, guilt edged mirrors and sumptuous carpet. Piano music was wafting out of another room mixed with a buzz of conversation as he passed by. A middle-aged gentleman in a smart suit suddenly appeared and approached him. 'May I help you, sir?'

'I was told to report to the desk, I believe there's a package for Mr Patrick Lawrence waiting for collection.'

'Ah, yes, I do know something about that; perhaps you would care to follow me.'

As they walked, the man engaged him in pleasant light conversation; Thomas thought he had an ease and charm about him.

As each member of staff passed him on the way, they respectively addressed him saying, 'Good morning, Mr Cartwright.'

When they reached the main desk, the man asked the clerk for the package. 'Yes of course, Mr Cartwright, I'll get it at once.' The clerk took a key out of the desk drawer and turned to open the door which lay behind the desk.

While they were waiting, the man turned to Thomas. 'He won't be long. Now what do you think of our hotel, have you visited us before?'

'It's just magnificent. To a blacksmith's son from Lancashire, it is something like I've never seen before, sir,' Thomas quickly added.

'Believe me, everyone is amazed when they see this building but there are still improvements to be made.

'I'm not sure how,' uttered Thomas, 'it takes my breath away.'

The man laughed. 'Tell me,' he said, relaxing his stance and leaning one elbow on the desk, 'how were you welcomed? I hope the head doorman greeted you politely as you came in?'

'He was very polite,' said Thomas, having no idea why this man was asking so many questions, but he felt at ease with him. His demeanour reminded Thomas of Patrick.

The man nodded. 'I expect he was busy on the door.'

'Extremely busy, sir, cars and customers were coming from everywhere. There is work out there for two.'

'How very observant of you.' The man became thoughtful for a moment before saying, 'Do you know, I was hoping to employ another man on the door, but so far, there hasn't been a suitable candidate.'

Thomas wondered if he had gone too far in suggesting there should be another doorman outside the building and was relieved when the man hadn't taken offence. The door at the back of the desk opened and the clerk came through with a small package in his hand. 'Here we are, sir.' He handed it to Thomas.

'Thank you' – Thomas turned to the other gentleman – 'it has been nice talking with you, sir.' As he turned away, Thomas suddenly remembered the man saying, *I was hoping to employ another man on the door.* Could he, dare he, he turned around, nothing ventured, he thought.

'Excuse me, sir, but would you consider me for the position, sir. I'm looking for employment, and I'm not having much luck. I'm honest and hard working.'

'Are you fit? There's a lot of standing.'

'Fit enough, sir.' Thomas was desperate and prepared to lie for a chance of employment, after all standing wasn't his problem.

'Then report to me the day after tomorrow sharp at seven in the morning, and we'll give you a trial. Come in any time before then to pick up your uniform.' The man looked over to the foyer. 'Now, you must excuse me, I have a few matters to attend to.'

On saying this, the man walked away. Thomas couldn't believe what had just happened; it was the easiest job interview he had ever had. Was the man in a position to offer him work, he decided to ask the clerk on the desk? 'Excuse me sir, who was that man who's just left?'

'Who, Mr Cartwright? Why he is our managing director.'

Thomas left the hotel with Patrick's parcel under his arm; he couldn't believe his luck in running into the hotel's managing director, what a day this was.

Patrick's telephone rang; he picked it up. 'Lawrence photographic studios,' he said.

'Patrick, Sam Cartwright here. Just to let you know your egg has hatched. He's taken the job.'

'Thanks, Sam, much appreciated, I can assure you he won't let you down.'

'I'll hold you responsible if he does Patrick, now about that drink…'

Thomas was full of his new job at dinner that evening. He described in detail how he had suggested to the Managing Director of Claridges that he needed two doormen outside the hotel. 'I thought I had gone too far, but do you know what, he interviewed me right there and then and offered me the job. I still can't believe it.' Eliza Jane, who was sitting next to him, hugged him fiercely. 'I'm so proud of you, Thomas, I knew you would do it. Anybody would be pleased to employ you.'

'Thanks, Lizzie, I've got a job, a real job.'

Etty looked at her brother across the table, she had picked at her food again, pushing the beef around her plate. She couldn't even look at the large dumpling that dominated the stew. 'I'm happy for you, Thomas, perhaps you'll feel more settled now,' she said.

The others all murmured their congratulations. Rory raised his eyebrows at Patrick, questioning his role in the job offer, Patrick merely smiled. 'Well done Thomas,' he said warmly.

Molly thought it was the right time to mention Jo's invitation to join the Lewisham Players. 'They are putting on a pantomime,' she said. 'I said I would ask if I could join because I thought we might have been moving on but as you now have a job, Thomas, I'm hopeful we're staying.'

Thomas looked at Patrick before replying. 'If Patrick will have us, then we will stay until after Christmas at least.'

'I would love you all to stay,' Patrick reassured them.

'Well, thank God we've got that sorted at last,' said Etty. 'I'm off to bed, all this excitement has done me in.' She scraped back her chair and left the room.

'Would it be all right if I went home with Jo tomorrow night then, she says her brother will bring me home.'

'Let me know if he can't, Molly, and I'll collect you in the car,' Patrick reassured her. If Thomas hadn't felt so carefree, he might have questioned the fact that his sister would be accompanied home by a stranger but he was a happy man tonight so he let it go.

After dinner, Patrick invited Thomas to share a nightcap with him to celebrate the new job. They settled themselves in the two large button back leather chairs on either side of the fireplace in the study. Patrick waved the whisky decanter at Thomas, as he poured a measure for himself.

'I'm not very good with spirits,' said Thomas sheepishly, 'I disgraced myself a couple of months ago after drinking whiskey. I had a lot on my mind and the spirits didn't help matters. I've never felt so ill in all my life.'

'Just a small one then,' replied Patrick, handing Thomas a thick tumbler with the amber liquid reflecting through the glass. 'I wanted to talk to you actually – I know we didn't exactly see eye to eye when we first met, I know you didn't like me very much but I really hope we can now start to become friends.'

Thomas swallowed some of his drink. The whisky burned his throat but left a warm contented feeling in his chest. 'It's not that I didn't like you, Patrick; it was just that I didn't really trust you. We didn't know you, you were a complete stranger, surely you understand.'

Patrick was about to speak when Thomas quickly added, 'I mean I couldn't understand why you should offer us so much help. I couldn't, and still can't understand why you would want to take five complete strangers into your home.'

'I needed a housekeeper, and if she came with four appendages, then so be it. I live a quiet life here, Thomas. I was lonely and you all seemed so close like the family I had never really had.' Patrick knew he would never be able to explain to Thomas the real reason he gave this family shelter and that reason was sitting laughing with his sisters in the dining room right now.

'We are close, very close as a family but somehow, since losing Ma and Da, we're growing apart.'

'Maybe that's my fault, Thomas.'

Thomas looked sharply at Patrick. The image of his hand on Rory's cheek flashed across his brain. What was this man all about? Rory had never mentioned it but he couldn't get that which he had inadvertently witnessed in the kitchen that day out of his head. He could never relax with this man, but he had to accept him for he and his family were living in this man's house

'No, not at all – you have done so much, given us so many opportunities.' Thomas struggled with his reply. 'Our lives are so different now to when we were living in Crossdale. There is something I have to say, Patrick; it concerns Etty. I know she cares for you, but I'm not sure you feel the same. I don't want her hurt, Patrick, do you understand? She went through so much with losing her fiancé in the war.'

Patrick smiled wryly, as he swirled his drink around the bottom of his glass. 'Thomas, I can assure you that I'm aware of my responsibilities towards Etty. Now how about another drink?'

Patrick refilled both glasses, then returned his chair, handing one to Thomas.

'Can I ask you something?' he said.

Thomas nodded; he was beginning to feel sleepy.

'You've never married? Why is that?'

I'd like to marry but my health's not good. I can't ask a girl to take me on with my weak heart, it wouldn't be fair.' He put the whisky glass to his lips and gulped on the contents. 'That's why I couldn't join up, because of my health. They wouldn't take me.'

'That must have been tough.'

The whiskey was relaxing Thomas, making him feel less on his guard. 'Tough isn't the word for all I've been through. I was spat at, abused in the street and beaten up on a couple of occasions. People thought I was a coward, a conscientious objector, but how could they know that I wasn't.'

'That's what's wrong with this country; no one has time for anyone any more, what has happened to love thy neighbour.' Patrick spoke with passion.

'War does that to people; I suppose in a way, I was relieved the army wouldn't take me. But believe me, I went through hell at home instead. I was prepared to go to war, and was one of the first in the village to volunteer at the recruitment centre. I needed to go and fight, be one of the boys – you know what I mean, stand up as a man. It was hard watching my old classmates marching proudly down to the station in their new ill-fitting uniforms. I watched them board a train that was to take many of them to their death. Then I had to deal with the all-consuming guilt of knowing that some of those lads died while I was languishing at home.'

123

'It was all so easy for me, living in the United States,' said Patrick, sitting forward in his chair, 'which makes me feel very guilty too.'

'The war has a lot to answer for,' Thomas said, draining his glass. He was feeling more equable than he had felt in months. 'I'll tell you this though, what I went through then is only a quarter of what I have suffered since.'

Patrick got up to replenish Thomas's glass. 'Tell me about your father, how did he die?'

Thomas looked down at his glass and swilled the whisky around before swallowing it in one go. He gazed at Patrick through a drunken haze. 'The doctor put kidney disease on his death certificate, but it was a lie. Doctor Green risked his career for us, so Da's crime would be covered up. He hung himself, my Da, my hero, the strongest and wisest man I have ever known, hung himself. I found the suicide note, no one knows but me.'

Thomas stared into his now empty glass, tears forming in his eyes. 'You know what hurts me the most? Do you know what holds my stomach in a vice-like grip, causing me agonising pain?'

'Tell me, Thomas.'

'I just can't forgive him for doing it.'

'Thomas, my dear chap, I'm so very sorry. I cannot imagine the hell you have been through. What a terrible, terrible thing to find out.'

Thomas laughed wryly. 'Oh but that's not all. At the same time, I discovered, another note and a birth certificate.' He looked up at Patrick, his eyes wet with emotion. 'Do I have your word that you won't divulge this to another soul, particularly not to Rory or the girls?' Patrick nodded.

'Rory is not our real brother.'

Patrick sat upright in his chair, gazing compassionately at the distraught man before him. Pondering on the revelations he had just heard, he rose from his chair and poured Thomas another drink.

Chapter 20

The following morning for the first time, Molly walked to work with reluctance. She was acutely aware she was to be closeted in the store room with old goggle-eyed Gambon for part of the day and was pondering how she would cope. It was now early October and a swirl of seasonal mist hung in the air adding to the dampness of Molly's spirit.

She met Jo outside the shop and they walked in together. Trying to concentrate on happier thoughts, Molly told her friend that she would love to have a meal with her and her brother and attend the audition for Cinderella. 'Thomas has just got a job, so it looks like we're staying put at least until after Christmas,' she explained.

Jo was thrilled, she clasped Molly's hand. 'That's wonderful news, Molly, my brother is really looking forward to meeting you, I'm always chattering on about you to him.'

'I'm sure he must hate me already then,' Molly replied, not in the least interested in meeting Jo's brother and momentarily thinking of Kit.

'Oh Molly, you are funny.'

'I won't be amusing after I've spent the day with goggle eyed Gambon, I can tell you that,' Molly warned.

'Perhaps, I could keep coming to the stock room with made up messages for you that should put a spoke in his wheel.'

'Don't worry, Jo, he surely won't dare try anything, after all it's his word against mine.'

'Yes, but Dolly Hunt was sacked because she spoke out and they believed him. Just be careful, Moll, that's all I'm asking.'

'Perhaps he'll forget with a bit of luck,' Molly replied.

Mr Gambon didn't forget however and was waiting at Molly's counter for her as she walked on to the floor.

'Ah, Miss Watkins, I've been waiting for you, today is your day to help me in the stock room, are you ready?'

'Yes, Mr Gambon, I'm sorry to have kept you waiting.' Molly's heart sank.

'No, not at all my dear, you are nice and early, you must be keen,' he leered, 'so let's get started, shall we?'

Molly reluctantly followed Mr Gambon to the stock room. As she walked behind him, several of the assistants on the shop floor gave her a knowing and sympathetic look.

Extracting a large key from his pocket, Mr Gambon opened the stock room door and stood aside as Molly entered first. It was a large airless room with boxes stacked high. In the corner was a step ladder to reach the top shelves.

He pointed at the highest shelf. 'Those are the boxes of gloves that seem to have been over ordered, we need to get the boxes down, open them up and count the contents against the invoice I have here.'

Molly realised that she was the one who was meant to climb the ladder and bring the boxes down. She turned to Mr Gambon who had shut the stockroom door. 'It's very warm in here, Mr Gambon, do you mind if we leave the door open?' She moved past him as she spoke, grabbing the handle and opening the door before he could object.

Molly became very business-like as she propped the step ladder up against the shelves. She hitched her skirt very slightly with one hand and gripped the ladder with the other. Mr Gambon held on to the ladder as Molly climbed up. She grabbed the first box, luckily, it was not very big, and handed it down to him. This was repeated twice before Molly suddenly felt something crawling up her leg, she tried to ignore it but the creeping sensation persisted, she threw her leg sharply to the side and shook it as if she was dislodging a spider. Nothing was said. As soon as she returned to reach for another box of gloves, the sensation returned. Mr Gambon was inching his fingers under her skirt and up her leg. Molly panicked; she wasn't sure what to do. If she kicked her employer away or complained loudly, she would have to face the consequences. Just as she was deciding that was what she would have to do, there was a knock on the open door. Mr Gambon snatched his hand away and quickly moved from the ladder.

'Sorry to interrupt, Mr Gambon, but Mr Cobb senior has called in un-expectantly, wishing to see you on an urgent matter.' Mr Gambon's secretary was a short, grey haired woman with glasses. She had given loyal service to the company for many years.

Mr Gambon coughed. 'Ah certainly, Miss Herbert, I will come now.' He turned to Molly who was still halfway up the ladder, 'that will be all Miss Watkins, thank you, you may return to the floor.'

Molly caught Miss Herbert's eye, as she descended the ladder and left the room. The secretary's face was expressionless.

The following evening after work, Molly took the short bus ride with Jo to her house in Lewisham.

Jo, after having the events of the stockroom described to her, was horrified. 'What a squalid, dirty, horrible man, just think of his poor wife and what a lucky escape you had, it was a good idea to keep the door open.' Jo sighed, she had been on the receiving end of Mr Gambon's unwelcome attention once or twice but nothing as horrifying as her friend had experienced.

'Do you think his secretary saw anything?' she asked

I'm sure she did but then…' She gazed out of the window catching sight of the Lewisham boundary stone – wasn't this where Kit said he lived? She prayed she might see him walk by?

'But then, what,' asked Jo.

'But then she can't say anything, she'd lose her job too.'

Both sat in silence for a moment each wondering what could be done.

'This is our stop, Moll, come on.' They sprung up from their seats, stumbling with the motion of the bus to the exit. Hanging on tight as the bus lurched to a halt, they got off.

Jo led Molly up the path of a large house next to a church.

'Is this where you live?' Molly asked incredulously.

'Yes, my brother's the vicar here, we live in the vicarage.'

Molly stopped walking. 'Jo what's your brother's name?'

'Christopher, Kit for short, look there he is now.'

Molly looked up and saw a tall blonde man on the doorstep. It was him, her Kit, the man on the train. 'But your name is Josephine,' she said bewildered that Kit had called her Grace.

'Grace is actually my name but my middle name is Josephine and I like it better so that's what I call myself. My family always use my proper name though. Why do you say that?'

'Because,' said Molly, 'I met your brother on the train coming down to London. He shared our carriage, and he said he had a sister named Grace.'

'So, you've already met, I can't believe it.'

Kit came forward to meet them. 'Hello again, Molly, it is so nice to see you. How's the family? I hoped Grace's new friend from Lancashire might be you.'

Rarely had Molly enjoyed an evening more. She and Kit fell into an easy friendship and once again, Molly felt she had known him forever. She auditioned for the same parts as Jo, which were, Cinderella, Dandini, the Prince and the Good Fairy. She laughed until tears ran down her cheeks when Kit read as one of the ugly sisters in a high falsetto voice. She was impressed with a young man reading Buttons. He had been introduced as John Draper; he was small with a baby like face that belied his true age and had a rubber like quality about it. His expressions were loaded with pathos, his acting excellent. Molly had warmed to him immediately.

At the end of the evening, the director cast, Jo with her long legs as the Prince; Kit as Vixen, one of the ugly sisters; Molly as Cinderella and John as Buttons.

Molly was concerned that on being given the lead role, she might upset someone – after all, she had only just joined them – but the congratulations she received from the rest of the cast soon dispelled her fears.

At the end of the evening, Kit walked Molly to the bus stop. Although Molly protested that she didn't need accompanying back to Sydenham, Kit insisted, just as Jo said he would. It was beginning to get cold in the evenings now but the lower temperatures meant a starry sky and the moon lay on his side as if to say, let the stars light the sky tonight, I'm having a night off. Standing at the bus stop, Molly drew her coat around her more tightly.

'I just can't believe it's you, Molly. I wondered if I'd ever see you again, never mind finding out that you work next to my sister at Cobbs. How did you find your way to Sydenham? Tell me what happened after I left you at Euston, I want to know everything.'

The bus drew up before Molly had the chance to answer but once on the bus and settled side by side, she regaled him with the story of how they met Patrick, explaining how he had taken them in and they had now all found work.

'Phew,' Kit whistled through his teeth. 'All part of God's vast plan – amazing isn't it – how the Lord provides. Are you happy living here, Molly? It must be so different to your small village back home.'

'I've never been happier, and especially now I'm going to do what I love most.'

'What, you mean acting?'

'No,' she giggled, 'making a fool of myself.'

Thomas and Patrick were still up when she arrived home. Kit declined the offer of a cup of tea, saying he should get back before the last bus.

Molly let herself into the house through the back door, and was surprised to see them chatting over toast in the kitchen; were they finally reaching an understanding?

'Did you get a part, Molly?' Thomas asked, he seemed surprisingly merry in Patrick's company.

'I certainly did, they want me to play Cinderella. Oh, and by the way, you'll never guess who Jo's brother is.'

Thomas shook his head, while Patrick looked bemused.

'Kit! Do you remember the Vicar we met on the train coming down here?'

Realisation suddenly dawned on Thomas. 'I don't believe it, Molly that's amazing. How is he?'

'Just perfect,' sighed Molly dreamily.

Chapter 21

Two weeks had passed since Etty received the news of her pregnancy. She was beginning to feel less sick, and so far, although she examined herself every day in the mirror for a bump, there was little to see. While externally, she appeared to be the same old spirited Etty, on the inside she was troubled and worried. Part of her thought she should return to Crossdale to tell David Jackson he was to become a father; she knew he would offer to marry her and her problem would be solved. Another part of her, however, recoiled at the thought of the claustrophobic life of being a grocer's wife in a small village. She knew it was not what she wanted, and she wasn't in love with him. She contemplated seducing Patrick, and passing the baby off as his – after all, Mr Barbour had assumed that he was the father. Disgusted at her deviousness, she briefly wondered what sort of girl she had become and then she answered her own question: a desperate one.

Etty knew no one suspected her pregnancy for a minute. She contemplated telling the family, but the thought of the ensuing recriminations from Thomas and the pathetic sorrow of Eliza Jane, ensured telling them was out of the question.

Since learning of her pregnancy, she had tried to end it by using some the methods she had heard from the girls in the munition's factory. She had sat in several hot baths, drinking gin taken from Patrick's decanter, but this made her feel even sicker. The factory girls had also talked about throwing themselves down the stairs. On several occasions, she stood at the top looking down, contemplating how to fall with as little damage to herself as possible, but lost her nerve. Tiredness was overtaking her; everyday, it was a struggle to go to work. She pleaded with God to take the pregnancy away, but it was very apparent that God was not prepared to oblige.

Eliza Jane was sitting at the kitchen table reading a letter from David, a letter she had already read it many times that day, since it had arrived with the morning post.

'It's a Lancashire post mark?' Patrick had smiled, as he gave her the letter.

Eliza Jane nodded, and looking at the envelope said proudly, 'It's from my friend, David.'

Patrick looked at Eliza Jane's animated face and felt slight envy as he remembered the feeling of how a letter from a special person could make you feel deliriously happy in an instant. 'Go and enjoy reading what your friend has to say, Lizzie,' he said with a slight note of regret in his voice.

Later that morning in the peace and quiet of the kitchen, Eliza Jane sat at the kitchen table with a pot of tea before her. She gazed with satisfaction around the clean room, and caught sight of the gas stove. She smiled when she thought of her first morning here, and the terrors that the stove held for her. It was now her best friend, so much easier than the big old black range at home. She knew her meals were good because they were all complaining about putting on weight; none more so than Etty, who seemed to be growing rounder every day. She thought about them all and marvelled at how far they had come in the three months they had been here. They had all seemed achieved a level of contentment, except for Etty; she seemed distant, as if weighed down by some unacknowledged trouble.

Eliza Jane sipped her tea; she could feel the rustle of David's letter in her apron pocket, refusing to be parted from it she kept it there to read again and again. Would she ever see him again, she doubted it. She delved in her pocket for the letter and opened it up, reading the last few lines again.

We still miss you and your family, but we are pleased that you have all found work in London.

Patrick sounds very nice. How do you all get on with him?

Jacob sends you his best wishes, he and Beatrice seem happy. Oh, and by the way, he says to tell you that Jack is proving to be a marvellous sheep dog and has settled well.

I will close now and look forward to your next letter.

Your friend

David.

Eliza Jane re-read *'look forward to your next letter'* several times before folding and returning the letter to her pocket. *Time to get down to the shops,* she thought. The thought gave her a little jolt of excitement and she wondered why. Moving quickly, she rinsed out her cup then snatched her hat and coat from the hook by the back door. She gathered her shopping basket and shutting the door firmly behind her, she set off.

Rory was trying very hard to be professional with his latest client. Lady Helen Giles was just perfect; she was so perfect that Rory was having difficulty concentrating on the job of photographing her. Her hair was the fairest he had ever seen. She had skin like translucent porcelain, and her eyes were the colour of Wedgwood china. Rory was smitten; he had never seen such a beautiful girl. She was sitting elegantly on the chaise longue, one slim ankle tucked discretely behind the other while appearing to examine a sheaf of lilies resting in the crook of her arm.

Her mother was watching while chatting with Patrick from another corner of the large studio, leaving Rory tongue-tied and unable to converse with this vision before him. 'Look to the right for me, Lady Helen,' he said. 'That's right, now hold that pose. Now look at the flowers but raise your eyes to the camera, now turn to the left and look straight at the camera. That's it, perfect.'

Standing up straight and moving back from the tripod, Rory said, 'I think we're done for the day.'

Lady Helen sprung out of her chair, gathering her coat and hat together. 'Thank heaven that's done,' she said.

'Most of our customers like having their photograph taken,' said Rory, slightly wounded.

'Oh, I'm sorry, was I being mean? I just find it all such a waste of time; there are so many more important issues in life then silly old photographs. I'm afraid publishing my birthday portrait in the Tatler to attract a suitable husband is very low on my priority list.' She looked towards her mother as she said this but Lady Giles although a matronly fifty-one years of age was flirting outrageously with Patrick.

'You don't want to get married then,' Rory said, finally finding his courage.

'Good gracious no, do you?'

'Eventually, yes, I do, but not for some time yet. My parents were very happy together until Ma died, then Da didn't cope very well without her.'

Helen gazed at Rory for a moment then leant forward and whispered, 'I don't ever want to end up married as miserably as my parents, I'd rather live alone.'

Confronted with her open honesty, Rory was growing in confidence. 'If you don't want to get married,' he said, 'what do you want?'

'I want women to be free, and no longer the property of men. There is so much I would like to do but being a woman precludes me from achieving it.' Helen suddenly caught sight of Rory smiling. 'You find this amusing, don't you? How typical of your sex you are – men don't think women have anything in their heads but fluff and cotton wool. When will you realise that women have brains? My father refused to let me go to Oxford University or drive a car. How can women fight such prejudices? Women held this country together during the war, and a great job we made of it too. We ran the railways without the slightest trouble, but now that the men have returned to their jobs, they're paralysing the trains with their strikes. There's unrest in this country, Mr Watkins, we're heading for problems.'

'Believe me, Lady Helen; I was only smiling because you remind me of my sister, Molly. She thinks much as you do – although I do believe that a certain gentleman has taken her mind off the plight of women and on to other matters just lately.'

'My point exactly, she's allowing a man to come between her and her ideals.'

'I don't think she is too upset about it.'

'Perhaps not, but I don't intend to let that happen to me. Come, Mummy,' she said sweeping out of the room, her mother thanked Patrick and followed her.

Her sudden absence left Rory with a lingering sense of loss.

Lady Helen sat next to her mother in their chauffeur driven car, as they drove home to Wescott Manor in Kensington. She giggled inwardly to herself. Why had she said all that rubbish about wanting to go to Oxford and women's rights, it was patently untrue, she cared nothing for such things except trying to get her father to agree to her having her own automobile then she truly would be free. She was glad she had thought of moving slightly while the photographs had been taken because then she would have to return to the studio to have them re-taken and that would be perfect. She had plans for the young photographer, oh yes; he would do very nicely to help her get what she wanted.

Lady Giles smiled at her daughter. 'I think the photographs will be wonderful, don't you, darling?'

'Absolutely mummy, just wonderful,' she replied.

As Eliza Jane stepped in through the open door of the butchers; she was aware that her heart was thumping loudly. She caught sight of Jim and smiled at him. He wasn't a handsome man but he was tall and broad shouldered with a ruddy face and merry eyes. Jim greeted her enthusiastically. 'If it isn't my favourite girl,' he said. 'What can I do for you today?'

With pleasantries exchanged, and the best steak and kidney purchased, Eliza Jane left the shop. She stopped a moment outside to consult her shopping list and heard her name being called. She turned around and saw Jim coming out of the shop and heading towards her. 'You forgot your change, love,' he said.

'You gave it to me Jim, I'm sure you did.'

'Did I?' he said airily. 'Well maybe there was something else I had to say.'

Eliza Jane waited, her heart beating a little faster, she was unable to read his expression.

'The thing is Eliza Jane…well the thing is, I wouldn't half like to take you to a variety show one evening how about it, would you like to go with me?'

Eliza Jane felt hot and bothered and slightly anxious, she had never ever been asked to walk out with a man before, and had absolutely no idea how to behave. 'I'm n-not sure, J-Jim,' she knew she was stammering but couldn't stop herself. 'I mean; we hardly k-know each other.'

'And we're never going to either if we don't give it a go. Come on, what night can you get off?'

'I can have any night off as long as I leave cold supper for the family,' she replied feeling slightly more courageous.

'I'll pick you up on Saturday then. I'll come to the house for you at half past six – I best get back now or the others will be wondering where I am. See you on Saturday, ta ta.'

Jim returned to the shop leaving Eliza Jane excited but nervous by the turn of events. She couldn't quite believe what had happened – had she really been asked out to the theatre. A shiver ran a circuit of her body and she drew her scarf snugly around her.

With an autumnal feel to the air, Eliza Jane decided to walk back through the park. A carpet of multi-coloured leaves had fallen onto the pathway. Suddenly, she felt like a child again, ridiculously happy and carefree. She had actually been asked out by a man and a lovely man too. She couldn't contain her excitement. Looking around and seeing she was alone, she delved into a pile of leaves, scooping them up and throwing them in the air. Then she lifted her skirt and rustled through them, shuffling her feet back and forwards. What was it about dancing through leaves that was so glorious – she didn't know and she didn't care. Looking up, she noticed someone approaching, thus propriety took over, and she strolled on with a deeply contented smile.

As she turned the corner, she caught sight of Ronald, the young blind man, sitting on the seat where she had previously seen him. She sat opposite him for a while to observe him. Suddenly, his stick fell to the ground; he began to pat around with the flat of his hand to search for it. Eliza Jane could see it had rolled under his seat, so she went to help. She retrieved the stick and placed it back into his hand.

'Thank you,' he said.

'That's all right; I was sitting on the bench opposite. It's a crisp day but warm in the sun.'

'Yes, the sun is warm, I'm not sure I will be able to sit here much longer when the days get colder. Won't you stay a while and talk to me, what is your name?' he asked.

Eliza Jane sat down beside him. 'I'm Eliza Jane Watkins.'

'How do you do; my name is Ronald.' He put his right hand out and Eliza Jane shook it.

'I know,' she said. She was feeling sociable and not in the least timid as she normally was with strangers. 'I've seen you here before with an older lady.'

'That's Grandmamma; she tends to fuss over me but I love her dearly. She worries about me.'

'You look very much like my brother,' she said, feeling an odd familiarity with this stranger. 'You could be twins and your voice is similar.'

'Handsome devil, is he?' Ronald smiled mischievously. 'Though I don't suppose he's blind like me.'

'Yes, very handsome,' she nodded in agreement, then suddenly blurted out what was on her mind. 'Have you always been blind?' she asked, feeling overcome with embarrassment for being so direct. 'I'm sorry, I didn't mean to—'

'I was blinded in the war.'

'You don't look old enough to have fought.'

'I lied about my age; I ran away from home and joined up when I was fifteen. Lots of chaps did, I wanted to fight for my country.'

'What happened?'

'I don't really remember.'

Sensing this was traumatic for him, she changed the subject. 'Do you come to the park every day?'

'Most days. Grandmamma thinks the fresh air good for me, and it's something to do. Before the war, I used to paint, and I was good, if I may say so myself. But of course, I can't do that anymore.'

'I'm sorry,' she said softly. 'My brother used to paint, but he won't do it anymore, not since our parents died.'

Looking straight ahead, Ronald raised his head. 'Why?'

Eliza Jane found herself telling him the story of Rory's painting, and the death of her parents.

'I'm so sorry,' he said, 'that is a sad story.'

Eliza Jane was amazed that this poor young man, who had been blinded in the war, should think her story was sad.

A car drew up outside the park gates. Noticing this, Eliza Jane told him and stood up to leave, promising that she would stop and chat when she next saw him. They said their goodbyes, and she made for home. *What a wonderful day,* she thought, firstly she had been asked out by a lovely man and then she had met a new friend in the park. She glowed with happiness all the way back up Sydenham Hill.

Thomas was famished; his day at work had been hard, and they had been so busy he had not had time to stop for lunch. 'Put the kettle on, Lizzie,' he yelled as entered through the back door. 'Do you have any cake?' He came into the kitchen to find Eliza Jane re-reading her letter from David. She put it down on the table, and got up from her chair to light the gas under the kettle.

Thomas picked up the letter. 'From David?' he enquired, turning it over.

She nodded. 'Actually, there's some news you should hear – Doctor Green has passed away.'

Thomas was shocked; he stood for a moment to contemplate that news, gathering his thoughts. 'Poor devil. I'm sorry to hear that. He was very good to us all. He'll be missed in Crossdale, he was a good'n, but it's probably a blessing in disguise.'

'Why do you say that?'

'What?'

'It's a blessing.'

'You wouldn't have wanted him to suffer,' Thomas said, thinking on his feet.

Eliza Jane scanned Thomas's face; he looked shifty, she thought, as if he was hiding something. 'Thomas,' she said firmly, 'he had a car accident. He was rushing to an emergency; he was killed instantly.'

'Well, I'm right glad it was quick then. Listen' – Thomas suddenly felt uncomfortable and wanted to be alone with his thoughts – 'I'd best get changed, hold the tea till I get back.'

'Thomas, wait, there's something I need to tell you. I should have told you before but I felt you had too much on your plate, so I kept quiet.'

Thomas froze at the stern face of his sister, as she took the kettle off the stove.

'I don't know how to begin,' she said looking almost ashamed, 'but I need to share this with you. I should have said something before.'

Thomas sat himself down at the table and Eliza Jane joined him at the table; she looked grave. 'I hardly know how to begin,' she said.

Thomas was alarmed. 'You're worrying me, Lizzie, what's the matter.'

'Just after Da died, I' – Eliza Jane swallowed back a tear – 'I, I overheard Mrs Fanshawe talking to Mrs Wimbourne and the Emmet's in the post office. Mrs Fanshawe was saying that she heard that Da…' She stumbled; a tear trickled from her eye. 'Oh Thomas, I can't tell you, I can't bring myself to say the words.'

Thomas reached out across the table and gripped his sister's hand. 'Tell me Lizzie, tell me what happened, just take it slowly.'

'She said that Da took his own life.' Eliza Jane searched Thomas's face for signs of shock but saw none.

Thomas nodded slowly. Still holding his sisters' hand, he whispered, 'Yes, I know. I found a letter from Da written before he died. I'm sorry, lass, but what you heard was right, our da hung himself in the Smithy.'

Eliza Jane screamed and Thomas kept a firm grip on her hand. 'Doctor Green and Jacob Pennington helped cover up his suicide for our sake – otherwise we couldn't have buried him next to Ma. How those village witches found out I don't know, but it couldn't be from Jacob or Doctor Green. No one must ever know, Lizzie, just us, do you understand, no one.'

He reached out and grabbed her other hand which was resting on the table. 'This is our secret.'

Eliza Jane spoke through bouts of tears. 'They were only guessing really, something that Doctor Green's cleaner thought she saw. Oh, Thomas, I can't bear to think of Da in all that pain, and not able to share it with us. Why would he want to leave us? How could he do that to us?'

'I know, lass, in his letter, he said it was breaking his heart to leave us, he called himself a coward, and asked for our forgiveness.'

'Can you forgive him, Thomas?'

'I'm not sure – can you?'

'I loved him so much for his strength and courage; he was my hero, always there for me when life got tough. Sometimes all I needed was one of his special hugs – I'd give anything for one now, and to see his dear face just one more time. But in the end, he was a weak human being, Lizzie, not a hero.'

'Perhaps you've never experienced the kind of love that causes you to curl up and die when it's taken from you. Please try to understand how losing Ma must have felt for him. I would like to see the letter, Thomas.' He shook his head. 'Please Thomas, I need to read it.'

'Yes, all right, Lizzie,' he agreed. 'You know I don't hate him; I just wish he had given us the opportunity to help him.'

'Perhaps we missed the opportunities, Thomas. The clues were there but we were trying to come to terms with Ma's death too – we were hurting and unable to respond properly to each other.'

'We must look after each other now, Lizzie,' he said. She nodded in response. Thomas gave her hands a gentle shake, which gave her a sense of togetherness before he left the room.

Chapter 22

Etty was sitting in the kitchen enjoying a pot of tea and some bread laden with butter. She was ravenous, she was always hungry these days and was putting on weight more quickly, than she would have liked.

Reaching for another slice, she glanced over to where her sister was working on the other end of the table and said as casually as she could, 'What do you make of Patrick, Lizzie? He's a bit mysterious, isn't he? I mean we know nothing about him, his family, or his personal life. We know he goes out occasionally in the evenings but where does he go, and who with? I've never heard him speak of any friends. He's over forty and there's no signs of any romance.'

Eliza Jane looked up from kneading her bread and thought for a moment. 'I think he goes to his club, but you probably know more about him than any of us; you spend of the most time with him. Anyway, do we actually need to know any more? He's a good person, and he's given us a lovely home and that's good enough for me. Why do you ask, as if I didn't know, you like him, don't you? I've seen you flirting with him?' She noticed Etty cutting another slice. 'And go easy on that bread, Etty, these loaves won't be ready for a while.'

'I do not flirt with him,' remarked Etty, plastering her third slice of bread with butter, 'but if I did, then at least I'm doing something about it than do nothing and moon silently over him like you do with a certain person.' Eliza Jane chose not to respond to the barb about her feelings for David but instead lifted her dough and slapped it down on the table with some force.

Etty continued. 'Perhaps Patrick was jilted a long time ago, and is forever sworn off marriage.'

Eliza Jane gave a hollow laugh. 'You sound like Molly, just because a man isn't interested in you, it doesn't mean he's had a sad romantic past.' She shaped her dough and placed it in two greased tins, before leaving it near the warmth of the oven to rise.

'Who says he's not interested,' Etty snapped, annoyed that her sister had pointed out that which she knew in her heart already. The challenge was there however impossible it seemed and she meant to take it on. 'I'll soon have him eating out of my hand and by Christmas, begging to marry me. Just you wait and see.'

'I have no doubt you can, you managed it with David.' Eliza Jane felt aggrieved that Etty seemed to be able to get any man she wanted, while she only wanted one who didn't appear to want her.

Etty squirmed at the mention of David's name; it made her think of his child nestling inside of her. She unconsciously placed a hand on her belly and felt the child suddenly move, an odd sensation like the gossamer wings in a light breeze fluttering inside of her.

'Can't you just forget David Jackson, Lizzie' – anger had overtaken her voice – 'he's three hundred miles away. You've got to let him go – you know you'll never be anything more than friends.'

'I know that,' Eliza Jane tried to sound confident in her response. 'Besides, I don't feel anything more than friendship towards him anymore.' She drew out a chair from the table and sat down wearily. 'Anyway, I've been invited out on Saturday – we're going to see a variety show.'

Etty's eyes widened. 'What by a man, no, I don't believe it, who is he?' she asked incredulously.

'James Harrison,' she said, enjoying the amazed look on Etty's face.

'Never heard of him, who is he?'

'He's the local butcher.'

Etty laughed sarcastically. 'The local butcher? Oh Lizzie, you're priceless.' She continued to laugh unkindly. Upset that Etty should mock Jim, and sneer at her, Eliza Jane pushed back her chair and fled from the room.

'Lizzie, Lizzie, come back, what about the bread!' Etty shouted. The baby moved again. 'Oh for god's sake,' she muttered sinking back in her chair.

Later that day, Rory sat alone at the kitchen table. He had a lot on his mind and was deep in thought. He had told Patrick the news that most of Lady Helen's photographs had not developed well. He didn't know what mistakes he had made to cause such a poor outcome. He had wanted to impress Lady Helen with his skills so much and everything it seemed had gone wrong.

Patrick was philosophical. 'I think Lady Helen might have moved as the shutter was pressed,' he explained, 'don't worry, I will telephone Lady Giles and explain the situation, we will offer a second sitting free of charge.'

Rory, usually so careful in his instructions to the subjects, wasn't sure how that could have happened. Remembering he hadn't been concentrating as he should caused him to flush with embarrassment. He hoped Patrick didn't notice his cheeks reddening with the memory of the sitting, and worst of all, Rory feared she might refuse to come back in view of her previous attitude to being photographed.

Eliza Jane came into the kitchen to check on the progress of dinner. 'Penny for your thoughts,' she said opening the oven door and cautiously and peeping in. She was thrilled to see that her puff pastry had risen beautifully. She gently shut the oven door, careful not to let too much heat escape.

She straightened up, pushing a stray hair out of her eyes by blowing upwards with her mouth. 'You look as I feel, Rory. What's the matter, lad?'

'I've disappointed Patrick with some photographs I took. They can't be used because they're out of focus.'

'You're still learning, lad, I'm sure Patrick understands – don't worry about it. Listen, I've been thinking about your twentieth birthday on the sixteenth – what are we going to do to celebrate? Patrick has been talking about us all going to the Ritz hotel for dinner.'

'What, no!' she wailed. 'He can't really think we'd fit in there amongst all those posh people. Oh, Rory, please, you have to tell him that we can't go to the Ritz. It sounds far too grand: I'd feel so out of place, and I've nothing to wear.'

Rory's previous gloomy expression relaxed into a smile. 'Etty would love it though, wouldn't she, can you imagine.' He noticed Eliza Jane's stricken face and tried to pacify her. 'He's only talking about it, nothing definite. So you shouldn't worry either.' He looked at his sister, pursing his lips, not sure whether he should mention her forthcoming evening out. He decided he could. 'So what's this I hear about you and your James?'

Eliza Jane giggled. 'He's not my James, Rory, but I do like him. I'm looking forward to my first visit to the music hall too.'

Rory was suddenly struck by the thought of taking Lady Helen out. He quickly pushed the thought from his mind, why would a lady like her look twice at a blacksmith's son from Lancashire, the thought was preposterous. 'Well, I hope you enjoy your evening, Lizzie, you deserve it,' he said.

'Right, we'll finish for tea there,' said Earnest Philips, 'well done every one.'

Earnest directed most of the Players' shows; he was very talented and the actors respected him.

Molly was hoping Kit would appear – she wasn't sure where he and the other ugly sister had dashed off to.

'They're having a costume fitting,' Jo said, reading Molly's mind, 'come on they'll be ages yet, let's go and have tea, I'm parched, it's thirsty work being royalty.

Reluctantly, Molly followed her friend to the back of the hall for tea. She was disappointed; Kit didn't seem to want to be with her as much as she wanted to be with him. Admittedly, he was working hard in his pantomime role but then so was everyone, but he always seemed busier than most with everyone seeming to claim his time. Just occasionally, Molly wished he would acknowledge her presence in company. He always saw her home but dashed off for the bus mumbling something about sermons not writing themselves. They had been for a walk in the park once or twice between church services on a Sunday and Molly had been to the vicarage for her Sunday dinner but they were always chaperoned by Jo. She longed to be kissed by Kit but it had never happened. All she received was a very light peck on the cheek. Molly was sure he liked her so why didn't he show it. Perhaps he was shy, perhaps; perhaps, perhaps; Molly could think of a thousand and one excuses for his lack of affection, but maybe he just needed time, but was she prepared to wait.

Chapter 23

Molly placed the hat gently into a large striped box, and handed it over the counter to the customer.

'Thank you, madam,' she said, forcing a smile. 'I'm sure the hat will be perfect for your special occasion.' She really didn't feel like smiling, once more Kit had walked her to the bus and seen her home and again, he hadn't even held her hand. She was beginning to wonder what the matter with her was. Didn't Kit find her attractive? She wished she could talk to her father about it; he would have reassured her that she was still his beautiful girl and that the reverend Christopher Howard did not deserve her. She began to tidy away the discarded hats tears beginning to brim in her eyes at the thought of her da. Hurriedly, she wiped them away.

'Rehearsal went well last night, Moll,' said Jo, approaching from her counter opposite to Molly's. 'Kit thinks you're absolutely marvellous as Cinderella.'

'Really, I wonder why he doesn't tell me that himself, in fact he barely speaks to me at rehearsals.'

Jo looked at her friend and saw tears in her eyes. 'Molly you're upset – oh my goodness, whatever's the matter.'

'I'm just being silly, I suddenly thought about my father and it came over me how much I miss him, and Ma too, of course.'

'I know how you feel, sometimes grief catches up with you when you least expect it. I still miss my parents, and I know Kit does too.'

'I'm surprised he has time to miss his parents, Jo, he never appears to have time for me.' Molly didn't mean to sound quite so aggressive with her reply but she couldn't help herself.

Jo was puzzled. 'What's brought this on? Kit really likes you, and I thought you cared for him.'

'Well, we're friends certainly,' Molly replied guardedly, 'but as for anything else, well it's too early to say.'

'Miss Howard, back to your counter if you please,' Mrs Roberts called out with a stern look in their direction. Jo returned to her counter pondering on what she had just heard.

Much to Rory's delight, Lady Helen returned to the studio to have her pictures retaken. Reaching out for Lady Helen's extended hand, he welcomed her into the studio.

'Thank you for coming back to see us again, Lady Helen, may I take your coat.' Helen shrugged her heavy fur coat from her shoulders and passed it to Rory who hung it carefully on the hat stand in the corner of the studio. 'I'll take extra care this time to ensure there are no mishaps,' he reassured her.

'I'm sure it wasn't your fault, Mr Watkins. Perhaps I moved at the critical time. I do hope you didn't get into trouble with Mr Lawrence.'

'He only beat me,' said Rory masking a smile, 'and sent me to bed without supper.'

'Is that all, then I think you escaped very lightly.'

They laughed.

'Lady Helen, do you think you could see your way to calling me Rory.'

'Is that your name?'

'No, I just like it that's all,' he joked

'Rory it is then – and I like the name too. In that case, you must call me Helen. Tell me about yourself, Rory, where is that accent from.'

'I am from a small village called Crossdale in Lancashire; my father was the village blacksmith there. I came to London a few months ago to collect a prize from the National Gallery. I won a painting competition.'

'How wonderful, you paint!'

'No, not anymore; photography is my new passion.' Rory was reluctant to tell Helen why he had stopped painting; he still had an overriding sense of guilt that he should have been in the smithy and not daubing paint on paper.

'Is your painting hung in the National?'

Rory nodded.

'Then I must go and see it.'

Rory suddenly felt brave and said, 'I would love to take you to see it Helen.'

'How divine, I should love to go with you. I am free on Saturday; perhaps we could have lunch afterwards.'

Rory was so thrilled that he totally forgot that lunch would cost money that he didn't have, perhaps he could scrape together enough, and he could ask Patrick if the restaurant he took them to by the gallery was expensive.

'I will collect you on Saturday then, now I suppose we must get these photographs done.'

As Helen sat still before the camera, she smiled inwardly as well as parting her lips in an outward smile. The plan was beginning to be a reality she thought and wasn't it just perfect he came from a working-class background. She couldn't wait to introduce him to her father.

'I can't make rehearsal tonight,' Molly said, as she and Jo tidied up their counter before leaving. 'I'm not feeling so well. I think I just want to go home.'

'You've looked pale all-day, Molly.'

'I've a headache, and that last customer didn't help, she was dreadful.'

'She certainly was; she must have had every single hat on her head without attempting to buy one. Listen, Moll, are you sure you won't come; it might relax you.'

She shook her head. 'No, I really couldn't concentrate, I'd forget my lines.'

'Get an early night then and I'm sure you'll feel better tomorrow.'

Molly was so disappointed in Kit's lack of attention that she doubted she would ever feel better again.

The following morning, she awoke feeling tearful; her head ached from tossing and turning through the night. Going over the non-existent relationship in her mind, wondering where she had gone wrong.

Autumnal mornings were well established, and with the occasional slight frost on the ground it was becoming colder. Stretching an arm from her warm bed covers made Molly shiver. She immediately pulled it back in, turning over to shut her eyes in an effort to erase Kit from her mind. She had been ridiculous, carried away by some fantasy relationship that clearly wasn't there. She struck her head hard on her pillow for her stupidity.

There was a knock on the door; she pulled the covers over her head.

'Moll, are you up yet?' shouted Eliza Jane.

'I'm not going to work today.' Molly let out a muffled holler from beneath the covers. 'I can't face it; I don't feel well.'

The door opened, and Eliza Jane made her way over to the bed and stood before Molly.

'What's the matter, are you sick?'

Molly nodded, she felt sick all right, heart sick.

'Perhaps you've caught what Etty had a few weeks ago.'

Molly weakly agreed. She felt guilty deceiving Lizzie, but she couldn't face going to work and seeing Jo.

'Stay here then, love – I'll bring you a hot drink shortly. I'll telephone Cobbs and let them know.'

The door closed quietly behind Eliza Jane and Molly dissolved into tears.

Saturday dawned frosty and cold. Eliza Jane woke with a mixture of dread and excitement invading her being. Tonight, she was going to the music hall with Jim. She had never been on a date before. So many worries flooded into her head: what should she wear? What if he tried to hold her hand, or even worse, tried to kiss her – what should she do? It wasn't that she didn't want to be kissed but how should she react? She had never kissed anyone who wasn't family before. She thought about asking Etty for advice but she had been so derisory about Jim that she felt she couldn't.

The day passed slowly. Eliza Jane went shopping as usual but carefully avoided the butchers. The thought of seeing Jim before he called for her was embarrassing, suppose he thought she was too keen.

On the way home, she popped into the park again, Ronald wasn't there, it was probably too cold for him, she thought, or she might have missed him. She sat on a bench, drawing her coat around her. The park looked different in a frosty half-light. The trees had shed their finery of the last two seasons. The ducks were swimming in a tiny space of water that someone had made by throwing a large boulder into the frozen pond. She was amused to see them slipping and sliding as they tried to walk on the ice.

At home in his room, Rory was dressing with care for his afternoon out with Lady Helen. Wanting to make a good impression, he had asked Patrick's advice about the restaurant near the gallery, and then made the telephone booking. Without thinking how he could fund further outings; he was willing to spend every penny of his savings on this special lunch

'You look very handsome,' said Eliza Jane who had arrived home to find Rory pacing the kitchen floor.

'Do I? I'm actually terrified, I don't mind telling you. What if we run out of conversation; what if the restaurant is a disaster; what if I'm so boring she never wants to see me again.'

Eliza Jane straitened Rory's bow tie; she had had similar thoughts about her evening with Jim, what if, what if, so many questions were crowding her mind. She took a deep breath, Rory wanted answers, and so did she. 'If the friendship is right,' she said, 'then the evening will be a success – just be yourself.' She gave him a reassuring hug, thinking how much he had matured since the day he had run away when Ma had died.

There was a knock at the back door and a voice shouted, 'Taxi for Mr Watkins.' Rory visibly paled now the time had arrived. He had never taken a lady out for before. He'd danced with the village girls, and walked a couple of them home but this was different, she was totally out of his class, she was aristocracy, he a working-class lad, but he really liked Lady Helen and he thought she liked him too. The day might prove to be one of the most important of his life.

'Taxi's waiting, Rory,' said Eliza Jane, as she gently shook him back to reality.

With a final hug for his older sister, Rory hurried to the door. He turned with the open door in front of him. 'Have a good time tonight Lizzie, you deserve it,' he said. Then with a quick wave, he disappeared down the path.

When the taxi drew up outside a large imposing house, Rory was perplexed surely the driver must have taken him to the wrong address? Nevertheless, in bold letters on a beautifully polished brass plate was the name Westcott Manor. He had never seen such an enormous house. The drive up to the front door must have been at least a mile long. He told the taxi driver to wait for him, and walked the couple of yards to the front door where he yanked on the bell that was hanging to the side. He heard the bell clanging as he let it go. Almost immediately, the door opened, and a rather pompous looking gentleman looked him up and down.

'Lord Giles?' Rory enquired politely.

'No,' he said affronted that anyone could be so foolish to think of him as lord of the manor. 'I'm Sedgwick the butler, whom shall I inform his Lordship is calling?'

'Rory Watkins.'

'Very well, please step in side and wait.'

Rory wiped his feet several times and entered the great hall. The cottage in Crossdale would have fitted in here twice over, he thought. He gazed at the sweeping staircase, several chandeliers and some historical portraits charting the family back through several generations. One in particular caught his eye; he went to have a closer look. It was Lady Helen, perhaps of a couple of years ago but obviously painted by a fine artist. The colours were superb; the way the light had caught her blue dress to the perfectly formed pink rose at her waist and the deep blue velvet of her chair – her Wedgewood blue eyes gazed out at him. She was adorable, he thought. The portrait before him inspired his artist's eye to such a degree that for a moment he wished he hadn't vowed to never paint again.

'Lord Giles will see you now, sir,' said Sedgwick, interrupting his thoughts.

'Actually, it's Lady Helen, I've come to see,' corrected Rory.

'Lord Giles will see you now, sir,' the butler repeated, turning away and indicating that Rory should follow him through the hallway.

They arrived at two large double doors which Sedgwick opened together in a grand manner: Rory stood in the doorway as Sedgwick announced him. 'Mr Rory Watkins, my Lord.'

The butler stood aside as Rory entered the room. He tried not to be overawed by its splendour.

Lord and Lady Giles were sitting like two bookends on a cream brocade chaise longue. Sitting between them with her eyes down cast, and her hands placed demurely in her lap was Helen.

Lord Giles struggled to his feet. 'Mr Watkins' – he shook Rory's hand – 'I believe you've already met my wife, Lady Virginia.'

Rory bowed over Lady Virginia's hand as Patrick had instructed.

'Do sit down, Mr Watkins, and tell us about yourself.'

'Well, actually,' Rory announced anxiously, 'I have a taxi waiting and a table booked for lunch – so perhaps we should be going.'

Helen addressed her father, 'Papa, the taxi is costing Rory money; perhaps if you let me drive us in mummy's car, then the taxi can be dismissed and then Rory can tell you all about himself.'

'I'll not let you drive your mother's automobile, Helen.'

She turned on her father. 'You're so unfair, Papa. If only you'd let me have my own automobile.'

'Go and pay your taxi driver, Watkins, then dismiss him. Johnson will drive you wherever you want to go.' Lord Giles turned to his daughter. 'We'll hear no more about automobiles from you, Helen. We've already discussed this several times, and the answer is still no.'

'Yes, Papa,' replied Helen meekly, noting to her satisfaction the surprise on her Father's face, as she was not usually so compliant.

Rory excused himself and anxious to make a good impression and do as he was bid, left the room and found his way back outside to pay the taxi driver He had been told by Patrick to give the driver a tip and by the look on the driver's face, as he pocketed the money, he must have been over generous.

By the time Rory had returned from dismissing the taxi, Helen had left the room.

'Do sit down, Mr Watkins,' said Lord Giles, indicating the chair to the side of them. 'Now tell us all about yourself and your family. What's your father's employment, and where were you brought up?'

Rory told the couple all about his upbringing in Crossdale, his father's business and then continued with how he came to be living with Patrick Lawrence.' He hoped Lord and Lady Giles might be impressed with the news of his painting hanging in the National but instead Lord Giles seemed to focus on his father's occupation.

'I see,' said Lord Giles, 'so your father is a small village blacksmith.' He exchanged glances with his wife obvious distaste on their faces.

'Was a Blacksmith, sir, both my parents died earlier this year. My brother and sisters and I have no one but ourselves.'

Lord Giles continued ignoring the news about Rory's parents. 'I admit I have never heard of Crossdale; in which county does it lay?'

'Lancashire, sir.'

'Oh, the North, no wonder it meant nothing to us, my dear.' His wife nodded in agreement.

'You say you have a brother, Watkins, is he the elder and if so, what regiment was he in during the war?'

'Yes, he's my older brother but the enlistment board wouldn't take him as he has a weak heart.'

'I hope you're not giving Rory a grilling, Papa,' Helen interjected, as she came back into the room.

Rory stood up. 'Not at all, Lady Helen, your parents have been very welcoming,' he lied.

There was a gentle knock and Sedgwick opened both doors to the drawing room to announce Johnson was waiting outside with the car.

Helen swiftly pecked the cheeks of both her parents before grabbing Rory's hand and pulling him towards the door.

After the couple had left, Lord Giles paced up and down in front of his wife, muttering angrily. 'He's a common blacksmith's son, with a brother who was ostensibly too ill to fight in the war, but most likely the truth of it was he refused to fight. Not only is he a northerner with no breeding or pedigree, but he was bought up in a tithe cottage for heaven's sake. Helen simply cannot be allowed to pursue this friendship. We have the house party with the Astors coming up next month, why it could ruin the whole weekend if it got out.'

'I agree, Cyril, but you know Helen, she's very wilful. I just don't know how you're going to stop her.'

Lord Giles sank wearily into the chair that Rory had recently vacated. 'There must be a way,' he said.

Sitting close together in the car, Helen apologised for her parents' attitude and her own small defiance when told she was not allowed to drive her mother's car.

'It's not even as if I can't drive,' she complained to Rory. 'I've practised many times in Mummy's automobile, although she doesn't know it. I wait until she goes for her afternoon nap, and then I drive out to visit friends. I'm a perfectly good driver but Papa is totally against the little woman, as he calls us, out on the road. Honestly, Rory, he's so old fashioned. He'll have an apoplectic fit when women finally become properly enfranchised. Sometimes I wish I came from a poor background like you. I would love to have brothers and sisters but now I've met you, I will have. I want to know all about them, Molly and Etty sound such fun and Eliza Jane sounds so wise. Oh, I wish I had sisters, I loathe being an only child.'

Besotted and beguiled, Rory listened adoringly to this wonderful girl's chatter. As he watched her animated face, he began to sketch it in his mind. How wonderful it would be to paint her portrait, to capture those beautiful eyes on canvas. Perhaps he could take up his brushes again, after all.

The restaurant was as pleasant as Rory remembered; he just hoped he had enough money in his wallet to pay the bill. The table for two was placed under one of the chandeliers and three lit candles had been placed on the table, casting a warm glow over Lady Helen. Rory could barely eat; he was so in love. Helen was having no such problems and was now tucking into her fourth course, much to his dismay. This was going to be expensive.

Lunch was wonderful, but took so long that Helen suggested they went another day to see Rory's painting. Rory readily agreed as it meant she wanted to see him again. As the meal drew to a close, the bill was discretely placed on the table beside him. Helen averted her eyes, as he picked it up and glanced at it. He could not believe how much they had eaten and drank and only just managed to find enough money to pay the bill. Patrick, thank goodness, had slipped a five pound note into his pocket. Rory had wanted to refuse but realised he might need the security it gave him.

Helen insisted Johnson drive Rory home first, and although he protested, for he would have liked to have escorted Helen to her home, he gave in. Now sitting in the back seat of Lord Giles's Rolls Royce and holding Helen's hand tightly, he wished the journey could go on and on.

'Helen,' he whispered, not wanting Johnson to hear him, 'would you like to do this again?

'What drive in my father's car?' She teased him.

'You know what I mean,' he laughed. 'Come out again with me. I enjoyed it, I hope you did too.'

'Of course, let's make an arrangement to meet next week.'

'I was thinking more of tomorrow – I can't wait until next week.'

'Tomorrow it is then, Rory dear,' agreed Helen, 'you may kiss me goodbye.'

Turning to see if Johnson was looking in his mirror to the back seat of the car, and having ascertained he was, Helen offered Rory her lips. The kiss was so sweet that Rory wanted another but Helen tapped him on the hand and admonished him.

'That's enough for now, sweet boy,' she laughed.

Johnson dropped Rory to his door. He climbed out of the car, waved to Helen then turned and skipped up the path, banging the gate behind him. As he let himself into the house, he could hear voices in the kitchen, surely Etty and Eliza Jane weren't arguing again? He stood and listened for a moment. As usual, Etty was trying to offer Eliza Jane some advice on how to look and dress for her night out. Helen said she would love to have sisters but sometimes Rory thought they were a mixed blessing. He left the girls to it and disappeared upstairs to sketch Helen in his pad.

Eliza Jane had managed to convince Etty that she didn't need any help with powdering her face or choosing her clothes before she went out.

'You're trying to turn me into someone I'm not,' she complained, 'just let me be.' Etty sighed making her displeasure known.

'Well don't blame me if he doesn't want to see you again,' she retorted striding out of the kitchen.

Jim had arrived on time to pick her up and they walked to the bus stop across the road. They were going to the Hackney Empire, which meant two bus rides across London. Eliza Jane looked at other couples on the bus and felt proud to be seen with Jim. He didn't seem to mind she was plain and overweight and for once she felt inconspicuous which for Eliza Jane was a rare occurrence.

'How long have you been a butcher, Jim?' she asked him, conscious of his warm leg against her thigh.

'It was me dad's business and his dad before him. Just after I got back from the war last year, Dad died, leaving the shop to me and my brother. That's him that's in the shop with me now. Well, he's six years older than me and has a wife and nippers. I know he would like to buy me out and one day it might happen, when I find the right opportunity. Now tell me about yourself and don't leave anything out.'

The music hall was a large, red brick building. They went into the foyer under the canopy over which the word Empire was written in large white letters. Jim had treated them to seats in the circle and Eliza Jane sat feeling like a queen, enjoying the chocolate that Jim had bought with him. After her initial shyness had worn off, she relaxed and began to enjoy Jim's company. The music hall was unlike anything she had ever seen before. From the gold walls and chandeliers to the plush velvet seats, she was astounded by it all. Jim looked at her animated face loving her enjoyment. There was something about his Lancashire lass he found very appealing.

There were seven different acts, including a magician, a juggler, a mime artist and even a ballet troupe. During one act, Eliza Jane had held her breath, almost clutching Jim's hand but not daring to, as she watched two men flying high in the air before catching their trapeze and swinging up on to a tiny platform before flying again. A man playing a trombone walked across a narrow wire that was set high above the stage. Every step made Eliza Jane gasp; she flinched during the more precarious moments and shut her eyes tightly until he was safely across, then applauded enthusiastically along with the boisterous audience.

The main act was a young man dressed in toff's clothes with a top hat and cane. He had been introduced as Miss Vesta Tilley, and it wasn't until *he* started singing that Molly realised he really was a woman. Eliza Jane was slightly shocked; she had never seen a woman dressed as a man before, though she did enjoy the catchy chorus of the song that they sang along to.

At the end of the show, they applauded loudly. Jim stamped his feet and put two fingers in his mouth to whistle his appreciation. Eliza Jane laughed at his antics.

'Well gel, did you enjoy your first music hall,' he said, as they shuffled out of the theatre.

'I loved it, I wonder how that trick was done when the magician made that girl disappear, I couldn't believe my eyes.'

'Ah, it's all done with mirrors,' said Jim tapping his nose as if he knew all about it.

They walked back to the bus stop, singing some of the songs they had heard, and dissolving into fits of laughter when they got the words wrong.

They said goodbye at the back door of Patrick's house. Jim took her hand but Eliza Jane withdrew it quickly, knowing that it was rough and red from housework. Jim persisted and gently took her hand again. 'I've 'ad a really good time tonight,' he said, meeting her eyes. 'I've enjoyed your company enormously. I hope we can do it again sometime soon, what do yer say, girl?'

She nodded. 'That would be right gradely, Jim,' she said teasing him with a proper Lancashire word.

'Does that mean yes,' he laughed.

'I would love to, Jim,' she replied.

'What about the back end of next week, we could go ter the pictures?'

Eliza Jane agreed, although she would have liked it to be a little sooner. Sensing her shyness, Jim let go of her hand and smiled at her. 'Well, I'll be orf then, I expect I'll see you in the shop in the week, we can firm up arrangements then. 'Nighty night.' And with a quick kiss on her burning cheek, he left her.

Eliza Jane floated through the kitchen and bumped into Patrick in the hallway.

'I thought it was you, Lizzie, did you enjoy the show?'

Eliza Jane's hand touched her kissed cheek. 'It was lovely,' she sighed, and then remembering she was in Patrick's employment, she asked, 'is there anything I can get you?'

Patrick smiled at her flushed face. 'No my dear, thank you. Goodnight, I'll see you in the morning – sweet dreams.'

Patrick disappeared into his study and poured himself a large brandy. He made himself comfortable in his large winged armchair beside the dying embers of his fire. Sitting forward he picked up the poker and inserted it into the fire wiggling it about a bit. Soon a small yellow flame flickered through the ashes which rapidly grew in strength. Satisfied that would do for now, he settled back in his chair picked up his drink and swilled the honey coloured liquid around in the bottom of his glass. It had been a trying day, he was finding it increasingly difficult to work alongside Rory, not because he was incompetent, nothing could be further from the truth, the real reason, and he really did not want to admit it to himself, was because he had fallen in love. Rory reminded him so much of another young man many years ago with gentle eyes and a soft mouth, his first love. He felt helpless, the Watkins were not aware of his problem, nor must they ever find out. Patrick had spent many years living alone denying his desires, but then there was always that fleeting face in the crowd that quickened his pulses. He had fought those un-natural feelings, as he knew them to be, with all his might and was succeeding until he first saw Rory in Trafalgar square. The situation was tearing him apart, he was surrounded by people, but he had never felt so lonely. He thought about Lady Helen. Patrick had photographed many young women over the years, he knew women, he liked the company of women and they trusted him, but there was something about Lady Helen Giles that worried him. He just hoped she wouldn't break Rory's heart.

Chapter 24

Molly was glad it was Sunday which gave her a day off work. She was so dispirited however that all day she mooched about and even refused her usual Sunday dinner at the vicarage. She had formed such exciting plans in her mind about her future with Kit, even trying out her new married name Mrs Christopher Howard. She had pictured herself sitting as Kit's wife in the front pew of church. She would be respected by the ladies of the parish, as they visited the vicarage for afternoon tea. She knew she would make the perfect vicar's wife but obviously Kit did not see it. The fact that Eliza Jane and Rory were so full of their new relationships made her feel even worse.

She had refused to come down for her lunch, preferring to read up in her room, but had finally been persuaded by Eliza Jane.

Patrick had taken to eating regularly with the family. He enjoyed their company and it was certainly better than sitting at the huge dining table on his own.

Over lunch, Eliza Jane and Rory were full of chatter about their outings of the day before, each trying to speak at the same time. Molly sat quietly, picking at her food.

'Molly, are you all right, you're very quiet,' Patrick asked, looking anxiously at her pale, sad face.

'I expect she's bloody tired of hearing from the lovesick, I know I am,' Etty remarked bitterly. 'Can we please change the subject?'

The doorbell ringing interrupted their conversation. Thomas put down his knife and fork and made his way to the front door.'

He swung open the door. 'Hello,' he said, 'do you want Mr Lawrence, he's having a meal at the moment but you can wait in the studio until he is free.'

'I'm Jo, Molly's friend from work, I was just wondering how she is.' Thomas was instantly taken by the young lady before him. He took a moment to absorb her rich auburn hair and delicately freckled nose.

'Is she up to visitors,' Jo enquired.

Thomas pulled himself together. 'What, oh sorry,' he said, 'I'm Thomas, Molly's older brother, come in, we're all in the dining room, I think she's feeling a little better.'

'Jo!' exclaimed Molly nervously, as her friend entered the room.

'Hello, Moll, Kit and I were wondering how you are. We both missed you at rehearsals again last night.'

Molly blushed at the mention of Kit's name. The others looked enquiringly at her.

'I thought you said the pantomime had been cancelled, Moll,' said Etty, gazing at her sister's burning face.

Molly stood up. 'I'm not coming any more, Jo. I'm sorry but you'll have to find a new Cinderella.' Then bursting into tears, she ran from the room.

'I'll go,' said Patrick, rising from his chair.

'No,' said Thomas, 'Lizzie, make Jo a cup of tea will you, *I'll go.*'

Patrick sat down cursing that he had overstepped the mark again.

Thomas made his way upstairs, knocking gently on his sister's door. 'Molly, let me in, please.'

'Go away! Tell Jo to go away too.'

Thomas felt the handle and found the door to be unlocked. 'I'm coming in, Moll. Now, lass, what's to do, eh?' Thomas sounded so like Albert that Molly burst into tears. She wanted her da so much it hurt.

'Oh, Thomas, I've been such a fool,' she told him between sobs.

'Nay, lass, why do you say that.'

Molly tried to explain to her brother how she had expected so much more from meeting Kit again. I thought he felt about me like I do about him but he just ignores me at rehearsals and then when he walks me home, he is distant and not at all affectionate. I think he regrets seeing me again.' She raised a tear stained face looking to Thomas for answers.

'I know he likes you, Moll, but some men are a little slow where women are concerned, your brother here included. Just give him time. Men can be a bit single minded at times. I bet when he's busy at a rehearsal, that's all he thinks about. He won't know how you are feeling, so maybe you should tell him, lass.'

'But what if he doesn't feel the same way?'

'Well, at least you'll know then eh, now come on, dry your eyes and come and see your friend. A flash of auburn hair flew across his brain which suddenly

156

gave him an idea. 'I tell you what. Do they need any help over there, I could make scenery.'

'I'm sure they do, Thomas,' replied Molly, 'I would like it if you came to rehearsals with us.'

'Good, that's settled, now come on, let's go down.' As they walked slowly down the stairs, Thomas smiled to himself, the idea to help with the scenery had only just occurred to him and was not entirely altruistic. Anything to see more of that pretty lass with the auburn hair who was currently sitting downstairs.

Jo looked up as Molly and Thomas entered the room. She rose from her chair and moved to greet her friend.

'I'm feeling much better now, Jo, I was just having a bit of a wobble about the whole thing, but I would like to come back to rehearsals if you'll have me and Thomas is going to come and help with the scenery.'

Jo reached out and gathered Molly into her arms. 'You've nothing to worry about you know, we all think you are wonderful.' She looked at Thomas over Molly's shoulder and smiled. 'And we would love it if you came to help.'

'Thank goodness that's all settled,' remarked Etty sarcastically, placing a cigarette between her painted lips, lighting it, drawing in then blowing out the smoke.

Thomas insisted he take Jo home on the bus; he didn't want her walking on her own, and he wanted to take the opportunity to get to know her. Patrick for once remained silent; he would have offered Jo a lift in his car, but felt by the dazed look on Thomas's face that he wouldn't appreciate it.

'I'll just get my coat then, won't be long.'

Soon Jo and Thomas were walking down the street together, Eliza Jane watched them from the dining room window. 'There they go,' she said, 'and if I didn't know better, I would think that cupid's arrow has struck in this house again.'

Etty groaned loudly making the others laugh.

On the top deck of the bus, Thomas and Jo drifted into a relaxed conversation. 'Tell me about the Players, Jo.'

'Kit and I have performed with them for as long as I can remember – we love it. We perform two plays a year, as well as a pantomime – it's a big commitment – we're only a small group though, and are always short of men, and we're always looking for set builders. So I do hope you can come and you didn't just say it to make Molly happy.'

'No, Jo, I meant it. I'm a carpenter and wood sculptor by trade; at least I was at home in Crossdale.'

'That would be wonderful if you could help. Molly could bring you to rehearsals?'

'I'll certainly come when I can. I work shifts at present at Claridges, but when I'm off duty, I'll be there.'

Having left Jo at her gate, Thomas turned and walked back to the bus the way he had come. He started to hum. He was suddenly feeling very optimistic. He finally had a job which paid him good tips on top of his basic wage and now he had met the most beautiful girl in the world. It was a while before he remembered his pledge that he would never marry, the thought bought him back to reality; he would have to be careful.

Chapter 25

The following night, Molly accompanied by Thomas arrived in the church hall for rehearsals. Molly was greeted effusively by the cast and Kit added, 'We missed you, Molly, are you feeling better?'

'Much better, thank you,' she replied, annoyed that Kit couldn't bring himself to say 'I missed you.'

Kit was also very pleased to welcome Thomas. 'Good to see you again, Thomas, it seems London has been good to you all since we met on the train. God is wonderful in his ways.' Thomas didn't so much feel it was down to God as to them, and he still wasn't prepared to accept that Patrick had a hand in the matter.

Kit was still talking. 'We really are pleased you've come to join us; we need all the help we can get on set building.'

'I'm looking forward to it,' replied Thomas.

Kit spoke to the room asking for silence, 'Listen, everyone; this is Thomas, Molly's brother, he's come to help with the set.' Much to his embarrassment, Thomas received a round of applause before he was taken by one of the Players and set to work.

When tea break was called, Jo put her arm through Molly's as they walked to the tea bar. 'Thomas is doing a wonderful job painting that back cloth, Moll. I'm glad he's here, he's a real asset to the backstage team.' An unexpected shiver ran down her back as she turned to look at him. He wasn't particularly tall and his skin was pale but he was handsome in a delicate sort of way. He had kind blue eyes and a wide mouth. She liked the way his brown hair, stuck up in places on his head even though he had obviously tried to keep it under control. Jo just thought he needed taking care of.

Molly interrupted her thoughts. 'He's fitted in so well, usually he's quite shy with strangers but he seems comfortable enough here.'

'It must have been a huge responsibility for him after your parents died, and very brave to bring you all down to London to find work.'

'Sometimes he seems to have had the all the problems and none of the fun. He always seems to have something on his mind. Eliza Jane says he's just taking his family responsibilities seriously, and not to worry, so I try not to. He's the best brother in the world.'

'I'm surprised that he isn't married,' Jo said, trying to appear casual, not giving away her interest in him.

'There was a girl up in Crossdale; she had hair much like yours.'

'What happened,' breathed Jo.

'I suppose he felt she wasn't right for him. I don't really know the details; you'll have to ask him.'

Thomas ambled over with his paintbrush. 'What are you two girls talking about?'

'Nothing important, come on let's go and get that cup of tea,' said Molly, swiftly covering Jo's confusion. She glanced at Jo who was smiling at Thomas. Molly laughed quietly; she had guessed right, her best friend had feelings for her brother.

After the rehearsal, Thomas and Jo walked ahead to the bus stop with Molly and Kit wandering slowly behind them. Molly watched her brother and friend chatting. If only Thomas could open his eyes to the possibility of romance, he deserved some happiness after all that he had been through. She turned to look at Kit walking beside her, dare she ask him how he felt about her; it would be the only way to find out.

'Penny for them, Moll, you're very quiet. You would tell me if something was worrying you, wouldn't you? Are you enjoying your part in the pantomime, is everything okay? You don't seem yourself. Jo tells me you were worried about your part, but really there's no need, you are wonderful as Cinderella, and the audience will love you,' Kit said, giving Molly her chance to ask the question uppermost in her mind.

'Kit, I need to ask you this and I hope I'm not being too forward.' She took a big breath in, wondering how to start. 'The fact is I'm confused about us; you see when we met on the train that day, I felt there was something between us, I thought you liked me as much as I liked you but I was obviously wrong. We never see each other outside of rehearsals except when I come to dinner on

Sundays and then you're always busy. I need to know how you feel, Kit, and please be honest in your reply.'

'Molly, I am so sorry I have put you in this position. Rest assured that I do like you, very much indeed and I also felt something passed between us on the train, but I have duties in the parish and to the Players that keep me busy and duties as a son and a brother too. It is all very difficult. Don't give up on me please, that is all I can say. I'm sorry I can't reassure you any more than that at the moment.'

Kit's cryptic answer frustrated Molly more than ever and she stayed silent until she got to the bus stop. In contrast, Thomas and Jo were chattering until they said goodbye.

Kit and Jo waved Molly and Thomas off on the bus and walked the few hundred yards back to the vicarage together almost in silence.

Jo took her coat off once in the house and began to climb the stairs, she turned halfway up and looked at her brother. 'You really are going to have to tell Molly about your promise to Mum and Dad, Kit, because I think she is in love with you. She's my friend and I don't want her hurt.' She continued climbing the stairs saying, 'I'm going to bed now, goodnight, Kit.'

'Goodnight and God bless, Grace.'

Jo stopped in her tracks to look at him. 'You know I prefer to be called Jo.'

'Sorry, Jo, goodnight.'

Kit disappeared into his study; his Bible was lying on the desk. He picked it up and opened it at random. He had prayed to God regularly for an answer with regard to his feelings for Molly. Scanning the page, he settled on chapter 20 verses 12 of Exodus. '*Honour thy father and thy mother that thy days may be long upon the land which the Lord thy God giveth thee.*' There was God's answer. His parents and Nora's parents had been very close friends and it was his mother's dying wish that he marry Nora and at the time, he had readily agreed to please her. He had never been sure if the mothers had hatched the plan together over the many cups of tea they had shared and whether Nora knew about it. Nothing had ever been said. They occasionally went out together and had an easy and simple relationship, like best friends. He was fond of her, who wouldn't be, she was a lovely girl, but he could never quite manage to ask her to marry him, and now he had met Molly, he knew it was going to be very difficult to honour his mother's wishes, but he knew in his heart that unless Nora released him from the promise, that is what he had to do.

Later that night, Molly lay awake listening to Eliza Jane's steady breathing. Life seemed to be simple for her older sister; Molly knew she had enjoyed an evening out with her butcher friend, Jim. He sounded so full of fun, and Molly hoped that the friendship would flourish. Eliza Jane deserved someone who would love and cherish her.

Molly's stomach lurched as Kit came back into her thoughts. She loved him to distraction, but all she could do was what he had asked of her and not give up on him. She wondered why it was so difficult, surely if she liked him and he liked her, what was the problem. She sighed and beating her pillow into submission she turned over. Why was life always so complicated?

In the room along the landing, Thomas also lay awake. Try as he might, he just couldn't get a certain girl out of his thoughts. Her ready personality, and glorious red hair, her bright blue eyes and scattered freckles; he had never felt like this before about any girl.

Down the corridor in her own room, Etty was gazing at her self sideways in the mirror. She was five months pregnant, and she knew she was beginning to show. She had tried not to eat too much so the baby would be small, but if she skipped lunch, she felt faint and couldn't concentrate on her designs. There were also times when she just wanted to eat and eat. She had developed a passion for cheese, and had great difficulty trying to curb her craving. In fact, she could manage a cheese sandwich right now and the more she thought about it, the more she wanted one. Without bothering to slip on the silk peignoir she had purchased at discount rate from the House of Harding, she slipped out of her door and silently descended the large wide staircase, making her way to the kitchen.

Eliza Jane stirred, she could hear Molly's sniffing and shuffling in her bed. She waited a while to see if it would stop, and when it didn't, she reached out for the lamp beside her bed and switched it on. 'Moll,' she called out, swinging her legs out of bed and going to her sister. 'Whatever's the matter, are you all right?'

'Sorry, Lizzie, I didn't mean to wake you.'

'Don't worry about that, dear.' She placed a hand on Molly's cool brow. 'Are you feeling ill again?'

Molly didn't want to tell Eliza Jane about Kit just yet so replied, 'I just can't get to sleep; I think I'm feeling a little homesick. You know, missing Crossdale, and Ma and Da.'

'I know,' replied Eliza Jane, 'I still miss everyone at home – even the sight of Jacob Pennington would do for me. The letters I get from David aren't enough, I want to see him again, Moll, I so want to see him again.'

Molly sat up in bed and hugged her sister. 'It's an utterly miserable feeling, isn't it? Loving someone when they don't love you back.'

Eliza Jane looked at her sister – where had the lively optimistic girl, who always felt something would turn up, disappeared to? She sighed inwardly.

'I'm going to make us a cup of tea, Moll. I shan't be long.'

Eliza Jane descended the stairs and turned down the corridor at the bottom. She noticed a light seeping beneath the closed kitchen door. She knew she hadn't forgotten to turn it off last night, but wait cupboards were being opened and closed. Warily, she approached the kitchen door and gingerly pushed it open peering slowly around the door. She let out a huge sigh of relief when she saw Etty buttering some bread at the table.

'Etty, you frightened me,' said Eliza Jane, entering the kitchen. 'I wondered who was there!'

Hearing a voice, Etty jumped, nervously dropping a slice of bread on the floor. She picked it up. 'Sorry, Lizzie, I was just hungry, I'll just go back to bed now.' And with that, she bolted for the door.

As she scooted past her sister, Eliza Jane caught sight of something that she had begun to suspect might be happening. Surely this couldn't be true, it was unthinkable. Sure, enough though she had caught sight of an unmistakeable bump under Etty's night dress. Etty was having a baby.

'Etty!' she called to her fleeing sister, who had gathered up her nightdress in front of her and was making quickly for the stairs. There was no reply.

Chapter 26

Etty had never been so miserable. She sat down heavily at her work desk and sighed. Inwardly. Even designing a wedding dress for the honourable Virginia, daughter of the Duchess of Hampshire could not lift her spirits; it only served to remind her that she, herself, was still unmarried and having a baby. Many times, she had been on the brink of writing to David to tell him about the pregnancy, but each time she had stopped herself, knowing in her heart of hearts that she didn't want to marry for the sake of propriety.

To make matters worse, after her sandwich making had been interrupted last night, she was sure now that her sister knew about the baby. She had better avoid Eliza Jane for as long as possible. She had escaped to work early that morning but she knew she would have to face her sister tonight, and was dreading it. Even if she worked late, she knew she couldn't avoid going home forever.

She would marry Patrick in a heartbeat, if only he would indicate he loved her. Although he was generous in a great many ways – even buying her a sewing machine – he was not generous in the way of love, and never gave her any indication that she meant anything to him.

Fixed in gloom at her desk, Etty thought about her parents. Ma would have been furious, she thought. She would have told her that the baby was no more than she deserved. Perhaps though, with Da's loving intervention, Ma would have grown to accept and even adore the baby. Thinking about her parents, induced a deep sadness and longing that she hadn't acknowledged before. She now realised that she actually missed them.

Etty pulled herself together when the supervisor, entered the room. During her short career, she had a got on the wrong side of Miss Bell several times. Plainly though it was evident that the latter was jealous of her; since it was obvious Mr Harding favoured Etty. It was difficult to concentrate on her work when she felt tearful and drained. She left her desk, keeping her head down so no one might see her distress and hurried to the ladies' room.

Etty sat quietly in a toilet cubicle; the peace and seclusion calming her agitated state. She heard the main door swing open, and someone using her name. Keeping perfectly still, she listened intently.

'That Etty Watkins is so stuck up,' said a voice that Etty recognised as Violet Cummings, her arch rival. 'Anyone would think she owns the company.' Etty heard a match being struck and then smelt the cigarette smoke.

'Did you see her fussing around old man Harding?' The other voice Etty knew as Ellen Bidewells, a seamstress. The two were inseparable and always gossiping. 'No wonder he likes her designs; I wonder what else she does for him.'

'Anyway, how did she become a designer? I heard she just made clothes at home as a hobby – she's had no training.'

'She's from the north, isn't she?' remarked Ellen.

'Yeah, I heard she arrived without a job or anywhere to live, and that her family were taken in by Patrick Lawrence.'

'Who's Patrick Lawrence?'

'You know,' said Violet enthusiastically, 'that good looking society photographer; he photographs people for all the best magazines.'

'Oh, yeah, I know the one. I wouldn't mind getting my feet under his table.'

'It wouldn't do you much good, girl. You know what they say about him?'

Etty listened, hardly daring to breathe, lest she should be discovered.

'No, what do they say?' said Violet.

'He's supposedly bent – you know, a nancy boy.'

'No! I hadn't heard that.'

'What, surely you knew its common knowledge.'

'Well if it's true, that Etty Watkins needn't think that she's so grand then, that's a turn up for the books, ain't it? Come on if you've finished your cigarette we'd best get back.'

Etty heard the tap running then door creak open and swing closed. She emerged stunned from the cubicle. She stood and stared at her reflection in the mirror above the sinks. She couldn't believe what she had heard, surely it wasn't true.

'Well, I will prove them wrong,' Etty said to her reflection. 'If it's true then surely, he could be cured, hadn't a friend's brother who was purported to be a nancy boy been made well again, he'd married and had children after all. I'll marry him and become Mrs Patrick Lawrence that will show them.' Etty nodded at her reflection in the mirror as if to seal the deal. Thus, satisfied and determined, she returned to her desk smiling broadly at Violet as she sat down. She wasn't going to let on she had overheard them. Trying to return to her design with renewed enthusiasm, it wasn't long before her thoughts preyed on her and she became tired and dispirited again.

Eliza Jane was making up the fire in Patrick's study and although she was busy, her thoughts were of Etty. She hoped that her sister would come home early so they could talk. She needed to know the truth. Sitting back on her heels, Eliza Jane wiped away a stray hair with the back of her hand, leaving black streaks from the coal dust on her face. It had suddenly occurred to her that the baby must have a father.

Eliza Jane was waiting in the kitchen when Etty returned from work. She looked pale and tired and Eliza Jane's eyes went straight to her belly. 'Etty, we have to talk,' she said with arms folded tightly

'Not now, Lizzie, I'm tired. I'm going to my room.'

'What about your dinner?'

'Not hungry.' She brushed past Rory, as he entered the kitchen.

'Whatever is Etty's rush – have you two had another fight?'

'No,' Eliza Jane replied with determination, 'not yet.' She followed Etty out of the door and climbed the stairs to Etty's room.

She knocked on the door and without waiting for an answer, she turned the handle and walked in.

Etty, who was lying on her bed, sat up quickly as Eliza Jane burst in. 'I said I didn't want to talk about it, Lizzie,' she warned, she had never seen her sister so purposeful before.

'Well I do, Etty, we need to get this sorted, it won't go away all by itself.' She sat on the edge of the bed and took Etty's hand in hers. 'Come on, I just want to help, talk to me please, you're having a baby, aren't you?'

Etty stared at the floor, how could she tell Eliza Jane that she was having David Jackson's child, it would break her heart, she just couldn't do it to her. She threw back her head and laughed loudly. 'Having a baby, good gracious Lizzie, what a thing to say, don't be so daft.'

'So your sickness a while ago was nothing, and I know you haven't had your monthlies for ages.'

'The sickness was temporary, probably a delayed reaction to the problems we have had to contend with, and I have washed my own rags out, why should you have to do it all.'

'I don't believe you, Etty. I know what I saw the other night. Come on, tell me.'

The silence filled the room then suddenly Etty held her head up high and looked her sister straight in the eye.

'Yes, I am going to have a baby, satisfied now.'

Eliza Jane ignored the sarcasm in Etty's voice and continued her steady questioning.

'Does the father know?'

'No, and it's none of his business.'

'Etty, is it Patrick, is he the father?'

Etty laughed ironically. 'After what I've heard today, you don't know how funny that is.'

'What have you heard?'

'Oh nothing, Lizzie, like I said, I don't want to talk about it.' Etty was determined that Eliza Jane was to be protected. 'So don't go on about it, all right.'

'Then I shall have to tell Thomas and he will see that you marry this man whoever he is.'

Etty didn't want Thomas or Patrick or anyone else to know. 'If I tell you, Lizzie, will you promise not to get upset and keep it to yourself?'

'Why should I get upset?' Eliza Jane laughed uneasily.

'Because it's David, David Jackson, he's the father.'

Eliza Jane searched Etty's face for signs that it was a joke, but she gained no such reassurance. Shrinking back from her sister, Eliza Jane stood up and doubled over clutching her stomach as if in pain.

'No!' she shrieked. 'How dare you tell such lies? I won't believe it, how can even sit there, and be so cruel.'

'Lizzie, please, look at me.' Etty tried to grab Eliza Jane's hands but was pushed away. 'Lizzie, you have got to listen to me, it's true, it's all true. It only happened once,' she said, as if that would make Lizzie feel better.

'Once was obviously all it took!' she yelled. 'How could you do this, only whores get pregnant out of wedlock? Ma and Da have would have been heartbroken. Not only that but you've let down the rest of us. What do you think William would have said? He'd have been horrified. Thomas will have to be told, and I don't know what Patrick will say when he finds out – he'll probably order us to leave.' Eliza Jane sank back on to Etty's bed and buried her face in her hands as her tears fell. 'Oh Etty what will become of us,' she murmured through her fingers.

Etty was incensed at the mention of her fiancé. 'How dare you bring William into this? I loved him with all my heart! If he'd survived the war, then I'd have been married, and this thing with David would never have happened. So, don't you preach William at me, it's all his fault for being killed!' Etty was trying to ignore her rising guilt, which was robbing her of her breath. 'Ma always said,' she continued, 'no good would come of me, and I'd be the death of her – so I suppose she has been proved right. According to Patrick's doctor, I'm four and a half months gone – so there's much I can do about it, is there?'

Eliza Jane stopped crying and lifted her tear streaked face. 'You mustn't do anything silly. Promise me you won't. It's David's baby too. Let me tell you this, Etty Watkins, if you don't tell him, then I will.' Eliza Jane swallowed hard before managing to add, 'I know he'll ask you to marry him; he'll do the gentlemanly thing.'

'I don't want to marry him – I don't love him. And I'll tell him about the baby if and when I'm ready – so don't you dare interfere with my business.'

Eliza Jane rose to her feet in anger. 'You allowed him to make love to you when you didn't even care about him? Your morals lie in the gutter – I'm ashamed to call you my sister.'

'I do care about him but only as a friend. There's no need to be so vile, Lizzie, but then I suppose you're speaking as a dried up prudish old virgin with no hope of ever getting a man to love her. It's such a pity that David never wanted to make love to you, especially as you've been hopelessly in love with him for years. Why you live for the few hurriedly written lines that he sends you every so often that masquerade as a letter, I really don't know. It would be laughable if it wasn't so pathetic.'

Eliza Jane struck Etty across the cheek with an open hand. 'How dare you!' she yelled.

Shocked to the core Etty covered her burning cheek with her own hand. 'I dare because it's true,' she spat out, then springing from her bed, she scrambled out of the room, slamming the door behind her.

All was not well at Wescott Manor that evening. As Helen had hoped, Lord Giles was waiting for her on her return from her next outing with Rory. She smiled to herself when he summoned her to his study, her plan was obviously working. It was just a pity she had to involve Rory, he was, it seemed, a little sweetheart and Helen regretted using him for her own ends. Lady Giles had retired early, leaving her husband to sort out their little problem.

'I trust you had a pleasant evening, my dear,' Lord Giles began amiably enough. He was sitting behind an oversize mahogany desk bequeathed to him by his father. In Lord Giles' view, the larger the desk the more important the person.

Helen sat on the arm of her father's chair and swung her free leg. Her father smelled of cigars and spirits. The top of the brandy decanter lay on the desk.

'Why, yes, Papa, very pleasant. Thank you,' she responded. 'He is such a sweetheart. Don't you think so; I know Mummy loves him.' She placed a quick peck on to her father's bald dome, then moved off the arm of the chair and sat on the stool by the fire. She held her hands out to warm herself.

'Have you a cigarette, Papa?'

Lord Giles opened his silver cigarette box and handed her one. She rose from the stool and placing the cigarette between her lips, she bent over to receive the flame from her father's lighter, the cigarette lit she inhaled deeply.

'Did you want to see me for any other reason, Papa?' She asked fixing her blue eyes on her father's face.

Lord Giles gazed fondly at his daughter, she was his world, and he loved her dearly. He had no idea how he could put a stop to this disastrous relationship and while his beautiful daughter stood smiling at him, it was difficult to think. 'Helen, your mother and I are concerned that this young man is of very lowly birth and plainly not one of us…' He began.

'Oh, phooey papa, the class system is rapidly becoming outdated. Queen Victoria has been dead some while now but you and mummy still seem to be living in the past.'

'Nonsense, my dear, England is built on the class system. Mother and I just feel that perhaps you should think carefully about what you are doing.'

'But I have, Papa, I have given it some serious thought. I like him, he's fun and I intend to see him again tomorrow.' Having planted that further nugget in her father's brain, she said, 'Well, I'm whacked; I must go to bed.' She turned towards the door then turned back. 'Goodnight, dearest.' She dropped a light kiss on the top of her father's head, stubbed out her cigarette in the ashtray on his desk then turning swiftly she swept out of the room.

Lord Giles poured himself another brandy, took a large gulp and then another. *Daughters!* he thought, why were women so bloody difficult.

Chapter 27

Eliza Jane hated falling out with Etty but it seemed to be something that was happening with alarming regularity. She was still feeling tearful as she brought Etty's harsh words to mind. She and Jim were walking back through the park in silence from their evening at the picture house. They had gone to see Charlie Chaplin in A Day's Pleasure; which Eliza Jane had been looking forward to.

'Blimey, Eliza Jane, you're quiet. You look like you lost a shilling and found a tanner. I know the picture wasn't one of Chaplin's best but you didn't even crack a smile. It's nothing I've done, is it?'

Eliza Jane smiled in spite of her disconsolate state.

'That's better,' said Jim, 'you're not half a good-looking gal when you smile yer know.'

'Oh, Jim, now you're really making me laugh,' she said, shaking her head at his stupidity. 'I've never been what you might call good looking but do you really think that about me?'

'You had better believe it, ducks – I don't know why you doubt yourself?'

'All through my life, people have compared me to Etty and Molly. They have the looks while I'm considered to be the practical one.'

'I meant what I said you are beautiful to me.' He took her hands in his and squeezed her fingers reassuringly. 'But somefings up with you so why not tell me all about it.'

Eliza Jane hesitated, if she told Jim about the baby and what Etty had called her, would he ever want to see her again? She couldn't risk it, but on the other hand, it would be nice to get his advice. She swallowed hard. 'Shall we sit down, Jim, just for a moment, I need to say something.'

Jim was worried, he was beginning to love this girl, and he couldn't face the fact she might not want to see him again. He sat down heavily beside her preparing himself for the worst.

'I don't know where to begin.' She took a deep breath. 'Etty said something to me yesterday that I can hardly bring myself to tell you.'

As the memory of Etty's words stung her again, Eliza Jane bit hard on her lip.

'I'm all ears, Lizzie, what's been said that's so terrible.'

Eliza Jane hesitated, swallowing hard.

'Come on, girl, it can't be that bad, she's yer sister for god's sake.'

'We were having an argument and Etty called me a dried up, prudish old... I'm sorry, Jim, but I can't repeat the last word she used, I'm too embarrassed.'

Jim was furious on Eliza Jane's behalf. 'Why on earth would she say something like that? What an 'orrible thing to say.'

'She's probably right, Jim, I'm all those things.'

He smiled, pulling her to him and giving her an enormous hug. 'Don't ever let me hear you say that again; you're insulting me too you know. Let me tell you if I 'ad to choose between you and your Etty, then I know who it would be – the gorgeous girl I have in my arms right now.'

Eliza Jane struggled to regain her composure; she wasn't sure that it was right to be hugging Jim in a public park. 'You haven't met her or Molly yet,' she said, 'wait 'till you do, then you won't look at me twice.'

'So, what was the argument about then?' asked Jim, reluctantly releasing her.

Eliza Jane hesitated, but knew she could trust him. 'Jim, if I tell you something, you won't think any less of me or my family, will you?'

'Course not, nothing you could say would alter my opinion of you – absolutely nothing.'

'Etty's going to have a baby.'

Jim was puzzled: new babies in his family meant celebrations and lots of knitting. 'But that's good news. Isn't it?'

Eliza Jane looked anxiously at the man she was beginning to care for. 'She's not married, Jim.'

'Whose baby is it, and is he going marry her?' Jim's voice sounded harsh. In his book, men stood up to their responsibilities and did the right thing.

'You remember I told you that I was writing to a man called David Jackson back home in Crossdale?'

'Oh, 'im, the one you used to work with, is he the father?'

Eliza Jane nodded, tears beginning to brim in her eyes as she thought of Etty's betrayal. She hastily wiped them away before Jim noticed.

'Well, there's a turn up for the books and no mistake. So, is he going to stand by her?'

'He doesn't know and she refuses to tell him, she's just burying her head in the sand, and hoping it will go away. She hasn't actually told any of us, but I guessed and asked her out right. I'm worried now because I threatened to tell David if she didn't. I may have gone too far, but I think he has a right to know.'

Jim gave out a long slow whistle. 'You're right; he needs to know the truth. Listen, if I were you, Lizzie, I would encourage Etty to tell 'im 'erself – don't interfere. You could always ask your bother Thomas, you know, discreetly like, and get his opinion.'

'I couldn't, Jim, Thomas has had enough to deal with, and he's only just beginning to look happy again. News like that could set him back months.'

'Well tell Molly then, she's a woman. She would know what's best to do.'

'I'm not making excuses, Jim, really, but Molly's also got troubles of her own, and don't suggest telling Patrick, because he might ask us to leave his house, and we've got nowhere else to go. The more I think about it, the more I know this has to be our secret, Etty's and mine, and that's how it should stay until she decides what to do.'

They fell silent for a while, staring ahead. She thought it would have made her feel better telling Jim, but now she sensed a sudden gulf between them. She touched his arm. 'Jim, we're having a big dinner up at the house for Rory's birthday, I'm cooking. Would you like to come and meet the family? Don't feel you have to but I would like it if you did.'

Jim hesitated for a moment. 'When was you thinking of girl?'

'Saturday evening; Rory's friend, Lady Helen, is also coming as well as Molly and her friend Jo. Etty, Thomas and Patrick will be there too.'

Jim was silent for a moment and Eliza Jane sensed his reluctance.

'I'm not sure I'm up to dining with a titled lady.' He sounded doubtful, but then he smiled. 'Of course I'll be there – miss a chance of sampling your cooking, not flaming likely. I'll send you up the best rib of beef I have from under the counter. Now come on, gal, it's getting brass monkeys, let's go home.'

Finally, Rory had managed to take Helen to the National Gallery to view his painting. She had hung on to his arm, as they wandered around and had been suitably enthusiastic about his talent. Rory glowed with pride as she congratulated him on his achievement. Shortly after they had viewed his painting,

Helen said was tired and suggested they take cocktails at the American bar at the Savoy. She hailed a taxi before Rory could demure and they alighted at the Strand.

'I don't have much money on me,' Rory hissed, as Helen led the way into the hotel.

'Oh, phooey darling, we will charge everything to papa, there is no need to panic; come on, two Manhattan cocktails are just what we need.'

Against Rory's better judgement, they were soon seated in comfortable chairs with their cocktails on the round table in front of them. The opulence of the American bar was surprising, the many lights glowed brightly and were reflected in the huge gilt mirror behind the bar, giving an artificial feeling to the room. Rory nearly choked on the price of the drinks but Helen took over and ordered the waiter to charge it to Lord Giles' account.

'Yes, Lady Helen,' came the reply much to Rory's surprise, she was obviously known in the bar. Rory memorised the cost of the drinks vowing to pay Lord Giles back when he had saved the money. He felt uncomfortable in the surroundings for he had only ever drunk the occasional beer at home before, not previously being old enough for visits to the Bluebell with Da and Thomas. He tried to relax and look as if he was used to drinking cocktails. Helen was amused as she looked at him. Poor chap was a lamb to the slaughter but he had suited her purpose very well. She felt it wouldn't be long before she would be the proud owner of a new automobile and if her father demanded she give Rory up to achieve it, then so be it.

'Well, birthday boy,' she said, 'I'm looking forward to meeting your family on Saturday. It's such a novel idea cooking a celebratory meal at home; Papa always takes me to the Ritz for my birthday.'

'Actually, Patrick wanted us to go to the Ritz for my birthday but Eliza Jane wasn't comfortable with that and suggested cooking at home. She's a wonderful cook, you will love it.'

'How delightful, Rory, it will be such fun to be with everyone. I know I'll enjoy it enormously.' She reached for her drink and drained the contents before putting it down on the table. She rose to her feet. 'Now, what would you like for your birthday – no don't tell me, it shall be a surprise. I have the very present in mind, and I can't wait for you to open it. Now kiss me, dearest, for I must go, I have an appointment I can't get out of.'

Rory attempted to prolong the farewell kiss but Helen drew away. 'Naughty boy,' she said, playfully slapping his shoulder. 'That's more than enough of that. You're very sweet, dearest, but I must be off. I'll see you with a whopping present on Saturday. Johnson shall drive me, so don't worry.' And with a final peck on the cheek, Helen walked away.

Chapter 28

Saturday dawned crisp and cold with a hint of frost on the ground. It was December the sixteenth, nine days to Christmas. Thomas, changing into his uniform in his shared room hummed to himself as he got ready for work. Tonight, Jo would be with them at Rory's birthday party, and he was greatly looking forward to seeing her again. With a bit of luck, he could take her home, provided Patrick didn't offer her a lift in his car. In fact, Thomas thought about asking Patrick if he could borrow his car. He felt quite capable of driving as part of his job at the hotel was to park the guests' cars.

He sat on the edge of his bed to tie his shoelaces and reflected on how far the family had come. He had to admit they would have struggled without Patrick. He was beginning to like him and perhaps even understand him but was still not entirely comfortable in his company; Patrick seemed few real friends but many acquaintances, but they still knew very little about him. Thomas acknowledged that the rest of the family seemed to think the world of him, particularly Etty, but unusually she didn't seem to be making much headway whereas men generally squabbled over her like birds fighting for a piece of bread.

He straightened up and positioned himself in front of the mirror, gazing at his reflection. As usual, he tried to dampen down his hair that stood up for fine weather. Ma had told him he had a double crown, which was supposed to be lucky. He had to admit he hadn't seen much evidence of that.

Thomas turned his thoughts to Rory, twenty years old today, but still very immature really. He regularly questioned his decision not to tell Rory about his true parentage, but would always arrive at the same answer; it would break his heart and serve no purpose. This was a secret he simply could not share. He had completely forgotten that he had confided in Patrick one night, having drunk more whisky than was good for him.

Eliza Jane, knowing the day would be spent cooking, decided to escape for some fresh air in the morning and took a walk to the park. Jim had sent up a magnificent rib of beef with a young lad on a bicycle earlier that morning and it stood proudly on the kitchen table waiting to be cooked.

She hoped by walking to the park she might see Ronald; she hadn't seen him for some time, and was beginning to miss him. She put on her coat, hat, gloves and scarf and set off at a brisk pace. After heading through the park gates, she made for her usual seat, and was pleased to see Ronald sitting muffled up against the cold on his usual seat opposite.

'Hello, Ronald, it's me, Eliza Jane, how are you?' She touched his arm, as she sat down beside him.

'Eliza Jane, how wonderful, I was just thinking about you. I hoped I'd see you today, if you know what I mean.'

'Well, here I am.' Eliza Jane pulled her scarf further into her neck and shivered; she had become warm walking and now suddenly felt cold. 'I don't know how you can sit here, Ronald, it's right chilly and is it safe for you to sit on your own in the park. I mean, you don't know who's around, you could be robbed.'

'I'm quite safe, Eliza Jane, if you look towards the park gates, you'll see my chauffeur's there, and watching everything that happens. Now tell me everything you've been doing, but first you can wish me many happy returns, it's my birthday today.'

'Is it? For heaven's sake, it's my brother's birthday today too. Well, happy birthday to you too. Are you celebrating; we're having a big party at my employer's house, and I'm doing all the cooking?'

'Which brother do you mean? The one that's lucky enough to look like me,' he smiled, 'or your older brother.'

'Rory, the one that looks like you.'

'I really would love to meet him one day?'

'I'll arrange it,' she said, suddenly struck with sadness for him for his blindness meant he would never be able to see the likeness. Her empathy made her bold enough to ask the question that had been worrying her. 'Will your eyesight ever come back Ronald, can you see anything?'

'I can tell the difference between light and dark, the doctors say its shock that caused it mainly due to my experiences in the war, but they believe it's only temporary. To tell you the truth, I don't hold out much hope of it returning, it's been eighteen months now. Sometimes I relive the pictures in my mind, hallucinations they're called. I'm back in the trenches with the smell of death all around me, I stand on the banks of river gushing forth red blood, then I look down and, in my arms, I see…' – he paused briefly – I cannot not tell you, Eliza Jane, just believe me these visions are horrific.'

Eliza Jane touched his arm; she hardly knew what to say to comfort him.

'I'm going to pray for you, Ronald, though I'm not sure God will listen – I rather abandoned him when Ma and Da died, and I haven't really acknowledged him since.'

'God will be keen to gather you back to the fold then, so let's hope he listens to you because unfortunately I also gave up on him a long time ago.'

Molly and Jo were both working until six o' clock that evening. Jo had brought her dress to work, so she could change for dinner in Molly's bedroom. It had been a busy day and much to Jo's disgust, she had been caught alone in the stock room by Mr Gambon. She told Molly about it while eating their sandwiches in the staff room. 'The cheek of the man,' she said, 'there must be something we can do about it.'

'What man?'

'Goggle-eyed Gambon; he had his hands all over me in the stock room, and he tried to kiss me. I had to push him really hard, and he fell onto some stock boxes. Then he had the nerve to tell me if I did that again, I'd be sacked.'

Molly tried to suppress a giggle, as she pictured the scene of Mr Gambon sprawling on the floor. 'What, he can't sack you. What did you do?'

'I just left him there and walked out. Honestly. Moll, someone has to stop him, he's a menace. There's absolutely nothing we girls can do about it. We should all band together, they can't sack all of us if we complain. Maybe we should go on strike, after all, if the men can do it. why not us.'

'Why don't you tell Mrs Roberts, I mean, the general about it?'

'Remember Lucy Gray?'

'That timid girl on jewellery, you mean?'

'Yes, that's the one – she made the mistake of telling the *general* when old Gambon did the same to her – and we never saw her again. That's quite a few girls lost their job because of him. Just promise me one thing though – next time I'm in the stock room and you see goggle-eyed Gambon heading for the door, just come and rescue me, otherwise I might also find myself out of a job.'

'Agreed,' said Molly firmly.

Jo took a bite of her sandwich and looked at Molly out of the corner of her eye.

'I'm really looking forward to tonight, Moll, I'm just sorry Kit decided he couldn't come.'

'I expect he had good reason, Jo, but it was disappointing. Things just aren't working out the way I hoped, I felt sure we liked each other.'

'He is always busy, Moll, try not to take it personally, I know he likes you.' Jo attempted to reassure her friend, she sighed inwardly, Kit must decide what he was going to do about Nora before Molly got hurt.

They continued eating in silence.

Lord Giles was pacing the floor of the library at Westcott Manor; Lady Helen sat demurely on an upright chair against the large mahogany table watching him. He suddenly stopped pacing and sat down opposite his daughter. He looked at her determined face before saying, 'Helen, I forbid you to go to that young man's dinner party tonight. This relationship must stop, before it becomes serious. Why he's probably a fortune hunter, I've met his sort before. I mean what sort of life could he provide for you? At best, he could house you in some slum dwelling in a backwater somewhere, with three or four children hanging around your apron strings. You'd be forever wondering where your next penny would be coming from, and I certainly would not be prepared to help you financially. If you pursue this relationship, then I will see to it you are cut off without a penny.' Her father flung his hands in the air. 'He'll never manage to attract the clientele that Patrick Lawrence has acquired to start his own studio. Lawrence has breeding and that matters. Why his father is the deputy Governor of the Bank of England. I know he and Sir Rollo fell out for some reason but you must see he has class, my dear, unlike your blacksmith's son.'

'He has a name, Papa, and it is Rory, and I really cannot believe you are holding Patrick Lawrence up as a fine example. Surely you have heard the rumours about him? Are you not aware of the gossip as to why he fell out with his parents?'

'Unfounded rumours, my dear. There has never been the slightest whiff of impropriety concerning Patrick Lawrence. He fell out with his parents over him going to America before the war – your mother was told that directly by Lady Lawrence herself.'

'There's no smoke without fire, Papa, that is all I am saying. Now let me remind you, that Rory is an accomplished artist – he has a painting in the National Gallery.'

'Yes, of his common blacksmith father.'

Helen decided she should squeeze out a tear to help her case, and she allowed one drop to slide down her cheek. 'Oh, Papa, have you no heart, I want to be with him, and I want to attend his party. Please, Papa.'

Lord Giles was distressed to see his daughter in tears and almost lost his resolve. He cleared his throat and tried to speak in a conciliatory manner.

'You must see this from our point of view, Helen. This is making your mother ill.' He paused; his words were having little effect. 'No, I'm sorry but I have to forbid this relationship, and so does your mother. I wish we'd never decided to pay for your *Tatler* photograph – a sheer waste of money if you ask me.'

Helen was about to agree, saying that she never wanted be photographed in the first place, but her father continued, changing his tone of voice. 'Now, my dear,' he said quietly, 'your mother and I are keen that you should meet Lord Ashman's son, Johnny again. He has just gained a very respectable degree from Cambridge, and has been taken on by a firm of actuaries. He would make a very suitable husband. Why Ashman and I were only saying at the club—'

Helen snorted loudly, talking over her father. 'From what I remember of Johnny Ashman, he is still wet behind the ears. Forget it, Papa, I don't wish to meet him. It's Rory I love, and Rory I shall marry.'

Lord Giles pushed a large veined hand through his almost non-existent hair then sank into a chair by the table. He looked at his daughter standing defiantly in front of him. 'What if we come to some little agreement?' he wheedled.

'I'm listening.'

'How would a trip to Paris in the spring suit you? Your mother is keen to go to see the fashions – though heaven knows why, whatever she wears looks like a sack on her.'

Helen stamped her foot. 'If you think a trip to Paris will make me forget the man I love, then you don't know me very well.'

'On the contrary, I know you well enough, so here's my final offer. Promise me you'll never see this Rory again, and I'll ensure that you and mother visit Paris with a large expense account. You can visit all the best fashion houses.

However, before you go, I think there maybe just time to purchase you an automobile of your own. What do you say, do we have a deal?'

Helen pulled a face. 'It will be very hard to give up Rory, Papa, but perhaps in time I can try to forget him.'

It was much later, when Lord Giles was confidently recounting the agreed deal to his wife that Lady Giles remarked how easily her daughter had agreed to his terms. Adding that she wondered just who had played whom.

The table in the dining room looked magnificent. Eliza Jane had polished the silver cutlery and candlesticks until they gleamed. She had placed a candelabra at either end of the table. She stood back proudly to admire her efforts then began to doubt herself. Was it too much? She wondered if Jim would feel out of place, but then Lady Helen would expect nothing less she reasoned. If only Ma was here, she would know what to do.

The kitchen door opened and Etty entered the room in a conciliatory manner. She looked beautiful and Eliza Jane felt a sharp stab of jealousy. Her pregnancy gave her skin a translucent glow.

She came and stood before Eliza Jane and reached for her hands. 'Lizzie, we mustn't fight. I'm just so worried about what I'm going to do.'

Eliza Jane gathered Etty in her capable arms, realising that was as near to an apology as Etty would ever make. 'I'm sorry, Etty, for insisting that David be told, it is your choice to make. Jim made me see that.' As soon as the words were out of her mouth, Eliza Jane knew she had said too much.

'You told the butcher,' Etty shouted, pushing her sister away, 'how could you discuss me with the butcher.'

'He's not the butcher, Etty, he's my friend. I needed to discuss my worries with someone and you didn't want Thomas or Molly told, so what was I supposed to do.'

'Just stay out of it, that's what I want you to do, just stay out of my life.' Etty turned on her heel and made for the door slamming it behind her.

Chapter 29

At seven o' clock, the family, Patrick and Jo gathered in the drawing room to await the other guests. Patrick began by pouring champagne for them all. The girls, apart from Etty, were excited, they had never tasted champagne before, and they giggled as bubbles rose to the top of their glasses.

'I can't taste it,' complained Molly laughing, 'the bubbles get in the way.'

Etty was sitting elegantly on the leather sofa, sipping daintily from her glass. She found the champagne rather dry for her taste but was not going to admit that she didn't like it to anyone. Besides, she preferred gin, and had already imbibed two glasses from Patrick's decanter that evening to help her relax.

'This is one of the best champagnes I've ever had, Patrick.' She pouted, raising her glass as a trophy.

'For heaven's sake, Etty,' Thomas laughed, 'get over yourself; it's the only champagne you've ever had.'

'Maybe, Thomas' – she smiled, inwardly seething – 'but I intend to have a lot more in the future.'

'Refills all around I think,' Patrick enthused, holding the half-empty bottle, 'and a toast to the birthday boy.'

'Would you mind if we wait until Helen arrives?' said Rory, looking at his new Cartier watch, a present from Patrick. 'I'm sure she won't be long.'

Etty was disgusted that such a present should be wasted on her young brother.

'Looking at that expensive watch won't make the time pass any faster,' she said, barely able to contain her envy.

Rory failed to note the contempt in his sister's voice and said, 'I can't wait to see her. I know you're all going to love her.'

'We can open another bottle when she's here, Rory, so come on, and drink up.' Patrick continued to refill Rory's glass.

Eliza Jane excused herself to check on the progress of the meal.

'Do you need any help, Eliza Jane?' Jo asked.

'No, really Jo, you relax and enjoy yourself – you're a guest, but thank you for the offer.'

Eliza Jane hurried to the kitchen, taking her champagne with her; she went to the sink and tipped up her glass pouring the champagne down the hole. She shuddered, feeling bad at wasting money, but she really didn't like the taste and she wanted to keep a clear head. She was actually worrying about Jim. Where was he? Had he decided not to come after her revelations about Etty? She couldn't blame him; why would he want to associate with such an immoral family. Taking a cloth and a large spoon, she knelt down before the oven feeling the blast of heat as she opened the door. Drawing the meat tray out of the oven slightly, she scooped up the juices with the spoon and basted the meat. She relaxed slightly in the knowledge it was cooking well.

By 7.55 pm, however, there was still no sign of either Jim or Lady Helen. Eliza Jane could hear laughter from the drawing room through the half-open door. She was glad that no one else seemed to share her fears.

Rory wandered into the kitchen; he kept glancing at his watch.

'What time did you tell Lady Helen to come, Rory? I shall have to serve the soup soon, or the meal will be overcooked.'

'Half past seven – I can't think what's keeping her. I'm beginning to worry.'

The clang of the doorbell interrupted their conversation.

'There she is now, thank goodness.' Rory scrambled down the hall to the front door.

'Where have you…' He began, then stopped as he looked at the large man standing on the doorstep with a bunch of flowers in his hand.

'I'm ever so sorry for being late. I'm Eliza Jane's friend, Jim. I'm pleased to meet yer.'

'Oh,' Rory was nonplussed, 'sorry, I was expecting someone else, but please come in. I'm Rory.' He held out his hand and Jim shook it firmly.

'Happy birthday to yer, mate, like I said, I'm sorry I'm late but I've been halfway up a tree this evening.' Rory raised an enquiring eyebrow. 'Oh it's a long story, mate, but at least I've got here.'

Hearing his voice, Eliza Jane came out of the kitchen and joined Rory at the front door.

'There's my girl, ain't you looking the bee's knees, Lizzie, sorry I'm late, girl, I'll tell you the tale later. I 'ope I 'aven't messed up your meal.'

'Course not, Jim, we're still waiting for one more guest, aren't we, Rory? Come and meet the others.'

Eliza Jane took Jim's hand and dragged him into the drawing room. The girls were sitting on the sofa, Thomas was leaning an elbow on the mantelpiece, and Patrick was sitting with his legs crossed in an armchair. He stood up as Eliza Jane brought Jim into the room.

'Everyone, this is my friend James Harrison. Jim, this is Patrick who you probably know by sight.' Patrick came forward and shook Jim's hand.

'You are very welcome, James,' he said warmly. Eliza Jane continued with her introductions.

'Meet Thomas, my older brother.' Thomas shook his hand.

'Then there's Henrietta or Etty my sister; Molly my other sister, and her friend, Jo, from work, and Rory who you met at the door.'

'Pleased to meet yer all. Sorry I'm late but I've been halfway up a tree tonight – I'll explain later, and please call me Jim; Lizzie's given me my Sunday name.'

'She does that to people, she's very precise in what she says,' announced Etty coldly. She really felt she couldn't bear to even look at this man as he was privy to her secret but she responded to him by regarding him coolly, challenging him to admire her.

Patrick showed Jim to a chair and presented him with a glass of champagne, which he accepted doubtfully. Champagne was not really his drink. He laid it on the table next to him, as he had no wish to offend Patrick on such a short acquaintance.

Patrick noticed his predicament. 'Thomas, shall we have some beers? I've had enough fizz – perhaps you would like one too, Jim?'

'That would be wonderful, Mr Lawrence, thanks very much.'

'Call me Patrick please' – he looked at Rory – 'do you want a beer, birthday boy?'

'I wish you'd stop calling me the birthday boy. I'm 20 years old and hardly a boy.' Rory was irritated and worried that Helen should be so late.

A small silence followed.

'Where the hell is she,' muttered Rory. 'I told her 7.30, she can't keep us waiting like this.'

'I really need to serve dinner,' Eliza Jane said gently.

'I can't magic her up, can I?' he snapped back, then quickly checked himself. 'I'm sorry, everyone. I'm just a bit on edge.' He rose to his feet. 'I'll go outside and look up the road to see if I can see her. Why don't you all sit down at the table, I'm sure she'll be here soon.'

Rory left the room abruptly, letting the door bang behind him.

'Perhaps we should do as he suggests,' said Patrick, offering his arm to Etty to accompany to dinner.

'The table looks beautiful.' Jo breathed. She looked at the gleaming silverware glittering in the tall candlelight.

'Ma worked in the kitchens of a large house before she married Da, and she used to tell me tales of how they did things,' Eliza Jane said proudly, pleased that someone had noticed her hard work.

Soon they were all seated and Eliza Jane began to serve the soup. Patrick sat at one end of the table with Thomas at the other. Etty sat next to Patrick, Rory's place was on the other side of him. Next to Rory was a vacant chair for Helen, then Jo who was on the left of Thomas. Molly sat on the other side of Thomas, Eliza Jane and Jim completing the table.

'So, Jim,' said Patrick, 'tell us the tale of how you found yourself up a tree on your way here.'

'It's a bit of a long story really,' said Jim, laying down his soup spoon and wiping his mouth on his napkin. Jim loved telling a tale or two particularly to a large audience. 'Now you'll have to picture this, next door to our shop is a wool shop run by Miss Perkins and Miss Perkins has a cat, a ginger Tom – a beautiful looking animal and her pride and joy. One of Miss Perkins' regular customers has a large, spotted dog, Dalmatian I think they're called and when she visits the shop, she ties this huge dog up outside Miss Perkins' shop. Now because he can smell the meat coming from our shop, he begins to strain on his lead. To cut a long story a bit shorter, the dog breaks free form his lead, and dashes through Miss Perkins' wool shop to find his mistress. The cat asleep on the counter wakes up, sees the dog jumps down of his perch and flees through the back of the shop into the garden and straight up the tree, where he taunts the dog who's now in a barking frenzy at the bottom. The owner of the dog catches him and marches him off but the cat stays where he is. He's stuck. Miss Perkins distraught for her cat dashes into our shop calling for 'elp to get her cat down, and I think you can guess who offered their services.'

'Did you manage to get it down?' asked Thomas.

'Well, not straight away, coz every time I climbs up me ladder and gets 'igher up the tree, the cat climbs up 'igher as well, and we goes on like this for some time until I run out of ladder – then I spend the next hour calling it, and offering it bits of my best mince to encourage it down. Now, even my best mince didn't do the trick, and it just sits there yowling and looking at me with its big eyes. Proper ignoring me it was, and me mince as well. In the end. I tells Miss Perkins I'm going out to see my girl as I'm goin' to be late, but I promise 'er that I'll try again when I get 'ome. Well of course, as soon as I climbs down and puts me ladder away, the cat hops down branch by branch and starts to eat me best mince that I dropped. It seems 'e wasn't stuck up the tree at all.'

Rory flung open the door interrupting the laughter that followed Jim's story. They all looked at him. 'Any sign of Helen, Rory?' Eliza Jane asked.

Rory shook his head miserably. 'Something must have happened to her. I'm really worried.'

'Why not telephone her house,' suggested Patrick, 'to see if she's unwell.'

'Yes, yes, I'll do that, thank you, Patrick. I'll use your study if I may.'

'Of course, go ahead.' Patrick nodded his head in agreement.

Eliza Jane cleared the soup plates, leaving Rory's on the table for him. With Molly's help, she replaced them with hot dinner plates in preparation for the main course.

When Rory returned, he had a thunderous look on his face and the general babble of light-hearted conversation once again ceased as they all looked at him expectantly.

'Well? What's the news, is she coming or not,' asked Etty bluntly. 'I mean we can't hold up dinner for much longer.'

Rory glared at Etty. 'You're the sole of tact and wisdom as usual, Etty. First of all, *she* is called Helen, and secondly, we don't have to hold up dinner any longer, as Helen's not coming.'

'Not coming,' screeched Etty, 'to your birthday celebration, who does she think she is?'

'Rory,' said Eliza Jane gently, 'why is Helen not coming, is she ill?'

Using his fist, Rory banged the table, splashing some of the contents of the soup bowl on to the starched, white cloth. 'Helen is not coming because she's gone to another party with someone called Johnny Ashman.'

'The cow,' snapped Etty. 'Who did you speak to on the telephone?'

'I spoke to the butler, and he told me that she'd left the house an hour ago, having been picked up by Ashman. Oh, and she left me a message, should I bother to find out where she was.'

'Which was?' Etty said, seething for her brother.

'Something along the lines and I quote, that it had all been terrific fun while it lasted.'

'I'm so sorry, Rory,' said Patrick sympathetically. 'That must be very hard to hear.'

Rory picked up his wine glass and swallowed the contents down in one go. 'You don't understand, Patrick,' he said. 'I don't think you will ever understand how it feels to be in love.'

Etty immediately got up and refilled Rory's glass with wine, then added another measure to her own. She clinked Rory's glass against hers. 'Cheers brother dear, happy birthday and welcome to the world of adults,' she said before gulping down her wine and draining the glass. 'Well Patrick,' she challenged, 'what do you say to that, have you ever been in love?'

'Sit down, Etty,' demanded Thomas, 'you're embarrassing Patrick and making the rest of us feel very uncomfortable.'

'I'll sit down when I've got an answer to my question, what have you got to say for yourself, or are the rumours I've heard at The House of Harding true?'

Etty was swaying on her feet as she refilled her glass. Patrick remained silent, staring intently at his drink.

'Nothing to say for yourself, eh,' she continued. 'Well let me tell you what people are saying about you. They're calling you a nancy boy.' She leaned over him putting her face close to his. 'Did you know that?' Patrick challenged Etty with a look. She gazed solidly back at him.

'Etty,' warned Thomas, knowing his sister had drunk too much and not wanting to acknowledge his innermost fears that Etty was right. 'Eliza Jane is trying to serve the beef; can we please just get on with our meal.'

'Of course, let her serve the beef, I'm not stopping her,' said Etty returning to her seat but suddenly losing her balance and falling heavily into Jim's lap. Giggling, she placed her arm around his neck. 'Hello, Lizzie's butcher friend. Do you think I'm pretty? Patrick doesn't, do you, Patrick? He would probably find you prettier than me?' She laughed uproariously.

Jim smiled. 'Pretty is as pretty does is what my old Ma used to say. Now be a good girl, and go and sit down.'

Molly rose from the table and walked over and pulled Etty off Jim's lap. 'You're drunk, Etty, and you've spoilt the evening for us all, and on Rory's birthday too. How dare you speak to Patrick like that, just because he hasn't

fallen at your feet like most men, you've no right, now sit down and shut up.'
Molly returned to her own seat.

'On the contrary, I can say what I like,' Etty slurred. 'Anyway, it wasn't me who spoilt the evening; it was a certain lady la-di-da.'

'Please don't call her that,' said Rory resorting to the whining voice that the others were all familiar with, when he was under pressure. 'I love her. Why wouldn't she come? I thought she loved me. She said she had bought me a present, but I don't care about presents, I just want her to be here.'

'Perhaps the butler got the message wrong,' suggested Molly.

'Don't be ridiculous, Molly,' interjected Etty, 'don't fill his head with such twaddle, she's a prize monster that one, and no mistake.'

Embarrassed by Etty's performance, Jo attempted to bring some normality back to the room. 'We had a very amusing customer in the shop today, didn't we, Molly?'

Etty however was not going to allow any digression. 'We hardly wish to hear about your day, Jo, Grace, or whatever your name is, dear.'

Thomas rose from his chair, his eyes flashing, and a red spot of anger on each cheek, his hands shook with fury before he rubbed his neck. 'How dare you insult my guest?' he yelled.

'I thought she was Molly's guest not yours,' Etty fired back at him. 'Ah, I see it now – our Thomas has a secret crush on your friend, Molly.'

Thomas was silenced, stunned in embarrassment.

'Shut up, shut up, shut up!' Rory hollered, saliva hurtling from his mouth. 'This is my birthday. The girl I love hasn't bothered to come to my special dinner, and all you're doing Etty, is upsetting everyone. Well, I've had enough of this; I can't take it anymore.'

Jim looked at Eliza Jane; her eyes were filling with tears and her lip trembling. He silently took her hand. Patrick stood as Rory threw his napkin down onto the table and marched towards the door.

'Where are you going?' Eliza Jane called to him, rising from her seat.

'To go hang,' he replied marching purposefully to the door of the dining room. Memories of overhearing the word spoken by Mrs Fanshawe leapt into Eliza Jane's mind striking terror into her heart. She screamed before fainting. When she came to and opened her eyes, her head was being cradled by Jim. She glanced over to where Patrick and Thomas were wrestling a struggling Rory to the ground. He was shouting that he should be allowed to kill himself and she screamed again.

Once Rory had been pushed down in his chair and was sitting sullenly gazing into his glass and Eliza Jane was recovered and sitting by him, Jim suggested he should leave.

'Perhaps I should go 'ome, Lizzie, I think you just need to be with each other right now.'

Eliza Jane looked up at him, she felt so tired and guilty about the evening as if it had been all her fault. 'You haven't had your dinner yet, Jim, and it was a beautiful rib of beef that you gave us, please stay.'

'No, girl, I'll see yer soon, promise.'

'I think I'll come too,' said Jo, sensing the party was well, and truly over, she started to get to her feet.

'I will see Miss Howard home,' offered Jim.

Thomas looked at Jo in desperation; she in turn sensed their need to talk.

'I'll see you at rehearsal tomorrow night, Molly.' She threw a reassuring glance at Thomas before following Jim out of the room. 'Goodnight, all.'

Exhausted and withdrawn, Patrick slowly got to his feet to see them to them to the door.

Rory continued to sit sullenly in the chair that he had been placed in by Thomas and Patrick. He felt more angry than ashamed, furious with them for manhandling him, and even more furious with Etty for causing all the trouble. He kept his eyes downcast into the bowl before him, apparently concentrating on the remains of his soup.

Patrick returned and slumped wearily into his chair at the table refusing to look at anyone he swallowed the remainder of his wine. When your whole world collapses, silence was your best defence.

Eliza Jane whose pallor was beginning to return to normal, tried to comfort her morose brother. 'We love you, Rory, please don't put us through what Da did to us, we couldn't…'

Eliza Jane suddenly stopped mid-sentence, realising she had said too much.

Etty quickly rounded on her. 'What do you mean, *what da did to us.*'

Thomas hurriedly tried to rescue Eliza Jane. 'Both Da and Ma's death was a great shock to us, that's what she meant. We couldn't go through it again.'

Etty was not about to let things go. 'Bbut you said *after what Da did to us*, Lizzy. What did Da do to us? After all, he couldn't help dying, so what was it he did to us?'

Patrick, having been confided in previously realised that Thomas was being put under pressure to explain the secret of his father's suicide. He took Etty's hand to avoid any further conflict. 'Etty, why don't you have an early night – you're overwrought; it's been an emotional evening. Leave it for now, there's nothing to be gained by discussing this now – just go to bed.' He looked across Rory at Eliza Jane, who nodded.

'If there's anything to say about Da, then I want to know too,' said Molly tearfully. 'What are you not telling us, Thomas?'

'I'm with Molly,' interjected Rory, suddenly awakening from his sullen mood, 'what secrets are you hiding from us, Thomas?'

Thomas looked at Eliza Jane, and then at Patrick, he sighed slowly and said quietly. 'I have some dreadful news, which I never ever wanted you all to know.'

'What are you talking about?' Etty snatched her hand from Patrick's grasp. 'It seems Eliza Jane is privy to this secret; and knows about this dreadful news, what is it?'

'Yes,' agreed Thomas wearily. 'Eliza Jane knew because she overheard Mrs Fanshawe talking in the post office. We kept it a secret for the best of reasons; we didn't want you all to be more upset, than you were. We wanted you all to believe in Da and his love for us, believe me; we stayed silent to protect you.'

Molly anxiously twisted her serviette between her fingers as she spoke, she looked from one sibling to another. 'Thomas, you're worrying us all now, and if you don't tell us, we can only imagine the worst.' She warned, her voice catching with emotion.

Thomas took another deep breath, 'Da didn't die of Bright's disease, he...'

'For God's sake Thomas,' shouted Etty, 'tell us!'

'Da took his own life; he hung himself in the smithy.'

Molly screamed loudly. 'No, Thomas, no, I don't believe you, how can you tell such lies.' She placed her hands over her ears to blot out her brother's words.

Rory went pale and said nothing.

The afternoon in the buttercup field with David Jackson flashed across Etty's mind, interspersed with horrific images of her father hanging from a rope on the very same day. She was suddenly engulfed by vitriol – someone must pay to assuage the feelings of guilt that was growing in her heart. She jerked to her feet, knocking her chair backwards onto the floor; it fell with such a clatter, it made them all jump.

'How dare you!' she screeched. 'How dare you keep something like that a secret? Who else was involved, who else helped you with your lies?'

'No one, I found a letter explaining things from Da.'

Etty rounded on Eliza Jane. 'And you! What did you overhear in the post office?'

'I overheard Mrs Fanshawe and Mrs Wimbourne talking in Emmet's shop; they'd heard certain gossip, so I confided in Thomas, who told me it was true.'

'So that just leaves one other person who I think knew about this.' She turned to Patrick. 'Perhaps someone could explain to me how it is that you came to know?'

'I told him, Etty.' Thomas got up and went to put an arm around a sobbing Molly. For god's sake, shut up – look at the shock on your brother and sister's faces that is why I kept it a secret.'

'You had no right to keep it a secret.' Etty kicked her chair out of the way and marched towards the door.

Eliza Jane watched her in disgust. 'What about you,' she yelled! 'You dare to take the moral high ground when you're keeping the biggest secret of all.'

Etty stilled for a moment, digesting Eliza Jane's comment.

She briefly considered her position and decided to deny the accusation. 'I don't know what you mean,' she replied her head held high, 'anyway, I'm going to bed, I've had enough for one night.'

'Oh, there she goes madam self-righteous.' Eliza Jane called after hers.

'I have no secrets.'

'You lie!'

'Etty,' snapped Thomas, 'what's this secret Eliza Jane's talking about?'

'You had better ask her,' Etty sneered. 'She seems to know all about it.'

'I'm asking you.'

'Well ask away, Thomas, because there's nothing to tell, now goodnight.'

As she began to close the door, she heard her sister say, 'Etty's having a baby.'

Etty banged the door on the stunned audience. She was making for the stairs when suddenly she felt a sharp pain deep within her. Groaning loudly, she hung on to the banister as she tried to climb the stairs to reach the sanctuary of her room, but the pain struck again. She put her hand down between her legs, it felt sticky. When she looked there was blood on her hand. Etty screamed for help as she doubled over in pain again.

The others flung the door open, rushing to her on the stairs.

'The baby,' she gasped, 'I'm losing the baby.'

Long after the doctor had come and the bleeding had stopped and the baby's heart beat pronounced strong, Patrick sat brooding into the night. The study fire had died down to a white ash, but there was still sufficient heat in the embers; not that he would have noticed the cold because he was deep in thought. He was feeling incredibly wounded that Etty should have heard such gossip about him. He was always very cautious about his private life, making sure he didn't frequent the bars or go down to Hoxton to meet the young men of the east end who would sell their favours at a price up back alleys. He tried to live a respectable life, he had built up the photographic studio steadily, his work now being much sought after. He was respectable and well liked, but he was also very lonely. Now his kind heart had finally caught him out. He had offered these five people a home and even jobs for two of them and as a reward, his life was beginning to be torn apart. Could he survive the scandal that was being brought to his door? Could he carry on, while his carefully built up reputation crumbled before him. The worst bit of it was he didn't know how to prevent it from happening.

Chapter 30

Eliza Jane carried the breakfast tray carefully up the stairs. She paused outside Etty's room, balancing the tray on her knee and holding it with one hand, she gently knocked on the door with the other.

'*Entre*,' came from within.

Ignoring Etty's affectation, Eliza Jane opened the door. 'Etty' – she put the breakfast tray down hurriedly – 'what are you doing up and dressed, the doctor told you to rest in bed for the next fortnight. For heaven's sake, get back to bed. Last night was a warning to you, take heed or you'll lose the baby.'

'I have to get to work – I cannot afford for Agatha Bell to pass off any more of my designs as her own.'

'Don't be silly, it won't happen,' soothed Eliza Jane. 'Come on, get back into bed.'

'It will happen. Listen, miss-goody-two-shoes, you've no idea what that woman is capable of. Why she told me that Mr Harding wouldn't like my latest designs because the hems were too short and the waist too low, but then she showed them to him as her own work and he loved them. They're now in production ready for the House of Harding Fashion show in April next year – designs by Agatha pour les jeunes femmes. Not only that, they say that Madame Gabrielle Souris will be visiting from Paris – imagine that, Lizzie, Gabrielle Souris will be looking at my designs but she won't know they are mine and that will give Violet Cummings an unfair advantage, she's already bragging about Mr Harding preferring her designs to mine. What if Madame Souris thinks the same?'

Etty may as well have been speaking Chinese, for Eliza Jane did not understand a word she was saying. She tried to reassure Etty. 'Well never mind about all that,' she coaxed, 'you must get back to bed and rest.'

'But I'm currently working on some new designs that are even more daring on the hemline. I am determined that Mr Harding will see these as designs by

Henrietta, so I have to go to work. The baby will be fine, the doctor said so, and if it isn't, well then that's a chance I have to take. Now go away, I need to make myself presentable.'

Etty strode to the door, holding it open for her sister. Eliza Jane knew she was beaten and retreated to the kitchen.

'How is she?' asked Thomas who was sitting at the table and lingering over a cup of tea.

'Determined to go to work, you know Etty.'

'I still can't believe it.' Thomas shook his head wearily. 'I don't know whether to be angry that she's landed in this mess, or sad that she didn't feel she could tell us. I mean, how long have you known?'

'I guessed,' said Eliza Jane, 'but she hasn't just got herself into this mess as you put it – there is a father you know.'

'Yes, whoever he is, he'll be made to pay when I find out. He'll have to support her; I'll make damned sure of that.'

'What if she doesn't want his support, what if she doesn't even want him to know?'

Thomas took a long hard look at Eliza Jane and discovering guilt in her face said, 'You know who it is, don't you?'

Eliza Jane shook her head. 'Etty must tell you, it's her decision. I promised.'

'Come on, Lizzie, remember we vowed to always be there for one another, tell me who the father is.'

'No, I promised Etty, I won't say unless she wants me to.'

'Patrick,' he suddenly shouted. 'He's the father, isn't he? Well so help me, I'll…' Thomas jerked upright from his seat. 'That's why she was baiting him last night – he's hurt her and she was making him pay as only Etty can.'

'Don't jump to conclusions until you've spoken to Etty.' Thomas made to leave, and she grabbed his arm. 'Where are you going? Don't do anything rash, please.'

'I'm going to work, I'm on with Wilson and he hates me enough to make my life a misery and I'm late.' He shrugged her off, slamming the kitchen door behind him.

Molly and Jo were already at work, and were starting to remove the covers from their counters while they talked.

'Really, Moll, stop apologising. None of last night was your fault. How is Etty this morning, I expect she has a king size headache.'

Molly forced a smile. 'I haven't seen her this morning but I expect you're right – she said some pretty weird things.'

Molly was careful not to say what had really transpired last night after Jo had left. As well as being ashamed of her sister, she felt an overriding concern for the baby. After all, the child was going to be her niece or nephew, and she was beginning to like the idea of becoming Aunt Molly.

Jo thought for a moment as if trying to find the right words, she wanted to know how Thomas felt about her but was shy of asking directly. 'Moll, do you think Etty meant what she said about Thomas, you know, and about me?'

'Etty spoke a lot of rubbish last night.' Molly began and Jo's heart lurched painfully. 'She had had too much to drink. All that talk about Patrick, why it's absolute nonsense; he's the nicest, kindest man in the world. I shouldn't let anything Etty says bother you.' Molly noticed the look of disappointment on Jo's face so continued, 'But on the other hand, I think she was right about Thomas's feelings bless him and I think you feel the same way.'

'I really like your brother, Moll, I do.'

'You need to talk to each other, Jo, it might surprise you what you find out.' As Molly uttered the words, she thought she needed to follow her own advice and talk to Kit again.

Rory and Patrick were keeping busy. Neither wanted to have the conversation that they needed to have. There was a detectable atmosphere between them and not only because Rory was suffering from a gigantic hangover, and had a terrible headache but because he was genuinely ashamed of his outburst. He should have seen Lady Helen for what she was, all that talk about women's rights did not equate with letting Rory spend his entire hard-earned wage on her. She used him; he could see that now. Well, no woman would ever treat him like that again.

At lunch time, they stopped for half an hour. Eliza Jane was out shopping so they sat in silence at the kitchen table, eating the remains of last night's soup.

'Rory, perhaps we should talk about the events of last night, clear the air, what do you think?'

'I don't wish to talk about last night ever. It was the worst night of my life. I found out that my father, who I loved, was a coward of the first order, and for that, I can't forgive him. I also discovered that the girl I thought was the sweetest, most compassionate and big-hearted champion for the underdog, was not what she seemed. I was used and I'll never let it happen again. I've learnt my lesson where women are concerned.'

'Don't judge all women by Helen's standards; that would be a great mistake. As for your father, remember how you felt last night when Helen didn't come to your party? Your father must have felt like that, only ten times worse when your mother died. He'd lived with your mother for well over thirty years. He knew he couldn't cope with life without her – surely you can understand that.'

'I think we had best return to work, Patrick, subject closed.'

Patrick got up and followed Rory through the door, as he did so, he blew out his cheeks in an explosive sigh. Buried in that sigh was the relief that another subject, one Patrick didn't want to talk about, had not been raised.

Thomas hurried up to the entrance of the hotel, straightening his hat and joined the other man already there. 'You're late, Watkins!' the man said, 'I don't like people being late on my watch.'

'I'm sorry, Mr Wilson, bit of a family crisis held me back but I'm here now.' Thomas took his place next to Bob Wilson, the senior commissionaire. He was a particularly nasty piece of work, and Thomas hated being on duty with him. Everything he did was criticised, which meant he often felt less than adequate in the job.

'You had better smarten up, man, or you'll be for the high jump if Cartwright gets to hear.'

'Yes, sir.'

Oh, but I forgot,' Wilson sneered, 'he wouldn't sack you in a hurry, would he?'

'What's that supposed to mean? 'Of course he would, I'm just an employee like you.' Thomas was becoming riled by Wilson's tone; he really didn't need this from him today. Thomas was tired and emotionally charged from the previous evening's events.

'Ah, but you're not really, are you, Watkins? You see that chap, Lawrence, who you're lodging with is very friendly with Mr Cartwright, in fact more than friends, in fact bedfellows you could say, if you get my meaning.'

'What are you talking about; Mr Lawrence doesn't know Mr Cartwright. I got this job on my own merits.' Thomas moved slightly away from this man who was baiting him, what was he playing at, Thomas was confused.

'Well, Watkins, you know what they say, don't you?' Wilson suddenly stood to attention and saluted. 'Morning, Mr Cartwright sir, nice morning, bit nippy but has the makings of a nice day.'

'Morning, Mr Wilson' – he looked over at Thomas and nodded – 'Morning Mr Watkins. How are you enjoying Claridge's?

'I am enjoying it very much, sir, thank you.'

'Well, Wilson, how is Mr Watkins getting along, is his work satisfactory; I have had reports he is a hard worker.' Thomas stood to attention.

'Mr Watkins is doing well, sir, under my direction, I am more than pleased with his progress.'

Mr Cartwright smiled. 'Good, that's the ticket, well keep up the good work.' He waved his hand behind him as Thomas opened the door and he disappeared through into the hotel. Thomas shut the door and resumed his stance next to Wilson.

'Thank you, Mr Wilson, I appreciate you telling Mr Cartwright that I am making good progress,' Thomas said gratefully.

'Well, it would look badly on me if I told him the real truth, wouldn't it?'

Thomas wondered what else he could do to get on the right side of the senior commissionaire.

'I don't know why you have taken a dislike to me, Mr Wilson, I try my best, I work hard, what have you got against me?' he asked.

'Yes, you work hard all right but I don't like what you stand for.'

'What do you mean what I stand for?'

'Well you're one of them, aren't you? Living with Lawrence and all. I know your job was given to you as a favour to a dear friend so to speak. Now that tells me you're probably part of their little game too. It was all so easy, wasn't it? All you had to do was turn up here looking good and you were admitted to the club, so to speak.'

Wilson coughed delicately into his hand as he spoke, raising his little finger at the same time in an effeminate gesture. Almost immediately, Thomas understood his meaning; Wilson thought he was a queer. How dare he! Without thinking of the consequences, Thomas flew at him, punching him solidly in the face. It made a horrible crack and the blood gushed from his nose.

Slightly dazed, Wilson staggered backwards holding his nose with his hand, he spoke viciously. 'You'll get sacked, Watkins, club or no club, or I'll personally see to it that your life is made a living hell,' he said

Thomas removed his cap, threw it on the ground, and shouted 'I quit' before walking as swiftly as his breathing would allow away from the hotel. His knuckles throbbed, his heart beat madly; he could feel it booming in his chest. He tried to steady his breathing, but was so incensed that it was proving impossible. He needed something to calm him down. He had only been drunk twice in his life, and although he hated the feeling, the thought of seeking oblivion in a bottle of whisky seemed more than appealing.

Thomas found a pub, he had no idea where he was, but after having walked for some while, he was pleased to sit at a small table on his own. There was little comfort in his surroundings; the pub had sawdust on the floor and a dim interior that matched his mood.

Swilling whiskey did little to calm his terrible anger. He drummed his fingers impatiently on the copper table while he tried to get his breath, before heading back to the bar for a refill.

'Are you all right, Ducks,' the bar maid said to him anxiously, worried by his flushed look and wheezy chest as she handed him another whiskey. Thomas nodded, as he slapped the money on the bar and slowly returned to his table. He stared down at his glass and thought about his life and his dear ma. He relived the panic of running for Doctor Green that morning when Ma had died. He remembered the agony of holding his da upright at the funeral. The horror of finding Da's suicide note and learning that Rory was not his true brother, came flooding back to him. The sadness of leaving Jack with Jacob Pennington brought tears to his eyes. He pictured sweet Jo in all her beauty, then in his imagination, he saw Patrick and Cartwright together, keeping secrets, laughing and plotting to get him a job because he wasn't able to achieve it on his own. No wonder his interview had been so easy; it was all a lie.

Bastard, thought Thomas, *queer bastard*. He knew there had been a reason why Patrick was not to be trusted. Right from their first meeting in the National Gallery, there had been something different about their host. He was one of those men that you hear about and snigger over with friends. That was not all; Patrick Lawrence also liked women too, for he had proved it by fathering Etty's baby. He bought and swilled down a fourth whiskey then stumbled out onto the street.

He hailed a taxi and sank gratefully into the seat, gave his address and promptly fell asleep.

He woke as the taxi drew up outside Patrick's house; he scrambled in his pocket for the fare then climbed out and staggered down the path to the kitchen.

Eliza Jane was not at home so he walked through the kitchen and down the corridor to the studio. He could hear Patrick's voice, then laughter from Rory and immediately he tensed in anger. He put his hand on the door of the studio, turned it and burst in.

'Hello, Thomas, I've just received a phone call from Claridge's, are you all right?' Patrick stepped forward and extended an arm to support Thomas.

'Cartwright rang you, didn't he? Well, I'm sorry that I ruined your little arrangement.'

'I'm sorry, I wanted to help Thomas, that's all, no harm done.'

'On the contrary, everyone thinks I am one of your special friends, Patrick, they think I am a queer, just like you, so plenty of harm done.' He staggered forward and took a swing at Patrick with his fist. 'Bastard,' he yelled, as his fist more by luck than judgement connected with Patrick's chin.

'For God's sake, Thomas!' yelled Rory, who had witnessed everything in silence. He pushed his brother back into the chair. 'What the hell do you think you're doing? Have you gone mad, what in Christ's name is all this about?'

'He's bent, Rory,' said Thomas slurring his words, 'a nancy boy, and he's given Etty a baby. He has no shame. Better watch out, lad, giving you expensive presents and the like, you might be next on his list.' He tried to take a deep breath to still his booming heart.

Patrick sat down rubbing his chin, stunned that Thomas thought he had fathered Etty's baby.

'Don't be so bloody stupid, Thomas, I know that Patrick likes men, so what, it proves he wouldn't have fathered the baby, doesn't it? It doesn't alter the fact that he is a wonderful teacher and man. He is still the same kind and generous person for god's sake.' Rory despaired of his brother. 'Why so bigoted, Thomas? You've always been a pacifist; you've never hit anyone in your life.'

'I was forced into being a pacifist, by my weak heart – don't you think I would have gone to war like everyone else but my health prevented it. Unlike that man over there, who escaped fighting by disappearing to America when the war began.'

'Thomas,' began Patrick, 'listen to me.'

'Listen to you, why the hell should I listen to you? I didn't want your charity but you gave it anyway, didn't you? You called up an old friend and got me a job at Claridge's. An old and very close friend, so I've heard. By rights, you and Cartwright should go to prison for what you do together; it makes me feel sick.' Patrick rose from his chair and began to leave the room. He suddenly turned back to face Thomas, he looked wounded beyond repair.

'We'll talk when you have calmed down. I'm going up to my room to clean up.'

Thomas made another lunge for him almost falling over. 'Come back here, you bastard, I haven't finished with you yet. What about Etty, you had better marry her or so help me—'

'Marry her! I'm not the father of Etty's baby. You must believe that.'

'You lie, of course you're the father, who else could it be?'

'It's David Jackson, Thomas,' said Eliza Jane quietly, as she walked into the studio after hearing raised voices. 'He's the father of Etty's baby, and would you mind telling me what on earth is going on here?' Then she burst into tears.

Chapter 31

Eliza Jane sipped her tea while trying to keep the cup steady in her hands. She looked across at Thomas who was asleep in the arm chair in the drawing room. She and Rory had struggled to put him there before he collapsed. Tears welled in her eyes again as she relived the drama she had come home to. What was happening to her family? They used to be happy in each other's company. Now they were fighting like strangers, tearing lumps out of each other in order to get through life. She thought of Ma and Da, which brought a deepened sense of sadness. 'Why did you take them from us, God?' she whispered. 'We needed them more than you, please help us Lord.' She prayed.

Thomas stirred and opened his eyes. He blinked then winced as he tried to move. He looked down at the grazed and swollen knuckles of his right hand. The horror of what he had done caught up with him. He felt ashamed. He didn't fight; he was known for his tolerance and gentleness. He usually had an open mind, let people live how they wanted to live was his motto. Now he saw with great clarity that he had become a wrathful judge – what was happening to him?

Eliza Jane noticing him move stood up, put down her cup and went over to him. She was rightly apprehensive, what sort of mood would Thomas be in. Her concern was mirrored in her voice, as she tentatively said, 'Thomas?'

'Lizzie.' He tried to sit further up in the chair. 'How is Patrick, I'm so sorry I hit him. I don't suppose he will ever forgive me and nor do I deserve it. When Etty comes home, we'll pack our bags and leave. We can't stay here now. Patrick will rightly tell us to go, so we best make plans.'

'I haven't seen Patrick; he went to his study and closed the door. Perhaps he will understand but it makes me weep for him when I think how kind he has been to us and how we have repaid him. I am so ashamed.'

'None of this is your fault, Lizzie, you have served him well, it's Etty and me who are to blame; we have no choice but to leave.'

'Where will we go, we don't know anyone in London.'

'We'll go back home, Lizzie. Jacob Pennington will put us up temporarily until we find somewhere. Etty needs to be back in Crossdale with David Jackson for the sake of the baby, and we need to be with her.'

'Thomas, think about this sensibly, what will we do and how will we survive? There's nothing for us in Crossdale.' Although the thought of her home village soothed her soul, Eliza Jane knew she would miss Jim too much. For the first time in her life, she hadn't even considered David. She began to panic; she didn't want to return to Crossdale. 'The others won't want to go back,' she said, hurriedly, 'they're settled now, and Etty doesn't want to be with David, I mean she hasn't even told him about the baby.'

'How can we possibly stay here now? I can't face Patrick. When I think what I called him. No, we must go home, it's the only course left open to us. We'll talk about it later when the others are back.'

'Why not come for a walk, Thomas. You've never been to the park. I know it's cold but the fresh air will help you think straight.'

'I could do with getting away from here, Lizzie. Let me get my cap and muffler and I'll be ready.'

They walked briskly down Sydenham hill to the park, and then sat for a while on a seat by the fountain, each lost in their own thoughts. 'Let's walk a bit more,' said Eliza Jane shivering, 'I'm getting chilly.'

They linked arms and wandered on. Gazing ahead, Eliza Jane let out a shrill cry. 'There's Ronald, you must come and meet him. He's the image of Rory; it's quite uncanny.'

Thomas allowed himself to be dragged towards a young man sitting on a bench. 'Ronald, it's Eliza Jane, I have my brother with me. Let me introduce you, Ronald, this is Thomas.'

Thomas took the young man's hand, taking in a sharp breath when he realised, he was a mirror image of Rory.

'How do you do, sir,' said Ronald, 'you're not the brother I'm supposed to look like, are you?'

'No, that would be Rory. It's absolutely amazing, you could be twins. Even your voices are similar.'

'So Eliza Jane tells me. I wish I could meet him sometime.'

'I don't think that will happen, Ronald, we're might all be going home soon, we're leaving London.' Eliza Jane sat down next to him.

Ronald turned his dark-brown unseeing eyes in the direction of Eliza Jane, he looked troubled. 'I'll miss our conversations in the park, Eliza Jane. Where's home by the way, I don't think you have ever said.'

'Crossdale, Lancashire,' said Thomas. 'It's a small village near Lancaster.' Thomas joined them on the seat.

'Crossdale!' Ronald exclaimed. 'I know Crossdale, at least I did. My grandmother and I used to live near there. We moved to London when I returned from the war; she wanted me to receive the best treatment for my blindness.'

Eliza Jane glanced up and saw Ronald's grandmother approaching. 'Here she is now, Ronald, we'd best be off.' She began to get up.

'No, stay, I've been telling her about my friend in the park, and I know she would love to meet you. Please stay.' He put out a hand as if to stop her from leaving.

Eliza Jane sat down again.

The old lady approached with a slight waddle, leaning heavily on a walking stick. She was small and plump and dressed in clothes fashionable at the turn of the century. Her grey hair was drawn back in a bun and a black hat was perched on top of her head.

'Hello, Ronald dear,' she said warmly, 'will you introduce me to your friends?' Thomas immediately stood up and offered his seat. She sat down heavily and rested her stick against the edge of the bench.

'Grandmamma, this is Eliza Jane and Thomas… Oh, I just realised I don't know your surname,' he said, turning in the direction of Thomas's voice.

'Watkins, Thomas and Eliza Jane Watkins, we're brother and sister.

'Watkins, you say?' The old lady paused while she digested that information then she continued. 'I'm very pleased to meet you both. It's nice for Ronald to have company. My name is Victoria Bennington.'

'Grandmamma, they used to live in Crossdale. It's a small world, isn't it?'

The old lady was silent for a moment, she appeared to Thomas to be momentarily taken aback but she quickly recovered replying, 'Indeed it is, Ronald, tell me Mr Watkins, have you brothers and sisters?'

'Yes, I have two other sisters and a brother, Henrietta, Molly and Rory.'

The old lady visibly stiffened and a shadow passed over her faded-blue eyes, but again she recovered.

'Well, it's been lovely meeting you both but perhaps we should go now, Ronald; it's getting very cold.' She leaned on her stick, as she rose from the bench and put her free hand under Ronald's elbow to encourage him to move.

'Will I see you again, Eliza Jane?' asked Ronald, as he rose onto his feet.

'I'm not sure, it really depends on the others, but should we leave, I promise we'll come to the park to find you to say goodbye before we go.'

'Don't you dare forget,' said Ronald, as his grandmother started to lead him back to the car. As she did so, she turned slightly and nodded at Thomas and Eliza Jane. 'It was nice to meet you, my dears.' She smiled.

'Likewise,' said Thomas, with a polite incline of his head. He was actually thinking how strange it was that when he named his siblings, the old lady seemed visibly disturbed and almost immediately wanted to leave. He turned to Eliza Jane. 'We'd best get back too, Etty and Molly should be home soon and we have things to discuss.'

Etty banged her fist on the kitchen table; the family were seated around it as usual. Thomas had recounted the day's events and warned them that were probably no longer welcome to stay with Patrick.

'You did what, you hit him?' Etty was furious. 'Is he all right, I must go to him.'

'Sit down, Etty, I'm the head of this family and you must do as I say for once in your life,' said Thomas raising his voice in exasperation. 'You have to go home for the baby's sake.'

'Why? I flatly refuse to return to Crossdale – my life's here now. I'm doing well at the Fashion House, and I love London. I simply cannot bury myself in a small backwater for the rest of my life.' She leaned forward and spoke passionately and with some venom. 'Let me tell you that I don't have to obey you anymore. This is not the dark ages, women have lost their lives to be on an equal footing with men, but perhaps that piece of history passed you by. Tell me why should I return home? I'm sure my baby would be happy to be born a cockney. I see no need to drag myself all the way back to the North.'

'David Jackson should be told that he's to become a father, and he will of course want to be near his child,' Thomas replied.

'David is the baby's father, when, I mean how, I can't believe it.' Molly was bewildered.

Etty was speechless. She looked accusingly at Eliza Jane across the table who cast her eyes downwards refusing to meet her sister's meaningful stare. Finally, she found her voice and with the eyes of her family on her wanting answers, she continued to bluff her way through. 'What,' exclaimed Etty, with a false laugh, 'first you accuse Patrick, and now David Jackson of fathering my child, who will be next?'

Eliza Jane looked up and reached across the table. 'Etty, stop it, I told Thomas that David was the father of your baby, I had to, he was beating seven bells out of Patrick at the time. I had no choice.'

'I suppose now everyone knows?' Etty appeared strangely subdued. She could deny the truth no longer.

'I didn't,' said Molly quietly, 'until now that is, and as far as I'm concerned, it's your business, Etty, so you sort it.' She turned to face her brother. 'Thomas, I'm not returning either. I'm enjoying my job, and I have a wonderful friend in Jo. What would there be for me in Crossdale. What about you, Rory? Surely you don't want to leave.'

'No, of course I don't, but I'm not sure how we can stay. Thomas has hurt Patrick badly – not only with his fists but with his words too.'

'He must apologise then,' said Etty, glaring at her older brother. 'He must offer Patrick an abject apology, and perhaps out of the goodness of his heart, he will see his way to forgive us, and allow us to stay.'

'I don't want you all to leave,' said Patrick coming into the kitchen and overhearing Etty's remark. His bleak and wretched appearance shocked the family. His face was contorted, his mouth was twisted, his eyes blank and lifeless and his shoulder length hair awry.

Thomas felt wretched. He had done this to Patrick and he could barely bring himself to look at him. 'Patrick, I'm so sorry, I was just so angry, something happened at work which I don't want to talk about and with the stress of last night and very little sleep, I just couldn't help myself. The last thing I wanted to do was hurt you but I have and I think it would be best if we leave here and return to Crossdale.'

'That would hurt me even more, Thomas, more than you know. I love having you all here. You're like the brothers and sisters that I never had.' In reality, Patrick could not bear life without seeing Rory every day, he needed him near and although that meant living with his secret feelings which he knew could never be reciprocated, he realised he couldn't continue without him.

'We have to go, Patrick; we'd be living a lie if we said your personal life didn't matter to us.' Thomas looked around the table at his family's obvious disapproval of his choice of words. 'Well to me then,' he added

'May I talk to you all?' said Patrick quietly. 'Please do me the honour of listening, and reserve any further judgement until I've finished?'

Their eyes fell upon Patrick, except for Thomas who stubbornly stared at the ground.

Chapter 32

Patrick drew out a chair and sat down, he placed his cigarettes on the table in front of him, then slowly and with great concentration, he placed his fingertips carefully together. He was aware of the air of expectancy in the room.

'My father,' he began, 'is Sir Rollo Lawrence. He's currently the Deputy Governor of the Bank of England. My mother was titled in her own right before she met my father. They married in 1874. For several years, they were not blessed with children. My father was utterly disappointed, and so I'm told, my mother was constantly in tears at her inability to conceive.

'Eventually in 1879, I arrived. Father was thrilled to have a son, and Mother triumphant that she had finally produced a healthy heir. I did not see too much of my parents in my formative years. My mother suffered with depression, so I was looked after by a nanny until it was time for me to go to preparatory school. She was a thin, mean looking woman with a huge mole on her face that sprouted three thick black hairs.' Patrick shuddered at the memory. 'If I was disobedient, she would use a ruler to spank me. If she wasn't hitting me, she was doing other unmentionable and personal things to me, which seemed to give her immense satisfaction. I apologise for being so indelicate in present company. I would stare at that mole with those three black hairs just to concentrate on something, anything really, while she touched me, then she would force me to touch her.

'Eventually, the time came for me to go away to school. I was relieved to leave my tormentor behind me, and I settled in as a boarder. I was just seven years old. I'm not sure why but school holidays and half term exeat were always spent at my aunt's house: a huge mausoleum of a building. I learnt later that my mother had been committed to a sanatorium, suffering from TB. My aunt was distant and my uncle was never at home.

'At eleven years of age, I passed the common entrance exam and went to Eton school. It was at Eton that I first understood the meaning of kindness and love. My housemaster was a young man, fresh from Oxford, and keen to make a difference. His name was Ruaidri McIntyre.

'It wasn't spelt like your name, Rory; it was the Scottish spelling. He was from Inverness, and had the softest Scottish burr to his voice.' Patrick appeared to drift for a while before continuing. 'All the boys thought he was a whizz. He was brilliant on the cricket pitch, and an amazing teacher in the classroom. By the age of sixteen, I was in love with him, and he, amazingly, with me.'

Patrick paused and reaching out for his cigarettes, he offered one to Thomas which was declined. Patrick took one himself and lit it, drawing on it deeply as he composed himself. Etty noticed how his hand shook as he did so.

He continued, 'We would meet in secret at the bottom of the woods that surrounded the playing field. We were always careful, so much was at stake, and no one knew about us until one day we were discovered by a fourth former who told the headmaster.

'My wonderful secret love was torn away from me, sent to trial and thrown into prison. I wrote to him regularly but I don't think he received my letters. I heard eventually that he had died at the hands of the other prisoners.

'I was expelled from school and sent home. My father was furious and refused to accept that I had loved Ruaidri. My mother, who had now recovered, tried to understand but was weak and frail; she failed to stand up to him. Their years apart had loosened their relationship.

'I was an embarrassment to them so they decided to seek treatment for my so-called *illness*. They took me to see a doctor who recommended a trip to a brothel as a cure. When that didn't work, he suggested cycling. A bicycle was duly purchased and I was sent off for long rides. Little did they realise these trips were actually a relief to me, as the atmosphere at home was so awful. I had a course of electric therapy, followed by hypnotism and finally, I was injected with a cocaine solution. I thought I was going mad.

'Believe me, Thomas; I would have done anything not to feel as I did. The love of my life was dead, I had leanings which disgusted my parents, and I hated myself so much I tried to take my own life but I was found in time obviously.

'When nothing was seen to cure me, my father suggested I leave and go as far away as possible, before I became an embarrassment to him at the bank. He gave me a large sum of money to ensure I didn't return. I decided to travel to Inverness to meet Ruaidri's parents, and there I found an apprenticeship to an elderly photographer who knew nothing of my past. I lived with Mr and Mrs

McIntyre for a while which made me feel closer to Ruaidri. I was the happiest I'd been for some time. Ruaidri's mother was so kind, and his father had a wonderful sense of humour. They knew about Ruaidri and me, and amazingly they accepted it and understood. They were rare people.

'I tried to take an interest in young women but I knew it was useless. I had loved Ruaidri with all my heart and I couldn't forget him.

'Eventually, I returned to London to protect Ruaidri's parents from the gossip that was beginning to emerge. They begged me not to go but I knew how difficult my presence would be for them. I said goodbye with a sad and heavy heart, for I loved them more than my own family.

'Now qualified, I had saved enough money to set up my own photographic studio. I tried to keep myself to myself but unfortunately, I met someone called Rupert from my school days, and he introduced me to his circle of so-called friends. I'm ashamed to say that in trying to forget Ruaidri, I engaged with other men, but none meant anything to me.

'I still hate myself; I cannot abide what I am. I try to forget what has gone before but I am a human being, Thomas, I have human frailties and desires, just like you. Do you not think if there was a cure, I would willingly submit to it? You have been beaten up and vilified by others, strangers who didn't know anything about you – surely you would know how it feels to be different. I ask for forgiveness from all of you, and I am asking you to stay. We all have our crosses to bear, and none so more than all of you.'

Patrick took a long thoughtful drag on his cigarette then continued, 'I'm not looking for sympathy, I just desire an acceptance for who I am, and what life has made me. I'll leave you now to discuss your future plans. Thank you for listening to me.'

Patrick stood up and walked shakily to the door but Molly, her eyes wet with tears, pushed back her chair and ran to him.

'You have nothing to apologise for, Patrick. Who are we to judge you, when you judge yourself so harshly? I would love to stay if you'll have me. The question is can you forgive us for being so ungrateful after all you've done for us. Look how far we've come since you took us in. We were just a sad little family with nowhere to go when you met us, but you have nurtured us, fed us, given us this beautiful house to live in – all out of the kindness of your heart. You've even found us jobs' ` she glared at Thomas ` 'and everything has been thrown back in your face. 'We should be the ones saying sorry.'

Thank you, Molly.' Patrick's brown eyes filled with tears, emotionally it had cost him dear to tell his story, but every word had been true. He looked down at her small frame with her beseeching blue eyes and tried to smile. 'I'd be delighted if you continue to live here.'

'Thomas, what do you have to say to Patrick?' Molly asked turning to him. She could see her brother's face was stricken with guilt. He was obviously having difficulty finding the right words, he rubbed his neck.

'I cannot begin to understand or accept what you are, Patrick, it is so wrong, however I hope in time I will learn to accept our differences and respect each other's point of view. I would however like to say I'm sorry for hitting you; I hope you will accept my apologies.'

Thomas tentatively put out his hand in an effort of reconciliation; Patrick took the proffered hand and shook it warmly.

Etty stood up and hugged Patrick and Rory rose smiled and clapped him on the back. Eliza Jane sat in numbed silence, still pondering on Patrick's story. She could not believe that anyone could have had such a sad life and still be so generous and brave.

Chapter 33

Early the following morning, Thomas sat nursing a cup of tea at the kitchen table. His mind was consumed with guilt and worry. He had walked out of a job he had enjoyed; he had wrongly accused Patrick of fathering Etty's baby, and he had spat so much venom at the poor man, that in spite of being forgiven, he didn't see how the family could continue to live in Sydenham, even though Molly, Etty and Rory had vehemently stated that they were staying.

He couldn't imagine returning to Crossdale, after a failed attempt of starting afresh in London and having to face the village once more. He didn't really want to go himself because of his feelings for Jo – though heaven knows what she would have thought of his recent behaviour. He was dreading seeing Patrick this morning too, although he had been forgiven.

He took a gulp of lukewarm tea and grimaced. Placing the cup on the table, he rubbed his sleep-deprived eyes. The fact of the matter was that he had no idea what to do for the best.

Etty interrupted his thoughts as she passed through the kitchen for her coat before setting off to work. 'Well, Thomas,' she snapped, 'I trust you're pleased with yourself. If it wasn't for Patrick's kindness, we would have been flung out into the streets with nowhere to go.'

'Don't start, Etty' – he turned to look at her – 'half of this mess is your fault. You brought shame to the family by doing what you did with David Jackson, and you were vile to Patrick on Rory's birthday so I'm not taking all the blame.'

'I suggest you just sort out the problem, Thomas,' said Etty airily, not taking any responsibility as usual. 'Losing your job was nothing to do with me, you managed that all by yourself.'

'There you go again, refusing to take the blame; nothing is ever Etty's fault, is it?'

'You're the head of the family, dear brother, you sort this out, but whatever you decide, I'm staying here with Patrick. Even after what he told us, I just can't believe it, I've made my own plans; you and everyone else can do what you like.'

'Can't or won't believe it,' said Thomas.

Etty shrugged. 'Does it matter?' She grabbed her coat from the peg and opened the back door.

'So what plans have you made?' Thomas shouted after her, but he was too late, Etty left banging the door behind her.

'Hypocrite!' he shouted. She couldn't have possibly heard but it made him feel better.

Rory and Patrick were setting up in the studio for their first portrait of the day. Patrick was checking the diary at the desk while Rory re-arranged the room, chatting as he did so.

'You know I don't want to leave, don't you?' said Rory, carefully placing a potted aspidistra on a small table. 'I like it here, and you've taught me so much. I just couldn't imagine being anywhere else.'

Patrick was worried; he loved Rory, what if he couldn't help showing his true feelings. He would try so hard to keep his love secret but it might prove impossible. He knew he should warn Rory as it might influence his decision to stay.

'Rory, stop what you are doing a minute,' he said coming out from behind the desk. 'There's something I should tell you, something that might make you feel differently about staying, you need to hear the truth.'

'This sounds serious,' Rory smiled, as he straightened up from moving a chair. 'Listen, Patrick' – Rory looked straight at him – 'I think I know what you are about to say and I think for both our sakes it is best left unsaid. Let's leave it there, shall we?'

'Rory, it's important to know that if you stay, you must be prepared to continue to work closely with me.'

'Of course, that goes without saying. I am learning so much.'

'I think you should know—'

'Patrick, please, you don't need to say anything more, I am staying if you will have me and that is final.'

Chapter 34

Dress rehearsal was going badly – lines were forgotten, props were not brought on to the stage at the right time and entrances were slow. Everyone said in the tea break that a poor dress rehearsal meant a great opening night, thus reassuring themselves.

Kit as usual was immersed in the dress rehearsal, and Molly was becoming irritated.

'It's as if he doesn't want to talk to me,' she complained to Jo.

'Why don't you talk to Kit after the show, and ask him what's going on. Perhaps he's thinking that your feelings have changed or perhaps…' Jo's voice trailed away before she said too much. Kit needed to make his mind up about Nora, she kept telling him that.

'Perhaps what?' asked Molly.

'Just talk to him, Moll, that is all I'm saying.'

Molly suddenly started to feel better. Perhaps she could take Jo's advice and talk to Kit again, but did she really want a relationship with a man who wasn't strong enough to tell her what was going on in his mind? Besides, apart from his initial pleasure at seeing her again, he hadn't really made any effort to woo her.

Molly thought of Eliza Jane and Jim, and how much they enjoyed and valued each other's company. Fun and laughter seemed to accompany them. She wanted that for herself, and had to admit that Kit was not stepping up to the mark. Almost at once, she decided, she would have it out with him, she owed it to herself to know where she stood.

'Thank you, Jo' – she grabbed her friend's hand – 'you're a really good friend.'

Molly returned to the rehearsal with renewed vigour and a sense of purpose.

Finally, at the end of the evening, she managed to get Kit alone in the corridor behind the stage. She had followed him out there and called his name to catch up with him.

Kit turned, surprised to see Molly behind him. 'Hello, Molly, what did you think to tonight? Thank goodness the second act was better than the first, I was beginning to lose hope.'

'Kit, can we talk, I'm confused.'

Kit immediately stiffened, he had been putting off talking to Molly about Nora for some time, but now the moment had come.

'Molly, there is something I should have told you a long time ago but I was hoping that I might never have to.'

Molly gazed at Kit with troubled eyes.

'Molly please, do not look at me like that because all I want to do is gather you in my arms and kiss you but I mustn't.'

Molly placed her hands on Kit's arms. 'I want you to kiss me, Kit; I have been waiting a very long time for you to do just that.' She lifted her face expectantly and Kit bent his head towards her, perhaps one kiss. Suddenly, he heard his mother's voice and came to his senses.

'No, Molly, it wouldn't be fair on you. Listen to me please.' He pushed Molly's arms down to release himself. 'I don't know where to start, except to say you are the most wonderful girl in the world to me and I care for you more than you might imagine.' He went on to tell Molly about his promise to his dying mother and the fact he had to honour that commitment. When he had finished, he held Molly's hand saying, 'Now you understand why we can never be more than friends.'

Molly was puzzled. 'Your mother died last year, Kit, I don't understand why you haven't kept your promise and asked Nora to marry you already. Why wait?'

'Simply because I don't love Nora, nor do I believe she loves me. I don't even know if she is aware of our mothers' agreement. Nothing has ever been said.'

'Perhaps you need to talk it through with her, see what she knows, why the poor girl has probably been waiting all this time.' Molly was feeling slightly irritated by Kit's lack of action. 'If you say you care for me, then you owe it to us to sort this out. Perhaps if Nora were to release you from your promise to your mother, then we might have a future. I love you, Kit, but I cannot wait forever.' Molly pulled down Kit's head and planted the lightest of kisses on his cheek before turning and walking away hardly able to see the corridor before her, from the tears in her eyes.

The following evening was the first night of the pantomime. Molly came home accompanied by Thomas late in the evening. She sat in the kitchen with the others drinking cocoa and reliving the evening.

'It was wonderful, the best night of my life. I know I've acted in pantomimes before but that was just to a village audience, this was a completely different experience. This was acting in front of people who I didn't know, and who don't know me. The audience clapped and clapped at my singing...'

Rory grinned, cradling his hot cocoa mug in his hands. 'They probably wanted to drown it out.'

'They loved it actually, and you should have heard them when I appeared in my ball gown. Jo and Kit were amazing, and John brought a tear to the audience's eye as Buttons. Many said that Thomas's scenery was the best the Players have ever had, didn't they, Thomas?' She did not pause to let him answer before continuing, 'Oh, I'm so excited – I'll never sleep, and I can't wait for tomorrow night to do it all again.'

'Take a breath and drink your cocoa,' Eliza Jane advised, rising from the table to wash out her cup.

'Oh, Lizzie, I'm too in love with acting to come back down to earth.' A moment of panic beset her. 'You're still all coming to see it on Saturday, aren't you?'

'We wouldn't miss it,' said Patrick, draining his cup. Cocoa with the family was now a nightly ritual, all six of them sat around the large kitchen table. 'I'm really looking forward to seeing it, I haven't been to a pantomime in years.'

'I'll probably be able to come,' said Etty, slightly jealous that Molly was the centre of attention. 'It depends on my work commitments – don't be too upset, if I can't make it.'

'Etty, I won't hear of you not coming,' said Patrick firmly.

'Yes, Patrick,' she replied attempting to be demure.

'Jim's really looking forward to going,' said Eliza Jane getting excited. 'It's going to be a great family night out, which is something we all need.'

'I wish Helen was coming,' said Thomas in a plaintive voice.

'Oh, Rory, just forget her,' snapped Etty. 'She was nothing short of cruel to you. That reminds me, I meant to tell you, she had an appointment at the House of Harding yesterday, and I watched from the window as she drove herself away in a rather smart car. It looks to me like something Papa might have bought her to encourage her to stay away from the poor blacksmith's son.'

'You don't know that,' Patrick remarked.

'I think I know how the female mind works.'

'Not all women think like you,' said Eliza Jane, which was met with a scowl.

'You didn't know her like I did,' said Rory looking pensive. 'She was honourable and fun. She wanted to help fight the injustices that face the poor.'

'If she wanted to help the poor, she could sell that car of hers – that would keep the poor in food for a year.' Etty was outspoken as usual.

'Etty,' warned Thomas, observing Rory's saddened face. 'Really though,' he said, wanting to return to talking about the show. 'Molly's right, the whole production was excellent, and we should have a full house every night. Now then,' he said, standing up from the table and yawning. 'I don't know about everyone else, but I'm tired and heading for bed. I have to get up early tomorrow to look for work.' He looked over to Patrick. 'I'll find a job, really I will, but on my own merits.'

Patrick held both hands up in acquiescence, but said nothing.

Gradually, they all rinsed out their cups and said goodnight.

Molly lay awake in her bed for some time. Her last thoughts before she finally managed to close her eyes were of Nora. Did she know of the wishes of Kit's mother? She was friendly towards Kit but then she was nice to everyone. Perhaps she would release Kit from his duty. Why would she want to marry a man that plainly didn't love her? Molly was confident that everything could be sorted. What had Kit said, she was a most wonderful girl and he cared for her more than he could say. His words gave Molly a warm feeling of hope as she drifted off to sleep.

Chapter 35

It was the last night of the pantomime: Etty, Patrick, Rory, Eliza Jane and Jim were all in the front row of the church hall. Thomas had decided to sit out front to join his family; he had been busy behind the scenes during the week, and had not seen the pantomime properly. He felt nervous for them all, but knew if the past five performances were anything to go by, he needn't worry.

There was an expectant buzz of excitement in the air. The audience were there to enjoy themselves after working hard all week. Children's cheeks were bulging with boiled sweets, and sticky finger marks were being left on the hall chairs.

The Lewisham Town Band struck up the overture, and the lights went down. The audience chatter quietened immediately, and Jim took firm hold of Eliza Jane's hand, squeezing it lightly.

As the pantomime progressed, Thomas noticed that a large man in the seat next to him, appeared to be on his own. He was puffing on a fat cigar which was making Thomas's eyes water. Out of the corner of his eye, he noticed the man never seemed to laugh or clap but sat up straight when Molly appeared. In the interval, Thomas dashed back stage and congratulated the cast as they were drinking their tea. 'It is so good, the audience love it,' he said encouragingly. When he returned to his seat, Eliza Jane handed him an ice cream. Jim had been to the kiosk at the back of the hall and purchased six vanilla wafers.

In act two, Cinderella was seen walking alone in the woods, and soliloquising about seeing the Prince again. Thomas was particularly proud of the stand-alone trees he had designed and made. They stood proudly, looking realistic placed around the stage.

Molly sang a beautiful song about her love for the prince. The audience clapped and roared in delight.

At the end of the show, the cast received three curtain calls, and one of the children in the chorus presented Molly with a bouquet of flowers. The family trooped around to the dressing rooms at the back of the theatre to congratulate Molly on her performance. They crowded around her.

'Moll, you were utterly brilliant,' said Eliza Jane, kissing her on the cheek.

'Yes, well done,' said Etty grudgingly, 'a good performance, though I could've made you a better ball gown if only you'd asked.'

'Well done, gal,' said Jim... 'An amazing performance, I genuinely laughed out loud.'

'Wasn't she good?' said Nora, coming up to them. 'She is a real find.'

'You were a wonderful good fairy too,' said Jim, in fact everyone was good.

Thomas walked over to where Jo was taking off her stage make up in front of the mirror. 'You were excellent too, Jo; I hope we can still see each other even though the pantomime is over.'

'I would love that,' she replied, thrilled that Thomas wanted to see her again.

As they started to gather up costumes and props to go back into the cupboard until the next production, there was a knock on the dressing room door. Jo went to open it. A portly, elderly, balding gentleman stood in the doorway twirling his hat. Thomas recognised him as the man sitting next to him in the front row.

'I wonder if I might see Miss Watkins,' the man said, he was perspiring heavily and still smoking his cigar.

'I'm afraid she's a bit busy at the moment,' Jo said, wondering why he wanted to see Molly and not really liking the look of him. 'Can I help you?'

'No, miss, I need to see Miss Watkins; I have a proposition for her.'

Hearing the man's request, and wanting to protect his sister from further excitement, Thomas bustled over to the door. 'Look, Miss Watkins is tired and needs to go home so I suggest you leave it for now.'

Thomas closed the door on the startled man.

'Who was that?' asked Molly. 'What did he want?'

He's probably some stage door, Johnnie,' said Patrick. 'In the West End, such men wait outside theatres hoping to take one of the actresses out to dinner. I think we should go home through the other door at the back.'

Kit stepped forward as they were leaving. 'Thank you, Molly, for making our show such a success, I will see you very soon, but right now, I have to talk to Nora.'

'Who the...why has he got to talk to the good fairy,' said Etty sarcastically. I thought you and he were...'

'It is all right, Etty, I know all about it, come on everyone let's go home and celebrate.'

Kit found Nora alone in the hall of the theatre when the others had gone. She smiled as Kit approached.

'It was a good run, Kit, Molly was brilliant, I hope she stays with us. I was just reliving some of the magic. I think everyone enjoyed it, didn't they?' Kit agreed. He took a deep breath in.

'Nora, I have been meaning to talk to you, let's sit down. She followed him to the front row of the stalls and sat beside him. 'Our mothers were very close weren't they, and spent a lot of time together before my mother died.'

'They were great friends,' Nora agreed. They hatched all sorts of plans for us, did you know?' She laughed lightly.

'Yes, I know and I'm sorry I haven't talked to you before.'

'I have been expecting it.'

Kit was worried, Nora obviously knew but had remained silent. 'The thing is, Nora, we have been out together a few times and I think we enjoy each other's company.'

'We certainly do.' Nora agreed. Kit started to feel uncomfortable, his collar felt tight and sweat was running down his back. Nora was not making this easy. 'I was thinking perhaps we should see a little more of each other.'

'In what way should we do that, Kit?'

'Well you know, perhaps you would like to come out to the theatre one night and we could see how we feel.'

'That would be lovely, Kit, how about tomorrow evening, you've nothing planned, have you? After all, the sooner we see how we feel, the better, don't you think?'

'Well, tomorrow is Sunday and I am rather busy on Sundays, it's the nature of the…' Kit suddenly caught sight of Nora who was trying to suppress a giggle, then as she caught his eye she laughed out loud.

'Oh Kit, you are funny, you should see your face, it's a picture.'

Kit was annoyed. 'I'm trying to do what is right here, and all you can do is laugh.'

'Kit, listen to me. I know our mothers wanted us to marry and I also know that they had no right to ask it of us. Let me put you out of your misery, though I'm sure being married to me wouldn't have been that bad. I am already engaged to be married to Captain Philip Nicholson; currently serving with his Majesties

Army in India. I am to travel out to marry him next month and we will set up home there. Now I happen to think that you are rather sweet on a young lady called Molly, so please forget about silly promises made at an emotional time and go and find some happiness, you deserve it.'

Kit was astounded. 'I had no idea you were engaged, when did this happen?'

'If you hadn't been so busy pretending to be being busy and trying to avoid conversations with both Molly and me, I might have had a chance to tell you. I wanted you to know before anyone else, I felt I owed it to you but I have not had an opportunity to do so.'

'I've been so stupid, I wish I had talked to you earlier, it would have saved so much heart searching. Congratulations to Captain Nicholson, he is a very lucky man and I know you will be very happy.'

Nora kissed him lightly on the cheek. 'Thank you, so what are you going to do now?'

'I'll go and see Molly in the morning, beg her forgiveness, then ask her a very important question.'

Chapter 36

The following day was Christmas Eve and Molly was tired. Luckily, it was Sunday so the shop was closed and she could relax. She took a book into the drawing room and sat by the fire, but was easily distracted from reading it. She had put so much into her performance throughout the week that it had exhausted her. She truly loved acting, and perhaps she really was as good as everyone had said. She couldn't wait for the Players next production, and hoped if Kit chose to follow duty instead of his heart, they would be able to work alongside each other without any bitterness.

If only Ma and Da had been in the audience – they would have loved seeing her in such a big production. The village pantomimes at home were very small affairs with make do costumes, and not much accompanying scenery.

The door opened suddenly and Etty walked in, she took up the seat by the window and opened her magazine. The two sisters read in silence for a while. Finally, Etty looked up and caught Molly's eye. She laid her magazine in her lap where it proceeded to quiver, as the baby kicked it from inside her tummy.

'What is happening between you and the vicar then?' Etty could never bring herself to be too interested in anyone else and often refused to learn people's names for fear she may have to involve herself. She always preferred an aura of mystery surrounding her.

Molly understanding this perfectly well replied. 'You mean Kit,' she said.

Etty nodded. 'I thought as you were going over to the vicarage every Sunday for lunch, you would soon become the vicar's wife.'

'I thought so too,' agreed Molly, 'but it's complicated. Kit's mother died last year and she made him promise on her death bed that he would marry Nora. Their mothers were inseparable apparently. Kit knows he should honour his mother's wishes but couldn't quite bring himself to do it. He also doesn't know if Nora was aware of the death bed promise. He was going to talk to her last night.'

'You mean it has taken him a year to find out if the good fairy knew of the plan, she must be running out of patience waiting for something from him.'

'Nora has never indicated she knew about the pact but Kit felt that he owed it to her to talk it through before becoming involved with me.'

'Right, let me get this straight, you, and he can only see each other romantically if Nora doesn't want him first. Well, there's nothing like being second best, is there, Moll?'

'It's not like that really, he's a vicar and it's his duty, I have no say in the matter.'

'Of course, you have a say, Molly, you should have given him an ultimatum for heaven's sake, are you a mouse? This is your future and you are letting someone else decide it for you. Kit is weak, Molly; he doesn't deserve you. Men do not deserve us women, they are all spineless creatures, bleating about how much they love us and doing nothing about it. For God's sake, Molly, do you really want to wait around for a few crumbs to fall from the vicarage table. I will leave you to it now, I have said my piece. I have to go and finish wrapping my presents but remember, don't be a doormat, you are worth so much more.'

After she had gone, Molly thought about Etty's words. Her harsh assessment of the situation had struck a nerve. Why hadn't she seen the incongruity of the situation herself? Had she been too blinded by her feelings? She had just accepted that Nora came first and had actually sent Kit to talk to her. Did she really want to be tied down into a permanent relationship, particularly one where she didn't feel important or loved?

The doorbell interrupted her thoughts, and she heard Eliza Jane thumping down the stairs to the front door. Molly strained to hear who it was. 'Hello, Kit,' she heard her sister say, 'come on in, Molly's in the drawing room.'

Molly hastily picked up her book, pretending to read before the drawing room door opened and Kit was shown in.

'Hello, Molly, how are you?'

'I didn't think I would see you today, Christmas Eve must be a very busy day for you.'

'Indeed, it is, but I spared the time as I needed to see you. May I sit?'

Molly nodded, and Kit sat beside her on the couch. He looked flushed and excited, almost as if he had been hurrying.

'Molly, when we parted at Euston station that day, I hoped with all my heart that I would see you again, but sadly you didn't get in touch.'

'I told you Thomas lost your address, and I had no way of knowing where to find you. I even thought about attending all the churches in Lewisham to track you down.'

'I take it you were as attracted to me as I was to you.'

'Yes, I was attracted to you but you know that already.' Molly was puzzled as to where the conversation was going.

'Thank you, that means so much. I couldn't believe it when Jo first brought you home. I was so thrilled to see you again.'

'As was I, Kit.'

They held each other's gaze for a moment before he broke the silence. 'I spoke with Nora last night, and it's all right, she's engaged to be married, I don't have to honour my mother's wishes, well I can't, she wouldn't have me. It was so funny, Molly; she teased me that I had taken so long to talk to her about things. She knew of our mothers' wishes but she didn't want me, isn't that wonderful?'

'It must have been very amusing,' remarked Molly stiffly.

'It was, all that worry and sleepless nights wondering if I should propose to her, well it's all over now, we are free to do as we please. Why you don't look very happy, I thought the news was what you wanted to hear.'

Molly thought for a moment, yes it was the news she wanted to hear but it was too little too late. If only Kit had fallen in love with her as much as she him, but it was evident because he hadn't put her first, that he had not. Etty was right. Perhaps in time, he would come to love her but Kit found describing his feelings rather difficult and Molly knew that in time, that would irritate her.

'I haven't got long, Molly, I have to get back for the children's Chris tingle service, but I needed to see you to ask you an important question.'

Molly gasped, surely, he wasn't going to propose, he couldn't, could he! 'No Kit, please don't,' she said quickly.

'Molly' – he took her hand, his eyes were moist – 'Nora has released me from a promise that I made to my mother and now I am asking you to consider being my girl. We could take it slowly, see how things go and in time perhaps you would consider becoming my wife.'

Molly was furious that Kit's declaration of love should be so shallow. Again, Nora had given him permission to court her and although she knew it was not Nora's fault, she was beginning to feel very second best as Etty had put it.

'Kit,' she said angrily, 'you have ignored me and put me to the back of your life so often over the last months that I didn't know if you even liked me.' She raised her hand to stop Kit interrupting. 'The fact is, if you had courted me properly, then I would now be saying, yes, let us try and see where this relationship could go, but right now, I am so angry that I just want you to get up, leave this room and shut the front door behind you. I have no wish to see you ever again. I suggest you try harder with the next girl you profess to love. Goodbye, Kit, forgive me if I don't see you out.' Molly looked away, her rage giving her the confidence she needed.

'Molly, please,' Kit said.

'Goodbye, Kit,' she replied.

Slowly, he got to his feet and whispered, 'May God bless you,' and then she heard the front door being shut gently behind him. *He couldn't even show any passion by slamming the front door,* thought Molly wryly.

After Kit had gone, Molly continued to ponder on her decision. Was she right to have sent him away, wasn't there a little part of her that would have loved to become Mrs Christopher Howard, perhaps but ultimately, she knew she had done the right thing?

There was a sudden commotion in the hall. Molly leapt to her feet and opened the door. She was amazed to see Patrick and Rory struggling with the biggest Christmas tree she had ever seen. They squeezed it through the door, pine needles scattering everywhere and after much pushing and pulling they managed to get the tree to stand upright in a large tub that Thomas had bought in behind them.

'It's beautiful,' breathed Molly, just perfect, she sat and watched as Candles in holders were attached to each branch ready to be lit later that evening.

The rest of the morning was spent turning small pieces of coloured paper into chains, using a flour and water paste, these were then draped over the tree. The whole effect was quite beautiful.

Thomas disappeared for a while then came back with a large wooden star that he had painted silver. Rory carefully placed it on top of the tree.

Patrick stood back from the tree to admire their handiwork. 'This is going to be the best Christmas ever for me,' he said, we must take a photograph to mark the occasion. You must all stand by the tree. Rory set the camera up, would you?'

Jim arrived that evening, bringing a large turkey with him from the shop. Eliza Jane was happy to see it had been plucked and cleaned, unlike poultry delivered for Christmas at home from Roy Hughes the butcher in Crossdale.

'This will barely go in the oven, Jim,' she laughed, 'it's so big.'

'We might have to cut its legs off, gal. But either, way it's going to 'ave to be cooked, or it will be saying either cook me or stick me feathers back on its blooming freezing wiv out 'em.'

The rest of the family who had gathered to admire the bird laughed. Later after dinner, they sat together in the drawing room admiring the candle light on the tree and chatting.

'You were right,' Molly whispered to Etty, 'I was second best; I won't be seeing Kit again, though I will miss acting with the Players.'

'Good girl,' said Etty, 'never let men get the upper hand, that's my motto.' She gazed across at Patrick. There was still work to do there if she wanted to put her plan in action.

'Here's to a wonderful Christmas day.' Said Patrick, raising his glass. little knowing what Etty had in store for him.

Chapter 37

'I can't believe it's 1920,' said Thomas to Jo, as they were walking in the park on New Year's Day. Although it was cold, they were well wrapped up, and were enjoying watching people ice skating on the frozen lake.

'Do you want to have a go, Jo? I can't do it but I'd be happy to watch you.'

'Why do you always say you can't do things, Thomas? I'm sure you could you know.'

'I'm not that strong, Jo. I had diphtheria when I was small, and it left me with a weakened heart.'

'You never told me before.'

'I thought Molly would have mentioned it.'

'No, all she said was I would have to ask you why you hadn't ever married.'

'I never felt it was fair to a girl, I mean who knows how my health might be in a few years, I wouldn't want to saddle anyone with an invalid husband.' Looking sideways at Jo, he sighed with unhappiness. 'I wouldn't blame you if you decided to call it a day, what I'm saying is I would understand if you decided to find someone else.'

Jo stopped walking and turned Thomas to face her. 'Do you want me to do that?'

'No, of course not, I just feel you should be given the option that's all. Perhaps I'm not what your parents would have wanted for you.'

'It's what I want that counts, my mother's wishes for Kit were bad enough and now he's lost Molly through trying to do the right thing. He's heartbroken.'

'I'm so sorry, Jo, I always thought they would be together, I don't know what got into Molly that day.'

'It's so difficult me seeing her every day, it's putting a strain on our friendship, I feel so sorry for my brother.'

They continued to walk in silence for a while. Suddenly, Thomas took her hand. 'Do you know what? I've just this second decided something thanks to you.' He lifted her chin so that he could look at her. 'I'm going to live life as I have never lived it before. I'm going to really live, Jo.'

He grabbed her hands and swung her around; Jo laughed loudly, the sudden exertion bringing colour to her cheeks. As soon as Thomas let her go, he started coughing and between trying to catch his breath while laughing and coughing, he had to sit down. 'So much for living life to the full,' he wheezed.

After Thomas recovered, they walked a little further, hand in hand. 'I'm so glad that you came to see me after Christmas, Thomas.'

'It was the best move I ever made but I haven't much to offer. I've no job, and only make meagre amounts from my carvings. I'm trying to find an outlet here in London as well as in Crossdale. Patrick has a building at the bottom of his garden for me to work in, it's not ideal but it does.'

'Perhaps I could talk to the buyer of fancy goods at Cobb's. They might be interested in your work; I could get you an appointment to see them.'

'That would be wonderful if you could.'

'Consider it done.'

'Jo, there's so much I need to tell you about us, and one day I will. You need to know if you are eventually going to become part of the family.'

'Is that your plan, Thomas, am I going to be part of the family one day?'

'I certainly hope so.' He pulled her close and very gently lowered his lips to hers, the first tentative kiss exploded into something deeper and it was a while before they drew apart.

'That's warmed me up,' she said, as they parted. Thomas took her hand again and they walked on through the crisp January air, puffing breath through open mouths and watching it curl and fade away.

'Look there's Rory,' Jo said, squinting into the distance and pulling Thomas's hand, 'on the seat over there. I wonder what he's doing here and who's that woman he's talking to?'

Thomas lifted his hand to his brow to shield the light, as he looked ahead. He smiled at Jo's natural mistake.' It's not Rory, Jo, but you would be forgiven for thinking it is, he's his double. The resemblance is uncanny. His name's Ronald and he was blinded in the war. He comes and sits in the park every day, no matter what the weather. Eliza Jane often talks to him. I was with her once. The lady's his grandma, he lives with her. Come on, Jo, let's go, and say hello.'

They walked rapidly to the seat where Ronald hearing footsteps and his Grandma seeing Thomas walk into view both looked up.

'Good afternoon, Mrs Bennington.' For some inexplicable reason, the old lady made Thomas nervous. He touched Ronald's arm. 'It's Thomas Watkins, Eliza Jane's brother. May I introduce my friend Jo Howard to you both? We were just out walking and saw you from over there. It's rather cold today, isn't it? No more than we would expect for January though. Did you have a good Christmas?' he gabbled.

'How do you do, my dears,' she said, 'won't you sit down? Ronald, move this way next to me so Mr Watkins and Miss Howard may sit down. We won't be staying long, for it's rather cold as you say, Mr Watkins, and it is rather icy, I'm afraid one feels the cold more as one gets older, and yes, to answer your last question, we did indeed have a very pleasant Christmas. I must say it is very fortuitous to have met you again, Mr Watkins, as I have been giving our last meeting a great deal of thought. It is very nice to see you again.'

'And you too, Mrs Bennington.'

Ronald smiled and interrupted. 'Actually Thomas, Grandmamma's correct title of address is Lady Bennington.'

'I'm sorry. Lady Bennington.' Thomas corrected himself

'Oh, don't concern yourself, my boy, you weren't to know.' She began to lean on her stick and edge herself forward on the seat before slowly rising. 'These old bones do not get any easier. Now then, Ronald, would you excuse me while I have a quick chat with Mr Watkins, I shan't be very far away, I hope Miss Howard, that you will keep an eye on my grandson for me? I won't be long, Ronald.'

Thomas stood up and walked the small distance with Lady Bennington away from the others. He was puzzled; whatever could she have to say to him in private?

'Mr Watkins, I'm sorry to take you away but I wanted to give you this.' She thrust a card into his hand. 'I have been hoping to see you again. I wonder if you would come and see me on your own, sooner rather than later, as Ronald tells me that you're soon to be returning to Crossdale. My address is on the card – there's something we must discuss of a delicate nature.'

'I am pleased to say we are not now returning to Crossdale, your Ladyship.'

'Ah, that is good, very good. But I would still ask that you visit me promptly, and please do not tell anyone about your visit until we have had our chat. I look forward to seeing you soon.'

She turned and walked the short distance back to her grandson. 'Come along, Ronald, time we were getting back.'

The old lady nodded to Jo. 'Goodbye, Miss Howard,' she said helping Ronald to his feet. 'Goodbye, my dears,' she said, as she steered her charge away.

'Phew, she's very grand,' said Jo, 'whatever did she want to see you about?'

'Oh, just to tell me how much Ronald values our company; he's very lonely for obvious reasons.'

He was mystified as to why Lady Bennington wanted to see him. Why did the name Bennington sound so familiar, he had surely heard it somewhere? Jo interrupted his thoughts. 'I say shall we have a cup of tea, if we can find a warm café, I'm parched.'

'Whatever you'd like, Jo, and I might throw in an iced bun if you're good,' he said, grabbing her hand and swinging it in his as they walked.

When Thomas arrived home, he could hear Eliza Jane and Etty arguing again in the kitchen. The Christmas truce not to talk about the baby seemed to be over.

As he entered the kitchen, he saw both women standing facing each other their arms folded across their chests, obviously neither prepared to give way. Eliza Jane immediately embroiled him.

'Thomas, tell Etty she's got to let David Jackson know he's to become a father.'

'Don't you dare, Thomas; it's up to me whether I tell him not – and at present, I don't feel inclined to.'

'I think if I were David, I would want to know so that I could prepare myself.' Then thinking of Lady Bennington and Ronald, he added, 'After all, the baby will have grandparents that will want to be involved. You can't deny them that.'

Etty thought for a moment then rejected the idea. Old ma Jackson, what sort of grandparent would she be, she hasn't an ounce of kindness in her body, and anyway I don't even want this child so why should they? This pregnancy is just an inconvenience – something to be got through, I cannot bring myself to tell him.'

'So who'll look after the baby after it's born,' asked Eliza Jane, 'if you say you don't want it?'

'I'll put it up for adoption or leave it on a doorstep; or perhaps you could look after it for me, your very own piece of David Jackson – how about that idea, Lizzie?'

'I hope you're not being serious,' said Thomas, aware that Eliza Jane's face had crumpled.

'Oh,' Etty sighed, she suddenly regretted the things she had said. 'I don't know, sometimes I hate myself for some of the things I come out with. I seriously don't know what to do for the best. I'm going to lie down for a while before dinner. I'm sorry, Lizzie; you must think me very hard?' She took Eliza Jane's hand, patting it briefly then she turned and left the room.

'I'm going to tell David,' Eliza Jane vowed, 'if she won't, someone has to.'

'Think carefully about it first, or she'll never forgive you,' warned Thomas

'How can I regularly write to David and keep this secret from him; it's just not fair to me or to him.'

'Be careful, Lizzie, that's all I ask. She's your sister.'

The doorbell rang, and Thomas made his way out into the hall. Opening the front door, he found the man who had wanted to talk to Molly after the final performance of the pantomime standing there.

'Yes, can I help?' he said.

'Sir, allow me to give you my card.' He raised his hat in greeting and took his cigar out of his mouth. 'You'll note that I'm the owner, impresario and artistic director of the Theatre Royal in Drury Lane. My name is Maurice Goldberg. May I enquire if I have the right address for Miss Molly Watkins?'

'Yes, Molly's my younger sister,' said Thomas, perusing the gentleman's card.

'Thank goodness, at last. Forgive me but since that night in Lewisham when I was forbidden to see her, I've been searching for Miss Watkins. I have a business proposition that I wish her to consider – is she available at this current time?'

'I'm afraid Molly's still at work.'

'Then may I enquire where she works, and I'll see her there.'

'I would rather be present when you talk to my sister, Mr...' – Thomas looked again at the card in his hand – 'Mr Goldberg. Perhaps you might call to see her later.'

'I'll call back at eight o' clock this evening, if that will be convenient.'

'Perfectly convenient.'

Mr Goldberg raised his hat once more. 'Good afternoon to you.'

'I'll tell Molly to expect you, good afternoon.' A lingering smell of cigar smoke wafted up the hallway as Thomas shut the door. *He might be a stage door Johnny but he obviously had money,* thought Thomas as he put the card in his pocket.

Thomas decided to walk down to Cobbs to meet Molly as she came out of work. Leaving the building through the front entrance, she caught sight of him approaching as she was calling goodnight to her work colleagues. 'Hello, Thomas, Jo's on half day today, so you won't see her, I'm afraid.'

'I know, I spent the afternoon with her in the park. I came to walk you home, Moll.'

'Did Jo say how Kit was?'

'Kit's throwing himself into parish duties, and also planning the next Players' production.' Thomas did not want to tell Molly that Kit was devastated for fear it would upset her again. She had felt quite sorry for herself over Christmas and was just beginning to perk up.

'Well' – smiled Molly – 'I'm honoured you came to walk me home, what's the occasion?'

By the time they had walked home through the dark foggy streets that made Thomas cough, Molly was almost dancing as she walked along beside him.

'Let me get this right,' she said. 'This Mr Goldberg, an artistic director and owner of a West End theatre, has a proposition for me, and he's coming back after dinner. Oh, my goodness, I can't wait to find out what it is. I wish you'd asked him what it was about.'

'I think he needed to talk to you directly, I don't suppose he would have told me anything.'

Molly couldn't wait to get through dinner that evening. They were eating in the dining room. The others had offered plenty of droll comments concerning the purpose of Mr Goldberg's visit.

'I expect he wants you to sell programmes,' joked Rory.

'Or ice cream,' Etty joined in.

'Shut up, both of you,' said Molly, her nerves jangling with anticipation. 'I suppose you think you're very funny.' She stood up from the table. 'Lizzie, do you mind if I skip pudding, only I want to tidy myself up before eight.'

'Go ahead; I'll keep you some for later.'

At eight o' clock precisely, Molly answered the front door to Mr Goldberg and ushered him into the drawing room. Thomas insisted on joining them much to her displeasure.

Mr Goldberg was seated and offered a glass of sherry, which he declined.

'Thank you no,' he said, 'I won't stay for long, but I do have a proposition for you, Miss Watkins. I came to see you in Cinderella performed by the

Lewisham Players. I'd been given a tip off that the young lady playing Cinders was really rather good, so I came to see for myself, and I must say I had to agree. You put on a very fine performance, Miss Watkins, and it was pleasure to see you both act and sing. Now let me get to the point. I'm putting together a touring theatre company. The troupe will perform three plays over two weeks in every area they visit. It will be a tight schedule, and will need complete dedication from the actors involved. The work will be hard; the actors will be staying in boarding houses in each town, which they will pay for out of their wages which will be one pound seven shillings and sixpence per week. Train fares to each destination will be paid for by the company. So, tell me Miss Watkins, what do you think?'

'About what, Mr Goldberg, what do I think about what?'

'Oh, dear me, I haven't said, have I? How silly of me. I'm just so excited by the project.' Mr Goldberg cleared his throat. 'I would like you to be one of my actresses, what do you say? It's a wonderful opportunity for a young lady such as yourself, is it not?'

Molly's face was a picture of disbelieving delight. 'It certainly is, Mr Goldberg. I can't believe it; the answer, of course, is yes. Yes, a thousand times yes.'

Thomas was concerned that Molly had been swept up in the glamour of the offer and decided to bring her back down to earth. 'Molly, don't be so hasty; we need to know more about this. Touring the country with a group of actors is no life for a young lady. Think what Ma would have said,' he warned.

'Thomas, please, I know what I am doing and I want to do this so much, I need to do this.' Molly's eyes shone. 'You don't know how happy it makes me to hear an audience clapping. It feels wonderful. It stimulates the very roots of my being, and lifts me so high that it takes almost forever to reach the ground again. Mr Goldberg is right; it is a wonderful opportunity and one I must take.' Molly turned to Mr Goldberg. 'Thank you, Mr Goldberg, thank you for believing in me, and the answer is still yes.'

'That's excellent news, Miss Watkins. I'll be in touch in the near future to discuss pre-rehearsal dates and your travel itinerary. Believe me, you won't regret it. My touring company provides each actress with a chance to eventually appear in my West End theatre.'

'You mean I could be appearing at the Theatre Royal one day?'

'Of course, you will, if you work hard enough. Now I really must be going.'

Mr Goldberg stood formally, bowed and kissed Molly's hand. 'Good evening, my dear. I look forward to you joining us. He shook hands with Thomas and quickly took his leave. As soon as Molly had shut the door behind him, she raced back down the corridor and burst through the door of the dining room. 'I'm going to be an actress!' she shouted, as she danced around the room. 'I can't believe it, I'm actually going to be an actress.'

The others, noticing her flushed face and bright eyes, did not have the heart to dampen her enthusiasm with their doubts and suspicions.

Chapter 38

Etty sat at a table in her room and gazed at the blank sheet of writing paper before her. She was emotional and confused. Were her family right, did David have a right to know about the baby? Putting down her pen, she cast her eyes over to the waste bin where several crumpled pieces of paper lay, all previous attempts at starting the most difficult letter she had ever had to write. She grimaced and sighed. How to tell a man that you hadn't seen for six months that he was about to become a father was difficult enough, but then to tell him you didn't want to keep his baby…

Picking up her pen, she turned it over in her hands. It was beautiful; Patrick had bought it for her for Christmas. She had given him a handmade cravat in rich burgundy silk, which he had worn ever since, though admittedly he had also regularly worn the waistcoat that Eliza Jane had knitted him too. She continued with the letter.

"Dear David," she stopped, pen poised, recollecting that summer's day last August, when the sun had been high in the sky, the sweet-smelling grass had made a soft comfortable bed, and the buttercups provided a warm yellow blanket.

Why had she done it? She hadn't ever loved David Jackson. She gave an involuntary shiver as the familiar accusing voice in her head criticised her for giving into temptation while her father had hanged himself in grief.

A tear rolled down Etty's cheek; she hastily wiped it away. She very rarely cried. Whatever was the matter with her? This pregnancy seemed to be making her an emotional wreck. She sighed, and continued the letter.

"Dear David,

I expect you will be surprised to hear from me but nevertheless, I thought I should write to inform you that I am having your baby. I know this will come as a shock to you, as it was to me, but the family felt you have a right to know. I have decided to give the child up for adoption. There is no need to come to London as my mind is made up.

I hope you are well and happy in your life.

Yours faithfully,

Henrietta Watkins.

Etty re-read her words, and then in total despair, screwed the paper up and threw it in the bin to join the others. She got up and surveyed herself in the mirror, cupping a hand under her small bump. She was six months pregnant and feeling physically well if emotionally distraught. Luckily, no one had suspected anything at work, although Violet Cummings had remarked that she had put on weight. In response, Etty had quickly retorted that she had always been too thin, and felt the extra weight suited her.

The baby moved and kicked randomly, which she tried to ignore. She did not want to feel anything for this new life growing inside her. If she disregarded what was happening to her, she felt she would be able to cope.

Lately, she had been formulating a plan in her mind, and the more she thought about it, the more excited she became. She selflessly intended to propose marriage to Patrick to save him from himself.

Mrs Patrick Lawrence sounded just right. Patrick would become the baby's father, for it would be his only chance to have an heir. They would both agree to lead discreet and separate lives while putting on a united front to the world. She would have very little to do with the child, as she would insist on appointing the right nanny. The plan was fool proof, David Jackson would never know the truth, Etty could continue to work at the House of Harding, and everyone would be happy. All she needed to do was find the right moment to propose.

Etty flung her writing paper back in her drawer then carefully laid her precious pen on top. As she closed the drawer, she caught sight of herself in the mirror, and hugged herself with immense satisfaction.

Thomas's hand was shaking as he tried to compare the address on the card he was holding with the name of the house on the large brick pillar before him.

East Cliff Mansion, he read, this was indeed where Lady Bennington lived. Shivering violently through a toxic mixture of cold and nerves, he pulled his overcoat tighter and adjusted the muffler around his neck.

He pushed open the heavy Iron Gate, and not wishing to draw attention to himself in case it clanged, he carefully shut it behind him. He walked down the long snowy path, using a set of tyre tracks to guide him. The tracks had been made by a black car that was standing outside the front door, already covered by a light sprinkling of snow. He had been asked to arrive sharply at three.

It was exactly three when Thomas pulled on the front door bell. The door was opened almost immediately by a man dressed in coat tails who seemed to be expecting him. 'Mr Watkins, please come in. Her Ladyship is in the drawing room; I'll take you to her.'

Thomas removed his cap and stamped his snowy boots on the boot scraper. Then with a quick polish of each shoe on his trouser leg, he entered the house. He gazed at his surroundings in wonder: Patrick's house seemed small by comparison.

The hall was large and square. The thick, royal blue carpet cushioned his feet making Thomas aware of his dirty boots. A large chandelier was hanging from the centre of the high ceiling, which cast a glittering light over all it surveyed. The stairs were wide and flanked by an ornate carved banister. Thomas's jaw dropped in amazement, he drew a breath in and almost forgot to exhale he was so overwhelmed; slowly, he followed the man to another large room.

On entering the room, the butler made a formal announcement. 'Mr Watkins, your Ladyship.'

'Ah, do come in, Mr Watkins. Will you take afternoon tea?'

Lady Bennington was sitting on a high-backed couch, her stick by her side. Her voice was but not imperious or imposing.

Thomas, still in awe of the house and worried about what he was going to hear, knew he wouldn't be able to eat or drink anything. Nevertheless, as it was impolite to refuse, he simply said, 'Thank you.' He felt breathless with nerves and took a deep breath into steady his beating heart.

A man was sitting by the window. He had grey hair parted halfway down the side of his head, and bore a large moustache. He had stood when Thomas entered the room.

'Allow me to introduce Mr Rudgewick to you. He's our family solicitor, and has been offering me advice on the matter before us.'

Thomas shook the man's hand before being motioned to sit on the chair next to a highly polished table, where a large carved eagle was displayed. To his great surprise, he recognised that it was the one he had made and sold through Laycock's Antiques.

'Everyone admires that piece,' said Lady Bennington fondly.

'May I ask where it came from?'

'Why yes, it was from Laycock's in Crossdale, you and your family used to live there I believe.'

'Yes, my lady, we did.'

Thomas thought for a moment wondering whether to claim ownership of the bird. Finally, he decided he would. 'My lady,' he said tentatively, 'I carved the piece.'

'Yes, I thought you did. I have one or two other pieces of yours sent by mail order from Laycock's. I admire your work, Mr Watkins; you are very talented.'

There was a gentle knock on the door, and the butler entered with a tray. Lady Bennington addressed him, 'Ah here is tea – put it there for me, will you,' – she nodded at the table in front of her – 'and that will be all, thank you. Oh, and Stevens, can you inform Master Ronald that I'm in a meeting, and don't wish to be disturbed.'

'Certainly, my Lady.'

The butler inclined his head slightly and then withdrew as silently as he had arrived.

Soon Thomas was juggling a delicate bone china cup and saucer in one hand, and a tiny sandwich on a plate in the other.

Note 'Mr Watkins'. Thomas swung his knees round to face lady Bennington, not daring to place his plate on the table next to him where the eagle was displayed.

'I have asked you to come and see me on a very delicate matter. First there's a matter on which I need confirmation. Your parents – are they Martha and Albert Watkins?' Lady Bennington glanced at Mr Rudgewick for support after asking the question. He nodded in agreement.

'Yes, my Lady, they were. Sadly, my mother died of a heart attack last June, and Da, I mean my father, followed suit a few weeks later with a disease of the kidneys.'

Lady Bennington gasped. 'I'm so very sorry to hear that. Martha's mother, your grandmother, worked for me at York Manor in Barton. Martha and my daughter, Elizabeth…' Thomas's had begun to tremble, almost spilling his tea. Observing this, Lady Bennington halted for a moment, before beginning again. 'Martha and Elizabeth became firm friends. Now, Mr Watkins, I have a long story to tell you.' Lady Bennington took a sip of tea; her hand had a slight age tremor as she lifted the cup to her mouth. She then replaced the cup onto the saucer and put it down on the table next to her.

'How shall I begin? Elizabeth was my only daughter, and I loved her dearly. Perhaps I was wrong to do so, because ultimately, she let me down. When she was eighteen, in 1899, she embarked on a tour of Europe accompanied by my late husband's sister. While she was away, she met a celebrated artist called Joseph Tyson. Elizabeth also painted, and unfortunately, I believe that is how they met. I use the word, unfortunately advisedly, because the gentleman was already married. His wife was American born and an invalid, so therefore quite delicate. Joseph had taken her to Italy in the hope that the winter sun would improve her health. Not long after their first meeting, my daughter and Joseph fell in love.

'Whether it was the hot sun or the beauty of Lake Como that induced temporary insanity, I will never know, but nature took its course, and two months after Elizabeth had returned to England, she found she was pregnant with Joseph's child. My husband, as you might imagine, was furious and ensured Joseph not to contact Elizabeth again. The baby was to be given away or adopted out. I took a more philosophical approach, understanding how much my daughter loved him.'

Lady Bennington took another sip of tea. Thomas did the same, burning his throat with the hot liquid. His didn't touch his sandwich.

'My daughter and I,' she continued, 'discussed the problem at great length, and it was Elizabeth's idea to ask your mother to bring the baby up as her own. My husband, keen to avoid any shame, quickly arranged an annuity to be paid regularly to your parents providing no more was said.

'On December the fifteenth, my daughter went into labour, forgive my indelicacies, Mr Watkins, but the story needs to be told. It was a long labour and on the sixteenth of December, Ronald was eventually born. Half an hour later, another child was born; my daughter gave birth to twins.

'Martha had been staying with us for some time, so that she could pass the baby off as hers in the village. Your father had agreed to the plan, and I believe your grandmother came to look after you all. As you may imagine, the fact there were two babies altered our plans considerably. Of course, in the very short time that it took to reconsider our course of action, my daughter became much attached to the boys, and could not bear to lose them. My husband was keen to continue with the original plan. Rightly or wrongly, I faced his wrath and intervened. Ronald stayed with us while your mother took Rory home with her. I knew separating twins was not really the right thing to do but my husband gave us no choice. We agreed never to contact your parents again, and Rory became a Watkins. Mr Rudgewick, you oversaw the legalities for us.' The solicitor stood slightly, agreed with the statement and sat again.

Thomas made an attempt to speak. 'No let me finish, Mr Watkins.' Lady Bennington raised her hand. 'My husband died in 1911, and I subsequently found out that my daughter had been secretly communicating with Ronald's father. By then, his poor wife had passed away, and Joseph was keen for my daughter to join him in America. He sent two tickets for a passage to New York. One ticket was for Elizabeth, and one for me to act as chaperone. Ronald would stay at school and come out to New York in the holidays, under the care of Joseph's sister. I would stay in New York for a while, and then return home after the wedding.

'You know, Mr Watkins, it's strange how the course of our lives can turn on a single event. We were all set to leave, when Ronald was sent home from Ample forth College, having caught a bad case of measles. Reluctantly, Elizabeth sailed for America without me. Horrifically, the ship was the Titanic. Now I'm sure, Mr Watkins, that you've heard about that ill-fated liner and the terrible loss of life. I'm sad to say that my daughter was among the casualties.'

Thomas could see that Lady Bennington was struggling with her emotions as she continued her story.

'Never a day passes when I don't think of my beautiful girl. My greatest regret is that I was not with her, but God had other plans for me. My grandson and I continued to live a peaceful existence together until war broke out. At the age of sixteen, a year into the war and like so many young men at that time, he ran away to join the army. He told them at the recruitment office that he was eighteen years of age.'

Thomas felt a stab of guilt slice through his heart.

'He returned from the war damaged with hysterical blindness, I sold York Manor and moved to London to seek the best treatments possible.' Lady Bennington paused; visibly weary from telling her story. 'I'm sure that my story has come as quite a shock to you, and I've asked you here today to discuss what's to be done.'

Thomas finally placed his cup and saucer on the table next to him. The sandwich remained plated on his lap. He looked again at his carved eagle while he reflected on his response. 'Lady Bennington,' he began. 'Your news has not come as a complete shock to me, as I already knew that Rory is not my blood brother. It is a secret that I've kept from my family since the death of my parents. I was sorting through their private papers when I came across a letter, from who I now know to be your daughter, to my mother, asking her to take the baby. I also found Rory's birth certificate. Is Mr Tyson still alive, and does he know about Rory? And why did your daughter call herself Elizabeth Tyson on the birth certificate?'

'Joseph is still alive and living in New York. He remains a very successful painter and illustrator. He has not married again. He sends me regular payments to cover the cost of Ronald's treatment but he's unaware that he has two sons. Ronald is aware that a gentleman from America sends him birthday presents but he has no idea that he is his father, just an old friend of the family. Elizabeth in an effort to legitimise her son called herself Tyson, rightly or wrongly that's what she wanted. Mr Watkins, I'm asking you to consider with me what should be done. I would, of course, love to meet Rory but I know that means both boys being told of the other's existence. It really was a chance in a million that we met as we did in the park that day, and I really cannot comprehend it, but it has happened and I believe it to be fate.'

'Are you saying that they should be told about each other, Lady Bennington?'

'Yes, Mr Rudgewick and I feel this to the best action. Ronald's doctors tell me that he has every chance of recovering his sight but his progress is slow. I feel that the shock of hearing he has a twin brother may just be enough to restore his vision. I would like to try it.'

'And what if the shock is too much and he becomes permanently blind?'

'His doctors feel it was shock that caused his blindness, so another shock may reverse the situation.'

'But what about the shock to Rory, and of course the rest of the family?'

'Mr Watkins, may I call you Thomas?'

'Yes, of course.'

'Thomas, there are two young men here who have been apart for nearly twenty years. I feel that's quite long enough to live without the other half of you

– do you not think so? I'm an old woman now, I want to live long enough to see Rory claim his birth right beside his brother.' She looked again at Mr Rudgewick; I am keen to re-write my will to include both boys. He nodded encouragingly again.

Lady Bennington turned to the elderly solicitor who had been observing the discussion. 'It's the correct thing to do,' she said, 'don't you agree, Mr Rudgewick?'

'Indeed,' said the old solicitor, 'Rory will be in line for a substantial inheritance from her Ladyship, and I don't believe we should deny that to the young man in question.'

Thomas swallowed hard, his mind racing. What would be the repercussions of such a move, how would Rory react? What would the others say? The implications for the family were beyond his imagination. He couldn't even begin to think coherently about it. Ultimately though, he knew that they should both be told the truth, and if he thought long enough about it, he would be glad to be relieved of his burdensome secret.

'You are right, of course,' he said with a little hesitation in his voice indicating his previous indecision. Rory should not be denied his rightful place, and I agree both boys should be informed of the other's existence. How do you plan to deal with this, Lady Bennington?'

'I'm glad that you agree with my assessment of the problem, Thomas. Mr Rudgewick and I feel that they must be told together, they need to hear the same words, and I'm the one that should tell them. Perhaps you might all come to tea on Thursday afternoon, when I'll break the news.'

'All the family?' enquired Thomas. 'Should they not be told alone, the shock might be too much for them collectively.'

'I'm not an autocrat but I do believe it will be for the best. Now let us have another cup of tea, this one has gone cold, and you haven't touched your sandwich. She turned to the solicitor. 'Mr Rudgewick, would you be so kind as to ring for Stevens?' He immediately obliged before resuming his seat.

Thomas sat back in his chair; his mind was reeling and he felt exhausted. He looked across at Lady Bennington, for her age, she was a remarkable old lady.

Chapter 39

The following morning while Molly and Jo were dusting and polishing their counter tops as Mrs Roberts was absent, they were free to chat. Molly had been telling Jo about Mr Goldberg's visit and offer. Jo was nonplussed at the announcement. Finally, she said, 'I suppose you'll be leaving now then.' Seeing Molly's excited face fall, she rapidly added, 'Oh don't mind me, Molly, I'm happy for you really I am, it's a wonderful opportunity, but I'm going to miss you. Cobb's won't be the same. I'll have to face the general on my own, and who's going to protect me from old goggle-eyed Gambon's wandering hands. Are you absolutely sure this is what you want to do? It seems to me it's going to be a hard life, with all those boarding houses, and being away from home for months at a time, and changing in dirty provincial theatre dressing rooms.'

Jo was not actually saying anything that in her quieter moments Molly hadn't already thought of, but she wanted this, she really did. She needed to act; somehow it was in her blood. Jo's words had irritated her – there was nothing more annoying than having your worst fears voiced back to you.

Molly snapped at her. 'That is exactly Thomas's view. Come on, Jo, I would appreciate a bit of support, but no, all you see are the negatives, and how my leaving will affect *you*. Are you jealous, is that the problem?'

'No!' Jo's face crumpled in horror that Molly should say such a thing. 'Don't be silly, Molly.'

'I didn't know I was being silly now, as well as reckless,' was the sharp retort. Why couldn't people just be happy that she was finally about to fulfil a long-held ambition.

'I didn't say you were being reckless – all I said was, are you sure it's the right life for you.'

'You are as bad as the others, Jo. What's the matter with you all; no one is pleased for me. Can't they see it's what I've been dreaming of forever?'

'Really,' retorted Jo, 'and I thought you were dreaming of my brother, but it appears not. Do you know how upset he was, and still is, that you turned him out of the house on Christmas Eve? I still can't believe you did that; I wasn't going to say anything but as we are talking frankly…'

'It's none of your business,' Molly interrupted quickly, 'that's between him and me, and I'm not prepared to discuss it with you. Suffice to say, I had a feeling that here was something better coming up for me and I was not prepared to be second best to Nora. You could have told me about your mother's wish, Jo, particularly as you knew I really liked your brother.'

'It was not my business to tell you, Kit should have done it.'

Exactly, of course he should as early as possible. Now I've got to go to see Gambon and tell him I am leaving.'

'How dare you, Molly!' Jo stopped polishing and stared at her friend. 'How can you stand there and say you felt something better was coming up for you, better than my brother, you mean. Is that what you're saying?'

'I didn't mean it in that way Jo and you know it. Whatever's the matter with you today?'

'What's the matter with me, there's something the matter with you, more like.'

In exasperation, Molly turned and started to walk away, then suddenly stopped, and turned back to Jo. 'If you can't be happy for me, then don't bother talking to me again.'

Molly once more turned away, and began walking.

'If that's what you want,' Jo called after her, 'then that's fine by me. You're obviously too high and mighty to bother with me now.'

Molly stopped in her tracks to consider a reply, then deciding against it, she continued onto Mr Gambon's office. Jo felt unable to swallow the lump that had suddenly developed in her throat as she went back to her counter.

When Molly returned home that night, she was in a foul mood. She and Jo had not spoken for the rest of the afternoon. She was cheered, however, by the sight of a typewritten letter waiting for her. She dashed upstairs to open it expecting it to be from Mr Goldberg.

The letter outlined rehearsal plans for the coming shows, and the towns they would be visiting when the company set off on tour. First stop was Southampton, followed by Bournemouth two nights later. Several other provincial towns followed with names Molly had never heard of. Last on the list was Lancaster. She giggled, imagine Mrs Fanshawe's face if she went to the Playhouse one evening to find Molly on the stage. The whole of Crossdale would soon hear about it. A shiver of excitement coursed through Molly's body. She refolded the letter and tucked it away in the drawer in her room. She ran back downstairs to tell Eliz Jane in the kitchen.

'Guess what, Lizzie, I shall be going to Lancaster with the company, imagine that! I could take the train out to Crossdale if I get time off.'

'That would be wonderful,' said Eliza Jane, 'but listen, are you free on Thursday afternoon at three?'

'Yes, I think so; we don't start rehearsals until Friday. Why do you ask?'

'You remember me telling you about Ronald from the park?'

Molly wrinkled her nose as she tried to recollect the name. 'You mean that boy who looks like Rory?'

'Yes, that's the one. Thomas and Jo met him and his grandma the other day, and she's invited us all for afternoon tea on Thursday.'

'Jo won't be going, will she?'

'No, I don't think so; it's a family invitation.' Eliza Jane was surprised by Molly's question. 'Why don't you want Jo to come, she's your best friend?'

'Oh, no matter, just wondering that's all. What time's dinner?'

On Thursday afternoon, the family set off to East cliff Manor for tea with Lady Bennington. Both Rory and Etty had said they were too busy to go but Thomas had insisted.

'Why does she want us all to go?' Rory asked, struggling reluctantly into his overcoat and hat in the hall way. 'Luckily, we're not busy in the studio this afternoon.'

'I told you, she was surprised to hear we were from Crossdale, and wanted to meet us all as she used to live near there.

'So where did she live near Crossdale?' Etty asked, she really couldn't be bothered to be sociable. 'I'll tell you what, this had better be jolly – I had enough trouble getting time off work for it to be a boring afternoon, listening to some old dear's account of life near Crossdale.'

Thomas chose not to answer but led his siblings through the streets to the Manor.

As they turned in through the gate, and started up the long path, they had their first glimpse of the house. Rory gave a low whistle. 'What a huge place,' he said, 'imagine owning this.'

Thomas felt the irony of his remark. 'It certainly seems to be a wonderful house,' he agreed.

'Well, at least we've arrived thank goodness.' Etty's feet were aching. She had found the walk arduous with carrying the extra weight of her pregnancy. 'I hope the old girl has got something nice for tea, I'm perpetually hungry.'

'Etty, quiet, there's someone coming.' Thomas straightened his tie and whipped his cap off his head. Rory did the same.

The door was opened by Stevens, who bade them to follow him into the house.

On entering the drawing room, Lady Bennington was standing supported by her stick to greet them. 'Mr Watkins, how delightful to see you and your family, do come in.' Molly thought how like pictures she had seen of the late Queen.

She shook hands with everyone and motioned for them to be seated. Thomas was pleased to notice his carving had been temporarily removed out of sight. It saved further explanation, he thought.

'Stevens, could you ask Ronald to join us, and then we'll take tea.'

'Certainly, my Lady.' Stevens inclined his head slightly then withdrew from the room.

'This is a beautiful room, Lady Bennington,' Etty began, her eyes having taken everything in before she sat down on one of the sofas next to Molly. 'The drapes are magnificent; what material are they?'

'Etty,' warned Eliza Jane.

'Please do go and take a closer look. I've been told that you're a designer with the House of Harding, so of course you'll be interested in fabric.'

Etty got up and walked over to the window. The curtains were rich blue and gold brocade. She felt the material. 'They're wonderful,' she said turning back to the room, 'and they match the sofa's perf—'

She stopped as Ronald was led into the room. She had heard he was like Rory but this was ridiculous. She wasn't the only one to gaze at him; Rory and Molly were both taken back. With Stevens' help, Rory was seated on the couch next to his grandmamma. The butler silently left the room.

'Ronald, our visitors are here. Thomas and Eliza Jane on the sofa to your right you already know, Henrietta and Molly on the sofa to your left and Rory in Grandfather's chair opposite you.'

Ronald spoke up looking straight ahead. 'Well, Rory, are we really alike or am I better looking?'

'You're far better looking,' agreed Rory politely, 'but our resemblance is uncanny.'

There was a knock on the door, and Stevens brought in a large tray bearing tea and sandwiches.

The old lady nodded at the tray approving its contents for her guests. 'We'll look after ourselves thank you, Stevens. I'll ring the bell for cake later.'

Again, the butler inclined his head and left the room.

'Henrietta, as you're standing, perhaps you would pour the tea.'

'I'll help you,' said Eliza Jane quickly fearing Etty might refuse.

'I believe you know Crossdale, Lady Bennington,' said Molly politely.

'Yes indeed, Ronald and I used to live about ten miles away in the village of Barton.'

Molly remembered Ma talking about Barton. 'My mother used to work at a big house in Barton; she was always telling us stories of York Manor. My grandmother worked in the kitchens there.'

'Yes, my dear, your grandmother worked for me and your mother alongside her. This brings me to the reason I've invited you all here. I have something to tell you, something that may shock you. I'm sorry to be so dramatic but Ronald and Rory, you must pay particular attention, as I have something very important to tell you both. We will just wait until everyone has a cup of tea and a sandwich, thank you Eliza Jane for handing everything round.' She watched as everyone helped themselves to a sandwich from the plate Eliza Jane offered them. 'Now then do sit down, my dear, and I will begin.'

Lady Bennington relayed the story much as she had done to Thomas. When she had finished, a stunned silence filled in the room. The tea had gone cold in the cups, and the sandwiches remained merely nibbled at.

Rory rose to his feet placing his plate on the table that once bore Thomas's eagle. 'I don't wish to be rude, Lady Bennington but I really can't believe a word of this. I was born to Martha and Albert Watkins; they were my parents, surely it's pure coincidence that Ronald and I look alike. It's been very nice meeting you but I'm sorry I must go now – Mr Lawrence needs me in the studio this afternoon. Thank you for tea, Lady Bennington.'

'Rory,' said Thomas quietly. 'It is true; I have the proof here in my pocket.'

Thomas produced Rory's birth certificate and gave it to him. Rory, almost losing the use of his legs, sank back into a chair. His face was white and drawn, his eyes wild and open. He studied the piece of paper.

Lady Bennington put out her hand, placing it on Ronald's arm. 'I'm sorry it's been such a shock to you darling, and you too Rory – I can't imagine how you must be feeling.'

Ronald suddenly rose to his feet, and began to feel his way to the door, handling the furniture as he passed. 'No please, leave me I can manage,' he said, as Eliza Jane got up to help him. 'I'm going to my room. Please accept my apologies everyone, but I don't think I'll stay for the cake.'

Eliza Jane noticed that Rory did not look at him as he passed by.

Etty, growing suspicious, had questions. 'Well, you don't seem as shocked as us, Thomas. How did you come by Rory's birth certificate? You've obviously known about this for some time.'

'I found it after Da died.'

'And you didn't think to tell us that Rory was not our brother, that little fact escaped you, did it? I can't believe you've been so devious.'

'I kept it a secret in honour of Ma and Pa. They obviously didn't want anyone to know or they would have talked to Rory about it. Besides, I thought it might be too much for Rory to bear. Just look at him, Etty.'

Etty looked over to her brother sitting forward in his chair, his dark head in his hands, he was shaking.

Etty like a dog with a bone continued, she needed to get to the bottom of why Thomas had kept it from them. 'Well, well, Thomas, the secrets you've been keeping, it's a wonder you've been able to sleep at night. I mean you didn't tell us the real truth about Da's death, did you? And now this, are there any more secrets to be told?'

'Etty,' warned Thomas, he was anxious that Etty did not air all the family secrets before Lady Bennington. He was shocked at Ronald and Rory's reaction, he was expecting the news to be hard to take, but Rory looked devastated.

Eliza Jane had also noticed that Rory was taking the news badly. She rose from the sofa and went over to him placing an arm around his shoulder. 'Rory, you're our brother, and always will be a part of our family regardless of your parentage. You know we love you, don't you?' She caught sight of Etty's cold stare. 'Don't look at me like that, Etty; this has come as a complete shock to me too.'

Rory shrugged away Eliza Jane's hug and suddenly sat up rigidly in his chair. The birth certificate was now lying forlornly on the floor where it had fallen out of his limp hands.

'Rory, please listen to me,' said Molly, leaving her chair to also give him a hug. 'You're still my baby brother and always will be. I love you, we all love you.'

He pushed her aside, and rose to his feet, his face now dark and scowling.

'How dare you, Thomas, how dare you not say anything to me? What gives you the right to play God? How do you think it feels to find out that you're not who you thought you were, that all those treasured beliefs you have held as you grew up are no longer true? I'm glad you're not my brother, you don't deserve to be. I can't forgive you for this.'

Rory stormed towards the door.

'Where are you going?' Molly asked tearfully.

'Home!' he said, through gritted teeth, his cheeks pinched and his mouth set.

Rory jerked open the door, but Thomas was ready to stop him and gripped his arm. 'Rory, please, I thought long and hard about telling you. I decided not to because I knew how much it would hurt you and us all. How do you think it's been for me? Looking at you every day, knowing this about you?' Thomas changed the tone of his voice trying to cajole Rory into accepting the news he had just been told. 'You're still the same man, Rory, except your father is still alive, and you have a grandmother and another brother who will love you just as we do.'

With a menacing stare, Rory broke free from Thomas's grip and left the room, slamming the door behind him.

Eliza Jane got up, and started towards the door after him.

'No, Lizzie, leave him,' said Thomas, 'he has a lot to come to terms with, and he's not a baby anymore.'

'I'm sorry, Thomas,' said Lady Bennington, her voice withered and weak with emotion, she suddenly sounded her age. 'There's no easy way to impart such life changing news. It had to be done, and I should have done it a long time ago.'

Rory walked briskly down the path to the gate finally breaking into a run. He couldn't even begin to process what it all meant. Why hadn't Ma and Da told him, why let him think he was a Watkins when he was plainly not. Then he remembered on the day he had received that letter informing him he had won a prize for his painting, Ma had said, *"Son before you open it, there's something we think you should know.'* Was she worried that the letter was from his real mother asking to see him and was she going to tell him then that he wasn't hers? He had been too excited to ask what she meant. He thought about what Molly had said, *you're still my brother,* which was swirling around in his head, jostling for space with much darker thoughts. His whole life had been a lie, they were not his siblings back there, they were imposters, and his whole identity was in question.

Patrick thought he heard the back-door bang. He slowly moved towards the kitchen, fearing someone had broken in. Opening the door, he jumped when he saw Rory taking a drink of water from the tap. 'You startled me,' he said, 'you're back early, where are the others?'

'You know, Patrick; I'll never get used to London water as long as I live.'

He pushed past his employer, leaving Patrick puzzled. *What's happened now,* he thought.

Thomas was mortified, he hated scenes, he ran his fingers over his head, in a helpless gesture making his hair stand up even more than usual. 'I am so sorry, Lady Bennington,' he said turning back from the door that Rory had banged. 'I can only apologise for Rory's behaviour. Perhaps we should leave.'

'Perhaps that would be best in the circumstances, but we must not apologise for either of the boys, this news has been as devastating as I thought it would be. They will both come around in time and I look forward to getting to know Rory properly.'

'Hardly surprising really, is it?' said Etty, fighting the incredible surge of anger she felt over the way Rory had heard the news. Anger from Etty was a method she used to prevent tears, and right now, she felt like loving the baby she was carrying fiercely and crying hysterically. 'I don't know you would expect anything different. They've both just received some life changing news, think how you'd feel.'

'Etty,' Thomas replied, 'there's no need to speak to Lady Bennington in that tone.'

'Not at all, Thomas, Etty has every right to speak her mind. Perhaps I could have handled it better but I'm not sure how. The facts wouldn't be any different no matter how you say them. I'll give Rory a few days to come to terms with the news, and then with your permission, I'll call on him.'

This agreed, they thanked Lady Bennington for tea, collected their coats from Stevens, including Rory's, as he had left it behind in his haste to leave.

Quietly and almost in shock, they left the house and walked down to the gate and were soon on the pavement heading home.

'Stupid woman,' complained Etty as they walked home. 'How did she think Rory would take the news as she put it, I just feel so angry about the whole business. She dresses as if still in the last century, with all her wealth too,' she added. None of her siblings replied, as each was travelling with their own thoughts.

Chapter 40

Thomas put his drink down on the kitchen table, yawned and then stretched back on his chair. He took his watch from his waistcoat pocket: a quarter past midnight. The others had gone to bed over an hour ago but Molly was still out with her actor friends for the fifth night this week. She was in the early stages of a two-week rehearsal schedule. They were performing three plays on tour, and Molly had been cast as the maid in each one. She was quick to point out that she was the understudy to the lead in one play. She had defended this position to Etty. 'I've got to start somewhere, and yes, it probably is at the bottom, but once they see how I handle my part, they'll soon give me better roles.'

The main part of the rehearsal process, however, seemed to be fun evenings out. One of them had a car, and they would pile into it, the girls sitting on the boy's laps, going for jaunts in the country. Molly had arrived home after one o'clock every night this week. She had repeatedly told Thomas not to wait up for her, but he had ignored her request, preferring to see her safely home.

Thomas shook his head wearily and yawned again, he was turning into his parents before his very eyes. "Old before his time" was frequently levelled at him, but he somehow couldn't shake off the shackles of family responsibility.

Jaded and drowsy at the kitchen table, he thought about Rory. In the past week, since the life changing news had been broken to him, he had railed at Thomas for not having prepared him for that afternoon at Eastcliffe Manor. Why had he not been told before, especially as it seems Thomas had shared the news with Patrick some months ago.

Lady Bennington had called to see Rory, as promised the previous day and though Rory was initially refusing to see her, he had been persuaded to at least hear what she had to say. He had been invited back to Eastcliffe Manor and had agreed to come.

Thomas took another sip of his drink; his family concerns seemed to be mounting. His thoughts turned to Etty: she still hadn't written to David Jackson.

According to Eliza Jane, she was only a couple of months from having the baby, and as far as he knew, she hadn't prepared anything for its arrival. There was no cot or nappies or clothes for the baby. In fact, Etty was still pretending it wasn't happening. He would have to talk to her again, make her see that plans should be made sooner rather than later.

Thank goodness Eliza Jane seemed happy and content, looking after them all and spending time with Jim. He was a good sort and seemed to think the world of her.

Thomas' thoughts then turned to Patrick. He had overcome his initial reservations, and was finally beginning to accept Patrick's predilections. He must be lonely though, he never seemed to go out anywhere, spending time reading in his study when not in his dark room. He would occasionally go to his club but Thomas preferred not to think about what went on there.

Thomas' thoughts turned to Jo; she was such a sweet girl, and so unhappy at the moment that she and Molly had fallen out. He knew he should do something about it. He sighed; he was falling in love with Jo, but knew it would prove fruitless if he didn't have any means of supporting a wife.

A crunch of tyres on the gravel driveway broke into his thoughts. He took the watch out of his pocket waistcoat: it was two am. This could not go on.

The car doors banged, followed by deep laughter, then Molly's lighter giggles filtered through the night. He heard someone say, 'I say, Molly, dashed jolly evening, what. See you tomorrow, don't be late.' There were several shouted goodbyes, and the gravel dispersed noisily under the car tyres.

Molly took a deep breath before she opened the kitchen door; she had seen the light was on and knew Thomas would be waiting.

'Sorry I'm late, Thomas,' she said breezily, 'but you didn't need to wait up for me, I'm a big girl now you know.'

'I will wait up, Molly, no matter what because I need to know you're safely in the house before I go to bed. Where on earth have you been until this time?'

'One of the boys suggested a trip to Brighton; it's only about forty miles away, so we all crowded into his car and flew down there. Unfortunately, we were stopped by a police motor cyclist, and by the time he had laboriously written down all our names in his book and cautioned us, time was getting on.'

'You had your name taken down by a policeman – whatever were you thinking?'

'He was perfectly sweet, so you needn't worry. We all gave false names. I was Amelia Snodgrass: I got the name from Pickwick Papers. We drove along the Sea front then someone suggested skinny dipping, but since it's the middle of January, so there were no takers. They really are such spiffing fun.'

'What is up with you, Molly, I don't recognise you anymore. You're using words like super and spiffing, where's the girl from Lancashire I used to know?'

'She's dead and buried,' she said, airily as if it didn't matter, 'along with two parents and a brother.'

Thomas winced outwardly. Along with picking up words from toffs, she was becoming difficult and thoughtless. 'Your brother isn't dead; he's still a part of this family, you said so yourself just the other day.'

'Yes, I know he isn't dead, but it doesn't feel the same any more. Look at the family he was born into – how long do you think he's going to stay with us when he inherits half of Eastcliffe Manor. With that money behind him, he'll soon change. In fact, life has changed us all – Patrick has his problems, Etty is having a baby out of wedlock and you've lost your job for being uncharacteristically aggressive. I'm not going to be sweet little *something-will-turn-up-Molly* any more. You have to make your own fortune in this life – you don't get anywhere by being nice.'

'Is that what your new friends have taught you? It's a shame you don't have any time for your old friends.'

Creasing her forehead, Molly gave him a quizzical look.

'I'm talking about Jo; she came around tonight to try and make it up with you before you leave for Southampton.'

'I'm going to bed, Thomas, it's late.' She was in denial over her lost friendship. 'I really can't think about Jo at the moment. She probably came to see you anyway, and only half hoped I'd be here.'

'She's very upset. The old Molly would have wanted to see her I think, don't you?'

'I told you, Thomas, the old Molly has gone, long live the new Molly. Now I'm off to bed, I have to be at rehearsals at eight, and I need my beauty sleep. Goodnight and sleep well.'

She left the aroma of cheap perfume behind her. Thomas sat morosely at the table. His eyes had misted over so he rubbed them vigorously, as if trying to erase sight of the "new" Molly. *What would Ma and Da make of their family now?* he thought. He hung his head and covered his face with his hands in despair. 'I'm doing my best, Da,' he shouted, 'I'm doing my best.'

He removed his hands from his face, swiping his glass from the table. The ensuing crash and splintering of the glass did nothing to alleviate his feelings of inadequacy and total disappointment in himself.

Thomas slept fitfully that night and the following morning, Molly was up and out before eight while Thomas feeling less than enthusiastic ate a solitary breakfast in the kitchen.

Charles Harding of the House of Harding swept into the design room, closely followed by the supervisor, Miss Agatha Bell. The designers sat behind their desks in the light filled room. Each desk had a lamp and a sloping tablet on which to rest their paper while they sketched. There were four designers including Etty sitting on stools at four tables in the middle of the room. Violet Cummings sat opposite Etty. She was a thorn in Etty's side, sniping and constantly trying to win Miss Bell's approval. She smirked when praised, looking across to Etty for confirmation that she had overheard the approval. Etty kept her head down, ignoring the other woman's posturing.

'Put your pencils down, ladies, I have an announcement to make.' Etty and the others put down their pens, turned their knees slightly and looked at him expectantly.

Satisfied he had the women's attention, Mr Harding began. 'You may have heard that Madame Souris is soon to be arriving from Paris and is deigning to grace the House of Harding with her presence. Madame is very well known in Paris for her unique and sought-after designs. While she is here, we intend to show her our designs, with the prospect of her purchasing some gowns for her shop in the Rue Cambon. I want you all to submit your best designs to me and I'll select those that I think represent the finest we have. She's arriving on March the twenty fifth, and will be with us for a while. She's most interested in the very English custom of dressing for afternoon tea.' Harding smiled and gazed around the table at his alert designers. 'Now I come to the most exciting news, Madame Souris and the House of Harding are to work more closely with one another in the near future, and there is a chance that one of you, if your designs are chosen, will have the opportunity to work with Madame in Paris. That is all ladies, so please return to your work.'

Mr Harding nodded briefly then left the room with Miss Bell following closely behind. There was a general buzz of excitement. Only Etty was quiet, she was rapidly calculating the dates; she might just submit her designs before the baby put in an appearance.

Violet Cummings leant forward on her desk. 'It's not worth your bothering, Watkins.' For a split second, Etty thought she was referring to her pregnancy but soon realised Violet was trying to intimidate her. 'After all, I am bound to win, whose designs have sold the most dresses this month.'

Etty had to admit it was true but replied, 'Your designs couldn't catch the eye of a frog, Violet, so if I were you, I'd just give up now.'

'We'll see.' Came the reply accompanied by a sneer.

Etty returned to her drawing. *March the twenty fifth*, she thought, so the rumour was true, Madame Souris was coming. The baby was due on April the first – that gave her plenty of time to submit her designs. She had to win; she could learn so much more if she went to Paris, she could still be married to Patrick to give the baby a name and leave the wretched child with a nanny. Paris would suit her plans very nicely. Violet spoke again, 'I was just saying to Ellen at break that you must be living off the fat of the land at that Patrick Lawrence's place. Violet leaned back in her chair to appraise Etty sitting in front of her. 'I mean you haven't half put on weight again lately, Watkins.'

'Do you think so?' Etty replied nonchalantly, already having formulated her next jibe. 'Mr Harding said I was looking beautiful the other day, so I suppose the extra curves must suit me. Perhaps you should put weight on too; you might get your designs passed a little more quickly.'

Violet sniffed, put her head down and went back to her work.

Rory was about to set off for his first visit to his grandmother's house. He really didn't want to go but Patrick had persuaded him that it was the right thing to do and suggested he drove him there.

'I don't need driving; it isn't that far to walk.' He noticed Patrick's look of doubt on his face. 'Don't worry, I will go, but whether I go again is a different matter. Thanks anyway for the offer, Patrick,' he added, realising he had been a little brusque, but he was finding it difficult to forgive the fact that Thomas had told Patrick the circumstances of his birth before him.

It was nearing the end of February and daffodils planted in tubs by the road side were standing tall with tight yellow buds and waving slightly in the breeze. Rory admired their composition as he passed them by and fleetingly thought he might like to paint them. He was dawdling really, suffering with a real anxiety about his visit he was in no hurry to arrive at East Cliff Manor. Eventually, he was ringing the bell and Stevens opened the door. 'Good afternoon, sir, her ladyship is in the drawing room, please follow me.'

Rory gazed in awe at the different paintings hanging on the wall as he walked through the hall. Soon he was shown into the drawing room where he took the small soft hand that was outstretched to greet him. There was no sign of Ronald.

'Rory, do come and sit, thank you for coming as I mentioned to you when I came to see you at home there is so much we need to talk about, and of course get to know one another. Some tea, I think please, Stevens.' Stevens nodded and withdrew while Rory sat down in the chair next to the table bearing the eagle. He gazed at it, surely it resembled the one Thomas had carved and left with Mr Laycock to sell.

'It is your brother's work, Rory; little did I know the significance when I bought it.'

Rory smiled wryly almost not quite believing her words. He couldn't believe anything anyone said to him lately. He changed the subject. 'Is Ronald coming to see me?'

'Ronald is up in his room at present, I have asked him to join us but he is refusing to listen at present.'

Rory was annoyed, he had made the effort despite the family mess surely Ronald could too. He said as much to Lady Bennington.

'I do agree Rory but he will not listen to me, perhaps you might…'

'Yes, just tell me where his room is and I will go and see him.'

Having received instructions, Rory left the room almost colliding with Stevens' bearing tea on a tray. He climbed the stairs and counted the doors down to the left, knocking on the third door down.

'Who is it?' a distance voice came from within.

'It's me Rory, can we talk?'

Ronald's stick made a tapping sound across the bedroom floor. When the door opened, Rory found he didn't know how to start. 'I don't know what to say to you, now I'm here,' he said, feeling embarrassed at his intrusion.

'What can we say; I know what about it's been a bloody shock, that might do, or even I can't believe we've got to twenty, and no one told me I had a brother. This is ludicrous,' he said, turning and tapping his way back into the room with his stick, feeling for familiar items to help him get his bearings. Rory followed behind wanting to help but realising Ronald wouldn't welcome it, he was more than used to the layout of his bedroom.

'So, you are the elder by half an hour,' Rory blurted out.

Ronald stopped in his tracks. 'That's what Grandmamma said.'

Rory desperately searched for the right thing to say; somehow now he was here, it was beginning to be important that he get to know Ronald. He tried again, 'We need to talk, there are so many questions, so much to think about. May I come in?'

Ronald shrugged an answer. Rory could see his face was blank and uncompromising but ignoring that, he went inside and closed the door. 'May I sit?'

Ronald said nothing.

'Ronald, whether we like it or not, we're brothers. Please don't make this harder than it already is. Talk to me.'

Ronald turned around; there were tears in his eyes. 'I have just learned that the man who sends me presents from America, whom I thought to be a distant relative is actually my father. He has never once wanted to see me or you for that matter, don't you find that strange?'

'He didn't know about me, he thought he only had one son, but yes, I find it strange. I also find it strange that no one ever told me I wasn't a Watkins. I always wondered why I was so dark and the others not. I find it strange that there's someone in the room who looks exactly like me and believe me that is very strange. I find it strange to think I had a mother and a father that I never knew, and will never know. Yes, I find it strange all right.'

'Just sit down,' Ronald ordered sharply

Rory looked around the room for somewhere to sit when he saw some canvasses stacked up against the wall. 'You paint,' he said enthusiastically.

'I used to until I got this,' Ronald pointed at his eyes. 'It seems from what Grandmamma is saying that our parents were both talented artists. I have a vague recollection of Mother painting.'

'May I look at your work?'

'Go ahead.'

Rory carefully walked his fingers through the canvasses, stopping occasionally and bringing one out to look at more closely.

'This is amazing; I love your work. I used to paint; in fact, it was my painting that bought us to London. I don't paint any longer though.'

'Why is that?'

'It's a long story.'

'I have all the time in the world, and I'd like to know,' said Ronald pushing himself into a comfier position on the bed using his legs. Rory noticed he had on different coloured socks, obviously he dressed himself.'

He patted the bed beside him. 'Sit down, Rory; I think we do have lots to talk about. By the way, did you ever get the feeling that something was missing in your life?'

'Yes, I did, but everyone looked at me like I was mad when I said it.'

Ronald grinned. 'Me too.'

Eventually, the boys came back downstairs. Lady Bennington was trying to read in the drawing room but she was so tense she couldn't concentrate. She smiled, as they came into the room to join her, Ronald tapped his way to a chair, and Rory stood not knowing quite what to do.

'More tea, I think, will you ring for Stevens, Rory, just pull that bell rope over by the fireplace, the other has gone cold.' Rory did as he was asked though feeling awkward that on the pull of a cord, a middle-aged man, probably older than Albert would appear and serve them.

'Grandmamma, I told Rory that you would have pictures of Mother to show him, will you find the box.'

'You've both got Elizabeth's eyes I think,' remarked Lady Bennington, as she struggled to rise from the sofa. Rory sprang forward, 'If you tell me where the box is then I can get it for you.'

'Would you, dear, it's in the top drawer of that bureau by the window.' As directed, Rory opened the drawer and found an inlaid box, he brought it back and handed it to Lady Bennington, who in turn patted the seat beside her indicating Rory should sit down. She opened the box and sorted through some old prints; finally, she settled on one or two and handed them to Rory.

'Here is one of your mother obviously before she had you, while on her painting tour of Europe, and do you see that man standing next to her? That's your father.'

Rory gazed at the faded print, photography was not so advanced then as now, but it was enough to see make out a clear image of his parents standing side by side.

'We seem to be very like our father in height and dark looks,' said Rory, turning to his brother. 'And look, we have definitely got his nose, but our Mother is so beautiful, Ronald, she has thick, dark hair swept up from her forehead and a charming smile.' Without thinking, he stretched out his hand containing the photo to Ronald as if he might take it and view the picture in the ordinary way. Realising his mistake, he became embarrassed. 'Oh Lord, I'm sorry, I forgot.'

'I wish more than anything I could see that photo again. Mother was beautiful, my friends at school always wished she was their mother when she came to collect me but I can't even remember the picture. Let me hold it,' said Ronald.

Rory placed the photo into his brother's hand, Ronald gazed down.

'Can you see anything at all?' Rory anxiously.

'Nothing,' was the answer.

The photograph was handed back.

Lady Bennington took the photo, kissed her daughter's image and replaced it in the box. 'Now I must tell you and I hope I have done the right thing but I've written to your father about your reunion. It was not an easy letter to write; it will be a shock for him.'

'Forgive me, Lady Bennington, but Albert was such a wonderful man, and a huge influence in my life that I'm not sure I have room in my heart for another father, particularly one who didn't even know of my existence.'

'I understand, dear, you're bound to feel that, but Joseph is a good man too, and I'm sure that he'll be very proud of the way Albert and Martha brought you up. It's my fault that Joseph didn't know about you, but it was done with the best of intentions. This has been a shock to us all, I never thought that I'd see you again, except in passing in Crossdale – even then, I could never have made myself known to you. Elizabeth promised Martha and Albert that she would never contact them again when she handed you over, and of course, we kept our word.'

Lady Bennington put out her hand, placing it lightly on Rory's arm. 'You must believe me when I say it's so wonderful to have found you after all these years. I know we all owe everything to Albert and Martha, and because they are no longer with us, it feels like an act of betrayal to be happy that we are together at last. I understand, Rory, really I do.' She hesitated feeling her way into the conversation. 'My dear, I wonder if you might now think of me as your grandmother, and address me as such.'

Rory looked fondly at the old lady – she was a dear gentle soul with an underlying steel core. He reached out and held the hand that was placed on his arm.

'I will try Grandmother, I will try.'

Ronald cheered. 'Why god bless us, everyone! said Tiny Tim,' he said quoting directly from Charles Dickens' novel, *A Christmas Carol*.

Rory laughed heartily, now becoming glad that he was a part of this amazing family.

Then suddenly, as if struck by some miraculous thought, Ronald opened his eyes wide as a flash of green silk blouse and a dear familiar face came into view. Disbelieving that he was actually seeing something, he blinked and looked again. Then, to his great astonishment, he could see a tall young man, sitting next to his grandmother – a young man who resembled himself.

He sat back in his chair; terror stricken.

'Ronald, are you feeling quite well, you have gone so pale.' Lady Bennington anxiously studied her grandson's face.

'I'm not sure, I suddenly feel very strange. I'm not sure what it is.' Then he relaxed, blinked several times more and sat forward suddenly sure of what was happening, he smiled broadly, puzzling his observers and said, 'You should always wear green Grandmamma, it brings out the colour of your eyes.'

'Ronald?' Lady Bennington hardly believed what she was hearing.

'I can see you, grandmamma, it's blurry but I can see' – he giggled like a child – 'and Rory too, by the way, I am the better looking one. I can see this room, and Grandpa's old chair from York Manor. I can see everything.'

Tears coursed down his face. Lady Bennington struggled up from the sofa with Rory's help and hugged him. 'Oh my boy, my lovely, lovely boy. I can't believe it, finally it's a miracle.'

Ronald looked over at Rory; he could see his brother had tears in his eyes also.

'Come here, Rory.' He held out his hand. Rory immediately went to him and they hugged.

Lady Bennington rang for Stevens; he was just coming along the corridor with a tray of tea so he appeared almost immediately.

'Stevens, ring for Master Ronald's doctor at once.

'Certainly, my lady – might I ask what the problem is, as no doubt the doctor will enquire.'

'Tell him that Master Ronald can see, Stevens, he can see!'

Stevens almost dropped the tray in shock but just managed to put it down on the table in time. 'Right away, my lady, that's such good news.'

'It's more than good news, Stevens, it's a miracle.'

'Yes, my lady,' Stevens bowed slightly and left the room. When he was alone, he took out his handkerchief and wiped his moist eyes. *God works in mysterious ways,* he thought, as he picked up the telephone and asked to be put through to Harley Street.

Chapter 41

Etty sat down heavily on the bed breathing hard. She had decided tonight she must put her plan in action. She would ask Patrick to marry her.

She had thought about this moment for so long now and with the upcoming design competition at work, she needed to get some security sorted for her baby so she was free to go if she won. It would be the perfect solution for both of them – if he was married, he couldn't be accused of being a nancy boy, she shivered with distaste at the words. She could vouch for him; he would be her husband. She practised saying it, *this is my husband Patrick Lawrence*, and it sounded good. Etty went to the mirror and looked at herself. He would be lucky to have such a beautiful wife. She applied some rouge and a touch of her new Elizabeth Arden lipstick. Satisfied with her appearance, she left her room and went downstairs where she headed to Patrick's study and knocked on the door.

Seated in his armchair by the fire, Patrick looked up from the letter he was reading when he heard the quiet tap. He hid the letter in his book then called, 'Come in.'

Etty opened the door and popped her head round it. 'Am I disturbing you?'

'Hello, Etty, not at all, please come in. What can I do for you?'

He observed her as she came into the room. She looked nervous he concluded, and had more makeup on than usual.

'It's more what we can do for each other, may I sit?'

'Of course, please do.'

Patrick drew up a chair next to his in front of the roaring fire.

'You're aware that I find myself in a delicate position,' she said nervously licking her lips as she spoke; it wasn't every day you asked a man to marry you… 'And it's my belief that you find yourself in one also.'

'I'm not sure what you mean, what delicate position do I find myself in?'

He noticed Etty's face flush red as she spoke.

'I'm referring to your private life.' Etty wasn't sure how to explain it any better.

Patrick crossed his legs and leaned back in his chair. As he did so, his book fell to the ground and the letter fell out exposed.

She went to pick it up. 'No, leave it, please,' he said, tension rising in his voice. 'I'll pick it up later.' He looked at her waiting for her to continue.

'I've thought of a way forward that will solve both of our problems.'

'I don't believe I have a problem, Etty, but do go on I'm listening.' He was afraid he knew what was coming.

'You and I both have reputations to maintain. Mine is already in tatters within the family and once it gets out that I am having a baby out of wedlock, then my career will be finished also. You also have much to lose. If word gets out that you're suffering from this er illness, then you would surely be in trouble.'

'I'm not ill, Etty.'

'Well what else can I call it? I loathe with a passion some of the names used to describe what you are, but I'm right, aren't I? It would destroy your business.'

'Yes, unfortunately that would be the case; people can forgive most things but—'

'I can't let that happen to you, Patrick, therefore I am willing to sacrifice my own hopes and desires to protect your good name.'

'How do you intend to do that?'

'It's simple; we get married – in name only of course. We would both be free to see whom we wanted, discreetly, you understand. I would be the perfect wife for you. No one would believe any gossip about you if you had a wife.'

Patrick smiled; her interpretation of the benefits for him would have been amusing if hadn't sounded so desperate. 'That's very selfless of you; could I enquire if there would be any benefit to yourself with this arrangement?'

'I've barely thought about that really, but since you ask, I suppose my baby could take your name, and be bought up with two parents. It would give you the child you are never going to have, and I know you would make a marvellous father. We could hire a nanny, and I could continue with my designing, surely you can see it's the obvious way forward.'

'You know my opinions on nannies; I would not subject any child to their ministrations.'

'Eliza Jane would look after the child for me. She would remain in your employ, wouldn't she?'

'My dear Etty, this has come as a surprise to me, it had not occurred to me that you should want to tie yourself down to a marriage in name only. Think what you would be giving up, a normal, healthy relationship with a man who adores you. I think you are a beautiful and talented woman, and I think the world of you, but I don't love you. You know that is an impossibility for me. I cannot love a woman in the way she would want or worship her with my body. You must understand, I cannot be cured, this is the way I am.'

'Please just think about it. I know we could make it work for the child's sake, if nothing else.'

'From what I understand, Etty, there's a man in Crossdale who could fulfil your wishes, if only you would let him. He is a man who earns a good living, and who once loved you, and probably still does. You deserve happiness in your life – you all do – but I can't provide that for you, as much as I may want to protect you. I'd be living a lie; we'd be living a lie. I appreciate your offer, but I can't marry you.'

Etty turned pale as she rose to her feet, he took her hand. 'I'm so sorry, my dear.'

She snatched her hand away. 'It was just a silly idea that popped into my head. You're quite right, of course you are; it would be living a lie. No matter, Patrick, forget I ever said anything, no harm done.'

She stooped to pick up Patrick's book and letter. As she handed them back to him, she caught sight of the letter head: Vogue, New York. Did he have other plans, she wondered. She quickly turned away trying to show that the rejection of her proposal was what she had expected, she laughed as she placed her hand on the handle of the door. Patrick stood as she left the room. 'Well I will say goodnight then,' she said stiffly and with that, she was gone.

After she left, Patrick sighed, he had had women throw themselves at him before but it had never meant anything but Etty was a different matter, he really liked her. Her courage, sense of identity and her spirit intrigued him, but she deserved so much more than a marriage in name only and he hoped he had let her down gently. He had promised Thomas he wouldn't break her heart but somehow, he didn't think Thomas would ever get to find out what had gone on that evening. Breathing a sigh of relief, he sat down again and opened his letter. He scanned the opening lines.

Dear Mr Lawrence

We have a vacancy for a photographer in chief in our New York office, and we would very much like to offer you the post.

Patrick put down the letter; it had driven him into contemplation. It didn't take him very long to assess that this was a most tempting offer that could resolve his immediate problems.

Upstairs in her darkened room, Etty lay on the bed, crying silent tears that were fuelled by rage and humiliation.

Chapter 42

Eliza Jane searched through the post and selected two letters, one addressed to her and the other to Thomas. She put those to one side and placed the others on Patrick's desk. She looked at the stamp on one of Patrick's letters, United States Post Office, she thought she might ask him if she could have the stamp when he had read his letter: Jim's nephew would love it for his album.

Going through to the kitchen, she sat down and looked at the two remaining letters again. The one addressed to Thomas was from Molly, she recognised the handwriting. She would enjoy hearing Molly's news later. The second letter made her heart beat just a little faster, it was from David Jackson. Eliza Jane worried that she was deceiving him about Etty when she replied, so somehow the sight of his handwriting, didn't have quite the same effect emotionally it once did. She smiled to herself, did she ever imagine the day when on receiving a letter from David, she immediately thought of Jim instead. He was the one who made her pulses race now, and best of all, he seemed to feel the same way. It was only a week ago that he told her he loved her, and had covered her blushing face in kisses, until she had pushed him gently away, giggling with delight. She flushed now with the memory of it. Returning to her letter, she opened it carefully, and unfolded the paper.

Dear Eliza Jane.

Thank you for your last letter, I love reading all your news.

I hope Molly enjoys acting with the touring theatre company; she was always good in pantomimes at home. I told Mrs Fanshawe that Molly was a professional actress now, this as you can imagine was greeted with a sniff, but she couldn't wait to go across to Miss Jemima's to tell her all about it.

Miss Beatrice doesn't work in the shop anymore; I think she is kept busy by Jacob. I have to say he looks well fed on his marriage and has put weight on, but they both seem happy.

Now I have some big news. Pop is willing to give me a couple of day's holidays and I was hoping that I might make the journey down to London to see you all. I'm sure you can book me into a lodging house for a couple of nights.

Please let me know as soon as possible when would be the best time to visit you.

Well, that's all for now, oh except I nearly forgot to tell you, Roy Hughes is retiring to Kendal and selling his butcher's shop. He's in no hurry but would like to move near his sister eventually.

Please write soon, I am so looking forward to seeing you all.
Best wishes from your old friend
David.

Eliza Jane went hot then cold; he mustn't come, Etty would be furious. He was better not coming. It was then that an idea grew in her mind, a devious idea that shocked her as it formulated. Suppose she asked Patrick if he would allow David to stay with them. They wouldn't tell Etty that David was coming, so it would be a surprise with no means of escape for her. David would have to be told he was the father of her baby.

She pondered on the rights and wrongs of the idea for most of the afternoon. When she wasn't thinking that, she was musing about Hughes butcher's shop coming up for sale. Should she mention it to Jim? He had said his brother wanted to buy him out, surely this was an excellent opportunity. The only problem was she couldn't envisage Jim moving to that wild place called Crossdale. She had a sudden vision of him calling Mrs Fanshawe *me ducks*. She would pay money to see that. Having finally decided on her plan Eliza Jane went to consult Patrick with regard to David's proposed visit.

Later that evening when they had all finished dinner and were sitting around the table chatting, Thomas remembered Molly's letter. 'Who wants to hear what Molly has to say?' he said, as he took it out of his pocket and opened it. Everyone looked up expectantly as Thomas began reading.

Dear all,
Well here we all are in Bournemouth. Southampton went really well with full houses each night. It really is lovely to be near the sea again after London.

The plays are good with appreciative audiences. I thought I was going to get a chance at playing Gwendolen in "The Importance of Being Earnest" yesterday, as the lead actress went down with a bout of sickness, but fortunately for her and unfortunately for me, she recovered in time.

I am playing my small parts with gusto. I hope it won't be long until I get a larger role! I know my chance will come. We've had a new director thrust upon us, he's very talented, but I don't think he's very keen on me!

The actors are scattered over several boarding houses. The accommodation is basic but comfortable. I certainly won't be making my fortune as I have to spend a good deal on where we stay, but it is all good experience.

We head to Plymouth next and I am hoping to have some time off to go and see the Hoe where Sir Francis Drake played bowls before the Spanish Armada. See my education wasn't wasted.

I hope everyone is well, particularly you, Etty, won't be long now.

I will write again soon.

All my love,

Your sister,

Molly.

'I'm so glad she reminded me the baby is due soon I'd quite forgotten,' said Etty with more than a hint of sarcastic boredom in her voice, sometimes Molly's cheerfulness irritated her jaded soul. 'Still, she seems to be enjoying it, that's the main thing.'

Etty couldn't have been further from the truth. Molly was feeling very miserable and home sick. The new director was Edward Bennett, aged thirty-five, he was short and stocky with a neatly trimmed beard and a slightly receding hairline that accentuated his forehead. His eyes were his best feature, being a mesmerising violet colour. He was both innovative and creative and although he picked fault with everything she did, Molly thought he was a wonderful director.

His criticisms were endless: 'Miss Watkins, we can't hear you. Miss Watkins, you are standing in the wrong place. Miss Watkins, please pick up your cue lines with a little more attack.' The others had suggested that she tackle him about his attitude towards her. Molly being a novice didn't want to upset him any further but said she would think about it. Meanwhile, she continued to try to please him.

The boarding house in Plymouth was horrific. The beds felt damp, and the breakfast consisted of lumpy porridge, watery smoked haddock, or fat bacon swimming in grease. Molly thought of breakfast at home, and wished with all her might she was back there.

The landlady was particularly disagreeable, and tended to walk around with a cigarette consisting mostly of ash between her lips. The ash would drop indiscriminately onto the food, and Molly always felt she got more than her fair share of it.

She lay on her bed, trying to perfect her lines. She tried saying them in different ways, deciding which sounded best. Why was she beginning to doubt herself, she had never had trouble with lines before? She put down her script and thought of Jo, she really missed her old friend and wished they hadn't parted on such poor terms. She could have been planning a wedding now, if only she hadn't been so pig headed; instead, she was miles away from home and feeling utterly miserable.

Fanny, one of the lead actresses put her head around Molly's door. 'We're going out, darling, are you coming? Jeremy knows a little dive that is perfectly divine, and is prepared to drive us there. Come on, you can't stay in this dump on our rare night off.'

'Give me five minutes,' said Molly, as she swung her legs down onto the oilcloth covering the wooden floor boards. She loved the other actors, they were inordinately kind to a new girl like herself, and besides, Jeremy usually bought her champagne.

Some hours later, after a night of revelry and free drinking, Molly was slightly the worse for wear. They had stumbled through the boarding house door, trying to be quiet, so as not to disturb the landlady. Unable to walk a straight line, Molly was being supported to her room by Jeremy, the lead male actor.

When they reached her door, Jeremy snuggled in close, nuzzling her ear. 'Aren't you going to invite me in, darling? We could polish off this off together.' He produced a small bottle of brandy from his overcoat pocket.

'No, I mustn't. I need a clear head tomorrow, go back to your room there's a good boy.'

'Don't want to, want Mollykins,' Jeremy whined like a schoolboy, as he tried to slip his hand under her dress. 'Jeremy wants Mollykins.'

'Jeremy, stop it.' Molly pushed his hand away; she suddenly felt quite sober.

'Come on, Molly, you've been flirting with me all evening.'

'That doesn't mean I'm prepared to go to bed with you. So please go back to your room, I'll see you in the morning.'

'You don't mean it, Molly, girls like you always say no when they mean yes.' He clasped Molly behind the head and pulled her close. His breath smelt of stale cigars and alcohol – the cologne that he wore which had pleased her at the beginning of the evening, now began to make her feel sick. He covered her face in kisses. She pushed him away but he was too strong for her and pulled her close again. Trying to fend him off, she struck him across the face. Immediately, he drew back, and raising his hand, he slapped her solidly across her face and lunged towards her. Molly screamed. Suddenly from nowhere, Edward Bennett appeared and grabbed a very inebriated Jeremy by the seat of his pants and unceremoniously marched him to his room whereupon he opened the door and flung him inside shutting the door behind him. He quickly returned to Molly who was leaning against her door with tears running down her cheeks.

'Are you all right, Miss Watkins?' he asked breathing hard from his exertions.

'Yes, I think so, thank you for coming to my aid, Mr Bennett.' Molly put a cool hand up to her stinging cheek.

'I suggest you should stay at home and attend to your lines in the evenings instead of visiting local hostelries,' he said, 'now if you are all right, I will say goodnight.' He nodded briefly at her before walking back to his room.

Molly scrambled for her door handle, turned it, opened the door slamming it angrily behind her. How dare he accuse her of not knowing her lines, she paced the floor her face still hurting while she walked off her rage. Purposefully, she strode to the door and turned the key in the lock, the click as she did it gave her some satisfaction, then she threw herself on the bed in floods of tears. She was breathing hard, panicked by the situation. What did Jeremy mean, girls like her? She hated this place; she hated the company but most of all, she hated the arrogant Mr Bennett. She refused to give in however – she wanted to be an actress, she needed to prove to the family that she hadn't made a terrible mistake.

The following morning after a restless night and having skipped breakfast, Molly presented herself at the rehearsal rooms. Fanny gasped when she saw her, 'Moll, whatever have you done? You look terrible, what's that mark on your cheek, are you all right?' When Molly had looked at her reflection in the mirror, she had noticed the small wound on her cheek, and thought that Jeremy's signet ring must have caught her. There was a bruise forming too. She looked over at Jeremy, who was talking animatedly with the other male actors.

'I'm fine, Fanny. I just caught my face on the door.' Just then, Jeremy and his group guffawed loudly. They turned to look at her, then Jeremy mumbled something, and they all laughed again.

What would Etty do, thought Molly, but she already knew the answer to that. Etty would have held her head high and carried on – and that is exactly what she was going to do.

Chapter 43

Spring was coming; Patrick could sense the arrival of his favourite time of year. The daffodils were shooting up into golden trumpets, and light-green leaves were appearing on the trees. Leafy Sydenham was beautiful at this time of year which made his decision to leave for America so much harder. He knew he couldn't keep Vogue waiting much longer for an answer – they wanted him in April, but did he really want to go? What would happen to the others if he decided to leave?

Perhaps he could let them rent the house and studio. Rory could continue to run it for him while taking a share of the profits. He loved Rory dearly and leaving him, although he knew there could not possibly be a future with him, would be painful. Was there no end to this loneliness for him?

He thought again about Theodore. He had bought him to mind when he received the letter from Vogue, although previously he hadn't thought of him for years. Was it possible he still worked for Vogue? Perhaps he needed to go to find out; it would be a new start. He would take a couple more days to think about it, before finally committing himself.

Eliza Jane was beginning to get nervous. David was due today but only Patrick knew about it. What if the plan backfired, what if Etty blamed her and never spoke to her again? She comforted herself that Patrick had thought it a good idea. David must know he was to become a father.

She also worried about seeing David again. She had loved him for so many years, but she could barely picture him now, would seeing him again bring back her old feelings. Fretting slightly, she continued to make up a bed for him. When she had finished, she inspected the room, feeling satisfied that it was ready to receive their guest. The house was quiet without Molly, Etty was at work, Rory out with Ronald, Patrick in his study and Thomas had left very early that morning to try and find a job.

Thomas had heard they were taking on men at the nearby laundry. They wanted drivers to collect the dirty laundry and deliver the clean back to the customer. There was some physical work but much of Thomas's time would be spent driving, a skill he had learnt at the hotel. At six thirty that morning, he had rounded the corner only to see a queue already forming outside the laundry. He joined the line as usual. This was the pattern of life now, join the queue of men, wait in the cold for a couple of hours only to be told there were only two vacancies. Most of the men were turned away disappointed, often the bosses chose a man from their old regiment to fill the job and of course Thomas stood no chance having never been allowed to join up. Jo had been as good as her word and had sought an appointment at Cobbs with one of the buyers. He had been successful and given a small contract initially for a couple of carvings, but not enough to provide a reliable income. Standing in line now, Thomas was desperate for a job but so were all the men in the queue before him. At least he didn't have children to feed or a wife to support like some of them, but without a job, Thomas knew a future with Jo was impossible.

He returned just before lunch, Eliza Jane was making some sandwiches. She was taking them to share lunch with Jim in the park. She looked up enquiringly as Thomas came in through the kitchen door. He shook his head. 'They wanted at least two years driving experience,' he explained. Eliza Jane put the kettle on the stove to boil. It was sometime later when she left Thomas brooding in the kitchen and set off down the hill. As she passed the park, she thought of Ronald, he didn't need to sit in the fresh air now his sight had returned and he and Rory seemed to go everywhere together. She was so happy that things were working out for them. Jim saw her as soon as she entered the shop. He signalled that he wouldn't be long and to wait outside. Through the window, Eliza Jane saw him say something to his brother, and then disappear through the back to collect his coat and hat.

'Best not keep her waiting,' shouted a customer, as he went through.

'Look, 'e isn't 'alf under the thumb already,' another remarked.

To the delight of the customers in the shop, Jim gave Eliza Jane a smacker on the lips putting his thumb up behind her back.

'Doesn't that bother you, Jim,' she asked, as they walked back through to the park. 'All that yelling and laughter?'

'Nah, it's only a bit of fun, Lizzie, they know just how I feel about you that's all.'

'How do you feel about me, Jim?'

'I just loves you, cos you're my gal, aren't you?'

He took her hand as they strolled along. 'Shall we sit over there?' He pointed to a bench. 'I can't stay long, girl, coz we're busy in the shop. It's a bit taters out 'ere.' Seeing she was puzzled, he explained, 'Potatoes in the mould, cold, get it. Cor blimey Lizzie girl, isn't it just my Friar Tuck to fall in love with a girl from Lancashire.'

'Now you are making fun of me, you don't normally speak like that. Let me guess, Friar Tuck, luck right.'

'I'm goin' to make you an 'onourary cockney.' He started to dive into the basket she had put on the bench between them. 'I'm starving.'

Eliza Jane produced thick ham sandwiches from her basket, made with fresh home baked bread.

'Feeding me like this only makes me love you more,' said Jim happily munching on his lunch.

'You might not love me when I tell you what I've done.'

'What 'ave you done; it can't be that bad.'

'Well,' she took a deep in breath. 'Patrick and I planned it together, but it was my idea. I had a letter from David Jackson a couple of weeks ago, you know the father of Etty's baby.'

Jim nodded, continuing to devour his sandwich.

'He wanted to come and see us, as he'd been given a few days off from the shop.'

'Nothing wrong with that – Etty's probably glad he's coming, saves her writing that difficult letter.'

'That's just it, Jim – she doesn't know. Patrick and I thought that if it was a surprise, then she couldn't do anything to avoid him. She would have to see him.'

Jim stopped eating; the sandwich in his hand that had been halfway to his mouth dropped to his lap. 'I can see why you 'aven't told her,' he said, swallowing, 'but I'm not sure it's the right fing to do. The shock might bring the baby on.'

'I know; I've done nothing but worry about it since.'

'Well, it's not too late, now. Why not tell her tonight?'

'He's coming tonight, there's no time. She's going to hate me, isn't she?

'You're not going to be popular; I must say. I take it that the others don't know either?'

Eliza Jane nodded miserably. 'Will you come for supper tonight, Jim; help me out, I need some support?'

Jim felt for her hand and squeezed it reassuringly. 'Course I will. What time, seven?'

'Seven would be just right.'

'I'll see you then girl, I've got to go.' Jim finished his sandwich then stood. 'Give us one more of them sandwiches, I'll take it for my break.'

With a quick peck on Eliza Jane's cheek, he headed back to work. It was only when he was nearly back to the shop, that he realised he hadn't told Eliza Jane his news.

Etty was home at the usual time. She seemed to be in a good mood for once, and offered to lay the table for dinner in the kitchen.

'I think we might eat in the dining room tonight, Etty, and set two more places. Jim's coming to join us,' said Eliza Jane.

'Do you know that you still blush when you mention his name; it's quite sweet really. I have to agree he's a good sort, and perfect for you. Hold onto him, won't you? Who's the other place for, have we got company?'

Eliza Jane tried to avoid the question. 'You're in a good mood tonight, Etty, you must have had a good day.'

'I had a very good day, Lizzie; my designs for Madame Souris are progressing well. I'm very excited by them.' She turned to head for the dining room before turning back saying, 'Who did you say the other guest was?'

There was a small knock at the back door before being suddenly opened, and Jim came into the room rubbing his hands. 'Ello girls, I've come for me dinner and I'm starving.'

He planted a smacker of a kiss on Eliza Jane's cheek before taking off his coat and laying it over the kitchen chair. He looked for signs of tension between the sisters and was pleased there didn't seem to be any.

'I'll get on and lay the table then.' Etty left the kitchen and headed to the dining room to set the table.

Jim immediately descended upon Eliza Jane. 'Have you told Etty yet?'

'Told me what?' said Etty, returning to the kitchen to ask what cutlery they were using this evening. She looked to Jim, and when he said nothing, she looked to Eliza Jane. 'What are you supposed to be telling me, Lizzie, that you patently haven't done yet?'

Eliza Jane turned her back and taking up a spoon went to the cooker, and using the corner of her apron to protect her fingers from the heat, removed a lid from a pan and stirred vigorously. This gave her time to decide how to tackle her reply. She was more than apprehensive, she was scared. 'The thing is, Etty, and please don't be cross but the other extra guest is—'

Jim walked over and put a reassuring hand on Eliza Jane's arm to steady her. She continued, 'The other guest is David.'

'David who?' asked Etty, expecting some new acquaintance to be introduced to her.

'David Jackson,' said Eliza Jane quietly

A stifling silence seemed to fill the room. Etty sank into a chair, paling visibly, she began to pant.

'Say something, Etty, please.' Eliza Jane anxiously watched her.

Etty looked up, her face was thunderous, and she was breathing hard. 'Oh, I'll say something all right, how dare you meddle in my affairs. I'll never forgive you for this. I suppose you arranged it all behind my back. You wrote and told him about the baby when I expressly said I would let him know in my own time. You've won, Lizzie – not only have you betrayed me but you've betrayed Jim as well. You couldn't wait to see David again, I suppose. Did you know Jim, that your best girl as you call her, is in love with the father of my child?' Jim looked visibly shaken. 'What, has she never told you how much he means to her? Why she's been in love with him for years. You don't stand a chance with her, Jim – not once the sublime David Jackson arrives.'

Jim took his hand away from Eliza Jane's arm and looked at her, silently demanding her denial. Eliza Jane said nothing. Jim stood away from her almost as if he didn't want to breathe the same poisoned air, he turned on her angrily. 'Eliza Jane I asked you if this is true,' said Jim, clenching his fists so hard that his knuckles were white. 'Are you in love with this man?'

'I don't know, Jim, and that's the honest truth. I used to be in love with him but he never loved me, it was all one sided and mostly in my imagination.'

Etty snorted, 'You didn't witness the fond farewell between them at the station on the day we left Crossdale. It was all very touching.'

'I've heard enough,' said Jim, 'so I'm going 'ome now cos I don't think I want to meet a man who gets one sister pregnant and 'as the other pining after him. I'm not prepared to play second fiddle, Eliza Jane.' And with that, he grabbed his coat and hat from the back of the chair before making for the back door.

'Jim,' shouted Eliza Jane, as tears flowed down her cheek, 'can't you see what she's doing, Jim? Look at her face, she's trying to cause trouble, and she's succeeding. Please, please don't go.' She tried to grab him but he was too quick for her. Not trusting himself to say anything, he opened the back door, went through and slammed it shut after him.

Etty smiled serenely as Eliza Jane collapsed in a heap on a kitchen chair. 'That will teach you to meddle in my affairs.' She spat at her.

'I was not meddling; it was David who suggested he came to see us, and I have not told him about the baby, I swear.'

'Do you think I believe you for one minute? You see, Eliza Jane, I'm too clever for you, no matter what you throw at me, I'll always go one better.'

The doorbell suddenly rang. The sisters looked at each other.

'Best go and let him in, Lizzie, but wash your face first, David doesn't need to know that you've been crying, does he?'

The doorbell rang again as Eliza Jane hurriedly wiped her eyes.

'Go on then, let the father of this baby in – I'm going upstairs to change.'

Chapter 44

Jim stood still outside the back door. He could hear Eliza Jane sobbing and felt wretched. What had he done? He had never let jealousy get the better of him before, and now he had told the only girl for him that he didn't want to see her again. What a fool! He slapped the flat of his hand against his forehead in despair. He turned preparing to go back into the house to make amends; his hand hovered over the door handle, but losing his nerve, he walked slowly down the path.

Did he really want it to end like this? He felt he had no choice; how could he continue to love a girl that was in love with another man? Love her he did though, so the only thing left to do was to prove that he loved and needed her. He would go back in and ask her to marry him, but it would serve him right if she refused, but he wouldn't take no for an answer.

He still hadn't told her his news – his older brother and his wife had offered to buy him out of the family business. It could mean a new start, and the chance to buy a new business for him and Eliza Jane – one they could build together. Finally, he would be able to run things his way, instead of answering to his brother. He started to turn back up the path, resolving to put things right with Eliza Jane, when a taxi drew up and a tall fair man stepped out carrying a suitcase. He stopped at the gate. 'Hello, could you tell me if this is where Patrick Lawrence lives?'

'Yes,' said Jim, trying not to compare himself to the good looking man in front of him. His cheery reply belied his feelings of inadequacy no wonder Eliza Jane loved him. He was what the women termed handsome. 'You must be David. Welcome to the best city in the world.' Jim opened the gate and shook David's hand.

'Nice to meet you, Mr Lawrence, I appreciate you allowing me to stay. 'Thank you also for all you've done for my friends.'

'Nice to meet you too, but I'm afraid I'm not Patrick, my name's James Harrison well I go by Jim. I'm Eliza Jane's friend.'

'Oh, you're the man she never stops talking about in her letters,' David replied, lifting Jim's mood of despair a little.

'Come on in, 'ere let me take that for you.'

Jim took the suitcase, as they walked up the path and rang the front door bell. When there was no response, he rang again. Both men waited apprehensively. They surreptitiously stole glances at each other. David, noting a pleasant looking man with a high forehead and a strong neck, and Jim seeing thick fair hair, a square jaw and an ex-army stance. He unconsciously patted his own receding hairline and stood taller.

David was nervous, it was eight months since he had last seen Etty and the others, and here they were living in this huge house with a man he had yet to meet.

He had felt a mixture of emotions on the long train journey down to London. He had missed Etty so much, but would she be pleased to see him? It would be wonderful to see the others too. Jim seemed like a good chap, he thought and hoped Eliza Jane was happy – she deserved to be.

Thomas opened the front door and couldn't quite believe his eyes when he saw Jim standing there with David.

'Look who I found arriving in a taxi,' announced Jim.

'David, my old pal.' Thomas shook David's hand warmly. 'You don't look any different, what are you doing here, lad?'

David laughed. 'It's only been eight months, you fool, but it's wonderful to see you. Didn't Lizzie tell you I was coming?'

Wondering what game Eliza Jane was playing, Thomas ignored the question. 'Come in, come in,' he said. 'Everyone's going to be so pleased to see you. Did you have a good journey? How was Crossdale when you left? You must give us all the news.'

David was ushered into a large finely appointed room, the like of which he had never seen before but he didn't have time to appreciate his surroundings, before he was pumping Rory's hand and being introduced to Patrick.

'It's wonderful to meet you, Mr Lawrence, Eliza Jane has told me how kind you've been to them. Now you're being kind to me by letting me stay, thank you.

'I've bought you down some of our best Lancashire cheese, a present from my pop.'

David handed a brown paper parcel to Patrick who sniffed it appreciatively. 'Thank you so much, I look forward to tasting it. Please call me Patrick, and let me get you something to drink, would a beer, do you?'

Patrick was in on it too, thought Thomas; he wondered if Etty was aware David was coming.

Soon David was sat down on a comfortable chair, his hat and coat whisked away, and a large beer placed in his hand. He looked around the room impatiently, where was Etty, he wanted to see her.

Jim made his excuses and slipped away to the kitchen, where he found Eliza Jane trying to cool her tearful eyes under the cold tap. 'Ello Ducks,' he said quietly, 'will you forgive me.' Eliza Jane turned and stared at him before running into his arms, and Jim hugged her tightly. 'I'm sorry, girl, jealousy got the better of me. He's 'ere now, I met 'im outside 'e's a fine lookin' chap.'

'Not as fine as you are, James Wilson,' whispered Eliza Jane shyly.

'Come and say 'ello to your old friend then.'

Jim took her hand and led her towards the door.

David stood up as Eliza Jane came into the room. He smiled warmly at her and kissed her burning cheek. 'Hello, Lizzie, it's so lovely to see you again. You're looking bonny.'

'Good to see you again, David, I hope your ma and pop are well?' Eliza Jane was feeling shy, particularly as Etty had told Jim that she was in love with David and Jim was watching.

'Indeed, they are, they asked to be remembered to you, as did Mrs Fanshawe when I told her I was coming.'

Eliza Jane smiled. 'Mrs Fanshawe, you surprise me. Still spreading gossip, I suppose.'

'Not much gossip to tell these days, except the new blacksmith's wife comes in for a bit of criticism now and again – the way she lets the three bairns run around the village. He took a sip of beer and looked around the room, where was Etty. 'I can't believe I'm here; it really is so wonderful to see you all again. I know Molly is away, and I'm dying to hear how she's getting on, but, where's Etty hiding?'

He laughed but stopped when he realised that everyone had grown quiet.

'I'll go and find her,' said Thomas, trying to keep calm, 'knowing Etty; she'll be trying to decide what to wear.'

Thomas breathed a sigh of relief, as he escaped from the tension in the room. He made his way upstairs to gently tap on Etty's door. 'Etty, David Jackson's here. I know it must be a surprise; it was for me too.'

There was no creaking of boards or movement from inside. Thomas knocked again. 'Are you there? Come on, lass, come down and say hello to David.'

There was no reply or any sound from within. Thomas tried the door, usually it was locked but this time the handle turned, and he slowly entered the room. 'Etty,' he warned her of his presence, should she be sleeping. His heart performed somersaults as he took in the scene before him – the wardrobe doors were flung open with clothes tumbling out. The drawers appeared to have been ransacked, the room a complete mess, but worst of all – Etty had gone.

Chapter 45

David stood up in expectation when Thomas re-appeared in the drawing room but on hearing the news that Etty had left the house, he sank down into his chair almost spilling his glass of beer. He was devastated. What had he done to deserve this treatment, except love her? On the long journey south, all he had thought about were her soft, blue eyes and the way her hair curled around her face. He couldn't wait to see her again, and now he had to face up to the fact it wasn't going to happen.

'Where is she, didn't she know I was coming?' He spoke plaintively, almost in anguish looking at Eliza Jane for answers. She gazed at him helplessly.

'Has she taken anything with her Thomas, such as clothes, money or a suitcase?' he asked.

'I'm sorry, David, her room looked as if she's packed and left in a hurry. I wish I could say otherwise.'

'But where would she have gone, and why has she gone is more to the point. Didn't she want to see me?'

David looked at the concerned faces before him, he could barely cope with his disappointment, was there something they were not telling him. 'Surely she could find five minutes to spend with an old friend.' He voice broke with emotion.

Eliza Jane's eyes filled with tears. She wanted to put her arms around him, tell him it was all her fault that Etty had gone because she had planned the whole thing but she couldn't do it. Jim squeezed her hand, willing her to tell David the truth. He felt for the poor devil. Rory and Patrick exchanged glances; Patrick shook his head – a gesture telling Rory that it was not his place to say anything.

'A cigarette, David,' suggested Patrick, offering him one from his case.

'What's going on here?' He ignored the proffered cigarette. 'There's something you're not telling me.'

'There's nothing going on as such, David?' said Thomas

'Then what is it, why has Etty gone?'

'For gawds sake,' said Jim, 'will someone tell the poor man, and then we can get out there and look for 'er. We're wasting time 'ere.'

He looked around the room at the blank faces in front of him. 'Well if you won't, then I suppose I'll 'ave to. David, there's no easy way to tell you this, mate, and it's not really my business, not being family an' all but—'

'What Jim is trying to say, David,' Eliza Jane intervened, 'is that Etty is having a baby.'

'Oh,' said David simply, looking dazed. 'When, err, I mean how – I mean, oh I don't know what I'm trying to say. I think I might have that cigarette now, Patrick.'

He took a gulp of beer as Eliza Jane took his free hand. 'The baby is yours, David. You're the father.'

David looked blankly at Eliza Jane then the picture of a hot sunny afternoon in July invaded his mind. He recalled the buttercup under the chin, the soft feel of Etty's curves and the hot sun on the sweet smelling grass. Suddenly, he understood.

Rising from his chair, he placed his beer on the table, and looked at them gazing steadily at him. He swayed on his feet, wondering what they expected from him. He fell back into his chair, as Jim rushed forward to catch him. 'Whoa there, careful, mate.'

Eventually, David found his voice. 'Thomas, please forgive me. Rory, Lizzie, please I never meant for this to happen. I wanted to marry Etty. I love her, but she won't have a bar of me. You must believe me that if I had known about the baby, I'd have insisted she became my wife.'

'David, you know Etty only answers to herself,' said Rory, thinking of his real mother and the controversy of his birth. 'Everything is on her terms, she neither worries nor cares about what others think. I don't think she would have done anything she didn't want to.'

'We must find her, bring her home. I promise we'll marry. I'll look after her.' David's thoughts were racing away with him. He drew deeply on his cigarette.

'What if she won't marry you? She didn't want you to know about the baby, David. No one was allowed to tell you. Believe me I wanted to so many times,' Eliza Jane said quietly

'Then I'll insist, Lizzie. She must marry me; we're having a child together.'

'I'm going out to see if I can find 'er,' said Jim, 'someone must have seen 'er.'

'I'll go with you, Jim,' said Patrick, he wanted to do something practical, seeing David's distress was hard to witness and he was worried about Etty, since he had turned her down, she had tried to avoid him which he hated. 'Meanwhile, let's think about where she might have gone, and who she knows. I'll get my coat and hat; we'll go in my car.'

'I'm coming too.' David jumped up from his seat.

'We'll all go,' said Thomas. 'Lizzie, you stay here in case she returns.'

As Eliza Jane shut the front door behind them, she sat down and exhaled deeply. 'Oh Etty, Etty, Etty – you'll be the death of all of us,' she whispered.

Two hours later, the men returned dispirited, and frustrated that they hadn't found Etty. They had been to the railway and omnibus station but no one had seen a woman answering her description. They had walked the streets in the hope they might see her but to no avail. Etty had completely disappeared.

Dinner had been impossible to rescue but Lizzie knew everyone would be hungry when they returned, so she had made soup and sandwiches which she laid out on the kitchen table.

'Where on earth could she have gone,' said David, his voice demanding an answer, 'you must have some idea.'

'London's a big place,' Patrick said honestly. 'She could be anywhere, but knowing Etty, she'll be somewhere warm and comfortable.'

'Try and eat something,' said Eliza Jane, 'we can search again in the morning, after a good night's sleep.'

'Sleep?' said David in despair. 'I don't think I'll ever sleep until she's found.'

'I can help until lunch time tomorrow,' said Rory. 'Then Ronald and I are going to Saville Row with Grandmother; it's all arranged. I need a new suit.'

David looked up. 'Grandmother, what do you mean?'

'Eliza Jane obviously hasn't told you this piece of news either. It's complicated but Albert and Martha were not really my parents. Oh they bought me up and everything but it turns out I'm actually a member of the aristocracy.' He smirked slightly feeling rather proud all of a sudden.

Thomas's eyebrows knitted together as a look of fury passed over his face. He quickly rose to his feet. 'This is not the time to bring this up, Rory, plenty of time to tell David of your new family when Etty has been found.'

Patrick also stood up. 'If you pull that face, Rory, I'm not sure I like the aristocratic you,' said Patrick.

Rory sullenly bit into his sandwich; he didn't like being put down by Patrick. There was silence for a while.

'What's going on?' asked David, gazing from face to face.

Eliza Jane drew up a chair next to David to explain how a chance meeting in the local park had revealed Rory had been adopted at birth by Albert and Martha. Rory has a twin brother, and she went on to tell him the whole story.

David was amazed. 'I can't believe this; it's like a tale in a book and all through a chance meeting in the park. You must be feeling very confused, Rory, everything that you knew and believed is lost. I feel very sorry for you.'

'On the contrary, David, I have lost nothing and gained a fortune.'

'Rory, please, that is hurtful to Lizzie and me,' said Thomas

'What I meant was that I still have my old family and now I have my new family, it isn't confusing at all.'

'All the more reason that the baby should know I am his father when he's born.'

'Well, I must be going, gel,' said Jim, as he got to his feet. 'It's getting late and I 'ave to be up early in the morning, duty calls.'

'Lizzie tells me you are a butcher, Jim.'

'I am indeed, man and boy.'

'Did Lizzie tell you that our local butcher in Crossdale is selling up and retiring? What about buying the shop and bringing Eliza Jane home to Crossdale, it might encourage Etty to come home. Oh, for god's sake, I'm sorry Jim, here's me planning your life for you. Perhaps you don't want to leave London, and I'm suggesting you and Eliza Jane get wed. It's none of my business, must be the ale talking.'

Eliza Jane's face flared red with embarrassment. Jim had never mentioned marriage to her, how could David be so forward. She kept the floor steadily in her sights, not daring to look at anyone.

'Nah, don't apologise, mate, that's not a bad idea. In fact, it might work out quite nicely,' Jim said happily.

He gazed down at her. 'Well, my lovely lassie from Lancashire, will yer marry me, gal?'

After coming off stage, Molly was frustrated. Once again, she had played a minor role with only three lines to say. Determined that this had to change, she sought out Edward Bennett who was backstage talking to the costume supervisor.

'May I talk to you, Mr Bennett?'

'We will finish this later, Edith.' She nodded and left.

'Yes, Miss Watkins, how may I help?'

'I don't believe that Mr Maurice Goldberg hired me to play maids,' she said, with as much assertiveness she could muster with Edward's violet eyes distracting her. 'I know I'm a good actress, please let me have a larger role in the next town. I know all the lines, and I've spent long enough watching Fanny play the part. Just give me a chance, please, that's all I ask.'

Edward gazed at Molly, she really was a beautiful girl, shame she was a Goldberg girl, usually that meant he was supposed to make an actress out of them though this one was slightly different, at least she had talent. He spoke harshly not wanting to let his guard down and show his attraction to her because as well as Molly being one of Goldberg's protégées, there was a reason that he couldn't allow himself to fall in love.

'Maurice Goldberg hired you because of your looks, and for no other reason. You're not the first girl he's thrust on this company, and you won't be the last. You're lucky I'm letting you play a maid – others before you haven't been so fortunate. I suppose he promised you a lead role in his West End theatre?'

Molly nodded. 'Yes, he did as a matter of a fact.' Molly was angry at his comments; a West End role was just what he had promised her. She stood in front of Edward Bennett. He was just a little taller than she was.

'I thought so,' he continued. 'Don't you realise what you'll have to do to achieve that?'

'I know I have to work hard, and show him what I can do, and if you won't let me have lead role experience, then I might have to tell him about your attitude. I wish he had put me straight into one of his West End shows?'

Edward laughed. 'There's a certain Miss Fleur Lamont who currently holds Mr Goldberg's interest. When he tires of her, she'll be sacked, and then he'll bring you out of the provinces into London where he'll wine and dine you at the Ivy. Nevertheless, be warned, once he has possession of you, he'll drop you like a hot brick. I've seen it happen so many times before, but in the meanwhile, I have to employ you as I see fit.'

Molly paled visibly at Edward's words; she had been stupid enough to believe Goldberg was genuine, now she felt ridiculous and naïve. Jo's words came back to haunt her:

Are you absolutely sure this is what you want to do? It seems to me it's going to be a hard life with, all those boarding houses and away from home for months at a time, and changing in dirty provincial theatre dressing rooms.

Tears welled up into Molly's eyes – her family and her best friend had been right, but still, she wasn't prepared to give up without a fight.

Edward noticed her tears and immediately wanted to reach out and draw her to him. He had been too harsh, Molly wasn't really one of Goldberg's girls, she was too trusting and gentle. He kept his arms firmly by his side to prevent him from holding her. Careful, Edward, he warned himself silently.

Chapter 46

Agnes Parkinson clicked her teeth in irritation and put down her knitting as the front door bell jangled. She glanced at the grandmother clock in the corner of the room, striking nine o'clock. 'Now who could that be,' she muttered to Perkins, her tabby cat who was curled up on the other fireside chair. He opened one eye and watched her heave herself onto her feet. As soon as she left the room, he lithely jumped from his own chair to settle down in the warm patch she had left vacant.

Agnes squinted at the young woman on her doorstep. 'Hello lovey, what can I do for you?'

'Aunt Agnes, its Henrietta Watkins, do you remember me? We stayed with you back in July last year – we're Cyril's friends from Crossdale.'

'Etty, love, of course I remember you. Come in, eh you're right cold I can tell. Come and get warm, have you eaten?'

Agnes flung the door open, drawing Etty inside. Etty's eyes filled with tears at the warm greeting, Agnes pretended not to notice – whatever problem had brought the lass here, it could wait until she had eaten.

It wasn't long before Etty was sitting in front of a big bowl of chicken soup and a hunk of bread and butter served on a small table by the fire. While she ate, they talked of everything but that which had brought Etty to her door. The soup was good and Etty ate eagerly.

'Aunt Agnes, that was wonderful, thank you.' Etty placed her soup spoon back in the empty bowl, as she swallowed down the final hunk of fresh bread left on her plate – she hadn't realised quite how hungry she was.

Agnes sat down opposite her, shooing Perkins off her chair, he looked reproachfully at her. 'Well now,' the old lady said sagely, 'you enjoyed that, but I'm noticing in spite of your loose sweater; you're eating for two lass, aren't you?'

Etty nodded. 'Would you think less of me if I tell you I don't want this baby, and I don't know what to do about it.'

'First things first, Etty love, how far gone are you, and where's the father?'

Etty explained about losing William in the war, and the afternoon spent with David in the buttercup field. She talked of their move to London and meeting Patrick, and her employment with the House of Harding. She spoke of Madam Souris and the chance to work in Paris, and of David's visit, and how she just couldn't face telling him about the baby.

'I panicked, Aunt Agnes. I didn't want to see him, and I couldn't think of anyone who would understand except you. So, I packed a bag and left while they were all downstairs.'

'Eh, lass, that's a right sorry tale, and no mistake and by rights, I should be shocked. But I know that we can sometimes get carried away by the moment.' Agnes grew wistful for a second as if remembering her own buttercup field. 'Why don't you want to see this man, is he a wrong'en?'

'No, David's the kindest, most gentle man I know. He would look after me, of that I can be sure, but—'

'You don't love him. Do you know, lass, your eyes lit up that bright when you were talking of your work and your designs, but when you mentioned the lad, your eyes lost their sparkle? You're up against it, Etty, although it's 1920 woman still don't have choices, they never have. Society insists on propriety, and women are expected to do the right thing. I think you have no option but to marry the lad.'

'Marriage is not something that I want now. I loved my William, he was everything to me, but he was cruelly taken. I'll never love like that again. I need to have this baby, and find someone to take care of it, so I can get on with my life.'

'Aye, I know, lass. I could never think about replacing my Earnest; although we were never blessed with babies. My guess is that you might feel differently when the child is born. Once it looks up at you with those big eyes, you might want to move heaven and earth to protect it.'

Etty shook her head. 'I don't feel anything except irritation with my swelling belly.'

'You will, lass, you will. Now don't you think we should let your family know you're safe – they must be worried!'

'No, please, not yet. Perhaps in the morning, if you would allow me to…' Etty suddenly doubled over in pain. 'Oh my.'

'When did you say you were due, lass?'

'I've got three weeks to go; it can't be coming, not yet.'

'Babies don't wait for due dates. I think we'd better get you upstairs and call the doctor.'

'Aunt Agnes I can't see a doctor' – Etty gasped with pain again – 'what will he think, I'm unmarried. They'll take my baby from me.'

'But that's what you want, isn't it, Etty love?'

'Yes-no, oh I don't know. I don't know what I want.'

'You'll have to think of something to tell the doctor, because this baby is on its way.'

Eliza Jane went to bed that evening with an enduring smile. Shivering, with part cold and part excitement, she quickly undressed, struggled on with her nightgown and dived under the covers, pulling them up to her neck. Then, drawing up her knees, she giggled, hugging herself. She wished Ma and Da could have known Jim. She felt confident that they, especially Ma, would have loved him, for he was similar to her da in many ways. Suddenly, she felt a pang of guilt at celebrating her happiness as she remembered Etty's unhappiness at David's visit, but the feeling soon turned to anger. How could Etty put them all through this worry? It was typical of Etty to steal the joy from the most important moment of her life. She had done this since they were small. When she had baked her first cake, and stood by proudly as Da took a slice, Etty had rushed forward with some newly hemmed handkerchiefs she had made for him. She had even embroidered Da's initial in each corner, and somehow, the cake was temporarily forgotten.

She complained to the wall, 'I'm not even allowed to enjoy a minute's happiness, Etty, because as usual, everything is about you.'

David lay in bed looking at the ceiling. Although he was exhausted, the reassuring oblivion of sleep seemed to evade him. His mind was working overtime, thinking about the baby and how things might turn out with Etty. If only he could talk to her, he was sure he could persuade her to return to Crossdale as his wife for the baby's sake because she wouldn't want to bring it up alone, and he was prepared to live with that knowledge because he loved her. She could help out in the shop that would be his one day. While they would never be rich, they would surely be comfortable. He felt sure he had enough love for the two of them.

Agnes puffed up the stairs with Doctor MacMillan behind her. He was a small Scotsman, near to retirement, and quite disgruntled he had been called away from his fireside and wee dram.

'She's one of my guests, Doctor, and I fear she's about to have this baby. She tells me she isn't due for another three weeks but she's in a lot of pain by the look on her face, and her waters have gone.'

Agnes opened the bedroom door, allowing the doctor to enter ahead of her. Etty was lying hunched up on her knees in the bed, she found the pain easier to deal with in that position. Just as they entered, she had a painful contraction. She moaned loudly.

'How often are you getting the pains?' Doctor McMillan asked her reaching for her wrist to take her pulse. Etty rolled over on to her back before answering.

'I only seem to have a few moments between.'

'I would like to examine you; would you mind if Mrs Parkinson stays?'

'No, please just help me, this pain is unbearable.'

The doctor leaned over Etty to expose her belly and examine her. 'Aye it's God's will, Mrs—'

'Mrs Lawrence,' puffed Etty. 'Mrs Patrick Lawrence.' Agnes thinking, she was confused by pain said nothing.

'Well, Mrs Lawrence, it's going to be a long night. Some hot water and a towel please, Mrs Parkinson; I need to wash my hands to examine the patient further.'

'Now, Mrs Lawrence, when Mrs Parkinson returns with the means to wash my hands, I will administer an injection, consisting of morphine for the pain and something to stop you feeling sick from the pain relief.'

Shortly after the injection, Etty felt drowsy and the pain lessened. Agnes made herself and Doctor McMillan a cup of tea and the night wore on.

At five fifteen in the morning, Etty finally gave birth holding tightly to Agnes's hand and with words of encouragement from the doctor leaning over her, she gave a final push and her baby was born with a hearty cry. Doctor McMillan quickly examined the child and reassured Etty all was well.

'You've a wee daughter, Mrs Lawrence, she's quite tiny but perfect in every way. A little sleepy from the morphine but that is to be expected. I'll be asking the midwife to call later today. Would you like to see her?' Etty shook her head.

'I'm so tired, doctor, I will see her later, as long as she's all right.'

'Of course, there is one more job to do with the after birth then you can have a cup of tea and a rest.' Doctor McMillan wrapped the baby in a towel and handed her to Agnes.

'She's so bonny Etty, she's got your colouring and a thatch of flaxen hair,' she said, as she laid her in the drawer that she had prepared earlier lined with pillows and towels.

'I'll go and make a pot of tea. Will you stay for a cup of tea, doctor? It's been a long night.'

'Thank you, no, Mrs Parkinson. I'll be away home and try to get a couple of hours' sleep before my morning surgery. I am rather tired too, my congratulations to you, Mrs Lawrence.'

The doctor slowly repacked his bag and with a final look at Etty, who was now sleeping peacefully, he left the room with Agnes close behind.

'I'm slightly worried about Mrs Lawrence,' he whispered, as they went downstairs. 'Usually mothers want to see their babies to count fingers and toes you know.'

'I expect she will later; I will keep an eye on the situation, doctor,' Agnes replied, not knowing what else to say.

'Good, thank you, you've been a great help. Well good morning to you, or should I wish you goodnight.' He allowed Agnes to open the front door as he wearily placed his hat on his head and set off to his car.

Agnes made a pot of tea and puffing with exhaustion she climbed the stairs to where Etty lay resting. 'I've bought tea and biscuits,' she said but Etty was sound asleep, snoring gently, while her daughter wriggled around in her makeshift cot.

Agnes put down the tray and went over to pick up the baby. 'You're going to need some food, little one, and while your ma's asleep, and I'm not sure what we can do about that.' The baby started to cry so Agnes wrapped her tightly in the towel, scooped her up and rocked her gently. 'Shh, my bonny bairn, Aunt Agnes will see what she can do.'

Realising there was no chance to rest, she went back downstairs with the baby and searched her cupboards. She found some evaporated milk in a tin that she used for rice puddings. Using some hot water from the kettle, she scoured a cup, and poured some milk out of the tin into it. After diluting it with water, she put spoonfuls of milk to the baby's lips. The child soon got the idea and managed to take some of the mixture.

With a full tummy in front of the heat of the fire, it wasn't long before the baby's eyes shut – closely followed by Aunt Agnes's. It was there that Etty found them two hours later, when she came downstairs fully dressed.

Sensing some kind of movement, Agnes stirred to find Etty about to leave the house. 'What do you think you're doing?' she blurted, her voice creaky from just waking. 'You should be in bed!'

'I have to go to work; I'll see you tonight.'

'Indeed, you won't, my girl – this baby needs feeding properly, and you need to rest.'

'I feel fine, just a little tired that's all. Can't you look after the baby until I come home?'

Agnes looked at Etty sympathetically. 'Don't you want to see your daughter, lovey?'

'I haven't really got time – I'm going to be late as it is. Please, will you help me just for today?'

'Yes, I'll help you,' said Agnes crossly. 'I'll help you get right back to your bed. Then I'm going to help you by telephoning your family to tell them the news. I think there may be a young man out there who's beside himself with worry, and has a right to know he has a daughter. Now go up those stairs, take your clothes off and get back into bed. I'll bring the baby up after I've made the call, but first I need the telephone number.'

Agnes stood up still holding the baby in her arms, and narrowed her stare. Etty knew she was beaten – for the third time in her life and she did as she was told.

Eliza Jane was putting the final touches to the breakfast table. She had finally drifted off to sleep in the small hours. She had dreamt that Jim was about to kiss her but when she opened her eyes, she found she was kissing David. The dream woke her up in a lather of embarrassment. Surely, she was over him by now, she loved Jim she knew that now. After all her doubts, he was the right man for her, of that she was positive. Why did the mind play such tricks? She was concentrating on straightening the cutlery when David came into the room. His eyes were heavy and dull from lack of sleep. His hair hadn't been brushed and his clothes looked as if he had slept in them.

'Good morning,' she said, 'how did you sleep?'

'I don't think I slept at all.'

'It took me a while to get off too – what with one thing and another.'

David was concentrating on pulling out a chair from under the scrubbed pine kitchen table. He lowered himself into it as if he was an old man, before looking up at her in surprise. 'Oh Lizzie, I forgot, I'm so pleased for you. Jim seems a good man; I hope you'll be very happy together. If we all weren't so worried about Etty, the news would be something to celebrate.'

Eliza Jane was stung by his words. She turned away to collect the toast, trying not to cry with disappointment that once again, Etty came first.

Oblivious to her condition, David probed her. 'Have you had any more thoughts as to where Etty might have gone?'

Eliza Jane shook her head, she turned to look at him. 'Etty always looks after herself. Don't worry; really, she'll be fine.

'I'm going to worry, even if she doesn't want me, I am obligated,' moaned David, 'the baby is half mine. I love her, Lizzie, you know that. I always have.'

'Then you must tell her, David, it's no use telling me,' said Eliza Jane, placing a steaming bowl of porridge in front of him, before sitting opposite him with some toast and marmalade.

'I have told her, and when we find her, I'll tell her again.' David picked up his spoon and they started to eat in silence.

Thomas and Rory entered the kitchen together. Rory began to sing. 'There she was waiting at the church, waiting at the church.' Eliza Jane smiled.

'Ha ha, very funny, Rory,' she said, 'sit down both and I'll get you your porridge.'

Thomas drew out his chair next to David who was gloomily eating small spoonfuls from his bowl, and Rory sat next to Eliza Jane's chair. 'We're thrilled for you and Jim, Lizzie, truly.' Thomas remarked much to Eliza Jane's joy; finally, someone was acknowledging her happiness. 'Ma and Da would have been delighted, and I'd be proud to have Jim as my brother-in-law,' added Thomas.

'Thank you, Thomas. I can't quite believe it; Jim did ask me to marry him last night, didn't he?'

'Indeed, he did,' Thomas looked over at David who was toying with his spoon and apparently miles away. 'Morning, David, cheer up, we'll find her don't you worry. She can't be far.'

Patrick came rushing into the kitchen; he looked relieved as he told them his news. 'I've just had a telephone call from a lady called Agnes Parkinson over in Islington; she runs a small guest house.'

'Aunt Agnes,' they chorused, with Eliza Jane adding, 'how strange, what did she want?'

'It seems Etty has spent the night there.'

David put down his spoon and looked up expectantly. 'You know where she is, can we go and get her? Islington, where's that, is it far?' He rose to his feet.

'Of course, but before you dash off to get your coat, there's something else you should know.'

David stopped breathing momentarily, until he noticed Patrick's serious face become wreathed in smiles.

'Etty had the baby, last night,' said Patrick. 'The doctor was with her, and she and the baby are fine. Congratulations, David, you're a father.'

David sat down again on his chair and blew out his cheeks with a huge sigh of relief. 'I'm a baby,' he said, gibbering. 'It's a father. I mean, oh, you know what I mean.'

David's eyes glistened, moist with tears. 'I've got a baby; I can't believe it. He rose from his chair again. 'Can we go now, Patrick, I need to see them. I need to see them right now.'

'Wait a minute, David; don't you want to know what you've had?'

'I've had a baby, that's what I've had.' David set off jigging around the room making the family smile.

'You have a daughter,' said Patrick finally, 'Etty had a baby girl.'

'A daughter! A beautiful daughter. I can't believe it, I'm the luckiest man alive.'

Patrick gazed at the new father with a mixture of envy and sadness. Envy, because he could never hope to have a child, and sadness, because David's troubles with Etty were surely only just beginning.

Chapter 47

'I've telephoned Mr Lawrence,' said Agnes. 'He's coming here to take you home.'

She had brought the baby upstairs to where Etty was sitting up in bed sketching. Agnes was tired, she was too old to be playing nursemaid. Although she sympathised with Etty's predicament – changing sheets, making up the fire in Etty's room and trying to feed a new-born baby in the middle of the night was not improving her temper.

'She's a dear little thing, Etty. Now just you hold her for a minute while I tidy the room.'

She tried to pass the baby over but Etty turned away. 'I can't,' said Etty screwing up her nose in distaste. 'I've no wish to see her. Please take her away.'

'She needs feeding poor lamb, she's hungry, look at her waving her fists. Please, you must take her and try to feed her yourself.'

'No, I can't. I just can't do it. Can't you give her some more evaporated milk and water that will settle her?'

'She's your daughter, Etty, your responsibility.'

Etty ignored the remark continuing to gaze at her sketch pad, making amendments and shading parts in. Agnes sighed knowing that she was beaten. *The sooner Mr Lawrence got here to take her home, the better*, she thought. She placed the baby back in the makeshift crib and went downstairs to boil some more water.

Etty looked over at the writhing mass of arms and legs that was her daughter. She felt no love for the child, only a kind of hatred for causing her so much pain coming into the world. *How could I hate an innocent baby?* she admonished herself, as the child began to cry.

Etty shouted, 'Aunt Agnes! She's crying! Hurry up with the milk!' Suddenly, Etty's breasts began to leak a sticky whitish fluid. The crying continued, and with no sign of Aunt Agnes returning, Etty started to panic. She swung her legs over the side of the bed and stood up.

'Shh, there there.' She soothed, gazing down on the now cross baby. The crying reached hysterical proportions with the baby almost turning blue with rage. Etty was frightened, instinctively she reached down into the drawer and scooped her daughter up. The child smelling food turned towards Etty and nuzzled her. Etty almost dropped her in surprise. She quickly placed the baby back into the drawer.

'Oh-no-you-don't, young lady, I'm not going to feed you,' said Etty said in a warning tone. 'Now look, I'm prepared to make a pact with you – you don't bother me and I promise I'll not be your mother. You don't want a mother like me, really you don't. I've real ambition – I'm going to Paris to work and you can't come with me – do you hear? Now just stop crying, will you? I'll find you the perfect mother, I promise, but it won't be me – now do we understand each other?'

The baby stopped crying, opening her deep blue eyes. For a frozen moment, mother and child stared at each other, and in that time, it seemed a firm understanding was reached. *Well at least you're pretty,* thought Etty, *thank heaven for small mercies.*

The doorbell rang; she quickly got back into bed as she heard recognisable voices coming up the stairs.

'I can't thank you enough for all you've done, Mrs Parkinson. We're so grateful,' she heard David say, 'and how's Etty and my daughter, are they well?'

'Why bless you, Mr Jackson, they're both very well. You must be so proud. Please call me Aunt Agnes, anyone who knows my Cyril is a friend of mine. Now go on up, Etty is third on the right at the top of the stairs. As David bounded up the stairs two at a time, Agnes turned to Patrick saying, 'I'll make us a nice cup of tea, Mr Lawrence; it might be as well to leave them to it.' She ushered him into the sitting room.

Etty's heart lurched as her bedroom door opened. She smiled sweetly, a sugary effort that didn't quite ring true. 'Oh, hello David,' she said as if she had only spoken to him yesterday.

'Hello, Etty,' David said, removing his hat. He hardly knew what to say. 'May I come in?'

Etty nodded, aware that she probably wasn't looking her best. 'Where's Patrick?' she asked.

'He's downstairs, talking to Aunt Agnes – how are you?'

'Awful,' she pouted. 'I never want to go through all that pain again.'

'I'm so sorry you had to go through it alone. If only you had told me, I could have been here. Why didn't you tell me? You at least owed me that.'

'You would have felt obliged to offer me marriage. I didn't want you to have to do that.'

'Would that have been so terrible?'

'No, it wouldn't have been so terrible, but I told you before – I can't marry you; it wouldn't work between us – we want different things from life. I couldn't bury myself in Crossdale and become a dutiful grocer's wife. There's a whole world out there and I intend to see it.'

'Please don't say no – just think about it. I'll do whatever you want – move to London if necessary, move anywhere you say, just let's be together, please.'

Etty wavered, if she agreed to marry him, would this buy her some time until after the competition with Madame Souris. She could never love him as he wanted but at least he wouldn't be pestering her. The plan had possibilities.

She smiled sweetly at him. 'Yes, David, I'll marry you, but you need to go home and make preparations. I will come back to Crossdale as soon as possible when I am stronger.

David looked at her. 'Did you just say yes?' he said, hardly daring to believe his own ears.

'Yes, I said yes,' said Etty impatiently beginning to doubt her ability to carry her plan through.

'Thank you, my darling. Thank you for making me the happiest man alive. I love you so much, you know that, don't you?' He leant forward to kiss her lips but she turned her face away, and the kiss landed on her ear. A short cry interrupted them.

'You had better say hello to your daughter then,' she said coolly.

David turned quickly; he hadn't realised the baby was in the room; she had been so quiet sleeping in her drawer. He walked softly over to her and knelt down beside the makeshift crib, and very carefully lifted his daughter out into his arms.

'Don't disturb her, David,' Etty grumbled, 'and don't bring her over here, she needs to stay where she is.'

David gazed in awe at his daughter. 'You're so beautiful,' he whispered just like your ma. The baby appraised him, seemingly staring at his moustache; she looked puzzled then crinkled up her mouth with wind as if she was smiling at her father. 'She smiling at me, Etty, she knows me, oh she is just so beautiful, my daughter, my very own daughter,' David continued to whisper, mesmerising the baby with his words. Finally, he turned to face Etty. 'Look Etty, look how beautiful she is.'

There was a knock on the open door, Patrick hovered over the threshold. 'May I come in?' Quickly, Etty patted her hair and rearranged her night gown.

David brought the baby over for inspection. 'Yes, do come in, Patrick. Come and see our daughter – isn't she just the prettiest baby you have ever seen?'

'She's very beautiful, you're a lucky man, my friend.'

'I know, I know,' David enthused, 'and Etty has agreed to marry me. I'm not only the luckiest but the happiest man today.'

As David placed the child back in the drawer, Patrick raised an enquiring eyebrow at Etty, who lowered her eyes, refusing to look at him.

'Well congratulations,' Patrick smiled, 'I'm very happy for you both. I'm sure your families will be delighted.'

'Thank you, Patrick, I know they will be.'

There was another tap on the open door and Agnes and Doctor Macmillan entered the room. The doctor had been concerned at his patient's lack of interest in her new baby, and had decided to return to re-assess the situation.

'Mr Lawrence?' he enquired, looking at the two men before him.

'Yes, that's me,' said Patrick looking puzzled.

'I'm Doctor McMillan, I attended your wife's birth.' The doctor turned to David, 'now if you would be so kind as to leave us Mr—'

'Jackson, David Jackson.' David was also puzzled – why did the Doctor assume Patrick was Etty's husband?

'Well if you excuse us, Mr Jackson, I'd like to talk to my patient.'

'But…'

'Mr Jackson, I have not got all day. I'm a fair busy man, you know.'

Agnes turned to David. 'I've got a pot of tea going downstairs, why not come and have a cup.'

David was about to refuse when Agnes half pushed him to the door. 'You can come up after,' she said.

Etty refused to look at David, as he made for the door.

'Mr Lawrence, I'm glad you're here. Your wife could have done with your support last night. I do not approve of men who fail their wives.'

Etty quickly interrupted. 'You were away last night, darling, weren't you? The baby wasn't expected until the beginning of April. But he's here now, doctor, and I feel so much better.'

'Good, now how is the feeding going, Mrs Lawrence.'

Patrick was speechless. What was Etty playing at, he was confused and angry that she should be duping the doctor like this and how was he going to explain this to David.

'She feeds really well doctor, like a trouper. There are no problems, she's a perfect baby.'

'Excellent, I'm glad to hear it.' The doctor turned to Patrick. 'Now Mr Lawrence, if you would just leave us while I examine your wife, then you'll be free to take her home. And send up Mrs Parkinson when you go down, thank you.'

Patrick meekly left the room.

Rory and Ronald were having a wonderful day together. Everywhere they went, people looked at them and smiled at how alike they were. The boys were amused.

They had taken the lift to the terraced gardens and café on the rooftop of Selfridges, the second largest department store in London. They were thrilled by the view of London from their elevated position. The day was clear with some watery sun.

'We must come up here and paint one day,' remarked Ronald, 'I'd forgotten just how wonderful it is up here.'

'I'd like that,' Rory answered, thinking how much he would like to start painting again.

Ronald looked over to the café. 'Grandmamma's waving at us, tea has arrived, come on let's go and join her.'

They walked briskly over to the table where the waitress was just placing a stand of sandwiches and cakes. Lady Bennington looked approvingly at her as she took her tray and left. 'Thank you, my dear.'

Rory kissed her lightly on the cheek before he sat down. 'Thank you so much, Grandmamma, for today. My suit is wonderful; it's the nicest piece of clothing I've ever owned. I always had Thomas' hand me downs until I grew taller than him, but never a suit like this.'

'I'm glad you're happy, Rory.' She poured the tea.

She gazed affectionately at her grandsons. 'You both do me proud; it's like dear Elizabeth never left me to have you two together at last. She would have been so happy.'

'I've just had an idea,' said Ronald, looking across at Rory, 'why don't you come home and live at Eastcliffe Manor with us – after all, it's where you belong with your own family.'

Lady Bennington took a sip of tea before replacing her cup in her saucer and saying, 'Give Rory a chance to become acclimatised to having a new family, Ronald. After all, he'll have allegiances to his brother and sisters.'

'But you belong to us now, Rory, and we've wasted so much time without each other, think about it, please.'

'It is very tempting; I have to admit, but my work is with Patrick. His studio is there, it makes life easy, but I have to say, that in such a short time, I've grown to love you both so much, and I feel I belong more to you than my other family. I heard myself calling Albert a common blacksmith yesterday, and Etty's antics have disgusted me. I've always felt different from them, and now I know why.'

Lady Bennington's eyes bore into her grandson. 'Rory please remember how much Albert did for you. He took you in and brought you up, knowing that you were not his own flesh and blood. As for Etty, don't judge her so – your own mother had the both of you out of wedlock. Twenty years ago, it was far more scandalous than it is now. Don't turn your back on the family who did such a good job of bringing you up. Surely, there's room in your heart for us all,' she chided.

'I'm sorry, Grandmamma. I just find it so hard to adjust between my real roots and my adopted family. It isn't every day that you find out you have an aristocratic heritage and a twin brother.' Rory was hurt, he thought he should be given credit for the way he had handled the dramatic change in his life, but all he seemed to receive were lectures on loyalty. Nevertheless, perhaps he should move to his grandmother's estate, after all it might impress a certain young lady. *Then we will see who is not good enough for Lady Helen Giles*, he thought.

Rory turned to his grandmother and took her hand. 'Do you know, on reflection,' he said. 'I think I will come to live with you both. It's the best thing all round – I'll tell the others tonight.'

Eliza Jane sat in the drawing room and gazed down at her niece. 'She's so beautiful, Etty, what are you going to name her?'

'I haven't given it much thought really,' said Etty, airily. 'I suppose something will come to mind sooner or later. Now put her down, Lizzie, I don't want her getting used to being held.'

'Babies need cuddles.'

'I'm sure they do. And I can assure you that when we're married, David will spend as much time as he can holding our daughter.'

Eliza Jane looked up sharply. 'Married?' she said, looking from her sister to David.

Etty smirked at Eliza Jane's surprised response. David smiled broadly.

'Your sister has agreed to marry me, Lizzie and I can't wait.'

Etty winced, 'Well you have to wait, David. First you have to go home and tell your parents.'

Eliza Jane looked sharply at Etty as she spoke. She couldn't believe Etty meant to marry David; it must be some sort of joke but she gave no indication of her suspicions as she spoke. 'Well, I hope you'll be very happy together. When are you getting married?'

'I was thinking by June,' said David, 'that should give us time to organise things.'

'No, David, that's far too soon. I think we should wait, perhaps until after Lizzie has married, after all we don't want to steal her thunder, do we?' Etty stretched her lips into a sardonic smile.

Eliza Jane took umbrage. 'That's never bothered you before,' she said, 'you've always been happy to steal the limelight.'

'I'm only thinking of you, that's all.' Etty stretched in her chair. 'Now, be a dear and make up the baby's feed in the bottle. You can feed her if you like, then when Thomas and Rory get home, we can have some tea, I'm parched.'

Eliza Jane placed the baby back in the crib that had been purchased by David on the way home from Islington, then left the room.

David sat forward on the sofa, now was his opportunity to ask Etty the question that had been worrying him. 'Etty?' he said.

'Yes, David.' She sounded bored.

'Why did the doctor think that Patrick was the father of your baby?'

'It's simple, David, you weren't there. I had to protect my reputation and avoid scandal and in the heat of the moment, I told him I was Mrs Patrick Lawrence. I didn't really know what I was saying; I was in so much pain.' Etty's eyes filled with crocodile tears. 'You do forgive me, don't you?'

'Of course, I do, I am just sorry you had to go through it all alone.' It was only later that it occurred to David that it wasn't actually his fault he hadn't been there.

'Good.' Etty's tears stopped, as soon as they had started. 'Now will you stay with the baby until Eliza Jane comes back – I think I'll go upstairs and rest a while, I'm very tired?'

After pecking David on the cheek, Etty swept from the room.

Etty lay on her bed, she felt wretched at her predicament – why in God's name had she agreed to marry David? She didn't love him, and it was the last thing she wanted to do. As for the child, what was she going to do with her? She had no instinctual need to look after her and no natural affection or bond. She rolled onto her side and silently wept.

Chapter 48

Eliza Jane set the table for six for dinner in the dining room that evening. The baby slept soundly in her cot in the drawing room having been given a bottle of Bengers infant food by David. He loved the way she had curled her finger around his as she sucked on her teat and gazed at him with big blue eyes. When she had finished, he carefully patted her back before placing her in her cot.

Etty had come back downstairs and had already taken her seat at the table before the others saying loudly. 'I don't think I could eat a thing.' Before tucking in heartily to her shepherd's pie.

Soon everyone was eating, and Eliza Jane asked Rory how his day out had been with Ronald and Lady Bennington.

Rory sheepishly stared at his knife and fork as he spoke, 'I really enjoyed it, we had tea in Selfridges, there is a great view of London from the roof garden. Actually, I do have something to say.' He looked anxiously around the table and cleared his throat. 'I thought I might move into East Cliff Mansion to be with Grandmamma and Ronald.'

The silence that followed made him swallow hard, he knew his plan wouldn't be received favourably but a silence was unbearable.

He gazed around the table. 'Doesn't anyone have anything to say?'

Thomas was furious inside but tried to remain calm. 'I don't think that's a very good idea,' he said. 'We're your family, and Ma and Pa would expect us to stay together.'

'But that's just it – we're not really a family, are we? Ronald's my true brother, my twin, and he wants me to live with him.'

'What about the studio, Rory, do you still want to work there?' Patrick put in quickly, anxious to avoid an explosion from Thomas at the mention of Ronald. All they ever seemed to hear these days was Ronald *this* and Ronald *that*. 'After all, you're wealthy enough not to have to earn a living now.'

'That's true, I don't have to work, but I enjoy it. Grandmamma's chauffeur will drive me to the studio until I learn to drive.'

'Listen to you, Rory, for God's sake, *Grandmamma's chauffeur*,' mimicked Thomas. 'Who on earth do you think you are royalty? You'll stay here with us, your common everyday family, do you hear? Don't let me hear any more about it.'

'Oh, let him go, Thomas,' Etty interrupted. 'He obviously doesn't want to be with us. After all, Eliza Jane will be leaving soon too, when she marries her butcher, won't you, Lizzie?'

'He has a name, Etty, but, yes, Jim and I will possibly be moving back to Crossdale. He's thinking about purchasing Roy Hughes's business.'

Etty was surprised at this. 'So you're going back to Crossdale.'

David smiled. 'You and I will be leaving for Crossdale too, Etty.'

Etty looked riled. 'Yes, well, that won't be for some time, will it?'

'All this talk of moving,' said Patrick seizing his opportunity to discuss his plans. 'There is something I need to discuss with you all. I've been offered a position with Vogue in New York; I worked on the magazine with them during the war. They've offered me an exceptionally good deal, and I'm more than tempted to accept. I could sell the business to you, Rory, if I decided to go, if you were interested. If not, then I'll sell the house and shut the business down.'

Thomas was beginning to feel vulnerable. Everyone seemed to have their future sorted, except him; he had no job and no prospects. He stood up, scraping his chair over the boards as he shifted back. His face was pale and his mouth set.

'I see,' he said bitterly, clenching his teeth between words. 'So, everyone is fine and dandy except me. What am I supposed to do, where can I go?' His eyes blazed at Rory. 'I'll tell you this, if you leave, I never want to see or speak to you again, do you hear me – never!'

Rory was furious. How dare Thomas humiliate him in front of everyone at the table, he wasn't Rory the youngest in the family now, he was important and of high birth, he also stood and faced Thomas across the table. 'You can't stop me leaving, in fact I have just decided to go and pack right now. I cannot spend another minute in the same room as you. You are a bigoted, selfish man whom the whole world does not revolve around, though you may think it does.'

'Who enabled us to move to London?' Thomas snarled. 'What, no reply. Well let me tell you, it was me, oh you may think it was your painting that bought us here but it was me who decided we could try our luck in London – otherwise we'd have all been separated at a hiring fair or worse still, languishing in the poor house. London has treated you all well but done nothing for me, I might just as well have stayed with Jacob Pennington after all he did ask me.'

'Jacob asked you to live with him?' said Eliza Jane incredulously.

Thomas was embarrassed; he had embroidered the truth in the heat of the argument, and was beginning to regret it. 'Well as good as,' he mumbled.

Rory with dark hooded eyes gazed at Thomas. 'If you'll excuse me, I'll just go and pack. Patrick, I'll let you know about the studio, because I think you should go to America, you deserve to follow your dreams – as we all do.' Rory stared meaningfully at Thomas. 'I hope you might reconsider your threats.'

Thomas scowled, 'Just go, leave us alone. Go to your rich family, and much good may it do you. I'm going out.'

Before Rory could leave, Thomas angrily made for the door. His hand steady on the door knob, he turned to listen to Eliza Jane as she tried to calm the rift. 'Thomas please and Rory, make up with your brother, I can't bear it, I love you both, I don't want to take sides. She turned to her sister who was ignoring the argument. 'Etty say something, they're your brothers too.'

'Don't involve me in all this,' said Etty, looking disinterested. 'Let them do what they have to do, I really don't care. I was just thinking how pleasant it would be to have a meal in peace one day, instead of this eternal bickering.'

The door slammed twice – Thomas left first and Rory followed, repeating the action. Both headed in different directions, Thomas to the front door, and Rory to their shared room to pack his clothes.

'I'm so sorry, David; your visit has been rather stormy,' Patrick said, more than used to the sibling squabbles.

David was astonished, Thomas was so angry. He had never been like this in Crossdale, so why was he so bitter now. He turned to Etty. 'Perhaps it would be best if I went home tomorrow and broke the news to my parents. They need to know they are grandparents now, and that Etty and I are to be married. I need to do it face to face; you don't mind, do you, love? I know mother will be upset that she cannot leave the shop to come to London and meet her granddaughter, so I'd best stay a while to help her through the disappointment, until you and the baby come home.'

'Yes, you must go home. I'll miss you of course, but I think it's for the best,' Etty said sweetly. Suddenly, there came a cry came from the drawing room. 'Oh, for heaven's sake, all that door banging has woken the baby. Would you go, Lizzie? You're so good with her.'

'I'll go' – David rose from his chair – 'after all she won't be seeing her daddy for a little while.'

Etty forced a smile through thin lips at her fiancé, thinking the sooner he went home, the better.

'Miss Watkins.' The junior assistant stage manager had been running to find Molly, and was now breathlessly banging on her door. Molly put down her script, although she knew every word of the part, she still practised every day. Crossing the small dingy room, almost catching her foot in the threadbare carpet, she opened the door.

'What is it, Arthur?'

'Miss Watkins, Mr Bennett wants to see you immediately.'

'Do you know what it's about?' Arthur shook his head.

Molly turned back into her room. She grabbed the key that hung on a nail next to a badly painted picture of the Madonna angled on the dirty wall. No matter how many times she straightened it, the picture always slumped to one side. Leaving the room, she locked her door carefully before following Arthur.

The boarding house was quiet. She had declined to accompany the other actors into the local town, amid cries of not being fun anymore. Since that night in Plymouth when Jeremy had molested her, she had avoided him and the others now finding them loud and lewd. She followed Arthur across the street and into the theatre.

Arthur knocked on the producer's door before opening it. 'Miss Watkins,' he announced, then retreated.

She entered the room. 'You wanted to see me, Mr Bennett?'

'I did, Miss Watkins.' He rose from behind his desk and walked towards her. 'Miss Fanny is indisposed and will not be appearing as Gwendolen tonight, so I'm prepared to give you the chance to appear instead. I'm taking a huge risk, and if the audience demand their money back because you are not up to the part, then you'll receive no wages this week. Do you understand? Now what do you say?'

Molly was thrilled, this was her chance, she spoke rapidly. 'I do understand, and I'll take the part. Thank you, thank you so much.'

'Do not let the company down, Miss Watkins. Oh, and by the way, there are two letters for you. Now off you run and learn those lines, I want you word perfect.'

'Yes, thank you, and I won't let you down,' Molly said firmly.

As she took the letters Edward Bennett gave her, a rare smile which had a strange effect on Molly's heart, perhaps she was just excited about her lead role she thought as she dismissed the feeling.

'Rehearsal at four,' he said, 'do not be late.'

'I won't,' she replied, her heart still beating slightly faster than usual, Molly closed his office door and ran back to her room in the boarding house. There sitting on her bed, she looked at the letters. The first was from Eliza Jane, she recognised the handwriting, but had no idea who the second letter was from.

Opening that one first, she quickly scanned the contents, her heart lurching when she saw Jo's signature. They had not spoken in the three months that Molly had been away.

Dear Molly,

I hope you are well and enjoying your new career. We miss you at Cobbs. Old Gambon is becoming more and more impossible, poor Letty Ashurst was sacked the other day for complaining about his behaviour to the General. Oh Moll, I wish you were still here, there is no fun in going to work anymore.

I know I am probably the last person you want to hear from as we parted such poor friends, but I hate the fact that we fell out, and admit readily that everything was my fault. Perhaps I was jealous, because you had found a way to escape. Whatever it was, I had no right to say what I did. I should have supported my best friend wholeheartedly.

I do hope you can forgive me, Molly; it is important to me; Thomas and Kit hate that we have fallen out too. They are both well and send their love to you.

I'm not sure if I should tell you this but Kit has met a nice girl and he seems quite taken with her. I'm pleased for him and I hope you will be too.

Please don't be cross with your old friend. I beg you write and send me all your news. I look forward so much to hearing from you.

Kind regards,

Josephine Howard.

Molly put down the letter, tears were stinging her eyes. She had missed Jo and regretted that their parting had been less than amicable. She was as much at fault as her friend. She would write back as soon as she was able. She thought about Kit, she was genuinely pleased he had found someone new but deep down inside, a tiny piece of her was upset that he had overcome his feelings for her so quickly.

Molly stood nervously in the wings with an elderly established actress playing Lady Bracknell. She waited for her cue.

The other actress offered some advice. 'You'll be fine, my dear. Just think of your motivation, mine is my pay packet.'

She laughed throatily, caused by a lifetime of gin and cigarettes. Molly nodded with obvious distraction, her first line whirling around her head. '*I am always smart, am I not, Mr Worthing?*' she repeated quietly to herself. Just before she went on stage, the line escaped her mind. She panicked briefly, desperately looking around her for help. Then suddenly, she was on stage, and remarkably the line came to her, and she delivered it perfectly.

At the end of the play as Molly took her forth curtain call this one on her own, the audience cheered, stamped their feet and applauded. She was exhausted but elated. She had been word perfect.

Backstage, Edward was waiting for her. 'You obviously can act,' he remarked much to Molly's joy, 'but don't go getting any ideas above your station, you're back to playing a maid tomorrow night. Molly nodded and walked back to her dingy dressing room. She sat down and examined her face in the mirror under the powerful lights that surrounded it. She laughed at her reflection saying out loud, 'Welcome to the big time, Miss Watkins,' before cleansing the greasepaint from her face.

Edward Bennett was privately thrilled with Molly's performance; she had stolen the show and Fanny had better look to her laurels.

Chapter 49

Eliza Jane was making up the fire the bedrooms. Although it was April, there was still a damp chill in the air, and everyone was reluctant to climb out of bed without some warmth in the room. She was trying to be as quiet as possible in Etty's room so as not to wake the baby, who was sleeping peacefully in her cot. She stood up from the fireplace, wandering over to the crib. She gazed at the sleeping infant, stirring deep maternal feelings in her. She loved this child already. David had returned to Crossdale with a cold send off from Etty. Eliza Jane did not see that marriage working.

Etty had returned to work, leaving Eliza Jane with the day-to-day care of the baby. She gently drew the blanket down from enveloping the infant's face. The baby looked so much like David with her fair hair and wide mouth. Sometimes it was painful to look at her, and after all, she was the result of Etty's betrayal.

She whispered, stroking the baby's head, 'You still don't have a name my little one, and nearly three weeks old. Never mind, Daddy will be back soon, and he'll give you one, whether your mother likes it or not.'

The baby stirred slightly, so Eliza Jane picked her up, gently soothing the child. 'Come along, little one. Time to have a fresh nappy before Mummy comes home.'

'Miss Watkins, you're to go to Mr Harding's office at once,' Miss Bell, the supervisor, commanded. It was two o' clock in the afternoon, Etty had just about given up hope of being summoned. All morning, one by one, her three colleagues had visited the office where she knew Madam Souris had been studying their designs, each designer had returned to their desks with no sign of what might have transpired on their faces. All except Violet Cummings who smiled serenely at Etty, as if she had some superior knowledge about the winner. Etty knew better than to show weakness by asking how they had all fared, and besides, everyone was under the watchful eye of the supervisor, Miss Bell.

Etty smoothed down her skirt, ensuring her blouse was tucked securely into her waistband. Thank goodness, by starving herself she had managed to lose weight and dry her breast milk up at the same time which pleased her, it was as if the baby had never happened.

'Ah, Miss Watkins,' Mr Harding beamed, from behind his desk, 'I expect you thought we'd never get around to discussing your designs. Do come in, you remember Madame Souris, do you not?' Etty gazed to Mr Harding's left where Madame Souris sat elegantly with her slim legs swept to one side. Her outfit was superb and fitted her fragile frame well, her jet-black hair was swept up into a stylish chignon, her face was made up and her eyes heavily outlined.

'*Bien sur, bon après midi,* Madame,' Etty was pleased she had remembered the few words of French that Patrick had taught her at her request. All was fair in love, war and design competitions, she thought.

'*Ah, vous parlez francais, 'enriette, bon! Eh bien, je suis heureux de vous announcer que vous avez un magnifique design ici.*'

Etty smiled; she had no idea what had just been said but she hoped it was complimentary.

Madame smiled also. 'Thank you ,'enriette, for speaking to me in French. I understand that you perhaps only know a few words, so we'll talk in English, shall we not? Now please sit down, and tell me why you 'ave chosen the colour lilac for your tea dress design, when the fashion is white, and you have included three quarter length sleeves.'

Etty sat on the chair Madame Souris indicated, tucking her legs underneath and leaning forward with her hands in her lap. 'Madame, before the war, ladies of wealth and status had servants to wash their white afternoon tea dresses; now, however, there are fewer servants, these women having found other forms of employment. I therefore thought that perhaps a coloured afternoon tea dress would be more practical, and I felt the sleeves would distinguish the dress from evening wear. As you can see, she pointed to her designs open on Mr Harding's desk, my next design is a heavily embroidered sleeveless, layered tunic with a large contrasting sash attached which is suitable for every evening occasion.'

Madame Souris stood and looked at the designs for a while before saying, 'Your ideas are very bold ,'enriette, but I like them. I can see that the ladies of Paris would find the practicalities of colour useful. However, we do not frequently go out to afternoon tea in our country – something I hope to change in time – so what use for the dress then?'

'Then I'm sure the coloured dress will be useful for lunch and general visiting.'

';enriette, do you understand about this collaboration between myself and the 'ouse of 'arding. It is in our mutual interest to join together to produce such fashion as to make that Chanel woman 'istory. We must ensure that we regularly have a presence in La Gazette du Bon Ton, our leading fashion magazine. Monsieur 'arding and I feel it would be beneficial to us both for an exchange of our most prominent designers. Now I believe you have had a little time away from work just recently, are you quite recovered from your ailment?'

'Quite recovered, Madame,' Etty replied, 'I was in quite a lot of pain but now it has completely gone.'

Madame nodded. 'Good then I 'ave decided, 'enriette, that I wish to take you to Paris with me. What do you say?'

'Thank you, Madame. I'm so excited that I don't know what to say except thank you – I would love to go; I won't let you down.'

'Tres bon, I am sure we will be 'appy together, 'enriette.'

'Excellent,' said Mr Harding, rubbing his hands together. 'However, a word Miss Watkins, please do not inform the other designers of your good fortune – I'll make an announcement tomorrow. Madame Souris will be here for one more week, will you be ready to leave for Paris with her then?'

'Of course, Mr Harding, I'll be ready.'

Etty walked to the trolley bus stop as if in a dream. She would soon be designing for the La Maison de Souris in Paris. She gave a little skip, of excitement, before remembering her family, how was she going to conceal her good fortune and future plans from them. She slowed down walking more slowly to her stop, losing some of her ebullience.

Jim had called in to see Eliza Jane at lunchtime with a large joint of pork from under the counter. He found her scrubbing the kitchen table, her sleeves rolled up and her apron on. She quickly removed it when she saw him. He suggested that she invite everyone to dinner that evening to mend the relationship between Thomas and Rory.

'Thomas won't come if he thinks Rory will be there,' she said unable to hide her disappointment. 'And vice versa, Jim, you know how they are.'

'Then don't tell them the other one is coming, gal. I mean, you don't 'ave to lie, just be somewhat evasive. Anyways, I just popped in quickly – must go, see yer at eight.'

A little later, Eliza Jane was cooking pork in the kitchen and trying to pacify the baby at the same time. She ran a hand over her brow, blew the wispy pieces of hair away from her hot face. Rocking the crib had not comforted the infant, so Eliza Jane picked her up and cuddled her.

Etty breezed through the kitchen door. 'You're spoiling that child,' she said, 'she's got to learn that she doesn't get things all her own way.'

Eliza Jane would have liked to have pointed out that Etty always had her own way, and had never learnt otherwise, but to avoid a row, she thought better of it.

'I think she's hungry, Etty – why not take her upstairs and settle her.'

'It's been a busy day; I need a bath. I'm sure you can cope for a while longer, can't you?'

Etty removed her hat and coat, hung them on the hooks and headed for the door to the rest of the house.

'No, I can't, Etty,' said Eliza Jane, surprising herself at being able to stand up to Etty, 'I'm actually rather busy. Jim bought a large piece of pork up at lunchtime with strict instructions that the whole family sit down to dinner tonight. He wants to build bridges between Rory and Thomas.'

'If everyone's coming that's all the more reason for me to relax in the bath,' then catching site of her sister's face, she added grudgingly, 'oh very well, give her to me. I'll feed her later after I've had my bath.'

Eliza Jane knew she was beaten, her sympathetic heart could not let the baby wait that long for her milk. 'No, Etty, leave her with me and I'll feed her. I could do with a sit down anyway.'

'Thank you, Lizzie, you really are so good with her.'

'I just know how long your baths take – the poor child will starve.'

Eliza Jane frowned as Etty left the room. She turned back to smile at the baby in her arms. 'Just go down in your cot for a minute while Aunty Lizzie prepares your feed.'

'You said Rory wouldn't be here,' hissed Thomas, following his sister into the kitchen.

'I didn't say he would and I didn't say he wouldn't,' responded Eliza Jane. 'Can't you and he just let bygones be bygones? Please, Thomas, Jim asked for everyone to be present tonight for some reason, let us just get through one meal without angry exchanges. Besides, Jo is here, I thought you'd be pleased.'

'I am, it was a lovely surprise, but let me make one thing clear. I'll sit at the table with Rory and that brother of his, but I'm not going to make pleasant conversation.'

The meal was a strained affair. Conversation was stilted, Rory was equally unhappy that Thomas was sitting across the table from him. Ronald and Patrick did their best to keep conversation flowing with little success, and even the usual effervescent Jim, appeared quiet and almost nervous.

'We received a letter from our father in America today, didn't we, Rory?' Ronald announced.

Thomas scowled and Jo placed a comforting hand on his arm.

'Yes, he wants to meet us, and is prepared to pay for our passage,' he added.

Patrick, listening to Ronald had an idea. 'Perhaps you could come over with me, it would be nice to have company on the ship.'

Rory shifted uncomfortably in his chair. 'I don't think we should discuss this in front of Thomas, Ronald.'

'Oh,' said Thomas, feeling aggrieved by the twins, 'so you do have some sensibilities left – enough to realise I don't want to hear news of your father when mine has barely left us.'

'What do you mean *mine*?' snapped Rory. 'Albert was a real father to me all these years, the only one I had. I loved him as much as you all did.'

'It's nice to know you cared about him,' replied Thomas sarcastically.

'I care about you too, if only you would let me. Just because I want to live with Ronald and Grandmamma doesn't mean I never want to speak to any of you again. You may not believe it but I still think of you as my brother and I hate us being at loggerheads.'

Jo placed her hand on Thomas' arm. 'Rory is right, Thomas, you are still family and I'm sure you still care about each other, think about it, don't destroy a lifetime with harsh words.'

Thomas looked at Jo, he loved this quiet girl and would do anything for her. He took a deep breath, formulating his words.

'I care but I cannot accept you wanting to leave us. I still think of you as my brother.'

'Really,' Rory answered bitterly, unable to accept Thomas's statement, 'I thought you couldn't wait to palm me off as Ronald's brother. I remember telling you that as your brother, I had a right to know the secrets you were keeping from me and you started to tell me that I wasn't your brother, but you managed to stop yourself in time. Do you know what, it all makes sense now?'

Patrick intervened. 'Much of this anger seems to stem from a misunderstanding between the two of you. The emotions involved in the recent revelation have affected you both, but your feelings are relatively similar, that is plain to see. You were brought up together, so in all but the accident of birth, you are brothers – can't you see that? Now shake hands, and act like proper brothers. Why I would give my right arm for what you two have.'

Reluctantly, Rory stood and looked at Thomas, while slowly extending his right hand. Thomas thought for a second then urged by Jo, he stood and reached across the table to grip Rory's hand. There was an awkward silence then in an effort to break the tension, Patrick turned to Jim and said, 'Now Jim, tell us why you really wanted us all here to partake of this magnificent piece of pork?'

'I wanted this to be a special occasion. Lizzie, my girl, a few weeks ago, you agreed to become my wife, and I feel now is the time to make it official like. Jim felt in his pocket and produced a small box.'

The room grew suddenly still.

Jim left his chair and opening the box knelt down on one knee. Lizzie held her breath. 'Eliza Jane Watkins, will yer do me the 'onour of becoming my wife?'

Eliza Jane looked at the ring – nestling in cream satin was a large ruby surrounded by several tiny diamonds. She gasped – in all her life, she had never seen anything quite so beautiful. 'Oh Jim, I can't accept this, please it's too much. You already know I want to marry you; I don't need a ring to prove it – it must have cost you a fortune.'

'I'm not one for fancy words but I do know that I love you more than anything, and I want you to wear my ring. I want the world to know you're my girl.'

He took the ring from its box and placed it on finger; it was a perfect fit.

'Oh Jim,' she gasped, gazing at the ring, 'thank you. It's just so beautiful.'

Jim got to his feet and with a whoop of joy, he grabbed Eliza Jane from her chair and swung her around. 'I don't care that we're in public, Lizzie – I'm just goin' to kiss yer girl.' He gave Eliza Jane the gentlest of kisses before hugging her tight. Everyone applauded.

'Listen, everyone,' said Etty interrupting the applause, 'I have just thought of a name for the baby.'

Everyone looked at her.

'I'm going to name her Ruby.'

Only Jo noticed Eliza Jane's face fall, as everyone focused on Etty, congratulating her on naming the baby.

Chapter 50

'How lovely, a letter to Etty I see,' said Miss Jemima to David, as he handed the envelope bearing Etty's address across the post office counter for a stamp. 'How are the family doing in London, did you enjoy your visit?'

'Very much, Miss Jemima, thank you, it was lovely to see them all,' David spoke warily, reminding himself that he could give away too much if he was caught unawares.

'What are they all doing?'

'All busy, you know, lots going on, well I must get back to the shop, you'll make sure the letter goes in the next post, won't you?' David smiled at Miss Jemima before turning on his heel and leaving the post office. As he walked across the road back to the Jacksons shop, he thought about his parent's reaction to his news that he Etty had agreed to marry him and he had a daughter. In his letter to Etty, he had written that his parents were thrilled with the news of their new Granddaughter but in reality, they were furious. Mrs Jackson called Etty names he hadn't even heard of, and Mr Jackson refused to accept the baby as David's.

He had overheard them one evening in their bedroom talking about Etty.

'She has obviously used all her wiles to catch our David, knowing that he might be worth a bob or two,' sniffed Mrs Jackson. 'None of this is our lad's fault.'

'How do we know the baby is his because I wouldn't trust her. She always seemed to let her parents down, and nicer folk you couldn't wish to meet,' Mr Jackson replied.

I had hoped he would see sense and marry Eliza Jane. I tell you what I'm glad that poor William Stanton had sense to die for his country, he would have had a life of misery with that lass's sharp tongue,' agreed Mrs Jackson, 'she smells money that one.'

David had turned from the door and made for his room deciding to ignore his parent's comments. They would love Etty and the baby as much as he did when she came home to marry him. He was sure of it.

Etty packed her old battered suitcase. She looked at it ruefully; she couldn't afford to buy a new one, so this one would have to do. She hid the case in her wardrobe all ready to travel. It had posed quite a problem packing for Paris; she knew she would look the poor relation in whatever she wore. Perhaps Madame Souris would be so horrified with her wardrobe that she would instantly offer her something more fashionable to wear.

That night, she had gone to bed early feigning tiredness. Eliza Jane had suggested, as Etty had hoped, to have Ruby in her room overnight so Etty could have some undisturbed sleep. In truth, Etty was wide awake; she lay in bed thinking of the morning when she would sneak out of the house at a very early hour and wait for the taxi cab that Madam Souris had arranged. She had suggested it wait around the corner so as not to wake the neighbourhood. It was all too exciting – the start of a new life.

The following morning, Eliza Jane took Ruby into her mother. Etty was already up it seemed, as the bed was empty. Then Eliza Jane caught sight of an envelope propped up on the dressing table. Her heart lurched, she suddenly felt nauseous and giddy.

'Oh no, Etty, not again,' she uttered in despair.

Patrick looked tired and drawn as he took his place at the kitchen table, next to Thomas. They sat in silence as they ate their breakfast, both looking up when Eliza Jane came rushing into the kitchen holding Ruby in one arm and waving an envelope with the other.

'Etty has gone; she's taken her clothes, but this time she has left a letter.'

Thomas stood up. 'For heaven's sake, I am getting so fed up with these drama's Etty keeps inflicting on us. Don't you agree, Patrick, how much more might she put us through?'

'I expect she has her reasons.' Patrick continued to butter his toast.

'What are her reasons, Lizzie, you've read the letter,' said Thomas

'Perhaps it is for Eliza Jane's eyes-only, Thomas,' said Patrick.

'Nonsense, we need to know. I'm sure after last time that she'll be perfectly safe but perhaps there's something we can do.'

'She's left for France,' said Eliza Jane flatly, her mouth slightly twisted with anger. 'I don't think she's coming back. She obviously won the competition at work.'

'Not coming back,' Thomas was incredulous, 'but what about Ruby? She has to come back for her, doesn't she? And what's this competition, what are you talking about, Lizzie?'

'She's been talking about it for weeks; haven't you been listening to her.'

'Not if I can help it, no.'

'It's an exchange programme between the House of Harding and some designer from Paris?' Patrick said simply.

'You see,' said Eliza Jane irritated at her brother, 'Patrick knows what I'm talking about, he cares more about our sister, than you ever will.' Patrick seemed to look uncomfortable, almost embarrassed at her words.

Thomas rubbed his hand over his face and up into his hair in despair. 'I thought she was going to marry David, and what about Ruby? She can't just abandon her baby.'

'Too late for that, Thomas, it looks like she has. This makes me so angry. I'd better read you her letter, and then perhaps you'll understand why I'm feeling like I do,' said Eliza Jane, handing Thomas the baby before pulling out a chair and sitting at the table. She opened up the sheaf of paper covered in Etty's flamboyant handwriting.

Dear Lizzie,

By the time you read this, I shall be on a train bound for Dover and the cross-channel boat. I have been given an opportunity beyond my wildest dreams by Madame Souris, to work with her design team in Paris. I know you wouldn't deny me this chance. I have talent, Lizzie, and I need to prove it to the world.

When we were children and sharing our hopes and dreams long into the night in our small bedroom in Crossdale, Molly always said she wanted to become an actress, you wanted to be married with your own family, and I wanted to design the best and most fashionable clothes possible. Well, Lizzie, all those wishes are about to come true. Molly is following her dream, you're about to become Mrs James Wilson, and now I have the chance to fulfil my destiny.

You will make a wonderful wife, Jim is so lucky to have found you, and he knows it. You will also make a wonderful mother, and it is my dearest wish that you bring Ruby up as your own child. You are probably going to move back to

Crossdale, and so David, dear kind sweet David whom I have hurt so badly, will be able to see his daughter every day.

I am begging you to do this, Lizzie, if not for me then for David. I cannot think of anyone who I would rather Ruby call mother. I will just be Aunty Etty, a rather glamorous lady that comes to see her niece occasionally. Ruby need never know that I gave birth to her. I will of course send you money for her when I am able.

I will write to David as soon as I have an address in Paris, but he must never be told of my exact whereabouts, he must be given the chance and every encouragement to find someone who will love him as he should be loved.

Please forgive me, Lizzie, as I hope Thomas, Molly and Rory will too, and try to understand.

I know you and Jim are made for each other and if you care to look in my wardrobe, you will see I have left you a present. I hope you like it; I know you will look beautiful.

I will be in touch in a few weeks but please just be happy for me, and know that I am following my dreams.

Your Loving Sister,

Etty.

There was a stunned silence. Patrick and Thomas looked at each other, neither finding the right words to describe how they were feeling. They didn't even know how they were feeling. It was all such a terrible shock.

'Poor David,' murmured Patrick, 'how will he take the news? He'll never get over this.'

'How about you, Lizzie,' said Thomas, 'what will you do?'

'What can I do but love Ruby like she's my own? I only hope Jim is as good about Ruby as Da was with Rory. History has a habit of repeating itself they say.'

'You don't have to do this you know,' said Thomas wearily not really believing in his own words, 'we could find an orphanage or something. Or perhaps David will want her.'

Eliza Jane shook her head, standing up she took Ruby back from Thomas and held her lovingly. 'No, if David agrees to it, then Jim and I will bring her up providing, he agrees when he returns from Crossdale. If we're blessed with other children, then Ruby will be loved just as much as they are.'

'It's not going to be easy,' Thomas replied.

'Did you ever feel that Ma and Da didn't love Rory as much as they loved us?'

'No, if anything. Ma doted on him more because he was the baby.'

'Exactly – I want to do this for David's sake as much as anything, and I'm sure Jim will agree. He's so like Da, you know.'

'What did she leave in her wardrobe for you. Lizzie?' Patrick enquired

'At first I felt I didn't want to look; I really didn't want anything from her but curiosity got the better of me.'

'Well. what was it?' insisted Thomas.

'It was the most beautiful wedding gown. Inside the lining, the label reads, Weddings by Henrietta. It is so beautiful that I just hope I do it justice.'

Chapter 51

Three days later, Jim returned from Crossdale having signed on the dotted line and bought Roy Hughes butchers' shop. He was full of the deal, and came around to see Eliza Jane as soon as he got home surprising her by grabbing her around the waist having crept into the kitchen quietly through the back door. She laughed. 'Da used to do that to Ma, always made her jump too.' She hugged him tightly, not knowing how to ask him about Ruby.

'Sit down, Jim, I will put the kettle on, we'll have a cup of tea.' Jim did as he was told before Eliza Jane continued, 'Before you tell me about your trip, there's something you should know.'

Jim grabbed Eliza Jane's hand and pulled her onto his lap and squeezed her tight. 'I know what you're going to say, Lizzie. David was in the Bluebell one lunchtime, he'd 'ad a letter from her "ladyship" breaking off their engagement and saying she had left Ruby with you.'

'At least Etty wrote to him then. I rather thought she wouldn't, but what of poor David, how is he?'

''e's a broken man, that's 'ow 'e is, and who wouldn't be losing the only girl you've ever loved, and so cruelly too. You know she returned his ring. 'e 'ad it all planned, 'ow they was going to do everything and all for nothing now.'

'How does he feel about us having Ruby? After all, he has every right to bring her up, she's his flesh and blood?'

''e would, Lizzy, like a shot, but 'is mother is refusing to 'ave 'er in the 'ouse. She says Etty's going is a blessing in disguise. She was never going to accept Ruby as family. I'm afraid Mrs Jackson doesn't 'ave a good word to say about our Etty. David thinks it's for the best. He'll be able to see 'is daughter every day but she'll not be told that 'e is 'er father – 'e's happy to be known as Uncle David. I don't 'alf feel sorry for the poor sod, and I like 'im, Lizzie, I really do. I've told 'im that we'll take care of Ruby like one of our own, 'e knows that, but I felt I needed to say it.'

'Jim Harrison you're the best fiancé a girl could have; no wonder I love you.' Eliza Jane kissed him heartily. 'Now tell me about Crossdale, what did you think?'

'Well girl, I'm not used to villages, and I'm guessing I might miss the smoke, but the shop 'as a good turnover, and the living quarters are all right, spacious an' that – nothing that a coat of paint won't fix. I was thinkin' we could branch out so ter speak. We could sell your meat pies. I think that might go down well. Upshot of it is the shop is all ours.'

'I can't believe it, Jim, our own shop.' With a thought crossing her mind, Eliza Jane's face suddenly fell.

'What's up, girl?'

'If we turn up with Ruby, people will put two and two together – they'll know she's not ours, the gossip will be horrendous. You don't know what village tittle tattle is like.'

''ow are they going ter know 'ow long we've bin married? They won't. Ruby could be our honeymoon, baby.'

Eliza Jane blushed to the roots of her hair at the mention of the word, honeymoon which made Jim laugh. 'I told 'em up there I was married but not whom I was married to. That'll be a surprise for 'em, Ruby could well be ours.'

'I would have had to marry you as soon as I got here really though.'

'And why not, any girl as gorgeous as you would be married as soon as a fella set eyes on yer.'

'Oh, Jim, I do love you.'

Just then, the baby wailed from the bedroom.

'I'll go to her; you make that tea, love,' said Jim.

The news of Etty's departure reached Molly as she was rehearsing for a new play in the church hall in Nottingham. Edward Bennett had finally relented and given her the opportunity to take a better part than the maid. Molly was thrilled and determined to show him what she could do, but it wasn't to be. Molly was so upset that Etty had gone to Paris, leaving her new baby behind her that she could think of little else. She wanted to be at home to support her family, not taking stage directions and forgetting her lines.

'For heaven's sake, Miss Watkins, you're standing in the wrong place again and totally upstaging Jeremy.'

Molly grimaced. 'Sorry,' she said. After being struck in the face by Jeremy after their night out, she thought he deserved upstaging.

'Miss Watkins, come on. You should know these lines by now – after all, you don't have that many.'

'Perhaps you were wrong to give Miss Watkins the part, Edward,' Jeremy sneered. 'It's obviously way beyond her capabilities, she's a rank amateur.'

'I do know my part; it's just I've had news from home that has upset me. My lines have gone straight out of my head.'

'Miss Watkins, we cannot afford for family worries to interfere with our career. Get off the stage, and come back when you think you can be professional.'

Humiliated and ashamed, she began to leave the hall as the other actors began a slow handclap. Molly fled to the cloakroom with tears spilling down her face.

'That's enough' – Edward put up his hand to stop the clapping – 'I suggest we all take a break and reassemble in thirty minutes. At this rate, we won't have an opening night.'

Grumbling, the cast moved off the stage and broke into little huddles to discuss their director.

Edward hating that he had again been unnecessarily harsh with Molly went in search of her. He found her in the cloakroom sitting beneath the coat hooks. She was sobbing into her handkerchief and his heart went out to her.

'Miss Watkins, please don't cry.'

Molly hid her face in her hands, unable to look him in the eye. He perched beside her on the narrow platform of the rail, and sat in silence while she continued sobbing.

He was aware of the smell of greasepaint coupled with a mustiness of an old building. The coats hanging there seemed to close in on him, and he pushed them away impatiently. His action made Molly look up. 'I'm not doing very well, am I?' she said, taking an audible breath in between sobs.

'On the contrary, you're a good actress, very good in fact.'

'But the others hate me, and you are always horrible to me. I never seem to do anything right for you. Why do you treat me so? You always call me Miss Watkins, never Molly, why?'

Edward couldn't help himself as all his bottled-up feelings of love surged to the surface. 'Oh Molly, can't you work out why I treat you so badly?' he asked gently.

'No, I can't.' She blew her nose hard on her wet handkerchief. 'I thought I'd been doing quite well. I received three curtain calls when I played Gwendolen but even that didn't seem to be good enough for you.'

'Do I have to spell it out to you?'

Molly gazed at Edward, and in that moment of looking into his violet eyes, she realised why his opinion mattered so much. It wasn't just because he was her director and her future career lay with him, his opinion mattered because, and here was the surprise, she was actually in love with him. She took another deep breath; she wasn't really prepared for this self-revelation.

'Yes, Mr Bennett, you do. Please tell me why you hate me so much.'

'I don't hate you, far from it.'

'What do you mean?'

'Perhaps this will tell you better than I can.' Edward cupped Molly's delicate heart-shaped chin in his hand and drew her towards him. Tentatively, he brushed his lips against hers, then realising that she welcomed this tenderness, he drew her into a long passionate kiss.

The kiss ended as suddenly as it started. 'I'm sorry, Molly. I shouldn't have done that.'

'I wanted you to kiss me, I suddenly realised I wanted it more than anything.'

'No, Molly, it must never happen again.'

'I don't understand, what can be so wrong?'

'I'm already married.'

Molly jerked to her feet in horror before fleeing the room.

'Damn, damn, damn,' Edward cursed. He remained secluded in the cloakroom for some time, contemplating what had just occurred and still feeling Molly's lips on his.

Molly arrived back at rehearsals at the same time as the others. She had washed her face, brushed her hair and gone over her lines determined to put her worries about Etty aside. She didn't want to think about that kiss either and she made sure she delivered a focused performance and received a spontaneous round of applause from the rest of the cast. When Edward congratulated her, she refused to look at him. She finished the rehearsal with such gusto, that she was in danger of overacting.

At the end of the rehearsal, Edward dismissed the cast but asked Molly to stay behind. The other actors glad to be let go after a tiring day trailed slowly out of the room whiles making plans for their night off. When they had left, Edward reached for Molly's hand and said, 'We need to talk, Molly.'

She reluctantly agreed, 'What's there to say – you're married. Where's your wife? With the children I suppose, waiting for you to come home.'

Molly hated her own sarcasm; it didn't come naturally to her.

'My wife left me two years ago,' he said, frowning at the memory. 'She met a South African jazz trumpet player and fell in love – I've not heard from her since and I have no idea where she is. Up until now, I have had no need to find her. Believe me, I wish with all my heart that I were free to court you, but until I find Marjorie and ask her for a divorce, we can't be together.'

'I'm so very sorry, it must have been terrible for you after she left. Will you ever be able to find her?' Molly took his hand and squeezed it lightly. 'You know Edward frankly, I don't care if you do, it may take forever to find your wife, but I will wait for you.'

'Molly, I can't ask you to wait in the hope of me finding and divorcing my wife. It may never happen.'

'Edward, do you want to give us a chance?'

'Yes, with all my heart, Molly.'

'Then I am sure something will turn up, now kiss me please.' For once, the director did as the actress ordered.

Chapter 52

'Grandmamma would think this dance is scandalous,' Ronald admitted, thoroughly enjoying himself. He and Rory were dining out in the elegant ballroom at Claridge's. Sitting at a table and sipping champagne, they were watching people dance the tango, fascinated by the shocking steps.

'Look how their bodies are together. Did you see that?' Ronald whistled long and low. 'See how she bends backwards,' said Ronald, as a couple danced past them.

Rory laughed. 'You have no idea what my adoptive mother, Martha, would have made of it.'

'I wish I'd met her; she sounds fearsome.'

'She was, but only in relation to us; she would protect us to the end. She and Etty clashed terribly; heaven knows what she'd have made of her deserting Ruby.'

Rory took a puff on his cigarette, then flamboyantly blew the smoke through his nostrils, as he had seen others do. 'Actually,' he said, 'I don't know what she would have made of me smoking, either.'

'You should have been in the trenches – you would have smoked then all right, to help steady the nerves.'

'I can't believe you went through all that. I was glad the war ended when it did or I'd have been called up.'

'Made a man of me though, nothing like a French Mademoiselle to practise on if you know what I mean.'

'You mean you're not a virgin?'

'Of course not, you mean you are?'

'No, I've had my share.' Rory was not going to reveal the truth. He changed the subject. 'Tell me more about our mother – what do you remember about her?'

'She was pretty with curls, so dark she could have been Spanish senorita – you've seen the pictures. My memories are a little hazy; I was only twelve when she died. She smelled of pears soap that I do remember; it was like an English

326

garden in full bloom.' Ronald's eyes took on a faraway look as he struggled to remember more. 'She painted beautiful landscapes; the ones done in Italy when she met our father are magnificent.'

'Yes, the one in Grandmamma's drawing room is painted by her – the colours are so vibrant.'

Ronald nodded. 'She was lots of fun. She would play cricket and tennis with me in the hols, but sometimes there'd be sadness about her, and her face would shut down as if she was in pain. Now I know why.'

'Have you thought anymore about visiting our father? Patrick was asking me the other day; he's going to take the job with Vogue and leaves in a couple of months – we could go with him.'

'How can we leave Grandmamma? She'd be all alone, except for Stevens and Mrs Willis – we couldn't possibly go.'

'I suppose you're right but I do so want to meet him.'

'So do I, believe me, but wait a minute – I've just thought of a solution. I think I might have an idea—'

'Well, I never,' a voice interrupted them, 'Rory Watkins, or should I say, the Honourable Rory Watkins.'

Rory would have known that scent anywhere; previously it had held intoxicating properties. Lady Helen draped herself over the spare chair at their table; crossed her long elegant legs and leant towards him.

Rory was surprised to see Helen. A few weeks ago, he would have relished the thought of seeing her again but somehow the sight of her made him angry. He didn't need her anymore; he had found the other half of him that had been missing and he was content. 'Helen, how nice, still busy fighting for the rights of the disenfranchised I suppose.'

Helen pouted with bright red lips. 'Don't be like that, Rory, I've missed you. 'I'm so glad I've seen you, introduce me to your brother, darling.'

'Lady Helen, my twin brother Ronald. Ronald, may I introduce you to Lady Helen Giles a one-time acquaintance of mine.'

Ronald got to his feet as Helen extended a hand, which he duly kissed.

'I heard about you finding each other, how very sweet, and here you both are. Rory, I'm so glad we've bumped into each other. I was intending to call on you to explain the night of your birthday.'

Rory stood up and stubbed out his cigarette in the ashtray on the table. 'Will you excuse us, Ronald,' he said, as he took Helens elbow and led her away from the table.

'You have no idea how things were for me that night. I was smitten to the point of being suicidal when you didn't come to my birthday party. That's how much I loved you.'

'It wasn't my fault, Rory; my parents wouldn't accept our relationship. I tried to tell them how much I loved you; I was devastated too you must believe me.'

Rory gazed at her. How he had longed to hear her say that she had loved him too, and here she was looking as beautiful as ever, explaining that she had been as upset as him.

She continued, 'But now it seems you're the Grandson of Lady Bennington, and it could be so different for us. My father would be happy with us seeing each other again.'

Rory was livid, he had obviously never been good enough for her, the bile rose in his throat. 'Really,' he said quietly, 'but I'm still the same person titled or not.' Rory put his lips close to her ear and whispered caressingly, 'Now here is what I would like you to do.'

'Anything, darling.' She wound her arms around him, snuggling close.

I want you return to your friends over there and never contact me again.'

'Well, there's no need to be quite so rude, darling.' She pushed him away. 'Let me tell you something however – you are an incredibly boring man, sweet but boring.' She leant forward and planted a kiss which left a bright, red mark on his cheek. 'Nice to see you again, toodle-pip.' She sashayed away, leaving a waft of gardenia perfume behind.

'Isn't life funny,' remarked Rory to Eliza Jane the following day between clients. Sitting drinking his morning tea, at the kitchen table he had recounted the tale of meeting Helen. 'Only a short while ago,' he said, 'I couldn't wait to see her again, but now she means nothing to me. Ronald thought she was an absolute horror and he's right – whatever did I see in her?'

'Who knows what we see in another person,' said Eliza Jane with all the wisdom of her twenty-eight years. It's a mystery, but I'll tell you this – I think it means you've grown up.'

'She told me I was boring, sweet but boring – do you think I'm boring, Lizzie?'

'The right girl won't think you're boring, far from it. Now I must get on – I've got these nappies to wash, and surely your next appointment is due soon.'

Rory consulted the watch Patrick had given him as a birthday present. 'Lord yes.' He drained his cup and made for the door. 'Where's Thomas by the way?'

'Trying to find work as usual, there's just nothing out there.'

'Well, he might not have to search for work soon.' He held his hands up at the sight of Eliza Jane's doubtful face. 'Don't ask me any questions, Lizzie – I can't say anything yet – it's just an idea that Ronald had.'

'Rory, you know he won't take charity – remember how angry he was with Patrick for arranging the job at Claridge's.'

'This is different, Lizzie, believe me if this plan works, it could be the answer to all of our prayers.'

'I'll believe that when I see it,' grimaced Eliza Jane.

'That sculpture of Thomas's that you've on the table in the drawing room is rather good, isn't it?' Ronald sat down beside Lady Bennington as she finished her afternoon tea and biscuit.

'Indeed it is, Ronald, along with the three other pieces I have of his work. Why do you mention it?'

'When I was blind, I used to run my hands over the eagle – I found it so comforting, the smooth feel of the wood grain under my fingertips. I could almost guess what it looked like, but now I can see it for myself, it gives me enormous pleasure.'

'I had no idea you used to do that; it certainly is a beautiful piece. Thomas is a very talented man. I'm only sorry that he sends everything back to Laycock's, and that I have to order from Henry.'

'I was thinking, Grandmamma, we have a large cottage in our grounds with a workshop attached – what was it used for?'

'Mr and Mrs Collins used it, you remember he was the grounds man and she was my housekeeper. When they left, I employed local people to come in daily, apart from Stevens of course The cottage has been empty for some time.'

'It's fully furnished though, isn't it? I went to look at it this morning; all it needs is a jolly good clean.'

Lady Bennington looked anxiously at her grandson. 'Do you and Rory want to move in there, to have your own independence?'

'No.'

'What then?'

'Grandmamma, you may or may not know that Patrick Lawrence has been offered a position in New York, which it looks likely he'll take. Eliza Jane is getting married next month and moving back to Crossdale, Molly is away with a touring theatre group and you know Etty has gone to Paris.'

'What plans has Patrick for his house and business? Does Rory wish to buy it from him?'

'No Grandmamma, but what is worrying me is that Thomas will have nowhere to go if Patrick's house is sold.'

'I see,' Lady Bennington smiled, 'Ronald darling, you must think I was born yesterday. I now understand where this conversation is leading.'

Ronald breathed in. 'You do?'

'Yes, my darling – you and Rory want to go to New York with Patrick to meet your father but there's only one little problem, me. You think I'll have no one to look after me.'

'Yes, Grandmamma, we need to know there's someone we can trust with your welfare while we are away.'

'Ronald, far be it from me to stop you and Rory exploring the world and your place in it. You're both young, now is the time. I've lived my life and I don't want you tied down to an old woman. Therefore, I have an idea, why don't I have a word with Thomas about us setting up in business together. I'll back him with my money for which I'll get a return on every piece sold. We'll invest in new tools and set up the workshop properly. Thomas will live rent free in the cottage for as long as he wishes. I'll have company and Thomas will have a home and a job.'

'Grandmamma, have I ever told you just how wonderful you are?'

'Not often enough, my boy. I'll choose my moment carefully to discuss this plan with Thomas – for I do believe him to be a very proud man, and I don't wish to hurt his feelings. Now run along and make your plans with Rory.'

Ronald leant in and kissed his grandmother soundly on her papery cheek. She smelt of powder and lavender, he breathed in deeply, it would be comforting to recall the scent when he was far from home.

Chapter 53

Eliza Jane stirred, opening her eyes slowly. She gazed around the bedroom happy to discover Molly asleep in the other bed, just like old times. Quickly, she sat up, there were fires to lay and breakfast to be cooked. Then she remembered there was no need to rush, for today she was to become Mrs James Wilson. With a contented sigh, she lay back down for a while, and thought about the first morning she had woken up in this room. Was it only a year ago? Now she was returning to Crossdale with a husband and a baby, Etty's baby. Here she was the plainest of the three sisters, as had often been pointed out by well-meaning but insensitive villagers, but nevertheless the first to marry.

When Molly arrived home late last night for the wedding, she had brought someone with her. She introduced him as her Director, Edward Bennett, but you only had to look at them to realise there was more to it than that. Although Molly was strangely reticent about the details of their friendship, her eyes positively shone with love, and Edward seemed to have difficulty keeping his arm from creeping around her shoulders at every available minute. He wasn't handsome thought Eliza Jane, like David or Patrick, but loving and dependable like her Jim – the man she was to wed in three hours at Kit's church in Greenwich.

She sat up again and swung her feet to the floor before padding quietly to the window, and pulling the drapes to one side. The sun was already high in the sky, glinting on the familiar rooftops opposite. Pigeons were fighting over scraps of food from last night's supper, and the neighbour's black cat was stealthily crossing the garden. Ma would have been pleased; a black cat was a lucky omen. Letting the curtain go, she started to put her dressing gown on to go and make up Ruby's feed. Molly awakened and sat up in bed yawning. Seeing Eliza Jane preparing to go downstairs, Molly intervened. 'Oh, no, you don't, back to bed with you, you're getting married today. Now, what were you about to do?'

'Ruby needs her Bengers.'

'Right, well I'm looking after Ruby – now tell me what she needs.'

'Are you sure, you don't have to you know.'

'Course I'm sure, how hard can it be? I watched you feed her last night. Besides I want to spend some time with my beautiful niece before she goes to Crossdale.'

Molly smiled, as she crossed the room and boldly picked up the squirming baby. She was heading for the door when Eliza Jane called out, 'Edward's nice, I like him.'

'Isn't he just?' she beamed with dreamy satisfaction.

Eliza Jane giggled as Molly left the room; it was wonderful to see her so happy too.

Thomas was up and dressed when Molly reached the kitchen. 'Good,' she said, 'now you can hold Ruby for me while I make up her feed.'

Before Thomas could object, a warm bundle landed on his lap. Baby and uncle looked at each other in surprise. 'What's this?' Thomas teased, getting in some practice before you have your own babies.' He looked up from the child, 'I must say Edward seems pleasant enough.'

'He is, but marriage and babies aren't going to happen for a long time yet.' Molly was anxious to change the subject before she had to admit that Edward was married. 'How are you and Jo, you know she wrote to me a while ago. I'm looking forward to seeing her today.'

'Yes, she mentioned she had; it really upset her you two falling out.'

'I know, it hurt me too, but hopefully it's all behind us now.'

Molly was busy mixing Bengers into some boiled milk in a jug. She poured the mixture into a glass bottle and attached the rubber teat. 'It will be a bit hot for her yet, time for a cup of tea I think.'

She looked over at her brother who was holding Ruby rather awkwardly. 'Are you all right there, Thomas, holding Ruby I mean?'

Thomas looked down at the child; her bright blue eyes captivating him. 'Yes, I'm fine, quite enjoying it really. I've never held her before.'

Molly set a cup of tea down on the table for Thomas. 'How are you really?' she asked, concerned about his welfare. 'You have done your utmost to keep this family together but we've all gone or are shortly going our separate ways. It's a shame Etty couldn't make it back for the wedding. She sent a post card of the Eiffel Tower though; just imagine seeing that in real life. The boys are off to New York with Patrick, and Lizzie's going back to Crossdale. Has anyone actually asked her if she wants to go back by the way?'

'You've not changed' – Thomas laughed – 'you can still talk for England. As for going back to Crossdale, well you know, Lizzie, duty comes first – wherever Jim goes she'll follow. I think she may find it strange seeing the smithy and our old cottage every day, but I think she's happy about it really.'

Thomas shifted the baby into a more comfortable position. 'I know she's worried that the village won't believe that Ruby is hers. David's mother might make life difficult for her too. I hear David has agreed to be called Uncle David, his mother's idea.'

Thomas screwed up his face in derision, privately he thought David had always been under his mother's thumb. 'Poor David,' he said, 'he's got an enormous cross to bear, I feel desperately sorry for him. But can you imagine how much that bird's nest on the top of Mrs Fanshawe's hat will wobble if she gets a sniff of the truth?' Thomas laughed. 'I think the Fanshawe woman worries her the most.'

Molly leant forward cupping her tea in her hands. 'So what are you going to do, are you going to marry Jo?'

'How can I, Moll? I've no job, no house and no money. She would be mad to take me on, and before you say something will turn up…' He suddenly noticed a damp patch on his trousers. 'I think this baby needs a change of nappy.'

After taking care of the baby, Molly took her back upstairs and laid her in her cot. Eliza Jane was sitting at the dressing table trying to pin up her hair. Molly laughed. 'Here, let me do it,' she said, picking up the brush. Usually, Eliza Jane wore her hair in a bun at the back of her head but Molly carefully brushed her hair to the side of her neck in a sleek chignon and added finger waves to frame her face.

'Oh, Moll, that is lovely,' breathed Eliza Jane. 'I actually look quite pretty for once.'

'Lizzie, do not let me hear you saying that again. You always have had a pretty face,' Molly said sternly, 'now put your dress on and then your veil.'

Eliza Jane wore a cloche veil of the sheerest lace with a coronet of pink flowers around her head. Her boat neck dress was made of sheer white silk and had ornate beading to the bodice that extended to her hips. Lace inserts formed elegant ruffles on the skirt, each finishing on a handkerchief point at her ankles. Around her hip was a pink sash to match the flowers on her forehead. Patrick had presented her with a double string of pearls that she now wore around her neck.

Molly stood back and looked at Lizzie's reflection in the mirror. Her eyes filled with tears. 'You look beautiful, Lizzie. Etty did a wonderful job on the gown.'

Eliza Jane had never worn anything quite so beautiful before. 'Do you really think so? It's not too much? I was just going to wear that suit she made me when we first arrived in London with a new blouse.'

'What, that suit's a year old and wouldn't do at all. Etty would say the same if she was here.'

'Let's be honest, Moll, Etty would be fussing about her own dress if she were here.'

Molly laughed. 'Yes, you're probably right, bless her. You know I was so upset and angry when she left for Paris leaving Ruby with you, but now I'm beginning to think she did the right thing. You'll be a much better mother to Ruby than she'd ever have been, and she'll make a magical aunt. I only hope she doesn't change her mind and want her back.'

'It's something Jim and I will have to live with, like Ma had to. Looking back, I suppose she must have always dreaded the arrival of the postman in case there was a letter demanding Rory's return.' Eliza Jane hesitated, there was something she wanted to ask but wasn't quite sure how to phrase it. 'Moll?'

'Yes, Lizzie.' Molly stopped adjusting the veil and listened.

'Will everything be all right, you know, tonight? I don't know what to do, people say it hurts, you know the first time.'

'Gawd, Lizzie, I don't know myself but I think if you love each other, the rest will follow, don't you? Now then I must get ready too. I bought one of my stage costumes with me, I wore it for the importance of being Earnest, I hope you like it. Just one last thing, I've been keeping some of Ma's favourite perfume, April Violets, let's put a dab behind your ears.'

Eliza Jane sniffed the scent, to have this little bit of Ma with her today was a comfort. 'I miss her, she would have loved today.'

'I don't think you ever get over losing your mother, do you? Even though they drive you mad sometimes. Not a day goes by when I don't think of her. She should have been here, they both should.' Molly slipped the dress over her head.

Eliza Jane turned and looked at her younger sister, as if noticing her for the first time since she had arrived. How petite she was, standing in her stage dress of pale blue, her blonde hair cut into one of the new bobs that were all the rage. *She's grown up,* thought Eliza Jane. Molly at twenty-two was now a young woman of the world. Previously, she would have felt a small stab of jealousy that her sister looked so pretty but today Eliza Jane had a new found confidence. Suddenly, she realised that in her own way, she was equally as pretty as her two sisters, and it was a revelation to her.

'You look beautiful, Eliza Jane,' Patrick said, as she came down the stairs. 'Doesn't she look wonderful, Thomas?'

'She certainly does.'

Edward smiled at the sight of Molly in her blue dress accompanying Eliza Jane into the room. 'Both sisters look beautiful,' he said fondly.

Patrick led the way to the car and settled the bride into the back seat before settling himself in the driving seat. Thomas climbed in beside Eliza Jane, trying not to crush her dress.

The ride to the church did little to settle Lizzie's nerves, and she tried to concentrate on her surroundings. People passing by peeped into the car, anxious to catch a glimpse of the bride which made her feel even worse. She began to feel nauseous as the sun beat into the car, accentuating the scent of the leather seats that had somehow fused with the aroma of her bouquet.

'Enjoy this, Lizzie, queen for a day, why I'm sure Queen Mary herself wouldn't look as wonderful as you do today,' Thomas remarked, as they sped along.

Eliza Jane smiled weakly.

Thomas sensing his sister's nerves added, 'Lizzie, it's not too late to change your mind you know, are you sure you want go through with it.'

'More than anything but let's get the ceremony over with, then I might start to feel a little better.'

Thomas squeezed her hand. 'Da would have been so proud of you. He should be sitting here instead of me, and I don't think he'd have stopped grinning all day.'

Eliza Jane felt the tears spring into her eyes. 'Do you think Da would have liked Jim?'

'They're very alike; I think they would have got on like a house on fire.'

Eliza Jane smiled pleased that Thomas thought that way.

Lady Bennington arrived with Ronald and Rory at the church just before Patrick drew up with the bridal party. Edward and Molly had followed on in Edward's small car. Jim's family and many of his customers had crowded into the church; all dressed in their finery to see their lad get hitched.

The church felt cool and smelt of damp kneeling stools and hymn books. As the organ music swelled, Thomas walked slowly down the aisle with Eliza Jane on his arm. Eliza Jane smiled at the congregation as she passed them by. She was beginning to enjoy her day. She could see Jim's from the back as he stood facing the altar and it looked as if he was anxiously fiddling with his collar. He turned to look at Eliza Jane progressing slowly down the aisle. Dressed in his Sunday best suit with a high collar shirt and white bow tie, he appeared as uncomfortable and nervous as she had been. She looked so radiant that he hardly noticed her dress, and later he said that he couldn't have told anyone the colour of Molly's frock. Taking a deep breath to steady his nerves, tears sprang to his eyes as his bride drew nearer.

Kit stepped forward to conduct the service as Eliza Jane handed her bouquet to Molly, who then slipped into the front pew. She caught Kit's eye realising with shock that through the intensity of his gaze, he still had feelings for her. Unwilling to respond, she turned away and noticed a young woman staring at her, Molly smiled at her but it was not reciprocated.

The service was simple but emotional. Everyone laughed as Jim said 'I do' rather firmly and Eliza Jane's voice quavered as she said her vows softly but she meant every word.

The reception was held at the Crown and Anchor on Sydenham Road. Jim was friendly with the landlord who had provided a feast of sandwiches, sausage rolls and pork pies for the wedding party. Eliza Jane had been saving sugar coupons for a while, and had made two fruit cakes.

Lady Bennington ordered several bottles of champagne as a wedding present.

Far from looking down her nose at her surroundings, she had joined in the merriment, announcing to whoever would listen that she hadn't had such a wonderful time in ages. The landlord had hired a gramophone which he placed on the bar and was encouraging guests to kick up their heels and dance.

Thomas gently waltzed Jo around the small dance floor. 'You're so lovely,' he murmured which irritated her. Why if he thought that wouldn't he commit to her? She knew he loved her and she loved him, but no mention was ever made of marriage. Maybe he really didn't really intend to marry. He had always said he was no catch but Jo thought otherwise. Was she wasting her time? When the music finished, she abruptly let go of his hand and went to find Molly in an effort to calm down. Thomas surprised by her reaction, was puzzled as to what he might have done?

Seeing Lady Bennington seated by a small round table on her own, he walked over to her. 'I get puffed easily but would you like to dance,' he asked.

'Bless you, Thomas; I'm too old for all that now' – she patted the seat next to her – 'but please do sit down beside me. I have a rather interesting proposition to put to you.'

Kit was sitting at a table holding the hand of the girl who had been staring at Molly in the church. Molly went over to say hello. The girl was rather shy and sweet looking. Kit introduced as Mary Harvey. Molly spontaneously kissed her on both cheeks; she congratulated Kit on the wedding service, and after a polite but stilted conversation, she wished them both well. Relieved that it was over, Molly moved away, she spied Jo watching Thomas talking to Lady Bennington and wandered over to her. Jo smiled.

'Mary's lovely, isn't she – they're just right for each other, she makes him very happy.'

Molly actually doubted this having seen Kit's eyes on her in the church but agreed nevertheless. 'I'm glad, Jo; he deserves it, where did they meet?'

'At the theatre group, where else. She joined to help with costumes and everyone likes her. Do you mind, Molly?'

'Not one bit; I'm just pleased to see him looking happy.'

'Edward's nice; he seems to think the world of you.'

'And me him.' She caught Edward's eye as he stood near the gramophone with Ronald and Rory and smiled over at him.

'So, tell me all about it; he's your director I hear?'

'That's right but there's not much to tell, really.'

She didn't want to reveal that Edward was married, why cause an upset today when it was not necessary.

'I envy you,' Jo sighed deeply, glancing again over to Thomas who was still talking to lady Bennington. 'You've got your life mapped out. For me, it's the waiting game. It seems that Thomas is no nearer proposing marriage than ever before, and I love him so much.'

'I know he loves you; he's told me he does – just give him time. He's come a long way from that vow of eternal bachelorhood – I honestly believe you'll get your proposal, don't give up on him now.'

Jim and Eliza Jane were waltzing steadily around the small space cleared for dancing. He smiled at his wife. 'Well, Mrs 'arrison.'

337

'Yes, Mr 'arrison,' answered Eliza Jane, causing him to laugh.

'I love you girl, we're going to be 'appy, aren't we?'

'I think we are going to be more than happy, Jim. I can't wait to go home tomorrow. Our own home.'

'But first we've got tonight,' he said, making Eliza Jane blush at the thought. 'I've a surprise for you. My family 'ave arranged for us to 'ave the best room at the best hotel in Greenwich. What do you think of that? I can't wait to get you alone, Lizzie, but you'll promise to be gentle with me, and me strawberry tart won't you, girl.'

Eliza Jane laughed. 'Strawberry tart. Ahh that means heart, doesn't it?' At that moment, she knew she had nothing to fear from her wedding night. Soon she was hitching up her dress and learning to sing and dance to *Knees up Mother Brown* with her new cockney relatives.

Ronald and Rory were sitting at a table with Patrick discussing their forthcoming trip to New York.

'We leave on the SS Scythia in August, sailing from Liverpool. I've booked a first class passage for the three of us,' Patrick remarked.

'I can't believe that we'll finally meet Joseph Tyson,' Rory said, excitement creeping into his voice.

'I know, we meet our father at last, Rory. Come on, let's go and get a drink to celebrate.' Ronald took his brother's arm, and began to drag him to the bar.

'Are you coming, Patrick?'

'No, you go on, I'll just sit here a while.'

Patrick watched them as they walked away with a mixture of emotions. He wasn't cutting ties with Rory but he knew that his feelings were hopeless. Molly approaching observed the wistful look on Patrick's face and realised what was happening. She sat down beside him. 'It must be very painful for you, Patrick,' she said candidly.

Patrick looked at her trying not to understand what she meant.

'Yes, it is,' he agreed, realising that to lie was fruitless. 'I have been in love with Rory since that very first day a year ago when I saw you all in Trafalgar square. I'm sorry my feelings are that obvious – here's me thinking what a magnificent job I'm doing covering it up. Do you think everyone else knows?'

Molly shook her head. 'I'm an actress, an observer of people, it wouldn't occur to anyone else.'

'I don't know what I'm going to do, Molly. I can never tell him how I feel, and each day is torture. I was trying to get away, forget him, but then I stupidly suggested he accompany me to New York.'

'I'm so sorry, Patrick.'

'We've never really talked properly before, have we, Molly? I was thinking I've never seen you look happier than today, but I detect just a little pain behind those bright eyes.'

Knowing that Patrick had lived a life of discretion, she knew she could trust him. She told him about Edward being married, preventing her own wedding, and he proved to be a source of comfort for her. 'Don't give up hope,' he said, 'there's always a way forward. You just have to find it and I know you will.'

Molly smiled. 'I think this is a case of physician heal thyself, don't you?' She sought reassurance that her secret was safe. 'You won't tell Thomas, will you? You know how he is; he'll be furious with me. He's such a stickler for propriety, and after all that business with Etty, I think my news might just finish him off.'

Patrick smiled, reaching for her hand. 'Poor Thomas, he does make life harder for himself than it needs to be.'

'You're a wonderful man, Patrick. Thank you, thank you for everything. Where would we all be without you? We owe everything to you. We love you like our own brother, and I hope and pray that one day you'll find love again and be happy.'

Molly kissed his cheek, and as she rose to her feet, she placed her hand fleetingly on his shoulder, before wandering away to find Edward.

Patrick surveyed the joyous scene before him: Eliza Jane was preparing to throw her bouquet while Rory and Ronald were standing at the bar laughing together; Thomas was talking excitedly with Jo at a table and Molly and Edward were dancing. Was it all down to him, he wondered? He couldn't be sure about that, but he knew that he had experienced, even with all the difficulties, the happiest and most companionable year of his life with these strangers from Lancashire. He watched Eliza Jane toss the bouquet over her shoulder; it seemed to travel in slow motion until it fell into Molly's waiting arms. He raised his glass and whispered, 'I guess something will turn up, Molly, eh? What do you say?'